I0822299

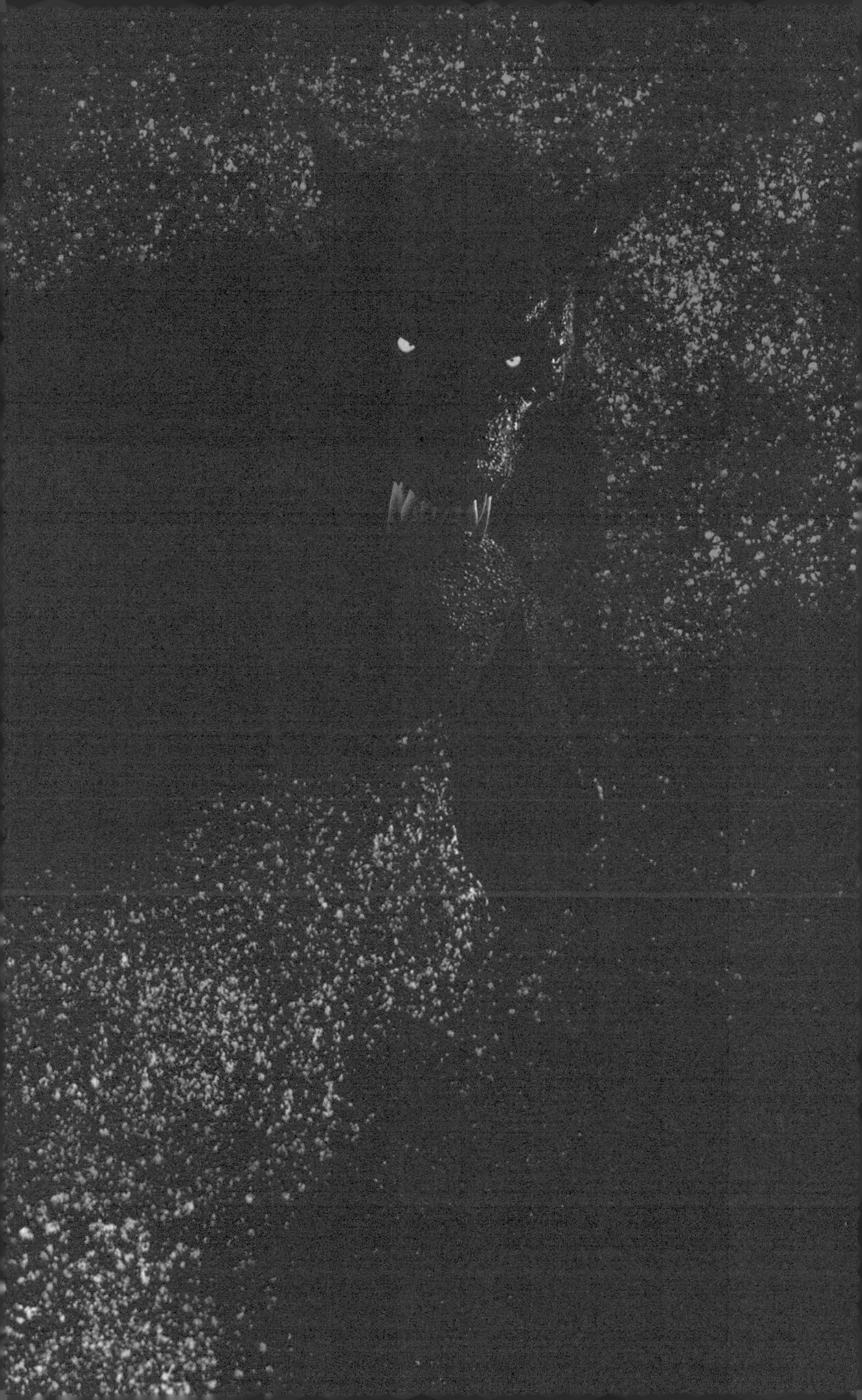

BOOK ONE OF THE BLOODBOUND TRILOGY

BLOODLUST

Devin Thorpe

Book Cover by Black Veil Arts

1st edition 2024

DEDICATION

For my readers, who are taking a chance on a new author. I promise I won't let you down. You are all Hellhounds now.

For my mother, who has painstakingly read every book of mine that will never see the light of day.

For my father, who taught me to never be embarrassed of my imagination.

For my girlfriend, who puts up with me living with my head in the clouds.

For my dogs, Atlas and Cato, who taught me there is strength in the pack.

UNDEAD EMPIRE

ASKAMYRE

SYGON

TYBER

THOREN MOUNTAINS

YUELTOPE

AREOPAGUS

VARNE

SKAAR

QUEENSMYRE

CARDONE

PAGEAN RIVER

NEVERGLADE FOREST

GALL

HOSH

UBAT

VEMEN

PENCE

THESSOLO

SCORPOS

SLAAVAN

VHEM

BLACKBLOOD MOUNTAINS

1

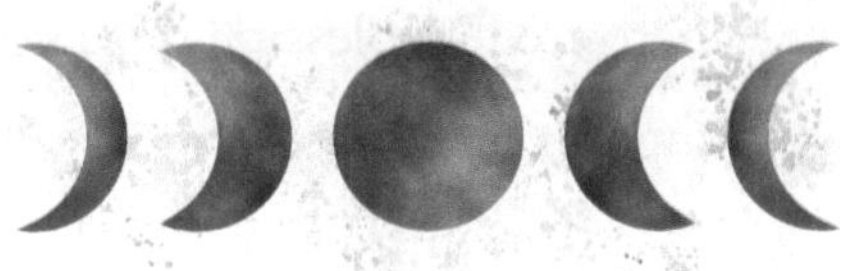

A Dream

"Good," I whisper with approval. Her feeble arms shake from the strength it requires to draw the bowstring. The muscles will adapt over time. She is already stronger than most boys at her age, though I would never admit it aloud. Her pride never needed inflating, even as a babe.

The unsuspecting elk lowers its head to the forest floor. Water patters against the surrounding greenery. The gods have heard the prayers of nearby villagers. This is the third day the sky has opened to shower the earth with its waters. The ground gargles for the sky to stop drowning it. The soil can take no more. The mud closes its doors and forces the water to gather in pools along the ground.

Such pools are convenient for grazing elk, who needn't look far for a source of hydration. And such rain is convenient for hunters, who needn't look far to find an elk's prints in the snitching mud.

Rain is good for more than growing crops. It fills the rivers with larger fish. Causes prey to seek for limited shelter. Washes away a hunter's scent on the wind. Camouflages him from being spotted. Dulls the senses of all prey alike.

But rain cannot prevent beings like me from sensing prey. My nose is not that of an ordinary mortal. Nor do I require tracks to find my prey. Bind my hands and blindfold me in an open field and I'll return home with a fresh kill fit for dinner. There are few blessings that come from my curse. The ability to never go hungry is one.

Sephora's arms shake the longer I make her wait. If her mind swells with impatient thoughts, she does a good job holding them in. I hear no groan from her mouth. I've trained her well, for she knows this isn't just about securing a warm meal for tonight. This is about training her body to be one with the bow. To get to the point where holding it drawn is an effortless motion.

The elk laps water into its mouth between bites from an eggrew leaf. The large leaves sag beneath the weight of water caught by their concave shape. Unlike most shrubs, the eggrew is known for its unconforming color. Where most new life at this time of year is different shades of vibrant green, the eggrew is a shade of midnight purple.

It is a type of nightshade, used by most to concoct herbal salves and medicines, though most chew it for its sweetness. Eggrew aren't abundant in most parts of the world, so those who sell foods and medicines from its blossom turn a pretty penny.

All I know is that elk who eat eggrew often have the most succulent meat.

"Okay," I whisper. "Fire when he picks his head up." I look down at my side. Sephora's back muscles twitch. Her breaths are strategically controlled. She's unfazed by the spasming in her forearms. Hyperfocus on the target negates the pain her body feels.

I take a moment to admire my daughter's might. She is the single greatest accomplishment of my life. Sephora is everything I'm not. She is her mother's daughter. I see Vesper's drive in her. Unwillingness to accept failure. Yet so gentle and calm. Like the tide of the ocean. Power to cause great damage countered by the power to heal.

Her eyes are like a ray of sun shining through lilac petals. Mine are midnight slate.

Her hair is silver as the north star. Mine is black as the starless night.

Her smile is the first blossom of spring. Mine is a raindrop amidst a tornado.

The elk raises its head from the glowing eggrew. This will be Sephora's third kill. She will need to put the arrow directly in its heart. If not, the massive beast will run for miles before it bleeds to death. We won't have time to track it with the sun casting its purple glow to the west.

I hear the bowstring twang. The air vibrates around us. The elk hears the noise and scatters. I look for a sign that the arrow has hit its target. The elk's chest seems unscathed as it takes off into the surrounding underbrush.

A dull pain enters my side as a force causes me to stagger a few steps. I look down and see an arrow shaft protruding from my ribcage. The shaft is buried in my chest to the feathers, the arrowhead emerging diagonally from my back.

The sight of the arrow in my side is confusing. The seeping blood around the wound doesn't make sense. I look up and see the elk is long gone.

I look toward Sephora. She has disappeared.

I fall to the ground.

The forest around me is gone.

Everything is dark.

There's a pressure around my mouth.

A strap pulling around my head. Hands clasping tight a contraption around my nose and mouth.

"You are an abomination before the sight of the gods," a voice spits at me as my body is lifted off the ground. Two people carry me through the darkness, then throw me back onto the ground. My body is shivering. It feels as though I've been pulled from the depths of arctic waters. I wear no clothes. My body is soaked in freezing sweat. My extremities are numb beyond all hope of movement.

The sound of silver bars slamming shut echoes in the dark.

I don't know *where* I am.

I don't know *who* I am.

I don't know *what* I am.

2

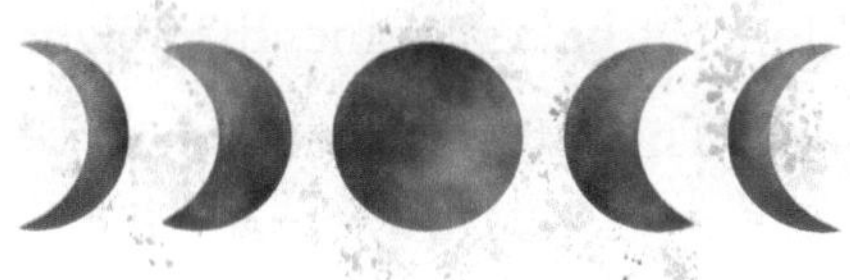

A Nightmare

Time doesn't exist in the dark.

The rising and setting of the sun is obsolete in the places it doesn't shine. The moon has little affect in places darker than night.

I manage to pull the arrow from my side over the course of several losses of consciousness. I am regaining my strength with every involuntary fainting spell. My mind cannot tolerate its current load of pain. I let it rest, mainly because there's little else to do in the dark.

I focus on the things I can control.

I wake.

Snap the arrowhead from the shaft.

Dark unconsciousness.

I wake.

Pull with all my might until the shaft is a few inches removed from my chest.

Return to the world of feverish nightmares.

Awake.

Yank the shaft with a single swift pull. Feel my body groan as the alien entity leaves its presence. I sigh with relief. My body loosens. My muscles scream their echoing aches. Sight returns to my unfocused eyes. Feeling returns to my fingers and toes with every passing shadow. Memories slowly return to my mind. Along with them comes the weight of regret. Moments from my past long gone. Things that can no longer be changed. The pain of loss and suffering.

I hallucinate often that Sephora is with me. Sometimes I see Vesper's slim silhouette against the cave wall. Their presence is comforting, even if the glimpses of them are nothing more than my fractured mind playing tricks on me.

My eyes grow accustomed to the dark once more. I can see the rocky tomb that keeps me captive. The silver bars that prevent my escape. There are no windows in this rocky forest. No avenues of outside light. Just the cavernous womb of the hollow mountain and those unfortunate enough to be trapped in its embrace.

I run my fingers over the scars that cover my body. Fidget with the muzzle that cuts into my face. Try not to focus on the pungent scent of the fecal matter and urine I've excreted in the far corner of my cell. Mold grows inside my muzzle. Moisture from my breath fermented with bacteria. Its scent is like a second home to me. The metal basket is like a second mouth. I've worn it so long that it feels like an extension of my own body. We are treated no better than rabid dogs. The Blackbloods muzzle us up like mangy beasts and throw us in cages like we are feral animals.

Inside these walls the only friends to be found are rats and shadows. Need to be careful of the rats though. They're the type to befriend you just so they can nip at you in your sleep.

My mind is running too fast. Need to get control of my thinking. It's easy to get lost in thought when they're all that keep you company. Sometimes I talk just to hear my voice. Just to make sure I'm more than a floating conscience.

I'm not the only one that does it. These cave walls are filled with the ramblings of its half-insane inhabitants. Prayers to deaf gods. Manic screams from those with less fortunate hallucinations. I don't let the frenzied echoes penetrate my mind. Doing so would catalyze my descent into madness. I merely listen to the echoes, then let them bounce from me like my ears are just another rock wall.

The Blackbloods get a kick out of hearing us go crazy. We are only animals to them. They feel no empathy toward us. How could they? We are nothing more than monsters in their eyes. We are the sons and daughters of Dagon. They're convinced we deserve nothing more than lives of torture and deaths of agony.

I won't give them the satisfaction. I hold my thoughts close to my heart. I do not cry out like the prisoners that surround me. I do not call out to Dagon for relief from this pain. Dagon is just another dead god to me. He wasn't there when I lost Sephora and Vesper. Why would he show his face now?

My ear twitches. Prisoners in my corridor fall silent suddenly. The air grows colder. I hear large, swollen feet dragging against the rocky ground. It carries with it the scent of decay. Its body is a walking enigma. A mockery of life. A perversion of Mother Nature herself.

Fellow prisoners don't dare speak in its presence. We have all seen the punishment that awaits if we break the silence while in its vicinity. I avert my eyes to the ground, knowing I will pay dire consequences for locking eyes with it as it passes. But my ear twitches again as its feet stop outside my cell.

My eyes hyperfocus on a puddle of my own piss. It looks like a miniature lake on my cell floor. I intentionally add to the puddle every time I need to go because of the rocks that raise around it. The rocks hold it in, like the rising walls of a bowl. Pretty soon they won't be tall enough to hold all the pee. Luckily for me, I am given little water, so the urge to go is never frequent. The piss is dark amber, reflecting the dehydration my body fights to stay alive.

Tutor Lundis told me as a child you can go weeks without eating and still survive, but only a few days without water before you will perish. It may sting and burn when I pee, but at least I still have been given enough water to continue adding to the puddle. Other prisoners are not so fortunate.

The Blackblood still has not moved from outside my cell wall. It stands there, silently. I don't dare look up to see what's happening. But not even my mind's attempt to focus on the puddle of piss is enough to distract me. Fear boils over from my heart and bubbles beneath my flesh.

"You are an abomination before the sight of the gods, Lycanthrope," the Blackblood grunts. It's the first time I've ever heard one of them call me anything other than Muzzled. "I've been told to bring you your earnings from your recent victory. I'll bet you don't even remember, do you?"

He's right. I have no recollection of what the Blackblood references.

"Your kind thinks you're so much better than us. You've brainwashed yourselves into thinking *we* are the monsters. At least we can remember all those we've killed, wolf. You can't even remember killing your own kind," the Blackblood chuckles, as if he's made some hilarious joke.

Keys rattle as he unlocks the silver bars, sliding them open. I keep my eyes low, knowing there is nothing separating us any longer. The air inside my rocky cell freezes. The hair on my arm stands. I suddenly remember how fickle I am. I am in hell itself. Only demons rule here. And now one stands before me, reminding me of my own mortality.

"Look at me," the Blackblood growls.

He puts me in a position where I can only lose. Disobey his order and I will be punished. Look at him and I will be punished.

I lift my eyes and feel the blood in my veins slow. It suddenly becomes hard to breathe. It feels like there's a hand around my throat. Saliva frozen in my mouth. My exhale is like frost against my metal muzzle. The runny mucus on my upper lip freezes.

Obsidian skin covered with bulging black veins. Black veins that carry black blood. Black blood that carries death. Its skin is decaying, like every day it survives is another day it has defied dying. It gains strength from the darkness. The light of the sun would dismantle its body to dust. That's why it's made the hollow mountain its home. That's why it only goes out in the night to wreak havoc on the outside world. These demons are nothing like the Undead, even if they themselves were once Undead.

The Blackblood virus has changed them. Demented them. Turned them to devils. Rotted their blood and perverted their minds. Their flesh corrodes away, covering their bodies in black blight. They grow wings like bloodthirsty bats. Talons like tyrfalcons. Fangs sharper than Fenryr.

We used to tell stories of the Blackbloods as kids to scare each other. But that's all they were. Stories. Silly tales we told around a dark campfire to frighten one another. Harmless fun because we didn't know they bided their time in the shadows, waiting to expand their kingdom of darkness.

My heart pounds harder in my chest. I don't know if it's the fear that causes the pain or the exertion it takes to push the cold blood throughout my body.

"Tell me, do you feel weak?"

He's asked me to speak. The last time I dared speak to a Blackblood I nearly lost my life. I'd like to think I've since learned my lesson.

I nod my head, knowing I will be punished if I do not answer him.

His massive body shifts, revealing something in his hand. He's holding a human's foot. My eyes quickly flicker and realize he's dragging a dead body behind him. A guttural laugh escapes his chest as he watches me come to understand. He wants to make a show of this. My miserable existence is nothing more than entertainment for him. "Like I said, I've brought you your earnings from last night's full moon."

He throws the human's dead body before me. The corpse lands awkwardly on the ground in front of me, bent in a disfigured shape. It is completely limp. Its skin is pale and cold, deprived of all life. "Bloodlust was pleased with your performance last night, so he's permitted you to feast on your killing."

Hearing the King's name spoken aloud is like being sentenced to death. The Muzzled aren't allowed to say his name. To do so is death. Lowlifes such as ourselves cannot speak the names of the Blackblood's royal leader.

I look down at the dead body. It has been ravaged. Barely recognizable, torn open so that it looks like its flesh is inside out. The blood has drained from its body and dried along its limbs. Whatever spirit once filled its beating heart is long gone.

I look back to the Blackblood, not knowing which sight is more horrifying. To stare at the Blackblood is to stare into the eyes of death itself. To stare at the carcass is to remind myself of what monstrosities I'm capable of when the moon is full.

"I was told to give you water to drink with your meal, but I see you've already filled your own bowl," the Blackblood mocks, laughing at the sight of my piss bowl. "Try not to eat too fast, you never know which meal will be your last."

The Blackblood slams the silver bars shut, disappearing into the night. I let out a gasp, my clenched throat finally loosening. My body slumps considerably and I realize I've been flexing every muscle I have left with tension.

I stare at the carcass left behind. It's been drained of its blood. The Blackbloods still have to eat too, after all. They've given me this body as a jest. They're taunting me. I've killed one of my own, though I have no recollection of it. Such is the curse of the full moon. The only night the Blackbloods remove our muzzles. The only night we are more a prisoner to our own minds than we are to them.

"Is that going to be you someday, daddy?" Sephora asks. My eyes shift to the corner of the cell where she stands. She's staring at the dead body before me with disbelief in her eyes. "Are you going to let them do that to you too?"

Her innocent eyes glimmer in the bleak darkness. Her platinum hair shines like the moon. Her presence breaks my trance of misplaced fear.

"No," I whisper unconfidently. "Daddy is going to break free from this place, Seph."

She looks back at me with doubt in her eyes. "You told me it's not right to lie."

I reply, "Then it's a good thing I'm not lying."

We lock gaze. She's more cynical than I remember. Like she questions my teachings. I want nothing more than to pull her in close for a hug. It's been days since I last saw her. It's been weeks since I've seen her mother. This isn't the first time I've told her I would break free, and look at the little progress I've made. She shakes her head at me.

"Prove it." She fades into the shadows behind her, leaving me alone once again.

I slink back against the wall behind me, too defeated to keep up the façade. We often lie to the ones we love. To save them from pain. All I love is dead, so I lie to their memory.

My bones ache. My muscles scream with fatigue. My vision is blurry. How death could be worse than this, I'm not sure.

I close my eyes and try to silence my mind. The thoughts scatter like flies, retreating to the subconscious so they can resurface at a later time.

I just need sleep, I tell myself.

Sleep will allow me to escape my current reality.

I close my eyes but there's little difference between the darkness of my cell and that of blindness. I curl my naked body into a ball, scraping my skin uncomfortably against the damp rock beneath me. I gave up long ago trying to find a place to cushion my head during sleep. Rock makes a poor pillow. Sleep still finds me though. My body is drained from the full moon still. And there is no telling what time of day it is in here. The sun could shine mercilessly outside and these walls would prohibit us from knowing.

I will sleep, because I need to prove to Sephora I'm not a liar. I will gather my strength. Bide my time. Wait in the shadows for when the moment is right. Then I will prove it to her. Her and Vesper both.

3

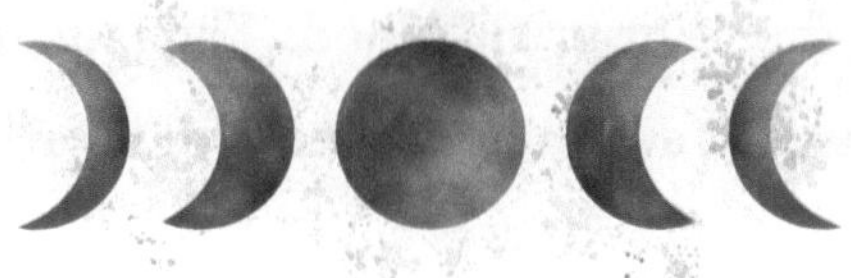

A Dream

"Now. Fire now," I command.

I don't look down at my daughter. My eyes look to the unsuspecting elk, licking its lips after minutes grinding eggrew between its molars. The bowstring twangs. The elk flinches. Blood spatters. The animal screams, a terribly awful noise to hear. Sephora drops her bow to cover her ears as the deafening pitch echoes for sympathy.

Humans aren't the only animals that beg for a swift death after they're dealt a killing blow. The elk takes off, sprinting into the woods with a red carpet of blood trailing behind it. If death is an entity an animal can run from, the elk is surely running fast enough to leave the reaper in the dust.

I see the arrow protruding from its belly as it vanishes behind a curtain of ferns. A stomach shot won't kill it instantly. Sephora's aim betrayed the animal. If we don't track it, the wound will fester for hours, killing the elk through infection or loss of blood, whichever comes first.

"Oh no," Sephora gasps, watching our dinner slip away from sight.

"Stay here," I order. My eyes glaze over as the beast within rises. I take note of Sephora's scent so I can find my way back. She smells of cinnamon cloves and smoke. It's a scent I've memorized over the course of her life. I could pick it out of a crowd of thousands. My heart flutters when I catch it on the wind. My daughter's scent, unmistakable from any other.

The wind carries the scent of elk blood. The rain attempts to fracture the trail of death, but not even a hurricane could conceal the bloody trail of dying prey from me.

My body takes over as bloodlust rushes to my head. My vision blurs as branches whip against my face. The forest comes alive around me to try to protect the desperate elk. Roots spring from the ground to ensnare me. Downfallen logs block the path. Loamy soil grabs at my heels like quicksand.

I hear the elk's panicked breaths. Smell the anxiety its pheromones excrete. Feel the tension in the air as it realizes it's running a losing race. Surely it hears me gaining on it. Smells my feral odor. Senses the predator within me. Blood fills my mouth as fangs rip through my gums. My fingers itch and ache as human nails fall to the ground, replaced by jet-black claws. My palms bleed as my fists clench, claws digging into flesh. The pain feels good.

I fight back against the beast within. My vision narrows as it seeks to take over completely, but I push it back. The sun is retreating on the horizon, but the moon tonight is merely a clipped toenail in the sky. The beast has no control over my body on a night like this, so I fight the darkness that converges on my vision.

A shrill cry from ahead sends a chill down my spine. The elk's sprint ceases. I hear its body thud before I see it dead on the ground. I smell a fresh wound bleeding profusely. I smell another. Hear a hiss between slurping. My body is no longer running. I push the beast back. Something's happened, that much I'm sure of. My mind needs to handle the situation with logic, not brute force.

I swallow the mouthful of blood that's accrued from my gums. The fangs shrivel. My claws retract. I still lean on the beast's keen sense of hearing and smelling to understand what's unfolded.

"Wait your turn, Midius!" a shrill voice hisses.

"You fool," someone growls back. "Look at its belly! An arrow! It's stuck like a pig!"

"And?" the shrill voice dismisses, failing to heed the warning.

"You are as stupid as you are undead, Gridion. Someone was hunting this elk. They will be tracking it."

I see them through the brush, squatting in a thicket of Ephesian ivy for concealment. There are two, and their appearance instantly gives it away. Undead scouts. I haven't seen them in many solstices, long before Sephora was born. And when I last saw any member of the Undead Empire, it was far from these parts.

My heart drops in my chest, something deep in me dreading what this means.

I try to push the panic to the back of my mind. Maybe there is some explanation for their migration. Maybe these are just vagabond outcasts.

Not likely, my gut says. *We aren't safe here anymore. Vesper and Sephora aren't safe.*

I need to get back to them. Our dwelling is only a few short miles from here. The scouts will find it within a single setting and rising of the sun. I was a fool for thinking we'd be able to live happily ever after here. We will live a life on the run so long as the Undead Empire continues to expand.

"Let them track it," Gridion cackles from beneath his mummified linens. "I prefer human to animal. Less gamey." The only exposed skin is his leprous lips, thoroughly covered in blisters from a day of sunlight exposure. Undead scouts aren't to be trifled with. Only criminals and crazies get assigned to scouting duty, I've gathered.

"The sun has yet to set. We must be cautious," Midius warns. "A human has twice our strength while the sun shines upon them."

"Good thing there's two of us then, eh?" Gridion remarks. "Let them come for their kill. I will flay the flesh from their bones and squeeze the juices from their heart."

Only two. The panic in my chest lowers. *Only two. For now*. I close my eyes and take note of their scent. Sulphur. Ash. Rotting flesh. Spoiled meat.

It's been years since I've come in contact with scouts. I've grown accustomed to Vesper's scent. Though Undead, she smells nothing like these two. Scouts are foul creatures. They don't have the pure blood Vesper does, and the days they spend in the sun doesn't help their case.

Luckily for me, their scent is unmistakable. A strategic advantage. I'll know when they are near, so we may never be caught off guard.

I am undetectable to them. If there is any benefit I gain from micro-dosing wolfsbane on a daily basis, it's the fact that my scent is erased. I inwardly thank my curse with silence. Without it, I would be dead right now.

I look at them once more before turning back. They are like lanky skeletons embalmed in human flesh. Their own skin is wrapped thickly with various dried fleshes. Some is from humans, others from animals. The flesh of mortals is designed to absorb the sun's light, acting as a barrier from its effects. It's the only way they are able to scout in the daylight. A loophole in the system. They mock Damon's curse by walking the earth without the moon's supervision.

"Dad?" a voice calls from the forest. My body tenses. *Sephora!*

The scouts snap alert. Gridion smiles. Midius lifts his nose to the air, picking up on the scent of cloves and cinnamon at the same time I do. They look at each other with suspicion. Gridion's smile disappears. Realization dawns. They come to the conclusion faster than I anticipated they would.

My worst nightmare becomes reality.

"Do you smell that? It can't be," Midius whispers. Gridion stands from the elk, no longer interested in its bounty. Gridion replies, "I know a Sylvian when I smell one." His voice is no longer joking. It's as if the scent has sucked all the humor from him.

Mention of the Sylvian name sends shivers through me. I haven't heard it uttered since long before Sephora's birth. I'd almost convinced myself it didn't exist. As if it was the name of some fabled family from childish bedtime stories. But hearing it come from the scout's mouth resurrects its weight in my mind. Brings back a life I'd long forgotten about. This changes everything. Now that they've smelled Sephora, I will have to kill them. I can't let them return to their clan with news of her existence. They move to pursue her. Not if I have something to say about it.

"Over here, Seph!" I call back to her, acting ignorant to the scouts' presence. "I think I've almost found it!" My voice is overly optimistic. I want them to think they've gone undetected.

I watch as my voice causes them to pause, forcing them to both turn in my direction and smell the sky once more. They smell no scent. I silently praise the wolfsbane once more. Neither scout speaks, knowing from the volume of my voice how close I am. They're like frozen deer, not knowing what to do. They've never encountered a human they can't smell.

My fangs and claws emerge simultaneously. I was going to leave the two alive, but Sephora's impatience has given us away. We won't have long. Scouts are to return to report at dusk. The sun is setting, so their disappearance will raise suspicion. Suspicion will require an investigation. Investigation will uncover their deaths. Their deaths will cause the Undead to wonder what was capable of killing them.

They will come for us.

Best get this part over.

"Where are you?" Sephora calls out, causing the scouts to flinch. Midius gestures toward her voice. He's indicating they should split up. Something tugs at my heart. Warmth washes over me. I'm feverish. I look up at the sky and realize a sliver of the moon is now exposed from behind cloudy coverage. The silver light bathes me, calling forth the beast within. Luckily for the scouts, the moon is far from full. That, paired with my constant dosing of wolfsbane, gives me ultimate control of the beast tonight.

I channel its power. I use only what is necessary. "Over here!" I call back to her, stepping forward from the Ephesian ferns. The moonlight reveals me to the scouts. Both look at me with surprise. Fear replaces the surprise. I'm met with horrified looks as they quickly realize what I am. The sun is now fully set, restoring them both to their full power.

But it doesn't matter. No amount of power in the world could make this an equal fight for them.

"Go! I will hold him off!" Midius cries, pushing Gridion away. The cowardly scout didn't need to be told twice.

Gridion pauses, the breath catching in his throat. He tries to cry out for help but blood gurgles from his mouth instead. Midius looks to his companion and sees the gashes along Gridion's throat. Blood pours from them. Gridion attempts to cover the wound with his hands, as if the blood can be held back. It seeps between his fingers like water from a compromised dam.

I realize I'm no longer standing among the ferns. I'm directly in front of Gridion, my claws wet with his blood from slashing open his throat. Midius gasps when he sees me standing a few short feet from him. Gridion falls to his knees, gasping for air but choking on blood instead.

"Why have you come here?" I ask. My voice is colder than the pale moon above.

Midius stammers incoherently. I need answers before I kill him. Need to make sure it is only coincidence that brings them here. Need to make sure they weren't alerted of Sephora's existence.

"Answer," I command, interrupting the scout's babbling.

"Blackbloods," he whines, "Searching for Blackbloods!" Midius spits the words out as if his life depends on it, because it does.

"What are you talking about?" I ask, my eyes narrowing. "There is no such thing."

The ground beneath us shakes. Midius and I both stumble from the earth's quaking.

"They've returned," Midius calls out. The whole world shakes violently around us, falling apart at the seams. The forest disappears, replaced by blackness. Cold rock takes its place. The feeling of superiority in my chest is gone. Dread and fear reside within me now.

The dream is over. I am back to reality. *They've returned*. The warning replays in my mind with cold deference. Maybe if I had heeded the Undead's words things would be different.

4

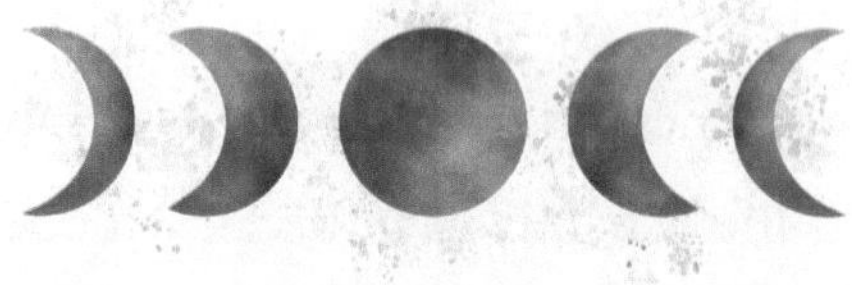

A Nightmare

I wake to the mountain walls around me trembling. The earth shakes beneath me. The rock comes alive, groaning with pain as it's bombarded from the outside.

"They're at it again," Ophy whispers excitedly, pressing his face into the silver bars. The silver burns him instantly, causing him to curse. He jumps away with heat blisters on his skin.

Sleep blurs my vision. Waking up is always painful. Leaving the world of memories for this hellish reality always fills my chest with despair.

"Not this again," Creon moans from down the dark corridor. "Somebody shut him up before he gets started." Creon's protest is met with concurrence from several other prisoners.

"Dagon will not forsake us. Not even this mighty mountain can prevent his vengeance!" Ophy shouts for all to hear. His shout bounces off the cave walls and echoes several times.

"Praise be!" Orton cries from further down the cell block.

"Here we go," Creon grunts.

I stare into my lap so Ophy can't see the smile on my face. There are only so many forms of entertainment in this hellhole, and listening to these lunatics is always guaranteed to make me laugh. I never add to the conversation. I let my long hair hide my face so no one can see me. I don't speak. I never do.

"We must turn to worship the almighty moon in this time of affliction!" Ophy calls. Orton chimes in, "The prophecy has sent our savior!"

"It's almost like they didn't see the Blackblood drag a dead body in front of all our cells," Creon reflects loud enough for us to hear.

"It was another one of Syrus's kills," Wren calls to Creon. Mention of my name intrigues me. They talk about me like I'm not here. Creon asks, "What's that, his eighteenth?"

"Twenty-fourth," Wren corrects. "He's close to reaching Crixus's record."

"Not if they put him against Crixus next moon, he won't," Creon laughs.

"Dagon has blessed Syrus! Sent him back with a gift from the latest moon! A weapon that can free us all," Ophy chants, jumping up and down in his cell. I can feel his eyes on me. His glare burns into me, worshipping me as if I'm Dagon himself. I don't dare look up to meet his gaze.

"What'd Dagon give him, eh Ophy?" Creon mocks, "Your dead god send our precious Syrus back with a key to our cells?"

"Forgive him, Almighty Dagon," Ophy repents. "His doubt will soon be put to rest, I'm sure of it."

Orton chimes in, "Some require sight of Dagon's works before their faith may blossom, so we pray you give our dearest Creon patience, Lord Dagon!"

"Amen!" Ophy cries, dropping to his knees.

"Amen," Creon adds, holding back laughter. "Now, pray tell what your lovely Dagon has sent back with Syrus, since Syrus is too shy to talk to us."

"Do not mistake his silence for weakness, Creon. He is the most powerful of us all," Orton warns. A half dozen cells mumble with annoyance. My face blushes beneath my greasy black hair. It is odd hearing people talk of me like this. Ophy and Orton worship me, thinking their god sent me. Creon and others think I'm unusually lucky, and others think I've only been matched against weaker opponents. My name circulates from cell to cell with every passing full moon, each prisoner taking note that I'm still here.

It isn't often a Muzzled lasts as long as I have. The average lifespan is eight fights. I've now tripled it. Some think I'm godsent. Others yearn to see my downfall. Such is the way of things.

"Surely we are doomed if he is the most powerful of us," Creon mocks. I half agree with him. I feel like I'm on death's doorstep. Every inch of my body throbs with pain. The slightest movement sends waves of protest to my brain. I'm malnourished and dehydrated. A mortal man would have died months ago, but the curse preserves me, refusing to let me pass on. Every passing moon is just enough to feed the beast within, allowing the feral creature to hibernate while I suffer. Creon is right. If I'm the most powerful of us, surely we are doomed.

"Dagon showed me his fight in a vision," Ophy sings for all to hear. This will be interesting. It wouldn't be the first time he's claimed Dagon showed him a snippet from one of my fights to the death. "The Blackbloods resent Syrus's abilities, so they look for any way to finish him off. Dagon showed me his most recent moondance. Syrus slayed one of his own, the body you saw dragged to his cell. Twenty and four kills, that's twenty-four. But the Blackbloods did not stop there, no, that was not enough for them. They unleashed Syrus on Undead archers! Behold! Only a single one pierced

Syrus, a gift from Dagon, for the Blackbloods forgot to remove it from his body!"

"A single arrow?" Creon shouts, obviously outraged. "You're getting worked up over a bloody arrow?"

Wren sighs, annoyed to a lesser extent. "Will you give it a rest, Ophy. Some of us are trying to rot in peace over here."

"Not any arrow, my fellow sinners! A silver arrowhead! Punctured his body and failed to kill him!"

The rant catches me off guard. I stare at the broken arrow through my matted hair. I was half incapacitated when I removed it, paying no attention to its detail. The arrowhead is covered in dried blood. How Ophy knows the contents of its forgery is a mystery. That, or he's full of shite. It's likely the latter. Silver kills our kind, weakens us with its mere presence. Its ore is mined from Phobos, a splintered meteor from the moon. Legend has it Damon sent the rock here as a gift to the Undead to have a fighting chance against our kind. The curse is tied to the moon, and only purified silver from the moon can cause our bodies damage.

Or so the legend goes.

There is truth enough behind it. There is a reason silver bars are our only barrier to freedom. The beast within would bend iron bars and flee this rocky hell. Our curse is helpless in the face of silver. Our kind heals at the rate of a mortal when pierced by it. All other wounds have little affect against us. When we wake from the full moon, the beast has healed us from any harm accrued in the darkness of night.

I look down at my ribcage. There is no longer a scar where the arrow punctured my body. No one would be able to know it was lodged in my chest several sleeps ago. I am healed, which leads me to believe Ophy's vision was nothing more than another inaccurate hallucination. I don't bother getting up to retrieve the arrowhead for examination. I don't have the strength to move. But any chance of Ophy being right this time is contradicted by my healed flesh.

"No, he's right Syrus." The voice catches me off guard. I haven't heard it in countless sleeps. I brush the hair away from my eyes, staring to the dark corner of my cell. "Vesper?" I ask in disbelief. Her purple eyes gleam from the darkness. All conversation from outside my cell is drowned out. My pain is put on pause. Suddenly, Vesper and I are the only two beings that exist in this world.

"The arrowhead is silver, Syrus. The man's vision is right. Bloodlust pitted you against several opponents this past moon. Your fighting has garnered great attention from the Blackblood King."

"Bloodlust doesn't care about our kind, Vesper. That's why he pits us against each other to fight like dogs to the death," I explain. I don't want to be discussing the latest moon with her. I want nothing more than to tell her how much I miss her embrace. The feeling her body brought when it held me. The butterflies in my stomach that fluttered when we kissed. I want to get lost in her amethyst eyes, not discuss the Blackblood's enjoyment watching me kill fellow Muzzled.

"Do you feel the rock shaking beneath you?" she asks earnestly. The question catches me off guard.

"Yes, it has shaken for many moons now. Fellow prisoners think it is Dagon himself attempting to break open the mountain. How silly a notion is that?" I let out a weak laugh, my lungs too tired to express humor.

"Whether or not Dagon has a hand in it, I'm not sure," Vesper admits, "But I do know the cause of the earthquakes."

I stare at her. My face is smitten with pessimism. "Unless it's Damon incarnate ready to blot out every Blackblood in existence, it matters little."

"It's the Undead, Syrus," Vesper replies. She says it as if it is good news. "They have found the Blackbloods and declared war. Their legions bombard the mountain with catapults."

"Ah, wonderful news, Vesper! And if they break through the impregnable mountain, we Muzzled will go from being slaves of the Blackbloods to slaves of the Undead!" I smile sarcastically. My muzzle cuts into my cheeks, discouraging the smile to last any longer than a brief moment. It is almost insulting to hear her talk about the Undead as if they are my savior. If there is any creature out there that hates my kind more than Blackbloods, it's the Undead. "In case you forgot, there's a reason they hunted us into the hills. The enemy of my enemy is not always my friend. Sometimes you just have two enemies who despise you equally."

"Bloodlust is planning on unleashing the Muzzled on them the next full moon. He will turn all of you from gladiator to soldier," she warns.

The notion seems unlikely, though. "He isn't stupid enough to do that, Vesper. There would be no controlling us if we were left to our own devices at the peak of the moon. The bloodbath would be greater than Crankshaw's Rebellion."

"He has little choice. The Undead are close to cracking the mountain open, and when they do, the sunlight will do more damage than any soldier ever could. The Undead don't know Bloodlust has enslaved the Muzzled. Pitting your kind against them will catch them off guard and turn the tide of the war."

"And the reason behind the silver arrow?"

"Bloodlust used you this past moon to test how well a Muzzled could kill the Undead. The Blackbloods have captured dozens of Undead prisoners of war. While you were in the arena still, he released twenty of them, each equipped with the same weapons they have on the battlefield outside the mountain, silver arrows included."

"And?"

"You killed every single one of them, Syrus."

I pause for reflection. She shouldn't know these things. She is only a figment of my imagination. A hallucination of my decaying brain. Her knowledge should be confined to the things I know, yet here we are, arguing with completely separate viewpoints.

If what she says is true then everything is about to change. The Undead have fought with silver weapons since Vespian's Moon. They realized the threat my kind presented and hunted us down until we were nearly extinct. After that, their weapons never returned to regular iron. Whether they grew used to the silver or awaited our return, they kept their silver swords sharpened and their silver arrowheads pointed.

I briefly glimpse at the broken arrowhead on the ground, not wanting Vesper to see me eyeing it. If what she says is true, I survived a fatal shot and my body has healed as if the arrow was nothing more than iron or steel. I avert my gaze, drawing my attention back to Vesper's presence.

Words don't describe how much I've missed her in my life. Living is empty without her. Loneliness is my only close companion. Yet nothing matters when I stare into her glowing eyes. War between Blackbloods and Undead is nothing more than ants rioting when I'm lost in her beauty.

"Vesper, why now?" I ask earnestly. "I've prayed every second of every day to see you again and you haven't returned. After all these months, why reappear now?"

"Because you've forgotten who you are, Syrus. I have come back to remind you."

"I don't know what you're talking about," I dismiss her response immediately. "I haven't forgotten who I am."

"The man I married would not let anything on this earth make him a slave."

"The man you married wouldn't have left his own wife and daughter to die," I spit back, venom in my heart starting to boil over. I am not mad at her. It is hatred toward myself that I harvest. Feelings I've repressed over many moons. Memories I've tried to forget so I can sleep.

"If you do not forgive yourself for that night, our deaths will have been in vain, Syrus," Vesper shouts. Tears cloud her violet eyes. "You did what you had to, Syrus. You saved thousands."

"And I'd have let them all die if it meant saving the two I love most!" I scream. I stand to my feet to face her, no longer bogged down by the pains of my mortal body. "My daughter is dead!" Tears stream down my face. Their salt brings a burning sensation to my cracked lips. "I deserve this punishment! I have brought it upon myself!" I admit aloud, an unbearable pressure lifting from my shoulders as I confess. These are feelings I've never allowed myself to speak, but Vesper's presence makes it all come pouring out.

I resent her for leaving me all alone in this darkness, yet I resent myself for being the reason she no longer walks this earth. It's an epiphany I haven't let myself revel in. It's the reason why I make no attempt at escape. It's the reason her words burn my heart with truth. She has always seen through any façade I've built. She knows me better than I know myself.

"You have punished yourself enough, Syrus," she whispers sympathetically. "Would you sooner go to your grave than forgive yourself?"

I wish I could touch her. I'd give anything to feel her tender caress. But she is merely a figment of my imagination. To touch her is to remind myself she isn't real. I wouldn't dare deprive myself of the first joy I've felt in months.

"I'd sooner avenge your death by killing this beast within me," I answer plainly.

"When will you get it?" Vesper moans. I recognize this tone of voice. She's vexed. I'm not saying what she'd like to hear.

"Get what?"

"Syrus, if you die, so will our memory," Vesper exclaims. "There is only darkness after this. Would you really prefer to walk into it without putting up a fight?"

"I do fight. Every full moon. My whole life, woman! Against my choice! Because of this damned curse that controls me! I am sick and tired of fighting!" My throat hurts from screaming but my emotions can no longer be contained.

"And I'm asking you to keep fighting," Vesper consoles quietly, realizing I'm past my breaking point. "If you truly love me, you'll keep fighting."

She begins to fade into thin air. I panic, reaching toward her. It's nothing more than instinct. It isn't fair for her to leave me like this. I haven't seen her in months. There's no telling if I'll ever see her again. There's a loud boom. The rock around me shakes violently. I hear Ophy screaming cheers in the distance. Several prisoners are howling. But all I can see are those violently beautiful violet eyes fading into the darkness.

Her words ring loud in my mind. *If you truly love me, you'll keep fighting*.

I'm alone again. The prisoners around me still shout at one another, likely debating the metaphysical lunacy Ophy preaches. The mountain still shakes as if it's coming alive.

I drown out everything. My eyes fix on the arrowhead. I need to discover the truth. If it is made from iron or steel, all these emotions are for naught. If it is made from iron or steel, I am just as mad as Ophy.

I grab hold of the arrowhead and crouch beside the bowl of piss. The metal beneath is hidden beneath dried flecks of blood. My eyes fixate on it as I submerge it into the dehydrated piss. I rub the arrowhead between my fingers, carefully removing the dried blood flake by flake. My hand begins to tingle as my fingers make contact with the metal beneath.

I lift the arrowhead from the urine and hold it close to my eyes. We are in the pitch dark, but the metal shimmers nonetheless. Jolts of electric current run down my forearm. I almost drop the arrowhead from the startling surprise. Holy shit. It is silver, I realize. I've been pierced by silver and survived!

I walk up to the bars that stand in my way from freedom and wrap my free hand around one of them. The hair on the back of my arm stands as it feels as though I've grabbed a bolt of lightning. I grit my teeth painfully. My mind focuses as the current of electricity sears through my body. The pain radiates, then slowly subsides like an evanescent note from a violin hanging in the air.

Goosebumps turn my flesh into a map of mountain and valleys. The numbing throb of pain remains, but it does little to weaken me any more than months of starvation and dehydration has. My gaze extends past the silver bar I grip. I lock eyes with Ophy. He is no longer shouting deranged slurs of religious quandary. He is watching me intently. His face has the look of one who has seen a ghost. But I am no ghost. I am a Muzzled gripping silver. I hold it just as a sage would grip a staff, or a knight a sword.

A warmth spreads through my chest and extends to my extremities. Light flickers within the contents of my cell, dispelling the surrounding darkness. The light shines into the rocky corridor, illuminating Ophy's face. Euphoria flows through me. The feeling is inexplicable. All traces of pain and agony disappear. Even Creon is silent now.

"Dagon's mercy," Ophy whispers, horrified at what he sees. He no longer has the face of one who's seen a ghost. He has the face of one who's seen a god.

The light is coming from my eyes, I suddenly realize.

"Oh my god," I whisper to myself. "I remember."

Darkness returns as I fall to the ground, unconscious.

5

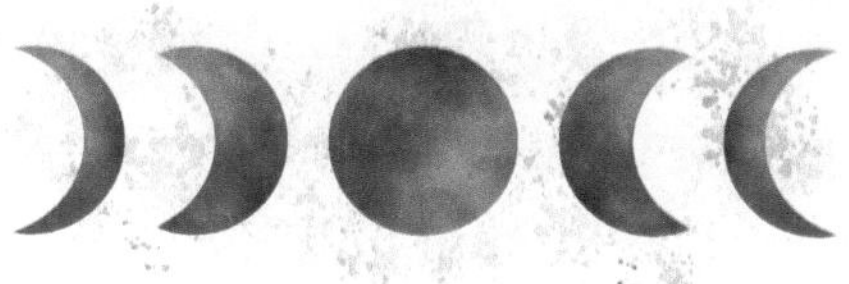

A Dream

"I beg you, father, tell us the story of Dagon and Damon!" I cry.

"Please, father!" Selena echoes.

The man laughs stoically. He's denied this request dozens of times by now, but he finds our persistence to be comical. "You already know my answer to that, children. You aren't old enough. The story will give you nightmares."

It's the same response he's given us for years.

"But Damon's eclipse is only a few short months away!" I answer. "And then I'll be a man grown! How can I be a Sylvian without knowing where my powers come from?"

The request makes sense to me, but father seems to think differently than I.

"Can't you just skip over the scary parts?" Selena begs. I don't agree with her logic. Half the reason why I want to know the story in the first place is so I can hear the scary parts. But beggars can't be choosers, so I will take what I can get.

Father pauses in the doorway. Contemplation strikes his figure. He is actually considering Selena's request. I can't believe it. This is the farthest we've ever made it toward breaking him down. He rubs his chin. I'm nervous to hear his response. My heart can't take another rejection. The anticipation is killing me.

"Fine," he announces loudly, "But only the basics. No scary parts. I'm talking to you, Syrus."

My ears perk up. Is this a dream? Did he just agree to tell us the story? I am in disbelief. "Yes, of course father, anything you say," I eagerly reply, sitting up in my bed. Selena looks to me with excitement in her childish eyes.

Father turns to us, his silver eyes glowing in the darkness of the night. Our dark eyes reflect the glow back at him. The light cuts through the night more powerful than the candle in his hand. He returns to our bedside, setting the candle down on the table between us. He sits politely on Selena's mattress, his body pointed toward me. Selena sits up excitedly. I try to conceal my excitement to preserve my dignity. I'm sure he can see it in my eyes, though.

"I guess the best place to start is the first eclipse. The sun was created to watch over us in the day, and the moon was made to guard us in the night. Thus they were, Solis, the god of the day, and Luna, the goddess of the night. But the two secretly fell in love from across the sky. They hid the love, knowing they were prohibited from being together."

"Why couldn't they be together?" I ask impulsively.

Father looks at me. The candlelight reflects off his pale face, dancing like fiery tides of the ocean on his skin. "The Creator forbid it, Syrus. The one responsible for all of creation. For if Solis and Luna were to fall in love, there would be no one to protect us in the day or night. All we know would be doomed to perish. But Solis and Luna thought themselves to be smarter than the Creator, so they traversed the stars to eclipse. It took years, but their love caused them to orbit toward one another."

"Is that how Damon and Dagon were born?" Selena interrupts.

Our father laughs. "I thought you two said you didn't know the story. Shall I stop there?"

"No!" I shout. "Selena was just guessing," I say, eyeing Selena scornfully.

"It was just something I heard in the castle, I'm sorry father," she apologizes.

"Hmm, if you say so. But yes, Solis and Luna eclipsed so they could express their love for one another. From Luna's bosom sprang forth twins named Dagon and Damon. And better yet, Solis gifted Damon with powers to protect creation during the day, and Luna gifted Dagon powers to protect the world during the night. Because of this, Solis and Luna no longer needed to protect creation, leaving it to their children instead. Their love affair continued, and creation began to notice the sun and moon's absence.

"The Creator soon learned of the sun and moon's sinful treachery and directed his wrath toward them. He punished Damon and Dagon for their parent's sin, turning their powers to curses. He made it so Damon would never walk in the sunlight of day again, and he forced Dagon to turn into a foul beast during the night. Without their protection, chaos ensued all across creation. Dagon wreaked havoc during the night, and Damon's flesh burned whenever he walked in the daylight. Solis and Luna were too encapsulated by love to notice creation's suffering. Meanwhile, the twins started creating offspring. Each of their bites infected the humans of the earth. Dagon's moonlit beasts multiplied. Dagon's sun-fearing soldiers spread."

"What of our ancestor, Sylvian, the third child?" I ask eagerly, connecting the dots on where the story is headed.

My father isn't annoyed by my impatience. He takes my excitement as something whimsical. Like it's comical how young and innocent I am. It feels demeaning in a humiliating way. My cheeks blush.

"Very good, Syrus," father commends, not adding to my embarrassment. "When the moon and the sun saw the peril their children Dagon and Damon had caused, they pointed their wrath at the Creator. They kindled all their rage and passion and eclipsed again, boring a third son. In the third son, they combined the gifts of Dagon and Damon in a single person, Sylvian, protector of the day and night."

I almost speak out again, wanting to guess what happened next, but I bite my tongue fast enough to dull the excitement. My father even pauses, anticipating me and Selena to interrupt the story again.

When he's satisfied with our patience, he continues. "The Creator expected his curse to affect Sylvian too, causing the sunlight to burn his flesh like Damon and the moon to turn him to a beast like Dagon. But to the Creator's surprise, the curses canceled out. When Sylvian walked in the sun's brightness, nothing happened. And when the moon was at its fullest, he was able to suppress the beast. Dagon's curse diluted the effect of Damon's curse, and Damon's curse allowed Sylvian to control Dagon's curse. Yet at the same time, Sylvian was able to control all the powers bestowed to him. In his creation, Solis and Luna had defeated the Creator at his own game, and Sylvian saved all of creation from Dagon and Damon."

"Is it true, father?" I ask, "Are we truly descendant from Sylvian himself?"

His brows furrow suspiciously, wondering where I'd gathered the doubt to ask such a thing. "You are named Syrus Sylvian, my son. Descendant from the great Silas Sylvian, who descended from Stoic Sylvian, who traced his origins all the way back to Sylvian the First. As are you, Selena," father whispers assuringly to my sister. "But family trees and namesakes do not matter, young ones. For on the darkest of all nights, you need only to see the glow of your silver eyes to know you are a Sylvian. 'Twas a gift from Luna to Sylvian, to light his way on the darkest of nights. Only Sylvians bear silver eyes, and only Sylvians can control the beast within."

"When will our eyes turn silver?" I ask.

"And when will we learn such powers, father?" Selena adds.

"It's for Solis and Luna to know, and for us to find out," he smiles back at us, his fangs showing beneath his lifted lips. "The time comes differently for everyone, but it seems to take longer for children who are impatient," he mocks, rubbing Selena's hair until it's a tangled mess. "Goodnight, children," he whispers.

"Wait, father!" I plead as he picks up the candle to take his leave. "You didn't finish the story! What ever happened with Sylvian? How did he defeat Damon and Dagon?"

"I guess that's a story we'll have to save for another night, isn't it?"

I groan deeply. There is no fighting him this time. He has already given into our demands once. There's a saying that beggars can't be choosers, and I am left with little choice this time around. I nod to him, thanking him after Selena does.

It was the last time I saw my father alive, for when I awoke the next morning, I laid in a pool of his blood, my entire family slaughtered around me.

6

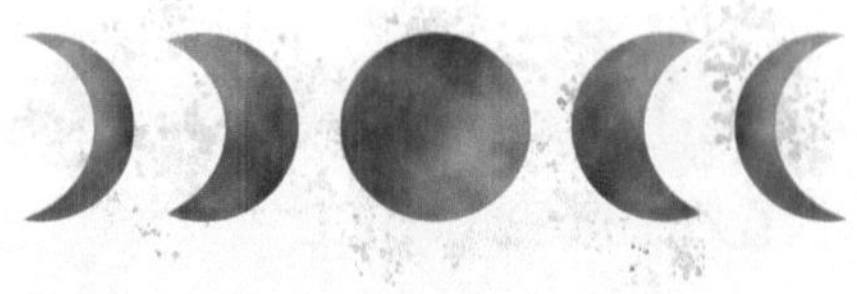

A Nightmare

I remember.

All these years I've spent trying to forget, but now I remember.

My life depended on me forgetting, but I remember.

For on the darkest of all nights, you need only to see the glow of your silver eyes to know you are a Sylvian.

My body is numb as I stare out into the darkness of my prison cell. The frosty air kisses my naked body. My hair stands like needles. A silent shiver runs down my spine.

My eyes no longer glow silver. They are the same pitch black I've known them to be since the repressed, bloody memories of my childhood.

The time comes differently for everyone, but it seems to take longer for children who are impatient.

After all these years, why now?

I've been a slave to Dagon's Curse all these years, a prisoner to the moon's wanton ways. Captive to the beast within, I've done unspeakable things because of my inability to control this curse.

Long forgotten was the promise that I could control the beast within.

When will we learn such powers, father?

It seems like a lifetime ago since my sister asked the question. After that night, I spent years hoping the day would come when I could control the curse. Then, when I realized no such power was coming, I spent years trying to control the curse myself. Micro-dosing wolfsbane. Locking myself away when Luna was at her fullest. Exiling myself from those I could harm.

That was all before I met Vesper, though.

"Dagon's downfall, I knew it was true," Ophy whispers from across the dark corridor. "You are him, aren't you? The Sylvian child that went missing all those years ago?"

I look up at him, my long, greasy, black hair hanging like a curtain in front of my face. It feels weird to see the reverence in his eyes. He looks at me like I'm a god. I've spent all these years repressing my past, all for it to explode in my face.

I don't answer him. My mind swells with a million thoughts. This all feels like some sick dream. Another cruel joke life has thrown at me to keep things interesting.

"We are saved!" Ophy screams, jumping up and down like a little kid in his cell. "Praise be! My visions were true!"

"You're hallucinating," I reply coldly. "You don't know what you're talking about."

"I saw the light too," Creon mumbles from a few blocks over. "If he's hallucinating, so are the rest of us." Creon is normally the one to argue against Ophy's delirium. Apparently there's a limit to his pessimism.

"I've heard stories of the runaway Sylvian," Creon says, "An old drunk in my village used to sit in the corner of the bar mumbling stories of olden days. Always thought they were fairy tales. He spoke of the royal Sylvian family, the direct descendants from Sylvian himself. Told the story of how their son murdered them in their sleep. Killed his parents and sister in cold blood."

My heart pounds in my chest. My blood pressure spikes as anger boils within. He has no idea what he's talking about. Memories from decades ago rise to the surface. The image of my parents torn apart limb from limb. My sister's bloody body on the floor. The surprised look on my mother's decapitated head. The puncture wounds in their skin. The torn flesh that looked as if a pack of jackals had ravaged their bodies.

Creon continues, "Turns out the Sylvian boy didn't have Sylvian's power after all. He was just like the rest of us, a slave to Dagon's Curse. So when the moon's fullness released his beast that night, the boy killed his family like a feral wolf kills an innocent lamb."

"Enough," I shout. My head feels as if it will explode. The beast stirs within. My brain burns. My limbs tingle. It feels like my eyes are on fire. I squeeze them shut to dull the pain. Light radiates from them again. Everyone is silent once more. I feel unstoppable. I stand from the pit of sorrow I've been sulking in and grip a single silver bar again.

It has no effect on me. It bends like taffy in my hand as I pull it to the side. I grind my teeth together, flexing my jaw. The strap of my muzzle snaps. The sound of it thudding against the ground is met by the dull echo of the rocks shaking beneath us. A war wages outside this mountain. A war wages within me. The world is filled with war, yet I've never felt so at peace.

I stare violently at my surroundings, seeing them with clarity for the first time. How have I let these fickle walls imprison me?

How could I have ever feared the Blackbloods?

How could I have run from my past?

How could I have forgotten who I am?

I am Syrus Sylvian, the last remaining Sylvian. The darkness cannot contain me. The beast within does not control me. The sunlight does not burn me. The moon does not command me. Sons of Dagon and Damon bow before me. Their curses are my gifts. Their damnation is my salvation.

The feeling fades. The light dissipates. Weakness returns to my bones all at once. It's too much to bear. A great weight descends on my shoulders. I can no longer stand. Too tired. I fall once more, unconscious.

7

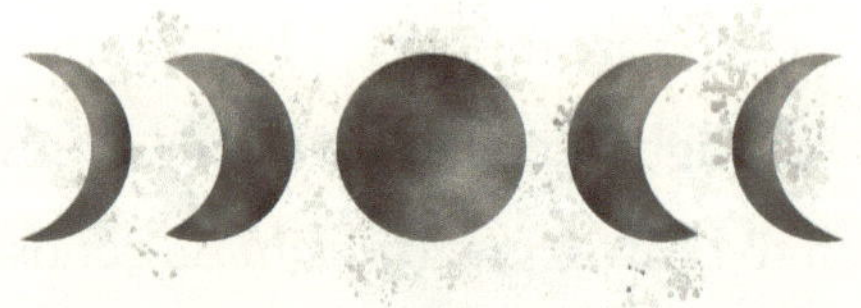

A Dream

Everything hurts. My mind is disoriented. My vision is blurred. My body is covered in blood. It's warm and sticky. The rocky ground beneath me is slick with it. The draft in the room chills my naked body.

I see my father's body first. It is motionless. I've never seen a being so dead as he currently is. Years ago, I snuck into a criminal execution in town square. Watched humans be hanged by their necks from the gallows for various reasons. I never forgot the way their bodies sickly swayed after their necks snapped.

Father's body doesn't sway, though. It is so dead it could convince an onlooker that it never possessed life in the first place. I'm shaking, unable to process what's happened. The parts of his face that aren't torn open or covered in blood are ghastly pale. His eyes do not glow silver anymore. His mouth gawks open. Blood trickles from the corner of his lips. The same lips that promised to tell the story of Sylvian's demise another time.

Father will never live up to that promise.

Father will never speak again.

I do not cry. I'm too confused to conjure tears. My head throbs like war drums pounding while an army marches. I can't remember anything from the time father left last night. I don't know how such a travesty could have occurred.

My mother's head lies several feet away from her body, staring at it like a snail stares at a shell that used to be its home. I may be too dazed and confused to know much, but I do know that heads are not supposed to be so unattached from their bodies. Her face stares with a look of horror at the bloody mess her body has become.

Selena lays not far from mother. Her limbs are a tangled mess of dislocated sockets. Selena's body caught the brunt of the damage. Her frail frame was defenseless against the assault. If the killer was able to slaughter mom and dad, Selena lost the fight before it began. Little flesh remains on her body, though chunks of it are scattered throughout our shared bedroom. Her bed is soaked in blood, as if the killer started their attack while she was sleeping. It looks as though someone has used her sheepskin mattress to mop up the blood on the floor. Its entire surface is smeared red.

I look down at my own body, rubbing the slick blood on my chest. I examine myself for my own wounds. I run my hands along my arms and legs, searching for the faintest sign of a nick or scratch. Nothing. I am covered in blood everywhere, but there isn't a single sign of injury.

It doesn't make any sense. I'm in shock. My fingers shake. My body feels as though it's been thrown from the highest window in the castle. I can barely move, much less find the strength to stand to my feet.

I desperately want to scream for help but my throat feels as though I've swallowed hot coals. My tongue is so dry that not even the Fountain of Youth could conjure saliva. Fever rises in me like lava before volcanic eruption. My eyes burn. My fingertips itch. My sternum feels as though it's been bludgeoned with a blacksmith's hammer. There's so much pain in my tailbone that I cannot sit without wincing. Every breath is a punishment to my ribcage. Every joint in my body is too swollen to bend.

I may not have external injuries, but I make up for it in internalized agony. Whoever did this must have fled before they could kill me. That, or they left me alive as a message.

A tear cascades down my cheek. How long have I been crying? I have no idea, but the tears come nonetheless.

This is just some nightmare. Another night terror I'll soon wake screaming from. Father was right, the story of Dagon and Damon has just given me nightmares. That's all this is. My subconscious mind is playing some sort of trick on me. Tutor Lundis taught me this. Said our mind has a way of communicating fears to us while we sleep. Said it's how our bodies deal with repressed memories and fears.

Oh, how I can't wait to tell him what I've dreamt about once I wake. I'm nearly proud of how realistic my mind has made this feel. My mother's face is identical to reality. It's haunting how well my imagination has painted the scene.

I twist my neck to look out the bedroom window. The light of a full moon kissing the horizon shines through. Dawn is coming, but night still reigns for now. I close my eyes once more. I'll wake soon, and when I do, this will all be some silly dream.

8

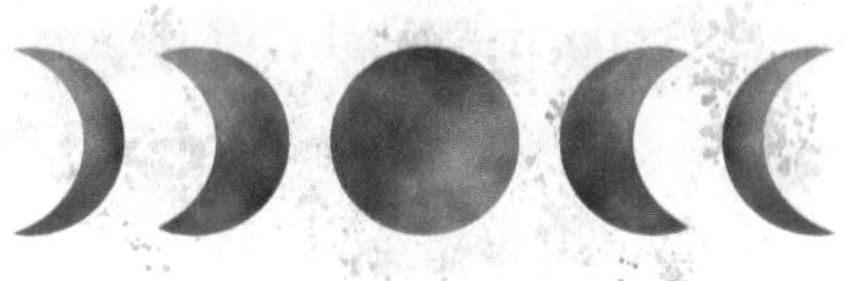

A Nightmare

When I wake, I'm just as naked as I was the night my family was slaughtered. Only now, there is no window with moonlight shining through. I'm no longer surrounded by my dead family. It's just me and the corpse of a nameless man I killed.

Tutor Lundis taught me this. Said our mind has a way of communicating fears to us while we sleep. Said it's how our bodies deal with repressed memories and fears.

Repressed memories. Terrible nightmares.

Because you've forgotten who you are, Syrus. I have come back to remind you.

I remember, Vesper. I remember.

There's no trace of euphoria to ease the depression I feel. My eyes don't glow. I can't even be sure that my silver eyes weren't a hallucination. I can't trust my mind after it's fooled me time after time.

I look over to Ophy for a sign of what's happened, but even Ophy has to sleep. He twitches in the far corner of his cell. He snores loud enough to wake the dead. No one else talks in our solemn corridor. All is silent, which makes me silently yearn for conversation.

I stare at the dead body the Blackblood left in my cell. It's hard not to wonder who he was or the things he did in a past life. Perhaps he was a carpenter or a mason. Maybe he was a husband and father like me. I'd like to wish he was a criminal to take the weight off killing another, but it likely isn't so.

His eyes are one of the only parts the beast within didn't harm. They are innocent eyes. Pale green like sea glass. His head is bald and covered with scars. His entrails hang from his slit belly like stuffed sausages above a butcher's block.

The wounds he suffered as a lycanthrope carry over to his human body. Our beasts clashed and his lost. An unfair way to go, forced to fight to the death with one of your own kind. We have little control of our bodies when the moon shines full. Any night could be our last in this dungeon. We have no sky to look up to. There's no telling how many days have passed between one full moon and the next.

Before slavery, our kind tracked the moon's movement and prepared for Luna's fullness. After generations dealing with Dagon's curse, we got good at minimizing our collateral damage. Developed ways of repressing the beast. Trapping it. Sequestering it.

But in the darkness there's little way of knowing when Luna grows full. We used to be able to tell as our bodies grew weaker by the day, but now we feel weak and feverish all the time. And so now we wait for our deaths and pray we wake the next morning, never knowing when a full moon will be our last. Then again, some of us pray we won't wake the next morning, knowing death can be no worse than this way of life. I am one of the few that doesn't pray. I stopped believing in gods at an early age. The Creator, Luna, Solis; they mean little to me. Dagon, Damon, Sylvian; they're all long dead. Just like my parents. Just like my sister. Just like Vesper and Sephora. Just like everyone I've ever loved in this world.

Anything that brings me joy in this world ends up dying, so I seek joy no more. My life is now this cell. Dark and cold and filled with despair. Twenty-four moons I've rotted in its womb. I used to count the days when I was first muzzled. But you lose track of Solis and Luna dancing in the sky in the places they don't shine.

Twenty-four moons. That's two years. Sephora could walk by the time she was twenty-four moons old. Her carcass has likely decomposed in twenty-four moons.

I married Vesper within twenty-four moons of meeting her.

So much can happen in twenty-four moons.

So little can happen in twenty-four moons.

A man can go crazy in twenty-four moons.

I stare up at the silver bars that hold me captive. One of them is severely bent. It looks as if a Blackblood itself has punched the bar as if to make it bow inward. They have the strength to do such. Silver effects them not, and their strength surpasses that of the Undead. I've seen them shatter the skull of a Muzzled with a single blow. We are fickle in our human form, and though we could likely kill them when the beast comes, there is a reason we all wear muzzles.

Well, some of us, I think. I stare at my muzzle. It lies on the ground, the leather strap that once dug into the back of my skull now snapped.

It wasn't a hallucination, I realize.

My trembling fingers rub the sores around my mouth that remain where the muzzle previously cut into my skin. Twenty-four moons of it shielding the Blackbloods from the dangers of the beast within me. Twenty-four months of blisters and chafe and infection.

The muzzles are a sign of their fear.

They fear what we can do when the moon favors us.

They fear us the way a trapper fears a feral wolf with nothing to lose.

Leash us, cage us up, restrain us with a muzzle, but we will silently await our chance to attack. And when they deceive themselves into thinking we are powerless, right when their guard is at its lowest, that's when we will bite.

Twenty-four months it took to free myself from my muzzle. Twenty-four months the Blackbloods have beat, tortured, and killed us. Twenty-four months and the monsters are comfortable enough to laugh at our miserable existence. Twenty-four months of watching us kill each other like rabid animals. Bloodlust sits on his throne every full moon, watching us rip each other apart because our beasts are too savage to form an alliance.

And now Bloodlust would use us like wolves unleashed on a herd of sheep. Expendable soldiers to send out against the Undead. He cares little whether we kill each other or kill his enemy. Regardless, he kills two birds with one stone by sending us to fight the Undead.

I stare at the broken muzzle, then the bent silver bar.

I am Syrus Sylvian, descendant from Sylvian the First. The Blackbloods have no idea who they've imprisoned. Now that I remember my identity, nothing will save them from my wrath. I will rip Bloodlust's head from his shoulders and watch his body leak black blood until his throne is too slick to sit upon. I will kill them all. These halls will flow with rivers of black blood.

I will lead the wolves as Sylvian the First did against Damon in the days of old.

I will learn to control the beast within; I will tame the wretched demon that has ruined my life, and I will make him earn his penance for the atrocities he's committed.

You may try, mortal man, a voice threatens from the confines of my mind. It is not my inner voice, though. The threat echoes in my head, but the thought did not originate from my own brain. Its voice was a sinister growl. The growl of a predator backed into a corner. The threat of someone with their back pressed against the wall.

I look around for a moment, though I know no one fills my cell walls. It's only me. Me, the corpse, and the darkness.

It speaks again, *I am the only reason you are alive. Your life belongs to me, weakling. Your Sylvian powers change nothing. I will not submit to your command*.

"Ah," I sigh. "So you'd rather stay here and submit to the Blackbloods?" I ask the beast in my brain. Never before has he spoken to me, and I can't be sure he isn't another deranged hallucination. Nevertheless, his defensive demeanor is almost comical to my manic mind.

You hear me?

"Yes, I'm finally looney enough to hear voices in my head that are not mine."

All your life I've spoken to you, and you finally hear me?

The voice is surprised. I'm caught just as off guard as he is. Here I am, having a conversation with myself. Or no. A conversation with a being within myself. Or maybe my mind has finally fractured and I'm off my rocker. I reply, "I hear you, beast of Dagon."

How?

"I am from Sylvian. I have the power to control your powers, I think."

I submit to no one, fool.

"That's odd, because it almost seems like you've done nothing to free us from this bondage," I reply.

Twenty-four times I've saved us from death over the past twenty-four moons. Have you no appreciation for my genocide? The beast asks the question rhetorically. He's proud of those he's slaughtered. I stare at the corpse at my feet, disgusted by its ravaged body. It's been here several sleeps. It's beginning to rot and smell as rats and pests feast.

"Yes, bravo for putting on a show for the Blackbloods. A real bang-up job you've done, beast. I could have hardly done better if you were to submit your powers to me."

I am the alpha here, human!

"Alphas do not have to announce their position as alpha," I chuckle. The feelings of euphoria slowly seep back into me. Damon's curse rises to counter Dagon's. I should be afraid of the beast, but I'm not. He's killed countless people. He's spilled more blood than an Undead consumes in an entire lifetime. And yet, his threats are empty to my ears.

How dare you—

"Your reign is over, beast. You have ruined our life enough," I reply coldly.

Ruined our life? I've never done anything but protect us, human.

"Tell that to my dead family." My voice is venomous, filled with hatred for the monster that lurks within me.

Your dead family? You think I killed your parents and sister?

"They didn't kill themselves, wolf."

I told you when you were a child, human. I didn't kill them. We *didn't kill them.*

"What are you talking about?" I ask. His words don't make sense. It's like being told the sky isn't blue and the trees' leaves aren't green. He killed my family and caused me to go on the run. He is the entire reason the Undead Empire took power. Without my father's rule, the Undead wasted little time claiming the throne.

I mean what I say, Syrus Sylvian. We didn't kill your family.

"You killed them, wolf. You slaughtered them and left me to discover your bloodbath."

I killed no one! I saved you from your own death that night!

"Saved me from what?" I scream at the lonely darkness as if he is sitting in front of me. "There was no danger!"

Oh how little you know, host. You are more foolish than I thought.

"Then enlighten me, beast. I have nothing but time on my hands. Show me how you so bravely saved us that night."

I have nothing to prove to you, simpleton.

"Fine by me. You're damned if you do, damned if you don't. Don't show me and I will continue to blame it on you; show me and you'll have obeyed my first order to you."

Silence.

Long, drawn out silence.

My vision blurs so I can focus on the sound within my mind.

Was it all a hallucination? Was the beast just another hallucination in my arsenal of ghosts? Another way for my mind to vent its lunacy as the loneliness of darkness takes over my mind. I hear nothing within the confines of my head any longer. I'm left to deal with the silence, all alone. There's a coldness in my chest. Numbness in my fingertips. Chatter in my teeth.

What I'd give for a blanket. A warm bowl of soup. A campfire. A tub filled with boiled water. The steam floating from a cup of warmed coco.

I flex my calloused toes. Rub the aches in my hip. Shift my starved weight from one buttock cheek to the other. Contemplate dragging myself to the bowl of piss for a drink. The thought of exerting effort deters me.

I only have the energy to shift my eyes between the broken muzzle and bent silver bar.

Broken muzzle.

Bent silver bar.

Twenty-four months.

The mountain rumbles suddenly.

The Undead must be attempting another breach.

The ground vibrates beneath me, further perpetuating the pain in my buttocks and hip.

I swivel my body and rest my head against the chewed-up thigh of the corpse beside me. I close my eyes and listen to the rock around us exploding like fireworks in the sky. The thought of the Blackbloods returning to another night of war is soothing to me. I hope the two armies slaughter one another.

I stroke my mangy beard until I fall asleep.

I sleep to replace this darkness with another.

I sleep so I'm no longer alone.

I sleep, and my mind whispers its deepest, darkest fears to me.

9

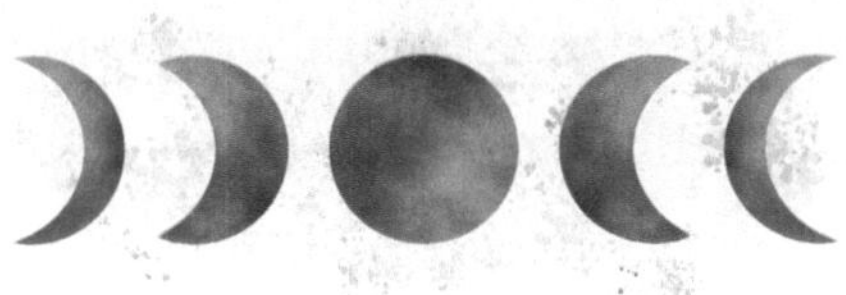

A Dream

"Master Syrus!" a voice breaks me from my trance. My teary eyes float from my father's corpse to my mother's. My mother's to my sister's.

"Master Syrus!" I can hardly see through the tear-blurred monochrome vision. The world has lost its color. The blood on the floor is black. The bodies are white.

The air is white. My heart is black.

I'm in shock, that much I know. But knowing doesn't make it any easier to break free from its grip. It feels like time is slow motion. My hands can't stop shaking. They have two minds of their own.

The tears on my face are stained red from the dried blood on my cheeks.

"Master Syrus! Look at me!"

Why is someone calling my name?

A hand grips my bloody arm.

I look up slowly from my father's carcass. My eyes follow the hand to its owner. Black shadows. White face. Black lips. Black eyes. White hair.

I recognize this man, though the shock tries to keep my mind bogged.

"V-ven-vent—" I mumble but my chattering teeth won't allow me to get the name out.

"Shhhh, child, we need to get you out of here." His face is sincere. His eyes are laced with worry. His grip on my arm is delicate, almost fatherly. When I lock gaze with his eyes the world's color returns. His eyes are a beautiful shade of lilac. His hair is layers of white and grey and silver. I study the lines of his face and recollection registers.

"I—I killed them Ventur..."

"It wasn't you, child," Ventur consoles, "It was the beast within. You had no way of controlling it."

"I'm a Sylvian," I sob, "I'm supposed to be able to control Dagon's Curse."

"You've not yet grown into Sylvian's powers, child. I need you to get up, Syrus. Are you hurt? Can you walk?" His voice is panic stuffed inside a calm façade.

"I can't leave them here," I reply, staring at my dead family.

"You must, Syrus. We have to leave now. The royal guard will discover what you've done, and when they do, you need to be far from here. They will hunt you down for your crimes. We need to leave now," he orders, applying pressure to my arm. My legs feel like overcooked pasta. I barely have the strength to think, much less walk. Yet Ventur pulls me from the ground nonetheless.

I don't have time to take in what's happening. He slings me over his shoulder and departs. My eyes remain fixed on my mother's detached head as we leave the room.

My head bobs as we descend that grand staircase. Flinches as we break through the castle's entrance doors. My eyes squint as the fading moonlight is replaced by the sunrise.

I hear Ventur scream out in pain as the light hits him. He continues to run as the sunlight burns his flesh. I feel the warmth of his body come to a fever pitch. Steam rises from his skin like smoke from a burning thatch building. His legs continue to carry us.

I can feel his flesh as it begins to blister. Ventur moans in agony as he fights the pain to carry me further from the castle. The sunlight shines beautifully across the castle courtyard, but the same beautiful light is killing Ventur with every step he takes.

I can feel the warmth of his cooking flesh through his bedtime linens.

He is Undead, and the daytime is not his to walk freely. Yet he was my father's right-hand man. My father's closest confidant. Ventur has been like a second father to me. Even now, he sacrifices his life so he can save mine.

The full moon taunts me as it sulks over the horizon. Dagon's Curse has finally possessed me after all these years. Dagon's cruel ghost silently laughs somewhere after watching me kill off the Sylvian family.

It has taken many generations, but finally Dagon has avenged his death. Luna mocks me as she disappears. Solis laughs as he sears Ventur's body. The Creator smiles at my misfortune.

I gasp as Ventur collapses beneath me. We both come tumbling to the ground, landing beneath the shade of a Bloodmaple. Ventur chokes for air as smoke exits his lungs. He is being burned alive before my eyes. I panic when I look at him. He is not the man who gripped my arm minutes ago.

His silver hair has singed from his bald head. His face is cracked and scarred and blistered. His eyes are no longer lilac, but instead glazed over with a foggy grey. Smoke rises from his body like roast lamb over a pyre. I'm forced to helplessly stare at him as he fights for every breath. And still the sun rises in the distance, waiting to consume Ventur with its gaze.

The Bloodmaple's crimson leaves protect Ventur with their shade for now, but when Solis takes his throne in the sky midday, Ventur's body will be reduced to ash floating in the air.

"Run," he gasps. "As far as you can!"

His voice is like sandpaper on cement.

War horns sound in the distance. Alarms sound from within the castle. They've discovered my parents' bodies.

Ventur was right. They will hunt me down for my crimes. Regardless of him being my father, I've killed the king. The queen. The princess. I slaughtered the entire royal family in a single night.

I look down at Ventur as he squirms uncomfortably toward the trunk of the Bloodmaple. He drags himself to a seated position, pressing his back against the tree's bleeding bark. Crimson sap leaks onto his head and shoulders. "Go now," he cries. No tears fall from his smoking eyes. "You are the last Sylvian, you must live!"

I am unable to speak. My throat is choked with a thousand griefs. It's all happening too fast to process. First my family, now Ventur. Ventur will soon die, and I will be the reason for his death.

"Deploy Scouts!" Someone screams from the castle. "Lock the castle grounds down!"

I stare at Ventur. He mouths something to me, but his voice can no longer speak.

A single leaf falls from above. The crimson maple leaf lands on Ventur's dying body. Orange veins run over its surface. It shrivels instantly as sunlight breeches the shade. The Bloodmaple leaf cannot withstand the sunlight once separated from the tree. The light hits Ventur's face as it pushes the shadows back. I see the look of agony in his blinded eyes.

He tries to scream the pain away but he is like a piece of crackling wood in a fiery hearth.

The sunlight hits my skin and its warmth brings me comfort. Dagon's curse has claimed me before Damon's could. I am safe from Solis's deadly gaze, unlike Ventur. But the moon will come for me in the night, and I will never again be safe from her.

I will run for now, but there is no running from the moon's beckoning howl.

She will find me in the night.

She will find me, and then no one will be safe.

I look down at Ventur and wonder if he should have let me be killed for my crimes.

How many more will die now that he's saved me?

My ear twitches as I hear Scouts sprinting through the castle courtyard.

I run.

I run, and I don't look back.

10

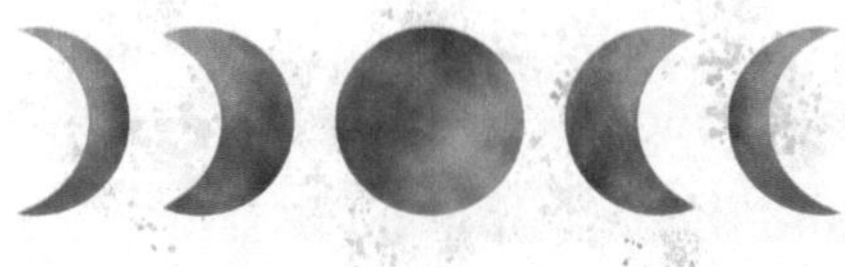

A Nightmare

Wake up! a voice screams within my head.

My eyes snap open. I'm suddenly alert. My panting breath freezes in the air in front of me. The running mucus on my nose turns to phlegmy icicles. The damp rock around me frosts. The humid condensation transforms my cell into a palpable blizzard. The cold penetrates my skin. The blood within my veins feels as though it is frozen. My heart fights to pump. My pulse rockets.

The sound of swollen, decaying feet dragging fills the corridor. One of them is coming. The air itself is devoid of warmth in their stale presence.

I stare at the bent silver bar and panic. The Blackblood will see it. My eyes shift to my broken muzzle on the ground. We are forbidden from taking the cage from our face. Several have in the past. They were taken away and never returned. Those who remained were smart enough to know what happened to them.

My mind rushes. I don't know what to do.

I suddenly feel like a child seconds away from a parent's scolding. Only it is not my parents who will soon discipline me. It is a demon from hell itself who will weigh me for my sins. I look at the muzzle and know I will be found wanting.

What was I thinking?

I wasn't. The hallucination of my Sylvian powers made me feel like a god for a brief moment. The fear in my heart now reminds me I'm no such thing. I feel more human now than ever. I am mortal, and I've sentenced myself to death.

No, a voice growls within me. *We stand and fight*, the beast commands. *The arrowhead. Grab the arrowhead*.

Another hallucination?

I shuffle on the ground to the bowl of piss and break through its frozen surface. The silver weapon is hidden at the bottom of my collected urine. I pull the arrowhead free, gripping it tightly.

My fingers itch. My teeth ache.

I know these feelings. I look down and watch my nails fall like bloody clippings to the ground. My hands tremble feebly from the pain. I spit bloody teeth from my mouth. I run my tongue along the inside of the fangs growing in their place. The taste of my bloody gums is oddly satisfying. The feeling of my claws digging into my palms is reminiscent of a past life.

Normally it takes immense focus for me to call forth these powers without the beast fighting for control. But now the Curse of Dagon comes over me effortlessly. I normally wouldn't risk relying on Dagon's Curse without consuming wolfsbane to give myself an advantage, but it's been twenty-four months since I've had access to the poisonous flower.

Something stirs within me, pushing back the coldness in my veins. The goosebumps on my skin disappear. The frosty air melts when it makes contact with my flesh. Mucus flows freely from my nose. My heart rate slows. I'm focused.

This is no hallucination.

The Blackblood's body comes into clear view in front of my cell. It stops and tilts its head when it sees the bent silver bar. Its body pivots to inspect me. Its slitted eyes dilate when they see my mouth no longer covered with a muzzle. A queer grin flickers at the corners of its mouth.

We lock eyes. It doesn't sense the danger lurking inside me. It smiles arrogantly, revealing its rotting fangs and charcoal tongue.

"Well, what do we have here?" The Blackblood exclaims. "The penalty for removing your muzzle is death, Son of Dagon. What say you?"

I stare at him without remorse. Fear flees my chest. My shoulders lift. I stand and step confidently toward the silver bars. The arrowhead tingles in my hand. I clench it tightly, cutting my palm open on its edges. Blood pours from the cracks between my fingers. I feel the metal's power coursing through me.

The beast within flinches, submitting control to me. Hallucination or not, his voice is dead silent.

"I'm no Son of Dagon," I reply coldly.

I can feel the eyes of others watching me. It has been months since someone in our corridor has openly defied a Blackblood. We learned our lesson long ago.

The Blackblood looks at me curiously. He's amused by my answer. I'm like a defiant ant crawling on his skin, not knowing his hand is moments away from crushing me. His muscles pulse, his rocky skin crackling with every breath. The Blackblood virus has not been kind to this monstrosity. From the looks of him, his body was meant to be dead decades ago. The virus has spread throughout his body so completely that black bones protrude from his leathery skin like sharpened stalagmites on a cavernous floor. The Blackblood's ribs are like obsidian spears tearing free from his chest. His spine is like a ridge of mountains and valleys. The webbing of his wings has long decayed, leaving only the exoskeleton of blackened bones behind. His rocky exoskeleton is like armor spread across every inch of his body.

If a Blackblood's level of dangerousness can be determined by how long they've been infected, this Blackblood is one of the most dangerous I've ever seen. What he's doing on patrol duty though, I have no idea.

"You're a mangy mutt is what you are," the Blackblood grunts hysterically. "I've no idea what Bloodlust wants from someone belonging to your filthy kind."

My ears twitch at what the monster's said. My fists slightly unclench. I look to him for clarity as he jingles keys to unlock my cell door. Then I see the mark on the back of his hand. The years of infection have swelled around the branding, attempting to cover it like moss over a stone. But the marking is still distinguishable. It's the mark of the Dread, the insignia for Bloodlust's royal guard.

This is no jailor that twists the key to my cell. This is one of Bloodlust's own imperial guards, I realize. He steps back as my cell door opens, gesturing for me to come forward. He is not here to kill me. He was sent to retrieve me.

"You've been summoned by Bloodlust himself," the Blackblood announces, loud enough for all prisoners around to hear. "Follow me, and don't you dare try anything without your muzzle on or it'll be your dead body that makes it to Bloodlust."

For fear of revealing the sharpened fangs, I don't dare open my mouth in response. I clench my fists and limp after the Dread Guard.

11

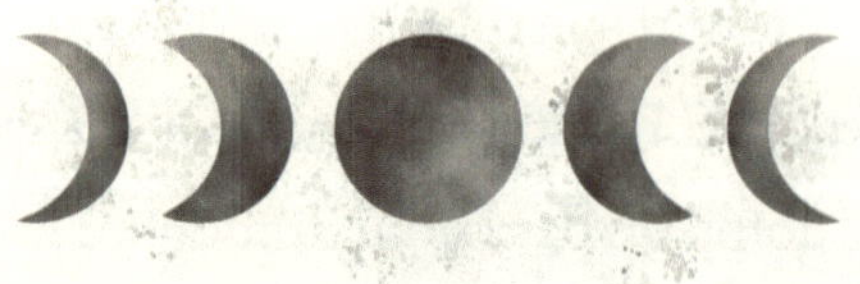

A Nightmare

I've never traversed the cavernous tunnels of this hallow mountain while cognizant. It is always my feverish, incapacitated body being dragged to and from the fighting arena. I do my best to take in every detail possible, mapping the tunnels out the best I can without writing the twists and turns down. If I'm to escape someday, I'll need to know where I'm going.

We are no longer surrounded by prison cells.

Now is your chance. Kill him.

No, I reply inwardly to the beast. He's right, though. We are walking alone through a narrow tunnel. The walls are so tight together the Blackblood's shoulders scrape against them with every step. If I kill him now I can make a run for it. But making a run for it is pointless if I don't know where I'm going.

I'll tell you where to go.

The voice pops in and out whenever it wants like a whisper in my ears. It reads my thoughts like I'm speaking directly to it. It's like my brain is cut in two, yet I can't read the thoughts of the other half.

I'm going insane.

You aren't going insane. You can finally hear me.

I'm filled with the irresistible urge to bash my head in until the voice stops talking.

You only hurt yourself if you do that.

I want to scream.

What good will that do?

It will shut you up.

Only dying will do that.

Great, maybe Bloodlust will solve all my problems in a few moments then. There's nothing I can do to drown out the insanity. Twenty-four moons and this confinement has finally broken me.

I follow the Blackblood into the open as the narrow corridor funnels into a vast chamber so expansive my eyes can't discern its limits. It is a crater in the center of the mountain, nothing but a five-foot rocky walkway between my feet and an indiscernible plummet to my death. My breath catches in my throat as I peer over the edge. Darkness bars my vision from seeing the bottom.

The hollow womb is filled with ice and emptiness. Frozen fog swirls in the open expanse. I can't tell how far the opening goes up or down or across. Cold condensation assaults my bare flesh. Black ice along the walkway seeks to send me to an early death. I listen to the Blackblood's sharp talons crunching through the ice to secure easy footing. My calloused feet don't have the same luxury.

I look up briefly. There must be a thousand stalactites dangling from the ceiling of the cave a hundred feet above. Some of them sway, others are motionless. They don't look like normal stalactites. They aren't—

Those aren't stalactites.

The beast's voice startles me. I stagger a step as my left foot slips on ice and comes close to sliding over the edge. I throw my arms out to catch myself, accidentally throwing the arrowhead from my grasp. I watch as the silver metal plummets into the darkness of the chasm. I don't hear it ever hit the bottom. There goes my only weapon. Instant adrenaline flushes my cheeks. I regain footing and collect myself. The Blackblood doesn't look back. It's apparent he cares little for whether or not he delivers me to Bloodlust alive.

I return my eyes to the ceiling and squint them tight. Epiphany and fear strike simultaneously. It can't be. No. No way there's that many of them. Thousands dangle from the ceiling, sleeping upside down. Their wings wrap around their bodies like cocoons. Their talons dig deep into the rocky ceiling to hold the weight of their corpses.

How could this have possibly happened without the outside world noticing?

The Acolytes destroyed the Blackbloods in the Holy Crusades hundreds of years ago. They struck Marduk down and burned his body so the virus would at last be eradicated from the face of the earth.

They obviously forgot a couple, the beast snickers.

Shut up! You do nothing but patronize me, I reflect inwardly. Look at me, screaming in my mind at my own insanity. Insanity begets insanity.

I could jump over this edge now and put an end to all the pain and suffering. Rejoin Sephora and Vesper and Selena in the afterlife.

I feel like a lamb being walked to the slaughter following after the Blackblood. The cave walls slowly become covered completely in ice as we march forward. We are close to the Blackblood King. I can feel it. The air freezes the closer we get.

Without warning the Blackblood stops and punches the wall beside us, shattering the ice like glass. The fragments fall, exposing the open archway they'd been covering. The Blackblood ducks into the alcove. This mountain is mined with more tunnels than the inside of an ant hill. I can no longer feel my feet from walking on the ice. The skin is long numb. Ice crystals form in my beard. With every blink my eyelashes threaten to freeze together. My throat burns from dryness. My fingers turn pale blue. I nearly go blind from the cloud of ice vapor.

I lose sight of my guide in the veil. The cold eliminates my sense of smell. I pray my feet don't fail me as I walk a gap between space and time. My frostbitten fingers scrape along the icy rock on either side of me. It is hard to breathe. It feels like being trapped beneath a sheet of ice in a body of water. My lungs ache to take their next breath, but any attempt at breathing is moot. My body is at war with the elements. I'm being frozen alive. My mind panics. I consider turning around for a moment, then think better of it. I have no idea of knowing which way is back. If I take a wrong turn and end up wandering this path much longer I will suffocate.

Left. Right. Left. Right. I count my steps to take my mind off its suffering. I can't feel below my ankles. Left. Right. Left. Right. I just have to trust my feet are still there.

I can't carry on any longer.

I stagger.

I fall.

It's no longer cold.

I can't feel anything anymore.

I'm dying, I realize.

My body is shutting down.

Is this really how I go?

A comfort rises in my chest.

If there is nothing but darkness after this life, I only hope it isn't as cold as the darkness I have felt while living.

I slip away into the world of nightmares.

12

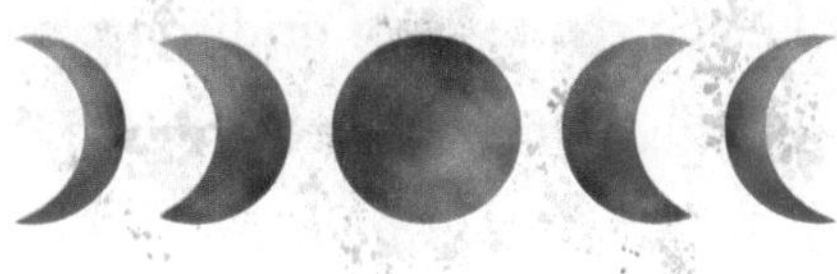

A Dream

I stare down at the valley in horror. It's been a year since the Undead scouts told me of the Blackbloods, but it wasn't until now that I believed the rumors. Sephora gasps beside me as she peers over the cliff. "Dad..."

"Shhhh," I quiet her. The sun is above so we are safe for now. By the time Luna wakes for the night though, we will need to be far from here. "Go to your mother. Tell her what we've discovered. Tell her it's true. The Blackbloods have returned." I whisper the words, almost as if I'm afraid uttering their name will further speak them into existence.

"We have to help them dad!" Sephora shakes her head. "You're going to help them, right?"

"Go to your mother, Seph. I'll be there shortly." I ignore her question, staring down with a pit expanding in my stomach.

Humans, thousands of them. Solis shines down on them with broad daylight. They're all naked and chained in shackles. Their only shelter from the sun is the shade provided from the surrounding mountain peaks. But mountain peaks cannot drown out the merciless midday sun. The heat is enough to melt skin. I stand hundreds of feet above them and even I can feel the waves of heat rising from the valley.

There are dead bodies all among them. Prisoners who couldn't survive the conditions. I even see rotting bodies and decayed skeletons. Chains still shackle their dead ankles to the rows of gridiron plates. The stench that rises with the heat is enough to make my eyes water. The unbearable smell of thousands of humans and their excrements being cooked beneath the sun.

How could such a thing be happening without the outside world's notice? The valley of death stretches for miles, humans laying on black rock, motionless. Two rivers flow on either side of the prisoners, both bodies of water out of reach from the humans. The rivers pan wide at the foot of the mountains. They create a moat around the prisoners, then exit the valley beneath the cliff I stand on.

Truth be told, the river is the only reason I discovered the death camp. If it wasn't for pitching our tent a mile downstream last night I would have never seen the bloated body floating in the black waters. The dead body was missing a foot, something that confused me at first. Now I understand he must have cut the limb off to escape the shackles. Cut the limb and crawled into the waters in a desperate hope to float toward freedom.

He likely bled out in the river's liberating embrace.

I watch them intently. The sun beats down on the black rock with all the heat it has to offer. The black rock accepts the heat gratefully, absorbing it to punish the humans that lay on its blacktop. They shift uncomfortably. Their moans harmonize every few minutes. Some dance from foot to foot, tolerating the fiery ground on one as long as they can before jumping to the other.

I am several hundred feet above but even I can tell they are bone thin.

"Dad?"

Sephora's voice breaks me from my trance. I thought she'd left me to return to Vesper. She's too young to see something like this. As her father, I'd prefer to conceal the horrors of the world as long as I can. Looking down at the death camp tells me I won't be able to preserve her innocence much longer, though.

"Are you going to save them?" she asks hopefully. She has Vesper's optimism, something I've always envied. But I've seen too much of the world to believe there's someone capable of saving these humans from their tragic ending. I know who is responsible for this atrocity. There is only one breed of monsters disgusting enough to collect humans like lambs for slaughter. This is the work of Blackbloods; I'm sure of it. The humans below are nothing more than livestock on a cattle farm to the beasts.

"You have to," Sephora continues, tugging at my sleeve. "The full moon is coming tomorrow. You can use Dagon's Curse to free them!"

If only, I reflect. "It isn't that simple, Seph," I reply, chewing the wolfsbane between my teeth. I've packed it in the space between my gums and cheeks, silently sucking it free from its poisonous juice. Its acidity and tartness caused my mouth to go numb hours ago. "I cannot control Dagon's Curse when Luna is full. I could accidentally kill them all," I say candidly. "There is nothing we can do for them, Seph. We need to move on before their oppressors do the same to us."

"It isn't right," she replies.

"The world isn't right, daughter."

"Doesn't mean we can't be, father."

Damn her optimism. It is one of my favorite things about her. It will be the death of me some day. "Someone else will come along, Sephora."

"We *are* that someone, dad."

I look down at her clinging to my sleeve. For a second my mind is tricked into thinking I'm looking down at Selena. I squeeze my eyes shut and focus my vision back on her. Her face is a spitting image of my long-dead sister. Caramel eyes twinkle the same color Selena's once did. I see the two girls I loved most in the world in her. How could I ever say no to those eyes?

"What would I do, Sephora? Sneak down there and break all their chains and carry them away? They're so weak they can't even walk." I don't know why I'm arguing with my daughter. I already know she's going to win. Putting up a fight is only a waste of both our times.

"What if it was you in those chains, father? What would you want someone else to do?"

"Go to your mother, Seph," I sigh. "I will stay here until nightfall. I need to see who is responsible for this, then I'll know by dawn what must be done. When the sun sets, send your mother to me so we may talk."

Sephora leaves, which means she's somewhat satisfied with my answer. She gets her stubbornness from me, no doubt. I've been on the run for so long that I've forgotten how to take a stand for something more important than myself. There's no time for morality when survival isn't guaranteed.

I've done a lot of things I'm not proud of to survive. Vesper has tamed me, and Sephora has reclaimed a shard of myself I thought was long gone.

I stare down at the death camp once more. What would my father have done? He was twice the man I've grown to be. I doubt he'd have hesitated in a moment like this. Silenius Sylvian would be down there now, leading the helpless humans to liberation.

I am overly cautious. I have my wife and daughter to think about. All these years I've perfected the art of keeping us hidden. If anyone were to discover the Sylvian bloodline still exists, the Undead Emperor would send all his forces after us.

I sense a storm coming. If the Blackbloods are behind this death camp and the Undead have caught rumor of their existence, all of creation will be consumed by war. By the end of it, either the Undead or the Blackbloods will remain. I can't say either would be ideal.

Part of me can't accept the Blackbloods returning. They've been extinct for hundreds of years. I used to tell Selena they would come for her in her sleep just to scare her. It was funny to me then because the thought of them being real seemed outlandish.

Looking at the death camp below makes me realize how terrified Selena must have been from my childish taunts.

I feel fear in my heart. Whatever is capable of committing such egregious sins against humanity is a force worth fearing.

13

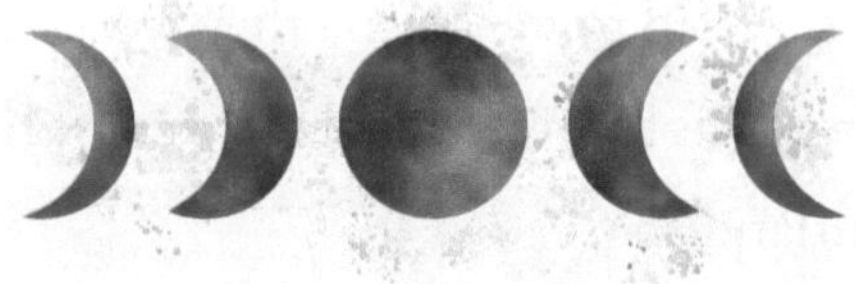

A Nightmare

I wake to the feeling of my corpse being dragged across merciless rock. My frozen flesh feels like a food grater is flaying me. A death grip clutches my wrist. A trail of frozen blood sits on my arm from where the Blackblood's talons dig into me. He drags me across the ground like a careless hunter drags its kill.

The shroud of ice vapor is gone. The narrow corridor of hellish ice is nowhere to be seen. I can breathe once more. My lungs deeply inhale, then regret it immediately. Coughing seizes my chest. The Blackblood doesn't pause as I writhe in a fit of coughing. He is the most savage savior I've ever come across. Doesn't look back to check on me. I could be dead for all he cares. The brute is on a mission to deliver me to Bloodlust. I get the impression he cares little whether I get there dead or alive.

I am too numb to resist the dragging. I would fight to gather my footing again if I could feel my body, but I'm merely a conscience floating in space. I feel nothing. I float between death's doorstep and life's misery.

The cave around us is a wide expanse of glowing ice. It glows like the Lights of Nightfall to the North. Blues and greens and reds and purples. A spectrum of beauty enough to make a grown man cry. Not me, though. My tear ducts are frozen solid.

It isn't the sort of sight one would expect to see when thinking about a Blackblood lair. I imagined a dark cave littered with skulls and bones stripped clean of all meat. Instead, the ice glows magnificently around us like one of the world's greatest wonders. It is the complete opposite from the dark, damp tunnel the Muzzled are imprisoned within.

"King," the Blackblood calls, pausing in his forward march. He releases my wrist and kneels beside me. I barely have the energy to scan his behemoth of a body crouching. "I have retrieved the prisoner you requested." The Blackblood bows his head humbly in the presence of his master. The position of my body doesn't allow me to see Bloodlust, and I no longer have the energy to twist for a better view.

All I can see is the beautiful ceiling, shining like the intergalactic cosmos above me.

"Tell me, Reynar, what did I ask of you?" A voice booms from some invisible place. The ice around us trembles as the stoic voice echoes throughout the chamber. The voice can belong to no one other than Bloodlust.

The Blackblood beside me raises his head to face his master. "You told me to retrieve the Muzzled who killed all the Undead last full moon, Bloodlust."

"Ah, and do you think I wanted you to bring him to me half dead?" The accusatory tone lingers in the air.

I eye Reynar beside me as he struggles to come up with an answer. I watch him hesitate.

"Better yet, do you think a Muzzled capable of killing that many Undead in this poor a condition should be treated delicately?"

"I—"

"Rise, Reynar." I am powerless to do anything but lay beside the Blackblood as he stands back to his feet. The shimmering spectrum of lights bounce off his black skin. I can feel the demon's fear. He hides it well, but there is no hiding fear in the heavenly lights that expose his features. The darkness is this beast's ally; he is vulnerable in this level of light.

A flash of cold wind rushes over me. A shadow passes over my helpless body like the angel of death. A sickening snap echoes, followed by the crunch of flesh ripping. Black blood gushes into the air like a fountain. The blood rains onto me, freezing like dark chocolate when it hits my frozen flesh. I flinch, squinting my eyes.

When I open them once more, I see Reynar's headless body drop back to its knees, then collapse lifeless onto the ground.

A creature who can only be Bloodlust stands above me with Reynar's decapitated head in his devastating grip. "You are discharged from duty, soldier," Bloodlust growls.

14

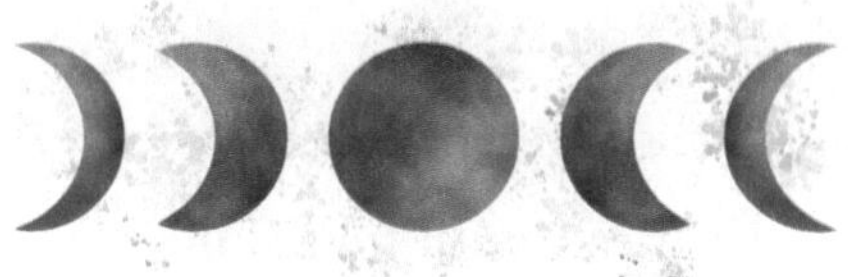

A Nightmare

The demon stares down at me like a god looking upon a mortal with pity. The lights of the illuminated icescape reveal his scarred, hideous body. Bloodlust's face is hidden behind the skull of a wolf. The skull is from some long dead Lycan, no doubt. I feel a tinge of sorrow to see one of my own be worn like a knight's helm. Fractures run across the surface of the wolf head. Dried flesh clings to the bone where the killer did a poor job skinning the beast.

The skull is a trophy of Bloodlust's superiority to our kind. His way of telling the world he has killed many of us, and he will continue to do so until we are eradicated from earth. The wolf's skull is big enough to cover his bulbous head, its empty sockets gazing at me like black pits of death.

I am nothing to this monster. Those of us cursed like Dagon are nothing more than prey to this hunter. He collects us. Fights us. Wears us like a hunter would wear a fur coat. But a fur coat wasn't good enough, so he scraped a wolf's head clean like a pumpkin and placed it on his head like a crown.

I cannot see beyond the bone. It is like staring at the dead corpse put in my cell. A constant reminder of the monster that lives within me. A gentle nudge to ensure I don't forget how weak I am.

Hatred doesn't describe what I feel toward this Blackblood.

My entire life has been ruined because of this monster.

My wife and daughter are dead.

Twenty-four moons I've starved in darkness.

Twenty-four moons the beast within has killed others of our kind.

There is little left of me but skin and bone.

And now I meet the leader responsible for my life's unfortunate demise.

Bloodlust.

King of the Blackbloods.

Slaver of Lycans.

Warlord against the Undead.

The Second Coming of Marduk.

"Tell me, Muzzled," Bloodlust commands. His voice makes the ice quake. Frost blows from the snout of his wolf helm. "What do you know of the Blackbloods?"

I lay before him, completely vulnerable. His monsterish foot is big enough to crush my skull with a single stomp. His body is clad with blackened muscle. Infected bones burst from his skin. Black veins surge like crawling worms beneath his flesh. Like snakes writhing to be let free, each of them carrying poisoned blood cursed with the Blackblood virus.

I cannot see his face, yet part of me is glad I cannot see it. Bloodlust's body is enough to tell me not even the face of a princess would be enough to redeem the quality of his physical appearance.

How does he expect me to speak when it feels as though the frost has bitten the inside of my throat?

"You were once the Undead," I croak uncomfortably. My face has long gone numb, my lips blue from the cold. Moving my jaw to form words feels like bending rusted hinges. "But the virus..." I struggle to move my tongue to finish the sentence. My teeth clatter uncontrollably. "Turns immortals to monsters."

Tendrils of icy smoke coil from the wolf's gaping jaws. I can't tell what Bloodlust is thinking behind the darkness of the helm. All I can see is the void in the empty eye sockets. Its gaze consumes me.

"We are not so different, Muzzled and Blackbloods," Bloodlust purrs. He has the voice of a panther. "We both have an evil within us that is outside our control. Dark urges that must be satisfied for us to survive."

He turns away from me and walks toward his throne. A massive slab of ice shaped to look like a chair. I can see the bones frozen within its translucent face. Skulls and skeletons dismembered throughout its base and backing. Bloodlust takes a seat on its edge, his charred arms clutching the throne's bony sides. "But you are no Muzzled." The accusation echoes throughout the chamber. The words chill my bones more than the ice in this room ever could.

He knows.

"How do you kn—?" I pause, not having the strength to say anything more.

"I had my suspicions after seeing what you did at our cattle farm. The suspicions were only reaffirmed watching you fight every full moon. A teacher never forgets a prized student."

I'm caught off guard. My brain doesn't have the energy to work through the statement. A teacher?

"Syrus Sylvian, the last remaining heir of the Sylvian household," he says the name with a sense of pride. The tone is one who admires the name and respects its heritage. "The boy who murdered his entire family because of his inability to control the beast within, now a grown man. What a disappointment you've become."

"I... I..."

"Look at you, so weak you can't even speak. Your ancestors were kings of this world. Not a single nation would ever dare cross the Sylvian household for fear of being slaughtered. In a past life, before this virus infected my veins, even I feared the family's power. I submitted myself to a life serving them. Your father was my greatest friend. Before you took his life."

"Who... are.... you?" I force the words out one at a time between endless fits of chattering teeth.

"*Vere mori skathen*." The Sylvian creed. *We conquer our demons*.

"Luh-lundis?" I say the name aloud for the first time in years. It can't be. It wouldn't make sense. But there are none who walk this earth who know the meaning of those sacred words. They have been erased from the histories. The Undead Empire has eradicated all knowledge of Sylvian creed. Wiped it from spoken language. Only those who walked by my father's side would be left with memory of our creed.

And those who walked by his side have been slaughtered.

All except... Lundis.

"What's left of him," Bloodlust replies.

"I don't... I..."

"Much happened after your family's demise, Sylvian."

My heart is racing in my chest. My head is spinning. It's all too much to process. My numb ribcage pulses rapidly. My childhood tutor is Bloodlust. The man who taught me everything I know. One of my greatest role models. The man who taught me how to be a man. Taught me to read and write and fight. The man I spent countless hours with.

All my suffering was enacted by this monster.

I can't make sense of it.

My family is dead because of this man.

The man that was once a second father to me.

He is the same monster that watched me kill the Muzzled moon after moon for his own amusement.

The man who taught me kindness is the one who enslaved thousands of humans to supply food for the Blackbloods.

The man who taught me compassion is the one responsible for my wife and daughter's death.

It's too much to bear.

My heart breaks.

Shatters.

Pain shoots down my left arm and leg.

I curl in the fetal position and let out a faint moan.

My racing thoughts disappear.

I am dying, I realize.

This is how I pass on from this world. Naked and afraid.

Frozen.

Unable to accept the betrayal of my former life's greatest mentor.

I watch as his perverted figure blurs.

His outline distorts worse than my memory of him.

The glowing light from the crystal ceiling fades.

Darkness replaces it.

15

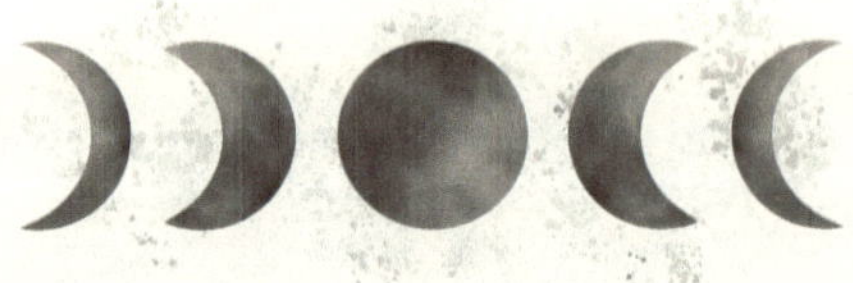

A Dream

I watch the sun retreat over the mountain's edge reluctantly. I watch the people below from a removed outcrop of rocks several dozen feet above. My worn grey coat blends well with the sunbeaten boulders. I draw my hood and wait.

The prisoners seem more afraid of the dark than they did the sun. Where they submitted to Solis's torturous ways hours ago, they now sit on edge, looking up at the sky. Some of them are panicking. They are much more active now that the sun is gone. They pull at their chains like lambs before slaughter. Just as animals can sense a storm coming, these humans can feel a palpable threat in the air.

I feel horrible for standing here and watching. Like a cruel man watching a predator stalk its prey without warning the prey what's coming. But in order to help these humans, I need to know what I'm up against. Freeing them only does so much if their adversary will be able to track them down the next night and enslave them again.

I hear a gurgled scream, followed by several others pointing in the distance. The entire valley is covered in nightly shadows now. I squint my eyes to see what they see, remaining motionless to avoid detection.

My blood freezes as the mountain explodes on the far side of the valley. It's so far away that it looks like a swarm of locusts has burst from the mountainous hive. The air is filled with them, their stark outlines ghastly in the dusk's evening glow. Their wings are torn tapestries beating the night sky to stay aloft, dark flags flapping violently in the winds of a hurricane.

An ungodly noise enters the air, echoing against the valley walls. It's the gut-wrenching, blood-curdling hiss of a hundred predators preparing for a feast. No one outside this inverted dome will hear the shrill cries of the prisoners below. They scream and cry and yank on their chains for liberation. There is weeping and gnashing of teeth.

The demons of the night sky descend on the helpless humans below. Their skin is black and grey so the darkness conceals most of what they do, but it's the echoing sounds that haunt my mind to fill in the details.

They do much more than drink the blood of their prey. I hear women screaming as the beasts steal all that is left of their sanctimonious bodies. Not just women, though. Men too, I realize. The demons mount men against their will, pushing their faces into the sand, forcing themselves on their demoralized spirits.

I catch a glimpse of one of the demons who's ventured near my outlook. She distances herself from the flock, expecting less competition on my side of the valley. Her body is a perversion of the Creator's intent in every way. All that remains of her hair is several white whisps that blow in the night breeze. Her face is sunken like the mummified remains of a being that died an eon ago. Her fingers and toes are talons. Wings like a featherless vulture. Black, leathery skin like a bat. She hovers over a human and grips his throat, lifting him effortlessly into the air in front of her. Her jaw unlatches, exposing rotting, blackened fangs. The man in her grip struggles violently. He kicks the air and claws at the grip around his neck, fighting the chokehold for one last breath of fresh air.

She smiles at him. It is the smile of the reaper when one dares to defy death. Her free hand fondles his genitalia, squeezing tightly around it. Blood seeps between her fingers as the talons remove all flesh between the man's legs. I see the man search for any way of screaming his pain for all to hear. All noise is stifled by the Blackblood's chokehold. His mouth opens for a silent scream like a fish kissing the air after being pulled from the water.

The Blackblood lifts her cupped hand to her nose, smelling the bloody manhood she's stolen from him. Blood pours down the man's legs from the wound like a woman during the moon's control. She licks the bloody mess in her hand, then devours it while the man watches. She pulls him close to her mouth, breathing the scent of his blood in his face. The man's face is so deprived of oxygen that it looks as if it might explode. The Blackblood licks the length of the man's face from chin to forehead. The black tongue is scaled in obsidian.

Something grips my shoulder. I jump, nearly cursing as I spin around ready to defend myself to the death. I'm met by Vesper's amethyst eyes glowing in the night. "Shhhh," she whispers. Her grip comforts me, making me realize how on edge I am. She wipes a tear from my eye that I didn't know was there. I grab hold of her in a tight hug. Silent sobs leave my body as I continue to listen to the desperate screams of a thousand humans.

"They've returned," I whisper in her ear. "Just when the world nearly forgot about them, the Blackbloods are back."

Our tears race each other to wet the barren rock beneath us.

16

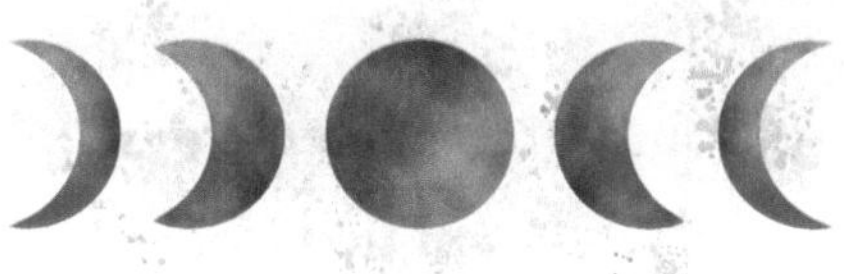

A Nightmare

I wake to the warmth of boiling water bubbling around me.

The first thing my eyes see is a dark sky full of stars. They glow with dull radiance in the overcast atmosphere.

"Am I dead?" I moan senselessly.

"You don't have my permission to die," Bloodlust purrs from a distance.

How long has it been since I've seen the night sky?

Twenty-four moons.

I'd lost all hope of ever seeing such a sight again.

I was sure death would take me before getting to leave the hellish dungeon of rocky confinement.

The fresh air heals my weakened lungs with each inhalation. The natural spring surges around me, the jetting currents massaging my frail body. It feels as though I'm comatose. A state of consciousness between life and death. A purgatory of past pains and future fears. My frost-bitten skin is numb from the overwhelming heat of the mountainous spring. I'm a block of frozen meat set in a cauldron to thaw. My blood slowly adjusts to the easy flow of pumping through my veins.

The clouds above move ever so slightly, exposing the crescent moon. It is merely a sliver in the sky. It is waning crescent. There is still quite some time before it will be full. It bleeds its fullness into the cosmos still before it refills for the next moon dance.

"What do you want from me?" I ask, my thoughts slowly returning to normal. The night air clears my confusion from unconsciousness.

"I am not the man you once knew, Sylvian." Bloodlust scoffs. "The virus has changed me. Blackened my heart. Perverted my nature."

"The Lundis I knew would sooner die than succumb to evil." I sigh, not looking away from the sky's beauty.

"The Lundis you know is dead, just as the Syrus I knew died the same night as his parents."

He has a point. It has been close to two decades since I last saw my childhood tutor. Two decades is longer than some are permitted to live on this earth. "You knew who I was, and still you made me fight all those moons. Twenty-four moons, Lundis. Twenty-four moons I starved in that cage. Twenty-four moons I killed others to save myself."

"Twenty-four moons I continued to teach you how to survive in this world, just as I did when you were a child," Bloodlust adds. I sit up, looking around to find him in the surrounding landscape for the first time. The water rolls down my head and shoulders. The chill of the night hits the condensation on my skin.

I now see that we are on one of the highest peaks of the mountain. The tub I lay in is a mere divot on the ledge of a cliff, a natural concave that leaks hot springs from the core of the earth. Several feet from the edge of the bath is a drop off with a kilometer long fall to the ground below.

Snow is packed loosely around the edge of the spring. Ice covers the mountain's crest. It has been two years since the air has kissed my skin. I've missed the Creator's beautiful world. It is summer, I realize. Summer of the second year, that is. Twenty-four moons I've been locked away. Eight seasons I've missed. But not even Solis is bright enough to thaw this mountain's tundra-scarred peak.

Bloodlust stands with his back to me, gazing off at the far horizon, deep in contemplation. His ghastly wings tuck between his shoulder blades. The wolf helm breathes frost into the night still. The stars above are just bright enough to expose the many scars along the Blackblood's infected flesh.

"Surely you aren't serious?" I reply. "What were you teaching me by enslaving and torturing me?"

"Advanced lessons," Bloodlust chuckles. "Lessons you were too young to learn before. Lessons you will need to learn if you're to retake the throne," he says stoically, twisting his head to look at me over his shoulder.

"Retake the throne? You must be bloody mad if that's what you think I'm going to do. I'd sooner jump off the edge of that cliff and plummet to my death."

"You still haven't figured it out, have you?"

"Figured what out?"

"Why running your entire life has made you lose everything," Bloodlust scoffs. "Your parents, your sister, your wife, your daughter, your kingdom. You've lost everything, Syrus. And still you run. When will you figure it out. It is not in a Sylvian's blood to run. The gods punish you for defying the very nature for which you were designed."

"You are the reason my wife and daughter are dead. You'd be wise to keep their memory out of your mouth, Blackblood." I warn, clenching my fists beneath the water.

"Your threats are emptier than your life's meaning, Syrus. Look at your reflection in the water. Tell me, do you recognize the man you see?"

I look down at the shifting water that surrounds me. A skeleton of a man looks back at me. His cheeks are sunken in from starvation. A scraggly beard consumes half his face. His eyes are deliriously mad. Like a raging lunatic. Bushy eyebrows and mangled hair down to his shoulders. I don't know who this man is that stares back at me. He is every bit as hollow as the heart that beats in his chest.

"How long will you run before you remember turning to fight is an option?" Bloodlust asks sincerely. "I did not teach you fighting as a boy as an empty gesture."

"I murdered the king of the old world," I mumble. "And you'd have me take on the Undead Empire to retake a throne that no longer exists?"

"You were a boy who didn't know how to control the monster inside of you," Bloodlust replies. "I didn't understand it when I was one of the Undead. I resented you for the chaos you threw the kingdom into. I wanted you to be found and executed as much as any other. But the virus has changed my perspective on things. Taught me what it's like to have a monster of my own, residing inside me, pushing me to do things I am not proud of. With that, I've come to realize it is not your fault for what happened. With that, I've come to forgive you."

"What in the seven hells happened to you, Lundis," I ask, desperate to shift the topic off of me, if even for a brief moment. My heart is pained to think back to that night.

Bloodlust turns to face me fully, his entire body tremendous with the starry night lit behind him. There isn't a trace of the zealous man I once knew. His entire body is consumed by the Blackblood virus. His veins bulge on the surface of his skin like black snakes crawling from head to toe. He is worse than any childish nightmare I had of the Blackbloods. The wolf helm atop his head peers down at me with judging contempt on its façade.

"There are many secrets you've yet to learn about the world we live in. Things your father would have taught you when the time was right, except that time never came," Bloodlust says with conviction. I'm split between the feelings of love I once had for him and the feelings of hatred I now hold toward him. "The only reason I escaped the massacre of your father's followers that followed his death was because he sent me away weeks before. It was a secret mission, one not even Ventur knew of. Your father had a premonition in the night. A vision, so to speak. In his dreams, he saw a black heart, beating upon a pedestal. Marduk's heart, he believed. The dream consumed him, appearing every night. Beckoning to him. Filling his head with nightmares of his death. The death of his entire family. Atrocities. He saw his kingdom fall. He saw the Undead rise. The sons of Damon claimed the throne. The sons of Dagon returned to slaughtering humanity. And worst of all, the Blackbloods returned."

Bloodlust looks down at himself, running his taloned hands down the length of his body. "He tried to dismiss the nightmares at first, communicated them only to me and your mother. I counseled him in secret, but the premonitions continued to plague him.

"We studied the histories together. It was written the Acolytes had cut Marduk's heart from his chest and drained his body of every drop of black blood left in his veins. But what happened to the heart was uncertain. Xander's histories said it was burned. Canterbury wrote it was frozen in rem-ice. Lysander's journals said it was locked away in a crypt within the Acolytes' ancient temple. Each record further contradicted what we believed to be the truth of the matter. And still, the black heart called to your father every night.

"So he sent me on a mission to find the Acolytes' lost temple. The rest is history," Bloodlust says, gesturing at his body once more.

"You found Marduk's heart?" I ask in disbelief, staring at the corrupted figure.

"And with it, the Blackblood virus found me," Bloodlust whispers. "By the time I was infected, your father was dead and the Undead Empire had taken the throne. Everything Marduk's heart had shown him came to pass, and I was forced into exile as the virus took over my body."

"You are the reason my wife and daughter are dead," I repeat, the memory of my life falling to ruins returning.

"You keep saying that as if it will change their fates. Point the finger all you want, Syrus. It will not change anything. What's happened cannot be changed."

"That doesn't mean it's forgiven," I spit back. The emotion returns. My blood boils at the sight of him. I'd push him from the cliff if he couldn't fly. I'm filled with the urge to rip the wolf skull from his head and bash his face in with it until there is nothing but a bloody puddle of blackened brain guts left. My fingertips itch for claws to grow. My gums ache with fangs pressing into my canines.

"I do not ask for forgiveness. I deserve it no more than you do. We will both be haunted by our actions for the rest of our lives. But fate brought us together after all these years. Teacher and pupil. The only remaining people in each other's lives who connect us to our pasts. This is not a mistake, Syrus."

"I'm not a Sylvian Lund—" I catch myself. This is no longer Lundis. "Bloodlust. I don't have the powers my father did."

"The wolf I saw the last full moon had eyes that turned silver when pierced by an Undead's arrow," Bloodlust counters, "You may have gone your entire life without Sylvian power to control the beast within, but you have it now."

So I'm not going crazy. The voice inside my head actually was the beast. I'd spent so much time in isolation that I was actually convinced I was no longer sane.

"Why now?" I ask, "After all these years… Why now?"

"Members of your family lineage received their powers at different ages. The power to control the wolf is not one easily understood. You are both Lycan and Undead. But the sun does not burn you, and now the moon will soon lose its grip over you, like your father before you."

"It's all a cruel joke. I needed these powers twenty years ago. Hell, I needed these powers twenty-four moons ago. They are useless to me now."

"Do you have any idea what I'd give to be you? What I'd give to have the power to control the demon that lives inside of me?" Bloodlust asks violently. He is angered by my pessimism. "You are being given a second chance, Syrus. A do-over. I would kill every Blackblood in my service for the chance to hold the reigns to the evil within me. You are being given that power and you don't even see the utility of it. You have the power to take back all that you lost!"

"And it will mean nothing!" I scream. "I have lost everything I love in the process, damnit!"

Bloodlust's hand shoots out faster than I can process and clenches my throat. His wings shoot out to either side of us and lift me from the spring into the coldness of the winter night. Three thrashes of the webbed wings against the air and we are propelled higher than the mountain's peak.

I'm suspended by the grip he has on my throat. I can't breathe. I'm suffocating. It feels as though I'm caught in a vice grip. The pressure in my head feels like it will soon explode from oxygen deprivation. All I can see is the hollow eyes of the wolf skull. The snout is a few short inches from my own nose.

The water on my skin freezes as we ascend into the air. The stars above laugh at me. The crescent moon is a mocking smile. The mountain is now far beneath us. The clouds wrap us in their empty embrace. "Fickle fool!" Bloodlust screams at me. Even as I choke I can smell the rot of his breath. "Look around us! Take a good hard look!" His hand releases me and my feet flail to find ground to stand on. There is none. I fall.

My stomach lifts into my chest as the clouds release me.

I plummet toward the earth like a comet set to crash. All those months I spent in confined darkness I wished for freedom. I'm finally freer than ever and I realize I'd give anything to be back in my rocky cell with solid ground beneath me.

I close my eyes for a moment and feel the fierce winds beat against me. The atmosphere burns my skin. Gravity rips at every inch of me. Vomit rises in my throat as I spin uncontrollably. The ground below grows rapidly. I can see the horizon in every direction through the tears that blur my vision. The edge of the earth radiates with signs of Solis waking for another day.

The fear disappears as I approach my death.

I'm weightless.

It feels euphoric.

Nothing in this world truly matters.

We are all just fickle beings destined to die.

The Undead.

The Blackbloods.

The Lycans.

The Humans.

We all make plans to force the world to serve us.

But we will all die, and with enough time, the histories will forget our existence.

Bloodlust was right.

My past blinded me.

Poisoned my mind.

It possessed me more than any beast of Dagon ever could.

I've let regret and guilt destroy my life, and only I'm to blame for that.

I realize I'm crying now. The violent winds dry the tears instantly, but they are there nonetheless. Wherever Vesper and Sephora are, I hope they forgive me. I watch as the darkness around me illuminates. My eyes glow silver. Euphoria rushes through my veins. Consumes me. The regret and guilt disappear. I feel as though I'm a god as my descent slows. The winds no longer beat against me. My body no longer flails uncontrollably. I gain composure. I feel the air bend to my will.

I'm no longer falling, I realize.

I am suspended in the air. The earth stretches to its end in every direction. I look down. I'm still several kilometers above the distant ground below. I'm flying, I quickly realize.

I am flying as though I am Undead.

But I am not Undead.

I am Sylvian. *Vere mori skathen*. We conquer our demons.

I fly, like my father before me, and his father before him.

My whole life I've wondered whether these powers would ever come.

The darkness submits to my platinum gaze.

I look back at Luna above me. Her crescent no longer smiles. It is more of a frown now that I see it from this perspective. She holds no control over me. The Curse of Dagon no longer holds me captive. The Curse of Damon is mine to wield.

"Who are you," Bloodlust calls out from above. "Say it!"

"I am Syrus Sylvian." My voice is crackling thunder on a stormless night. My eyes shine bright through the darkest night. "The gods have taken everything from me. Now I will make them pay for their insolence. Now I will take back all that belongs to me."

The light from my eyes disappears. My head grows faint. I lose footing. I'm falling again. I'm too tired to process what's happening. I'm too tired. All I know is that I'm falling. Too tired. The euphoria fades. Tired.

Falling.

Darkness.

17

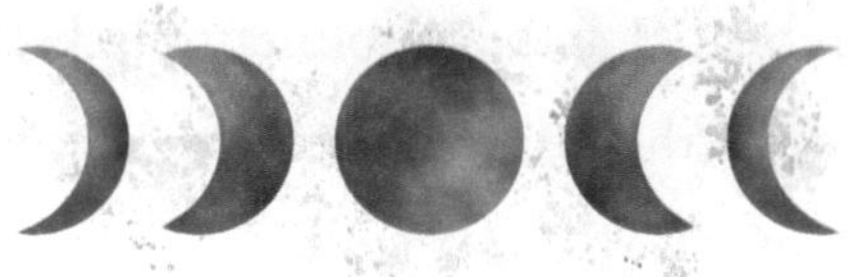

A DREAM

By the time Solis rises to claim the day most of the damage is done.

The screams from prisoners stopped hours ago. Any fight they put up was in vain. Any retaliation only furthered their torment. I was forced to sit and listen alongside Vesper as the Blackbloods fed on the humans like pigs being eaten alive. The demented creatures killed very few of the humans, they made sure of that. They need the humans for feeding, red blood is the only thing that satiates the Undead, even those who've been infected with the Blackblood virus.

A human's body is like an endless supply of food for the monsters. With enough time permitted in between, the blood will regenerate. Round up enough humans to collect from and a group of Blackbloods can easily rotate between groups of humans like a farmer rotating crops on an annual basis. Tutor Lundis taught me about it as a child. He wasn't supposed to teach me the histories of the Holy Crusades. Father thought it was too bleak a subject for a child, so Lundis taught me the histories in secret.

Marduk and the first Blackbloods waged war against the Acolytes. The Undead locked themselves in crypts for the duration of the war, knowing a bite from a Blackblood would cause their own blood to become infected.

Humans, though, are immune from the virus. Immune, yet powerless, I now realize as the sun rises to reveal the night's massacre.

The Blackbloods retreated to their mountainous keep at the first hint of dawn, leaving behind the thousands of humans they gorged on. Vesper is just as speechless as I am as we hold hands in the aftermath. Two bystanders who've just witnessed a genocide.

I look down and see a mother holding a child in her arms. She rocks with the body in her lap, back and forth, back and forth. The little boy's body is limp like undercooked meat. The boy's shackles rattle as the mother rocks his body vigorously. All the rocking in the world won't bring her son's soul back. A pit grows in my stomach, knowing that could be Sephora. These demons have no moral guideline. Prey is prey to them. A child is no more than the weakest link among the human race. The virus blackens their souls as much as it does their blood.

"They're in no state to make a run for it, Vesper."

There are thousands of them. I can't break their chains and carry every single one of them to freedom. There are not enough hours in the day to contemplate such a miracle.

"We must do something, Syrus. To continue living with knowledge of such an atrocity would be worse than dying."

I want to scoff at her dramatics. Saving them would condemn all I know and love in this world to die. The Blackbloods will catch our scent all over the valley. They will hunt us mercilessly and flay our skin until we've given them every last drop of blood our bodies have to offer.

"Look at me," I say, grabbing her wrist. I turn her to face me, but even after all these years I'm caught off guard by her beauty. The morning light sparkles in her heliotrope eyes. She flinches as the light crests above the surrounding mountains. I see her pale skin begin to flush with redness. She needs to leave. Retreat to a cave to await Luna's return.

She pulls away from me and retreats to the nearest tunnel. She stands helplessly at the threshold of shadow and daylight, eyeing me from afar. "If there was a way, would you have me take it?" I ask earnestly, seeing the concern in her eyes. She knows just as well what this means as I do. She may be an optimist, but she is not a fool.

The lives of many for the life of one. The life of her lover for a chance to save a thousand strangers. I told Sephora that someone else would come along. Someone will, but it won't be until it is too late. Vesper and I both know many more will die before the coming war ends with a victor. No action I can take will prevent that war. One man can't save the world.

I desperately wish fate hadn't chosen me to be the hero of this story. Heroes often lose everything to claim the title. Losing Vesper and Sephora isn't worth playing savior. They are all I have, and yet they'd ask me to save those who are too helpless to save themselves.

The sun creeps slowly into the sky, pushing Vesper to slowly follow the line of darkness on the cave floor as it retreats further into the mountain.

"We don't choose our destiny, Syrus," she whispers. The cave's echo carries her delicate words to surround me.

"The moon will be full when it returns. Use the tunnels to run as far as you can while Solis is awake. Then, when the daylight fades, take Sephora above ground and run far away from here," I warn. I never believed I'd speak these words. I can see the tears in her eyes. "I will let the beast out when Luna looks upon me. When I do, you need to be far from here. I cannot control it."

She's shaking her head as she continues to step back into the cave's darkness. She knows this will be the last time she sees me.

"Promise me," I demand. "I need your word you will flee. This monster within me... It will know your scent. It will know Sephora's. I can't hold it back when it takes over."

"I can't leave you." Her words are choked with sobs. I rush into the cave's mouth and plunge into the darkness. I press her up against the rocky wall and pull her body close to mine. She's cold. I'm warm. I transfer my body heat to her. She chills my blood with a single kiss.

The sun stands still for us as we remove our clothes. We kiss each other's bodies like jackals nipping at the carcass of some long-dead animal. I lay on my back, the sun's brilliant light shining on my chest and face. She mounts me where the sun doesn't shine, the curtain of shadows cutting off at my waist. I feel myself enter her. Hear her let out a stifled moan.

Solis averts his eyes as she rides me like a stallion beneath her. I grip her thighs tight, biting my bottom lip as I feel her insides pulse around my member. It has been so long since we last basked in each other's lust. She's so tight that I can barely fit, but her muscle memory stretches to take what I've form fitted her for.

The shadows empower her. The sun strengthens me. We are star crossed lovers. Solis and Luna eclipsing against all odds. Forbidden love incarnate. I watch as she twitches, climaxing atop me. The weight of pleasure nearly makes her double over. Her pulsing insides cause me to finish. I grip her tightly as we twitch together. She moans as she feels me fill her cavity, licking her lips and fondling her breasts. We don't speak. Words won't do justice. Euphoria overwhelms us.

"I love you," she says. We don't say the words aloud often. Don't want to strip them of their meaning. In this moment, though, I know it is likely the last time I'll hear her say it in this life. In this moment, I regret not saying those three words more to her while I could.

"I love you," I reply, meaning it with my whole heart. For a split second we revert to the vulnerable kids we were when we met. She is the girl who saved my life. I am the boy who ruined hers.

"Give them hell, then come find us," Vesper says. I appreciate her optimism.

"Sephora will need you now more than ever," I remind her. "If I don't make it, she will be the last Sylvian."

"You will make it," Vesper reassures. "The gods have failed in every attempt on your life thus far. You've proven yourself too stubborn to kill." She smiles. A tear falls from her eye down her face. It drips from her chin onto my naked chest.

"Do you need a strand of hair so you can track us on the morrow?" she asks.

"I could smell you and Sephora on the wind from miles away."

"Then we will be waiting for you."

"I want to say goodbye to her," I announce as she stands and begins dressing herself again.

"I won't allow it," Vesper says. "You'll see her tomorrow. A goodbye is not in order."

I nod to her. Fighting her on this is pointless. She knows if I see Sephora now then I will lose the strength to do what needs to be done. She's a smart girl. She will pick up on my emotion. She will know I am likely not going to return.

"Tomorrow," I say.

"Tomorrow," she repeats, backing away into the darkness of the cave. The sun's light creeps after her. I watch as she fades into the cave's bowels. "Tomorrow," I whisper, lying to myself.

18

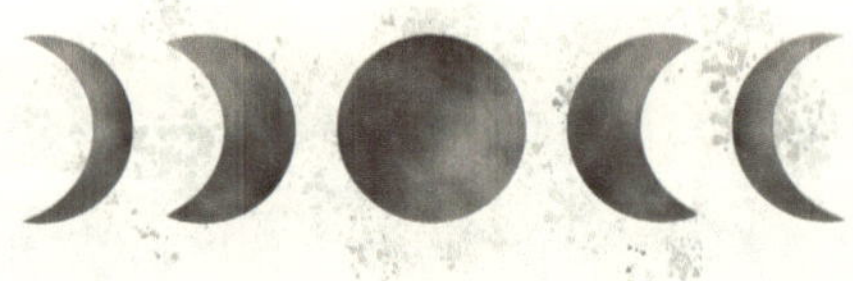

A NIGHTMARE

I wake to the sound of shackles clinking along icy rock. The cold has returned to my bones. The numbness subtly creeps in like a squatter claiming an abandoned home. The ceiling above me is no longer the stars in the sky. I stare once again at the glowing crystalline rooftop of Bloodlust's throne room.

I briefly wonder if the dream of me flying was nothing more than a hallucination. Another made up fantasy from my increasingly deranged mind. There's no way of knowing. I cannot trust myself.

Still, the chains clink.

I conjure the energy to sit up. I'm at the foot of Bloodlust's bone throne. I face one of several entrances as two Blackbloods hold the chains to several Muzzled prisoners.

"—Tear your wings off and shove them up your arse!" a prisoner threatens. I know the voice, though I don't recognize the man. It is Creon's voice, though I have never seen him before. He's a short, stout man. Though the months of starvation have impacted him the same as me, his body is laden with muscle still. He is a few inches too tall to be a dwarf and a few inches too short to be average. His naked body is covered with thick hair from his neck to his toes, yet his scalp is bald as a baby's butt. Other than that, I've never seen such a hairy man. His beard is not the scraggly mess that hangs from my chin. It is thick and full and extends to his stomach.

The Blackblood that holds his chains whips around and backhands Creon across the face. The force of the blow is nearly enough to take the hairy man off his feet. Creon absorbs the blow and manages to stay standing. He yells, "That the best you got?" I watch as he spits a bloody tooth from his mouth at the Blackblood's feet.

The other three Muzzled move silently, without protest. None of them wear a muzzle around their mouth anymore, though the scars from the muzzle is still etched around their lips. Each of them holds a look in their eye that is the perfect mix of ferocity and fear. They each tremble the same way I did as I was brought before Bloodlust. The cold penetrates their bones, no doubt. The fear penetrates their minds, with certainty.

Two of the prisoners are she-wolves. Their naked bodies are covered in dirt and filth, yet attractive all the same. The one closest to me has the look of one ready to lose it all. She does not fear death. She eyes me for a split second, then moves her eyes to Bloodlust behind me. She scans the room. Her eyes are constantly shifting. Analyzing. Plotting.

Her skin is naturally tan, like rich caramel. Her hair is jet black, like my own. She has dark eyes that give a sense of natural beauty. Her bound hands cause her arms to press her breasts together. Her hips sway in a way that captivates my attention. Twenty-four moons I've gone without the touch of a woman. I swallow, then move my eyes to the next prisoner.

The next woman makes it no easier for me. I clench my jaw as my eyes look over every inch of her body. She, unlike the first, has pale skin and autumn red hair. Blue eyes like the reflection of water in glass. Freckles that line her skin like scales on a serpent. She holds a look in her eyes fierier than her hair. She is petite yet tone. Her abs are etched in pale stone. I can see the striations of muscle in her thighs with every step she takes. Her crotch is covered with a carpet of blood-red hair. I force myself to look away, knowing I'm aroused just by the presence of the she-wolves.

The final prisoner has skin like coal. He is darker than the night is long. And unlike Creon, he is taller than even myself. His arms are so long they could likely hug the thick base of an oak. The member between his legs swings like its own loose limb. It is thrice the size of Creon's and twice the size of mine. Must not be cold, I think to myself. The man is wiry; little muscle remains from the months of starvation. His dark skin indicates he's from the Isles of Skaar, where the men and women have been burned by the sun. I didn't know there were Lycans amongst their population, yet it doesn't surprise me. The Curse of Dagon is not impartial to those it infects.

I turn to face Bloodlust, slowly picking myself up from the icy floor. "What is the meaning of this?" I ask.

"Meet your pack," Bloodlust replies in a low growl.

"My what?"

"Before you, I've assembled the fiercest Muzzled fighters Dagon has to offer. They've proved their skill for several moons now. They each have as bloody a past, if not bloodier, than your own. They will be yours to command. Your own wolfpack, if you will," Bloodlust chuckles.

The girl with the black hair stares at Bloodlust with more hatred than I can fathom. She eyes the wolf skull upon his head, likely searching for his eyes in the darkness of the sockets. She looks at me with the same level of anger, likely thinking I am on Bloodlust's side. She doesn't even know who I am. Probably thinks I am nothing more than a pawn of the Blackbloods.

"A pack for what? You still haven't told me the meaning of all this?"

"I taught you better than that, pupil," Bloodlust sighs with disappointment. "They are going to be your strongest allies in retaking the throne."

"No," I dismiss immediately. "I work alone. Always have. I don't need four Lycans slowing me down every full moon."

"Oh, you work alone, do you?" Bloodlust repeats. "And look where that has that gotten you." He gestures to the expansive cavern. "Some miracle worker you must be." His laugh bounces off the cave walls and echoes around me.

"I haven't even learned how to control the beast inside myself," I yell. "How in the seven hells am I supposed to control four other wolves?"

"Sylvian the First turned Dagon's entire army of wolves against him. United all Lycans under his cause against their master. I see no reason why you can't learn to control four," Bloodlust replies.

The prisoners look at me with suspicion at the mention of Sylvian's name. "Bloody hell, are you telling me Ophy wasn't off his rocker?" Creon cries. "You're him? The Sylvian kid who murdered his entire family?"

I stare violently at Creon. The accusation hurts, but the truth hurts worse. "I am," I say, locking eyes with the dark-haired woman.

"Oh wonderful," Creon says sarcastically. "Let the man who killed his own parents lead us into battle! What could go wrong?"

"Do they know something I don't?" I ask Bloodlust. "What battle is he talking about?"

Bloodlust shifts upon his throne, paying attention to only me as if we are the only two in the chamber. "They have already been instructed on the plan. You are to lead them to Sygon before the next full moon. The Undead Empire has taken siege of the human kingdom and turned it into an impregnable encampment. The walls are lined with archers day and night. My forces cannot get within a thousand yards of the city without being spotted and shot down. Our war has come to a stalemate in Sygon, and I cannot defeat the Undead Empire without the city falling."

"I fail to see where that is my problem," I reply coldly.

"Watch your tongue Sylvian," Bloodlust growls, "You may be coming into your own powers but you owe me."

"I owe you nothing. Any misery my actions caused you are met threefold with the torture you've unleashed on me the last twenty-four moons."

"No," Bloodlust growls. "That is not what I speak of. You owe me for this," he says, then shouts, "Bring her out!"

My nose twitches.

Cinnamon and cloves. It's a scent I've memorized. I could pick it out of a crowd of thousands. My heart flutters when I catch it on the wind.

Sephora?

I hear the clatter of more chains against icy rock, this time coming from a tunnel to my left side. A Blackblood emerges from the darkness of the cave's mouth, his bulky outline blocking the prisoner he drags behind him. Bloodlust announces, "You are not the last Sylvian, Syrus. Allow me to reintroduce you to your daughter."

The Blackblood guard moves to the side, exposing the teenager behind him. "Sephora!" I cry. Her eyes beam at me in disbelief. I am in dismay. Is this another hallucination? I sprint toward her and throw myself at her. She is no figment of my imagination. My arms feel her frail figure as they wrap around her. My body warms as I pull her freezing body tight in my embrace.

"Dad?" she chokes up in disbelief.

"It's me," I sob. Her hands are weighed down by the chains. She can't hug me back. "I'm so sorry, Seph," I cry aloud. "For all of it." I can't control the emotion that takes over. This is my daughter. Twenty-four moons I've thought she was dead. Twenty-four moons she thought I was dead.

"I needed you to think she was dead," Bloodlust laughs as if this is all a big game to him. "You had to remember who you are without coercion of your daughter." This is just a reminder of how much Lundis has become infected by the Blackblood virus. The monster that sits on the throne is not the man I knew as a child.

"It's so dark," Sephora whispers to me. "So cold." She barely has the strength to say more.

"It will get warmer now that we are together," I promise her. My tears fall into her hair. My clutch is so tight that I worry I'm suffocating her. "Have they hurt you?" I ask in a low tone so no one can hear me.

"I can assure you my guards have withheld from their wanton ways with the child," Bloodlust interrupts. His hearing is keener than I expected. "Strict orders from myself that no one harm the child. Aside from the initial harm that caused you to think she was dead, that is."

My hands touch her neck delicately. It has healed remarkably. I do not feel the slightest bump from where it was previously snapped in front of my own eyes.

"Her Sylvian blood healed the wounds we inflicted on her when we imprisoned you," Bloodlust croaks. "Your lady wife was not so fortunate, but that is no reason to not celebrate the life of your daughter. I hope you see now that we are very much not even, Syrus."

I turn to face him, not releasing Sephora from my protective grasp for a single moment. "What do you want from me?" I growl. I search within me for the powers of Sylvian but don't find the euphoric feelings anywhere. I am a mortal before a king of demons.

"I've told you what I want, Syrus. Sygon. Take it back from the Undead before the next full moon sets. It is the first step of you reclaiming the throne, and the first step toward me winning this war against the Undead. Defy me and Sephora dies. Fail me and Sephora dies. Do anything other than what I command you, and Sephora dies. I feel these instructions are somewhat simple to follow, are they not?"

I grind my teeth violently. My grip tightens around Sephora. I search again for anything within myself that could allow me to kill Bloodlust and run off with my daughter toward freedom. Nothing. The beast does not speak to me, offering to lend his powers. My eyes do not turn silver. I have no choice but to comply with the demon's orders, yet every inch of me burns to rip out his jugular with my fangs.

"Our goals are more aligned than you think," Bloodlust continues. "I simply want to see my kind survive and prosper. And to do that, I need you to sit on the throne, not the Undead. I have the plan to achieve this, you only need to learn from me as you did when you were a child. Then, when this war is over and you've eliminated my enemies, I will deliver your daughter to you."

The Muzzled prisoners watch me with dialed curiosity. I am their pack leader, so they now watch to see what I do when I've been backed into a corner. They watch me because they want to know if they can trust me. If I am to lead them into Sygon, Dagon knows they need to be able to trust me. It is a suicide mission, like walking into the belly of the monster itself.

"When this is all over, and I have reclaimed the Sylvian Throne, just know I will come for you," I warn Bloodlust. "And I will hunt your kind more violently than the first Acolytes hunted Marduk. Our sides may be aligned now, but I swear on my father's honor that I won't rest until I've separated your head from your shoulders and turned your skull into my own crown."

Though there is venom in my voice, my threat does nothing more than cause Bloodlust to laugh. His deep, coarse, scratchy voice booms with laughter, like a human threatened by an ant. He does not take me seriously. He has known me since I was a babe swaddled in diapers. He is the only person who has known me since my very inception. He does not take such a threat seriously.

"I look forward to that day, Syrus Sylvian. But until then, the enemy of my enemy is my friend. Now, let go of your daughter."

I look down at Sephora's beautiful face. The twenty-four moons we've been separated have changed her appearance. She is older. More serious. Her cheekbones are sharp like her mother's. Her eyes no longer have the childish glow of optimism. Her face is no longer flush with hope. She is pale and cold, yet more beautiful than ever. She has grown into an adult over the past twenty-four moons. I can't let her go. I did that once, and it is my greatest regret to this day.

"Syrus," Bloodlust says menacingly. "Let her go," he repeats slowly.

I stagger my stance defensively. "No," I reply.

"Dad," Sephora cautions. "It's okay." She raises her shackled hands to rub my wrist lovingly. Her fingers are ice cold to the touch.

"I can't," I tell her, loud enough for Bloodlust to hear me.

"You truly are your father's son," Bloodlust chuckles. "You know your mission. When you wake, I expect you to carry it out, for your daughter's sake."

"When I wake?" I repeat, confused. I hear movement behind me and turn just in time to see the Blackblood guard's fist on a crash course for my skull.

Pain, then darkness.

19

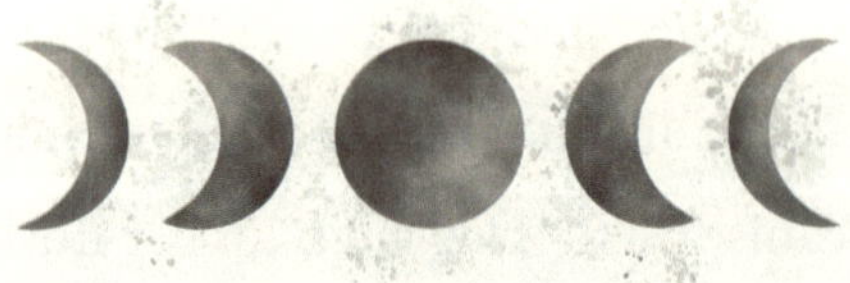

A Dream

My body screams from the effort it takes to carry on. The sun beats down on me like alcohol poured on an open wound. The sand absorbs its heat and burns my feet and ankles. Heatwaves flash in the air before my eyes. The chains I break are hotter than molten lava.

Sweat drips from my body and evaporates before it hits the ground.

Yet I persist, breaking the chains from their post with a little help from the beast within. My palms burn from the heated metal. It's like grabbing coals from live flames. I drag the prisoners' half-dead bodies from the sand and throw them in the rushing water of the nearest river.

The rapids grab hold of their tortured souls and carry them away instantly. Whether or not they live will be up to them, but their lives being left to fate leaves greater odds of survival than remaining chained in this valley of death.

I drag them two at a time, knowing the sun has reached its peak in the sky and will soon descend for the night. When Luna rises there will be nothing

I can do to hold back the beast. I have to work fast, for any who remain when the moonlight takes over will be doomed.

The lifeless bodies have just enough energy to groan as I drag them to the river. The water brings new life to their movements as they sink. Fight or flight responses return as they thrash in the water for air. Other bodies aren't so fortunate. A few never rise to the surface again and settle on the river floor to rest eternally.

The water mocks me as the sun leeches all moisture from my body. Solis punishes me for my heroics. Burns my flesh with every broken chain. Pulls sweat from my pores with every muscle I strain.

My vision blurs as I go about my business. I turn my mind off to lessen my suffering. My movements are senseless and minimal. Violent yank. Metal breaks. Feet drag through sand. Throw body in river. Violent yank. Metal breaks. Feet drag through sand. Throw body in river. On and on and on again.

Until I come to the child. I have to wipe the burning sweat from my eyes to make sure. When I see the mother's dead body wrapped around her baby boy's broken body I freeze. It is the mother that called out in the night for her dead child. Now she, like her son, has passed on from this world. Her naked body clings to his corpse. Both bodies are bloody and bruised. Burnt and barren. Beaten and broken.

I feel a sense of urgency as a cloud passes overhead, giving me the first feeling of eerie relief since I embarked on this mission. Shadows fill the valley as the sun disappears. Shadows, followed by darkness. It comes on like an unforeseeable storm.

I look up in the sky and see the menacing clouds. They blot out Solis and fill the desert air with moisture. I feel a drop of rain smack against my forehead as I look up.

"Dagon no," I curse as I look around. Thunder rumbles in the distance. Lightning flashes within the pitch-black clouds. I look up on the mountain's ridges and realize I'm no longer alone.

When the sun goes away, the Blackbloods come to play.

A Blackblood screeches when it sees me from within one of the mountain's cave entrances. A dozen more peak their skeletal heads from a half dozen other caves. They all look to the sky, noticing the storm that comes. They emerge one by one, like wasps swarming to protect their hive. There is no longer any daylight around to turn them to ash.

I spin slowly and notice them materializing along the domed walls that surround the valley. I look at the prisoners around me, then look at the broken chains behind me. For the first time I allow myself to reflect on the progress I've made. When I see how many prisoners remain shackled I realize I've barely made a dent. A breeze rushes down the mountain walls. It carries their scent along the valley floor. I scrunch my nose as the putrid odor of fresh manure on a hot summer day swells around me. A human wouldn't need to have my heightened sense of smell to know when these demons are nearby, I deduce.

Prisoners around me wake in a panic as the shriek of several dozen demons rips through the air. Thunder roars. Lightning flashes behind them. The clouds open and release their rain all at once. The lightning illuminates the sky for a split second. There are hundreds of batlike creatures swarming. The lightning disappears and darkness conceals them once more.

"And so it begins," I sigh.

20

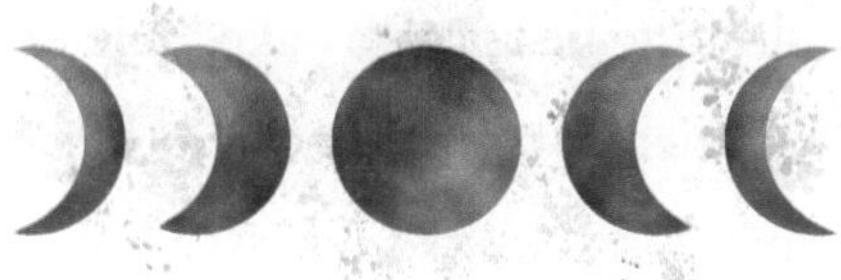

A Nightmare

"He is out cold," a distant voice announces.

"Well we're going to need him to wake the fuck up if we want to make it out of this alive," another adds.

"Fuck that," a man counters, "We don't need him. I say we take off and head for the hills. Nothing's standing between us and freedom anymore."

"They'll kill his daughter."

"Who cares? The man's a murderer. Haven't you heard the story of Syrus Sylvian? Killed his whole family."

"The girl is innocent."

"You're going to let some purebred princess stop you from living happily ever after?"

I open my eyes just in time to see the woman with jet-black hair and caramel skin grab hold of Creon. She pins him against a boulder while he innocently scoffs.

"My father sold me to the Blackbloods for a dozen coppers," she spits. "If he hadn't betrayed me, I never would have ended up a slave to them. If this man has the balls to save his daughter, we're going to help him." Her voice is a low growl, each sentence its own threat.

"Easy now," Creon assures. "I was simply making sure we considered all our options. Besides, sleeping beauty is awake." He points at me.

I look around at the bunch of misfits, each clothed in cheap rags stained with Dagon-knows-what. I'm slumped against a boulder myself, my upper half propped up. I lift my eyes to the sky and see we are at the base of a mountain. The sun glares back at me with violence. It's been twenty-four moons since I've seen its brutal light. My eyes flinch and my hands do their best to shade my face from the harsh glare.

"Where are we?" I ask, my throat drier than the deserts of Scorpos.

"The Blackbloods dropped us off outside their mountainous fortress. The Undead that lay siege every night retreated to Sygon when Solis rose," the woman says as she releases her grasp on Creon. Creon wipes at the permanent wrinkles on his shirt.

I stare at the woman as she offers me a hand. Her clothed physique hides the natural curves of her naked body, but the image of her flesh is seared into my mind. I reach for her hand. When we touch skin I feel a spark. She pulls me to my feet without effort and our chests collide. I hold her hand a moment longer than I should. I feel the callous of her palm. The scars from her past.

We lock eyes. I feel her breath on my neck. Smell her natural aroma. Memorize it. Tea olive and eucalyptus, if I had to describe it.

The others notice our silence, so she instantly breaks the trance. "Name's Crixus," she announces, ripping her hand away and pushing my chest so I stagger backward. I nearly fall back on my butt but the boulder catches me. She's stronger than she looks, and I'm weaker than ever.

"Crixus?" I mumble aloud, confused. "Like—the Crixus everyone talks about?"

"Talk is cheap," she replies.

Creon and I lock eyes. He nods at me to answer my question.

"How many moons have you survived under the Blackbloods?"

"Why does it matter?"

"Your name is legendary amongst the Muzzled. I just didn't expect you to be—"

"A she-wolf?" she finishes.

I look to Creon. He's slashing his throat figuratively with his index finger. I'm treading thin ice. "Yes," I reply, knowing she's caught me.

"My sex has nothing to do with my skill. The beast within me has survived twenty-eight moons under slavery. It is ravenous."

I see a look in her eye like a roaring fire seeking to devour. A hunger—no—a starvation that cannot be satiated. I know why Lundis chose her to assist me, though I did not expect her to be female. The name Crixus echoed the cavernous halls of our prison with every passing moon. The name preceded itself. Crixus was an unknown legend none of us had ever seen.

I avert my gaze from her consuming eyes. "I've been acquainted with Creon already, unfortunately," I say, looking to the other woman and the black-skinned man. "But I'm unfamiliar with you two."

"I'm Jasmine, but everyone calls me Lockjaw," the redheaded woman chirps, cheerful as a singing bird. I look her up and down, trying to see why she has been chosen for this mission. She's tiny and tone, her height no more than sixty inches. I've never heard either name she goes by.

"The other bloke doesn't talk," Creon chimes in. "Has no tongue. Must have lost it in Skaar or something." I look at the black man, tall as an oak and lanky as an ape. He opens his jaw to reveal pearly white teeth. I look for a tongue. Creon is right. The black man makes no noise. He stands there, motionless. His eyes communicate to me everything he needs to say.

"Etch your name on this boulder," I say to him, handing him a rock sharp enough to make markings.

The man drops the rock and shakes his head, confused.

"Ha!" Creon laughs. "Don't you know they don't teach reading and writing in Skaar, Sylvian?"

"What's so funny about not knowing how to read and write?" Crixus asks menacingly to Creon. His laughter cuts short as her eyes sear into him. He stutters, quickly trying to find a justifiable answer.

"Not all were fortunate enough to be of noble birth," she continues. "Not all could afford a private tutor like our dear Sylvian leader." The statement is every bit accusatory as it is an insult. My birth status means nothing to Crixus. Where some would admire my bloodline, she sees it as nothing more than entitlement. *Talk is cheap.*

"Enough," I interrupt. I look back to the black man, knowing he needs an identity. "You will be known as Scar, the wound, not the Isles." Scar nods affirmingly.

"I heard your talk as I awoke, Creon," I say, turning to the stocky man. His face becomes instantly defensive. "If you want to run, you have my leave," I say. "But if you're going to do it, I'd rather you do it now. Wait any longer and your betrayal may get us killed if we choose to rely on you."

My words catch him off guard. Any figurative collar he thought he wore is now removed. I've dropped his leash and told him he can run. There is nothing stopping him. I won't chase after him, and he likely has the speed and skill to be far from here by nightfall. The Blackbloods will never find him again.

"The same goes for any of you," I add. "I understand the injustice in Bloodlust forcing you to follow a man you don't know. I won't force anyone to take Sygon by my side. It is a suicide mission, anyway. We are just as likely to die trying to get to the city as we are once inside its walls. If you want no part in this, all I ask is that you leave now."

I stare at each of them in their eyes, and they each stare back into mine. I wait in silence for Creon to turn and run. He shifts uncomfortably from foot to foot, not sure what to do. Contemplation is heavy on his mind. Crixus, however, contemplates nothing. Her face is etched with determination and loyalty, though I haven't earned these feelings.

Lockjaw smiles stupidly. She looks like a dog wagging her tail at the sight of her master. "I'm content here," she affirms. "I've nowhere to run. Besides, we all must serve a master in this life. I'd rather mine be one who offers freedom than one that enjoys oppression."

Fair enough. I nod, hoping I'll come to know her past in time.

Scar kneels and picks up the jagged stone I offered him as a writing utensil. Instead of writing, he drags it across his open palm, slicing his flesh open as he stares at me in the eyes. His face doesn't flinch from the cut. He makes it look as if it was no more painful than a child's pinch. Blood drips from the wound as he pulls the arrowhead away. He holds the sharpened rock to me. It's a symbol. Tutor Lundis taught me of the Skaarians long ago. Said they were a primitive culture that still sacrificed burnt offerings to their foreign gods.

I take the rock from him and use it to slice my own palm open. I do my best to hide the pain, but my face flinches nonetheless. I draw it quick, without time for reflection, then drop the rock at my feet. Scar bows his head and extends his bleeding hand toward me, palm open to the sky in submission. I place my wounded hand atop his as both our cuts begin to close. By the time I slide my hand away, the cuts have disappeared. Only the blood remains.

“I’ll stay, but I’m not bloody cutting my hand open for you,” Creon says, breaking the silence. Scar stands to his feet and wipes the excess blood on his stained pants. “Dagon knows I’ll likely bleed for you in time.”

“Blood is guaranteed. Death is likely, Creon. Tell me, are you willing to die? Because we need to know you won’t decide to run when you stare death in the face,” I warn. I try to be as genuine as possible. I don’t want this to come across as a challenge to the man’s pride. I need him to make this decision for himself, not join halfheartedly because it’s what everyone else is doing.

“I said I’ll come, damnit,” Creon groans. “What do you want from me? Just because I don’t bow down and kiss your shoes doesn’t mean I’m not a man of my word.”

“I agree, but I heard you trying to convince the group to leave me while I was unconscious moments ago. You’re not necessarily the kind of guy I expect to protect my back out there.”

“Then why would I grab this?” Creon asks, pulling something from the waistband of his pants. It’s a cylindrical tube filled halfway with black fluid. He throws it to me and I barely grab it before it shatters on the ground.

I raise it above my head, watching as it blots the sun’s harsh rays from hitting my eye. “What is this?”

“What do you think it is?” Creon laughs. “That, my friend, is one hundred percent pure black blood.”

I look back at him in disbelief. Crixus and the others do the same. We are all as speechless as Scar.

“Where exactly did you get this?” I gawk.

“When they brought us to Bloodlust’s chambers there was some headless bloke on the floor. His black blood was spread around his body in a frozen puddle. I kicked a chunk off with my heel before they released us. Me and Lockjaw went to the closest village to get food for the journey.

Kind old lady had a pan over the fire for a stew she was making. Defrosted the blood, stole a vial, it was rather easy. You get the picture," Creon concludes as if it's just another day in the life for him.

We all look at him as if he's some diabolical genius. I can tell by the others' looks of amazement that they had no idea he did this, nor had they thought to do it themselves.

"And what exactly did you plan on using this for?" I ask.

"Oh come on!" he moans in return. "You're supposed to be the leader. That, Master Sylvian, is our ticket to Sygon." He has a perverted smile on his face. "Bloodlust said it's been taken over by Undead. Sent us to take it back. Do the math."

"We don't have to kill them all," I realize aloud, staring at the obsidian liquid.

"Bingo!" he shouts. "Now come on, if I had the foresight to do all that, do you really think I am going to betray you? I was just joking about making a run for it. It's what I do. Complain a little, make a few jests, rub a couple people the wrong way. It's all just fun and games, Sylvian."

I can't take my eyes off the vial of blood. This changes everything. We no longer need to take the kingdom by storm. We can infect its inhabitants from within. Create chaos. Cause confusion. Then, as the citizens are crushed with panic, we can kill their leader.

"Welcome to the pack," I say, tucking the vial of blood into my own waistband. Creon sarcastically bows. Crixus still looks at him with skepticism, but he has earned my respect. I don't actually care whether or not he betrays us. I'm merely putting on a show for the other followers. I am better alone, and now that I have this vial, I know I can accomplish the mission, with or without these Lycans. If Creon betrays us, I will slaughter him worse than any Undead ever could.

I take comfort in knowing that.

"The road to Sygon is long," I redirect the conversation. "We must make haste if we are to travel by road."

"But you haven't ate," Lockjaw questions.

"There will be plenty of prey for me to eat in Sygon," I reply coldly, marching northwest.

The others follow without protest.

21

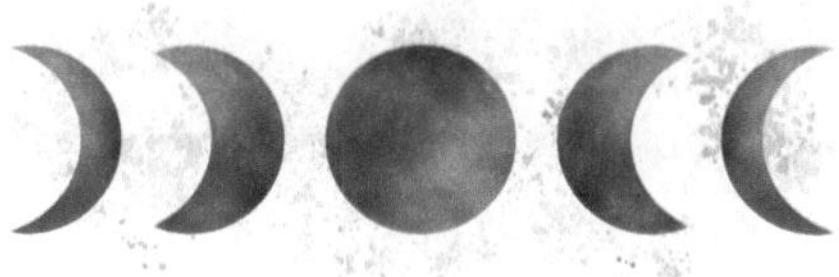

A Nightmare

We don't light a fire to warm us through the night.

We trudge through Vemen, a backwater marshland a week's trek from Sygon.

We could have traveled further, but the dark is our enemy. Night is when war emerges. Undead, Blackbloods, and all the parasites that feed off the scraps.

We wade in the marshy waters like still reeds. I harvested enough wolfsbane in the wilderness of Pence to erase our scent. To be double sure, I've forced our pack to smother their skin in the muds of the marsh. Undead can smell Lycans from miles away. Blackbloods from dozens of miles. We see their silhouettes soaring through the darkened clouds above. Blackbloods head to Sygon. Undead head toward the mountains. The two forces collide in battle in the airspace between. The clouds boom with the thunder of war chants and lethal blows.

"I thought the Undead were afraid of Blackbloods," Lockjaw whispers, staring up at the overcast night sky with fear in her eyes.

"They were," I say. "Back when Marduk sought to take over all of Creation. They locked themselves in underground crypts, fearful the infection would devour their population."

"What changed?" Crixus asks.

"No idea. I have been locked up for the duration of this war."

"What about the Acolytes?" Lockjaw asks. "Will they come back?"

"Doubtful. The Holy Knights rose as a necessity. Now that the Undead have found their courage, the humans have no reason to interfere in this war."

"How in the seven hells are we supposed to sleep in this marsh?" Creon interrupts. "Or am I the only one who realizes we still need sleep?"

I've lost count of Creon's complaints. Crixus and Lockjaw had been tallying them throughout the day but neither had known what number came after twenty. We stare at him in silence.

"Yes? No? Anyone? Staring up at the Undead and Blackbloods getting it on get you guys too excited to sleep?"

"He's right, you four should sleep. I will keep watch," I say.

"Finally! I mean, geez, if I wanted to stay awake at all hours I would have stayed in my cell and listened to Ophy rave like a lunatic."

"Where are we supposed to sleep? We are in water," Crixus points out the obvious.

"Lay on your back. Your body will float," I reply. Her statement makes me wonder where she is from. I realize I know little to nothing about these people. Have they ever seen a body of water before? Do they know how to swim? Surely Scar knows how to swim. The Isles of Skaar are surrounded by water. Hell, their main profession is crabbing and fishing.

I'm asking these people to die for my mission, and I don't even know them.

I curse inwardly.

What would my father think of me?

I am not a leader.

I've been a lone wolf so long that I've forgotten how to connect with others.

"I don't know how to—"

"We will sleep from dawn to noon in shifts," I cut Crixus off. I don't want her to admit to the others her inability to swim. I don't want anyone to be forced to openly admit their weaknesses. Not yet.

"Until then, we will march on, slowly. We can arrive in Gall by morning and lodge with the Galatians. Can your complaints hold off until dawn, Creon?"

"It will be a stretch, but I will manage." He smirks in the darkness.

The water ripples as we trudge slowly through the muddy depths. The sound of war echoes above like an endless storm. The Undead fly to meet the winged demons.

The darkness makes it hard to see.

The dense fog of the marsh impairs our sight further.

We are forced to listen to the screaming and hissing from both sides of the floating battlefield. Luna did not raise to protect the night tonight. The night of the new moon. We have two weeks, give or take. One week to get to Sygon. One week to take it over.

Unless we die.

Then none of it will matter.

"Tell us a story from your childhood, Syrus," Lockjaw asks as we wade through the waters. "I need something to drown out the sound of flying death overhead."

"What would you like to know?"

"You were the bloody prince of the Sylvian Kingdom," Creon laughs. "Surely you have a story or two you can share."

"Okay," I reflect. I've spent the better part of two decades trying to forget my childhood. The memories are painful. It has been easier to drown them out than confront them face to face. But the night is long and the road ahead only gets more difficult.

"My father took me to the ancient ruins of Cardone when I was a child. I remember it vividly. The final resting place of Sylvian the First. The graveyard of Dagon and Damon. The uninhabited wasteland so dark that even ghosts fear to travel there. Father took me there as a child to teach me there is nothing to fear, but fear itself. We walked along the fossilized ashes from centuries ago as if they were nothing more than a nature trail. Touched the rubble of buildings whose names are long forgotten. Saw the beauty of nature reclaiming what once belonged to it. Vines consuming stone. Grass growing from cracked cobblestone.

"In truth, it wasn't dark at all. It was one of the most beautiful sights I've seen in all my life, and I've traveled many places. But no one lives within a dozen miles of Cardone. Superstition haunts the city and its surrounding land. Laymen think it is cursed. Say the soil itself is poisoned. Rumor that those who travel there will never return."

"Who is Sylvian?" Crixus asks humbly.

We each stop and look at her with dumbfounded looks. She isn't embarrassed in the slightest. "You all keep saying his name. I have never heard of him until being told to follow Syrus."

"Have you been living under a rock your whole life?" Creon laughs. "You chose to follow this man without knowing who he is?"

She shrugs her shoulders innocently. "Should I have told them I'd rather go back to my cage?"

"How old are you?" I ask.

"I don't know," she replies, plainly.

"Where are you from?"

"Varne."

I wish I hadn't asked the question. But now that I know, there is no forgetting. I look silently into her eyes as we march through the marsh, side by side.

"Varne?" Creon cries. "You were a whore before the Blackbloods caught you?" This is all very hysterical to him. Creon seems to be the only one other than me who has heard of Varne. Scar and Lockjaw showed no recognition at the utterance of the city's name. "Dagon's sake, I knew you were too bloody attractive to have been a former housewife!"

"Watch your tongue," I bark.

"What?" he asks playfully. "Varne is a city of thieves and whores! Place is a total dump. Buddy of mine used to call it the armpit of the Empire. I call it the butt crack. Not even the Empire itself is willing to stoop to the level of lowlife it takes to clean up that dumpster fire. Old friend of mine fucked a whore in Varne and woke up drugged, bound, gagged, and a dozen coppers short. A dozen coppers! Can you believe that? We're not talking silver or gold here, those thieves and whores will cut your balls off for a copper tooth. Hell, I bet that's why 'ole Crixus here survived twenty-eight moons."

"I have survived from moon to moon my entire life. Bondage to the Blackbloods changed nothing for me," she replies coldly.

"Enough," I growl. Lundis taught me all I needed to know of Varne as a child in geography lessons. The kingdoms knew it was the central port of sex slaves. The kingdom's greatest whoremongers resided there, sending their slaves to every corner of the known world. Father tried multiple times to eliminate their egregious trades of prostitution but failed. Lundis said for every whoremonger father tracked and killed, two rose in their place. They are filthy cockroaches profiting off the violation of others' bodies. Men and women and children. Varne is an equal opportunity employer for sex slaves. Men go there to purge their dark desires and sell their souls to rape slaves sold for a few coppers.

Lundis said father was forced to stay his hand when the whoremongers threatened to spread sexual curses throughout the realm through their agents. Infectious diseases that would create a pandemic. You cannot exterminate a colony of roaches, Lundis taught. You can only do your best to keep them contained to a single area. And so Varne was the limb father was forced to cut off from the kingdom so the other cities could flourish.

"Sylvian was my ancestor," I whisper. "The third son of Luna and Solis. The slayer of Dagon and Damon. He embodied both of their curses in one. He was both Lycan and Undead. He could walk in the day and control the beast in the night."

"So he was a human?" Crixus asks.

"Not exactly," I explain. "The curses canceled in his person, but he could call on their powers nonetheless. He had the flight and fangs of the Undead. He had the inner beast of Dagon, too, only he could control it when the full moon shined on him."

"And you have these powers too?"

"Not exactly," I repeat. "I was not born with these powers, and when I was ten, the Curse of Dagon claimed me."

"Oh," she says, finally understanding the rumors of my childish genocide. She looks at me, not with pity in her eyes, but with compassion. "And Damon's Curse?"

"I never got it," I lie, thinking back to my flight below the waning crescent. "My father was descendant from Sylvian. My mother was human, the last descendant from the last living Acolyte, Lysander. I have spent most of my life convinced the powers of Sylvian would never be mine to wield. But that all changed the last time Luna was full."

"It's true," Creon interrupts. "I saw the glow of his silver eyes myself. Thought I was hallucinating at first, but Bloodlust confirmed it."

I nod weakly. "Ay, something is happening inside of me. I don't understand it. Can't explain it. But it's like some force inside of me has woken."

"Is it true what they say about you?" she asks meagerly. "That you killed your family?"

"Ay," I acknowledge. The image of my mother's headless body lifeless on the floor flashes.

"We have all done things we are not proud of," she whispers to me, gently rubbing my wrist. I pull away instinctively, frightened by the spark I feel when her fingertips brush my skin. The hair on my forearms stands, excited by the contact. My heart flutters briefly. I break eye contact and continue to push forward.

The marshes are no longer at our chest. We've made great progress, I realize as I focus on our surroundings. The still water sinks to our knees. The reeds are sparse. The frogs no longer sing their symphony of nightly croaks.

"She's right," Creon laughs, obviously reminiscing over some horrid memory from his past. "I killed an entire village of innocent humans the first moon Dagon's Curse took me." He admits the truth as if it's a funny joke, but I know the truth behind Creon's charade. Humor is the only way he's been able to cope with the atrocities he's committed in life, though he'd never admit it. Laughter is the only thing that has kept him from slitting his throat with a silver blade.

Lockjaw chimes in, "My parents were tax collectors. They used to chain me up and loose me on debtors that wouldn't pay when the moon was full.

Then they'd claim their property and rent it to other debtors. They used me like a weapon. Sometimes I forgot I was their daughter."

"My masters used to sell me to soldiers," Crixus adds. "The night of the full moon, they'd lead me to a stone cottage a few miles outside of Varne. The soldiers would pass me around, mounting me like a group of stallions on a cheap mare. But when the moon shined bright, I'd take my revenge. When I would wake the next day, their bodies would be mutilated, and my masters would loot everything in their possession." She recites the memory with a smile on her face. Unlike me, she wears her past on her sleeve like a shield. To her, Dagon's Curse has not been a curse. It has been a gift. A power to protect herself from her oppressors. The beast within is her greatest ally.

We each stare at her in awe. She tops each our stories unknowingly. An awkward moan vibrates from Scar's throat. When I see his sparkling teeth exposed behind a smile, I realize he's laughing.

Creon joins him, then Crixus laughs herself. The sound of laughter draws my attention to the lack of thunder above. The battle no longer rages in the night sky. The Undead and Blackbloods have withdrawn from conflict for the night. Dawn approaches. Solis will soon rise, exiling the armies to their underground crypts to rest and regroup.

My feet find solid ground. We rise from the marshes onto the banks of Gall, where we too will rest for a few hours.

"I suppose now is a good time to tell you I'm wanted for murder in Gall," Creon announces as we shuffle toward the impoverished village on the horizon.

I sigh.

"How recent?"

"Years ago."

"Who?"

"Their sheriff."

"Wonderful," I exhale sarcastically. "We will sleep here. I'll take first watch. At noon we will make for Gall and hope Creon's past exploits don't get us noticed."

"Great plan Sylvian, I doubt any of us could have come up with one better than that. Wake me at noon, I need all the beauty sleep I can get."

All but Crixus retire to making makeshift cots on the muddy banks of the marshland. They sleep spread apart, scraping together heaps of mud to sculpt pillows. I sit on a misshapen log. Crixus sits next to me, staring off at the marshland that's now illuminated by the early dawn.

"Your daughter," she whispers, "How long has it been since you've seen her?"

I look over at her, but her eyes don't leave the marshland's horizon. The reflection of dawn ebbs and flows on her beautiful face. Her cheekbones are pronounced, her nose petite and angular. Her lips are succulent. The early morning breeze makes her hair dance about her face.

"Twenty-four moons," I reply.

"And her mother?"

"Dead."

"How?"

"Blackbloods."

"Ah."

"Yeah."

"You are a good father."

"I don't see it that way."

"Why?"

"The Blackbloods killed my daughter too. If it wasn't for being a Sylvian, she would still be dead."

"Do you believe in the gods?"

“No.”

“I don’t either, but stuff like that makes me think I should.”

“Why?”

“Your daughter gets a second chance now, and because of her, so do you. And through you, so do all four of us. I thought I was going to die in the darkness of those mountains. But now I stare at my first dawn in over two years. All that fighting and killing I did will haunt me till the day I die. But in moments like this? Moments of true beauty? It all seems worth it. And maybe, just maybe, there’s something out there responsible for it all.”

She doesn’t look away from the rising sun, and I don’t look away from her beautiful complexion. I realize suddenly that she makes me feel nervous. Not in a bad way, but in the way Vesper made me nervous when I first realized I loved her. I force myself to look away and repress the fluttering in my stomach. She is nothing more than a distraction, and I cannot afford to be distracted.

My daughter’s life is on the line.

“You should get to sleep,” I tell her.

“I don’t want to miss a moment of the sunrise,” she whispers, still in awe of its beauty. “I will take the first shift and wake you when it is over.” I’m reluctant to pass our safety into her hands, but she briefly breaks her trance to look me in the eyes. I flinch at the beauty behind her dark pupils. “Trust me,” she orders gently.

“Okay,” I answer, ripping my gaze from the endless voids of enticement her eyes present. I leave her on the rotting log by herself and lay down in a bed of nearby cattails. The ground is stiff, but my body cedes to exhaustion almost immediately.

Darkness.

22

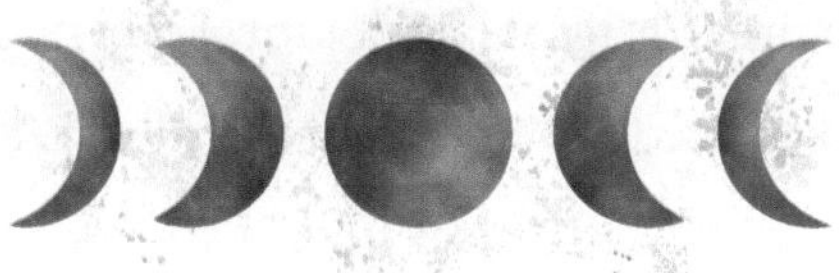

A Dream

"Come on!" I scream up at the swarming Blackbloods. They are like a storm of locusts in the sky. I rip a chain from the pole the prisoners were tethered to. I quickly wrap it around my fist, then grab another and snake it to my side like a lasso.

I have little time to formulate a plan.

My conscious mind takes a backseat as instinct takes over. Deep down I know this will be the day I die. I knew that going into this. I only hoped I'd have more time to free the slaves. But the gods are cruel. I knew this, so why did I expect them to show kindness this time around?

The first Blackblood dives from the sky like an owl after a field mouse. I can see its ugly grin. Its rotten teeth. Its unparalleled confidence.

I have never stood toe to toe with a Blackblood, but after watching what they are capable of, I won't take any chances. When the demon closes the distance on me I flick my wrist in its direction. The chain lashes in the open air to meet the diving beast. Like a lasso snaring a bucking bronco, the chain whips around the Blackblood's neck. I cheer inwardly, yanking the demon into my control. Its wings fight against the restraint but are too weak to parallel my force. I pull the monster down to earth to fight me like a mortal man, then deliver a punch to its face hard enough to wipe the devilish grin off its mouth.

It crashes hard to the earth on its stomach. I waste little time mounting its back. I pull the chain around its neck taut. I feel its spine crack beneath me, then feel its head concede to my strength. The skull rips clean from its body and soars through the air. Black blood spurts onto the desert floor. The rain falls to wash it away but the blood is too plentiful to be absorbed by the sand. My chains are now slick with black blood. I can smell the putrid scent of rotting eggs. It fills my nostrils with its wretched odor.

I turn in time to catch the next assailant as it flies overhead. My chain lashes out, this time missing its neck but catching its wing. I yank the chain, ripping the wing clean from its socket. Gravity does the rest. The Blackblood spins to the ground like a one-legged duck swimming in circles.

It spirals out of control until it hits the ground hard enough to make the earth quake. It doesn't have time to get up before I've stomped its head into the ground, crushing its skull like a rotten pumpkin. The black blood splashes onto my cheek from below.

Something grabs my shoulder and I turn, throwing my fist blindly. My chain-studded knuckles connect with its cheekbone. It hisses hysterically, then opens its mouth to bite me. I duck under its lunge and put my hands into its mouth. One hand grabs its upper jaw, the other grabs the lower. I rip the jaws apart like they're nothing more than the wishbone of a turkey. The skull separates with ease. The body falls to the ground with nothing more than its bottom jaw atop its neck.

I whip the chain blindly into the sky and miraculously grab hold of another demon, knocking it off its trajectory. Instead of pulling this one to the ground, I adjust its flight to cause a collision with another of its kind. The two crash together and fall like ducks during hunting season.

I'm panting. There are too many.

A force crashes into me from above, knocking me onto my back. A Blackblood mounts me, hissing violently. Rotten spit flings onto my face. Its wretched breath causes me to flinch. My skin crawls as my claws rip its eyes from its sockets. My fangs instinctively bite into its jugular. I toss the suffocating body off me and jump back to my feet. I spit the jugular out. Black blood fills my mouth and drips from my chin.

Rage takes over and a second wind fills me. My fatigue slips away. I'm in a fever dream as Luna slowly takes her mantle in the sky behind the timeless storm. Thunder rumbles. Lightning cracks across the landscape. Rain pours like a flood prepared to drown the entire earth. My whip cracks tirelessly. My fists flash. My claws slash. My fangs devour.

The Blackbloods fall at my feet like swatted fruit flies. I kill them one by one, but they litter the ground in dozens. I'm blinded by my bloodlust. My vision is consumed. I am no longer myself. The beast slowly takes over as time fades from reality. The chains eventually slip from my grasp. My hands are slick from black blood and rainwater and sweat. My clothes have been ripped from my body. Scars litter my flesh but I feel no pain.

I'm losing control, I realize, but I don't care.

If there is any time I don't mind the beast within taking the reins, it's now.

I scream as my bones snap. My skull cracks as a snout grows from my nose. My flesh stretches over the elongated, canine nose. Whiskers rip through my skin. Fur sprouts all along my body. All the while my claws lash at the assailants that surround me. My fangs treat the Blackbloods like a feast for a fasted monk. My vision tunnels, darkening around the edges. The beast is waking.

The bones in my body continue to break and grow. My muscles double in size. My femurs turn to hindlimbs. I feel a tail swipe the ground behind me. My flesh is no longer detectable beneath the thick coat of black fur that covers my body. My wolfish ears twitch as the rain patters against them. I try to speak but only a low growl exits my mouth.

Something stabs my back and I howl like a wounded dog. The Blackblood responsible for the pain is now dead on the ground. When did I kill it? I don't remember. My memory is feverish. My actions are uncontrollable. Bodies fall around me like gnats consumed by a flame. I am forced to watch as I devastate the Blackblood army. There are loose, decaying limbs in every direction I turn. I'm turning the desert to a graveyard.

A force pins my beast to the ground. When I look up I see five separate Blackbloods holding us down. That's a mistake. I blink for a moment. Now only two hold us down. I blink again. We are back on our feet. We stand on five dead Blackbloods. The darkness is closing around my vision. Soon, I will lose all consciousness and the beast within will be the sole operator of our body.

My nose twitches at the scent of something familiar amidst the storm. *Vanilla and coffee*. I'd recognize that scent anywhere. I could smell it from miles away. I panic, looking around. The Blackbloods circle me by the dozens. They form a ring around me. They've surrounded me like a wild hog circled by a hunting party. Something glows outside the ring. Something purple. It flashes around the outskirts of the Blackbloods, dropping bodies faster than I can register.

I catch a brief glimpse of it as its claws rip a Blackblood's throat from its neck. Vesper locks eyes with my beast.

No! I scream inwardly, but all the beast does is howl painfully, going back to work on the surrounding foes. The darkness is converging. All I can see through the veil of shadows is the flickering flash of purple light spinning like a planet orbiting Solis. I want to scream. I want my body back. I want to push the beast back. I want to hold the reins again. I cannot protect Vesper from myself. I cannot protect her from the Blackbloods. I cannot protect her from the monster I'm becoming. All I see is darkness.

Darkness, and a purple star in the distance.

And soon, the shooting star vanishes, consumed by the darkness. The smell of vanilla and coffee is overwhelmed by sulphuric death.

Vesper, I sob inwardly as I fade from consciousness.

The gods are cruel. Why did I expect them to show kindness this time around?

23

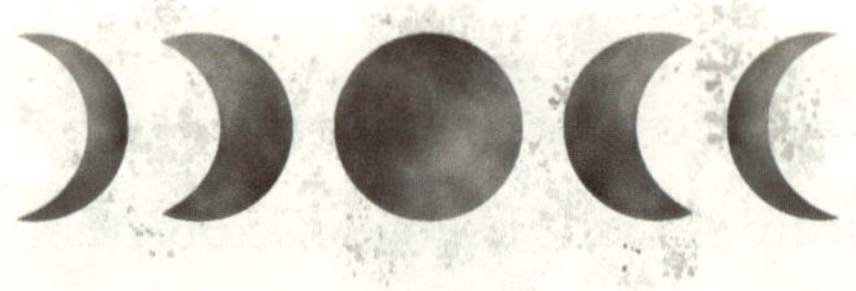

A Nightmare

I wake to the sound of a female screaming.

My body snaps alert.

The delirium of the sleep world washes away immediately.

I'm on my feet before my brain can order myself to wake up.

The scream turns to a moan, then a childish giggle. My eyes scan from side to side for signs of danger.

A tender hand grips my wrist. I spin and end up facing Crixus. Her finger is raised to her lips. "Shhhh," she whispers. "Everything is okay."

I grunt in confusion, trying to understand what she could possibly mean. Crixus laughs at my confusion. Solis is now high in the sky. Scar still sleeps where I saw him drop at dawn, but there are only impressions in the mud where Creon and Lockjaw laid. "What's happened?" I mutter in sleep-dazed confusion.

A female screams, but now I'm awake enough to hear the delight in its tone. "Creon and Lockjaw are—uhm—they've taken to each other,"

Crixus chuckles. The scream turns into a moan of pleasure again, followed by more giggles. I hear Creon's rough grunt. "You like that?" he asks from somewhere in the distance.

My cheeks flush instantly, realizing instantly I've just misinterpreted intercourse for a damsel in distress. My shoulders instantly sink, the weight of panic replaced by relief. Lockjaw moans, "Just like that... oh... yes... don't stop..."

"How long have I been asleep?" I ask, squinting at the glaring sun. Creon roars like a grizzly bear, panting deeply. Crixus covers her laughter with her hands.

"Long enough to miss three of Lockjaw's—uhm—peaks," Crixus laughs uncomfortably.

They are finished from what I can tell. Both cease their animalistic noises and huff and puff from concealment. "That was long overdue," Creon sighs.

"I'd say so," Lockjaw giggles. "That was one of the quickest rounds I've ever had."

"Ay, let's not forget my one brought you three."

"Then I guess I owe you two more," Lockjaw says flirtatiously.

"What's the meaning of this?" I ask, barging in on them. They lay a few dozen feet away in a bed of crushed cattails. They are both laying on their backs staring up at the sky. Both of them are naked and sweaty. I can see Creon's seed dripping from between Lockjaw's legs. Neither of them attempts to cover their nakedness. We have all spent countless moons in our nakedness. We are used to the feeling of being without clothes.

"Can you blame me?" Creon asks, unashamed. He nods at Lockjaw's naked body. Her pale, freckly skin is flushed red from the fresh fucking. Her fiery hair is spread around her head like a field of molten lava.

"Is this a joke to you?" I ask. "Need I remind you that you were the one who asked to stop for sleep?"

"And sleep I did. Lockjaw was the one with sinister intentions on her mind," Creon defends. "Tell him, red."

"It's true," Lockjaw admits. She isn't embarrassed. She has the same wide smile on her face that never seems to disappear. "I couldn't sleep. Women have needs too, ya know. I sought my rest and recovery through other means, and now I feel ready to take on the world."

I stare at them with contempt, but it's hard to be mad. Crixus is at my side now, and it's hard to be scornful when I see the look of entertainment on her face.

"Any day could be our last out here, mate," Creon laughs. "Can you a blame me for not wanting to die with full balls?"

"Put your clothes on, we leave in five," I order. I'm not here to babysit these adults. They can fuck whoever they want so long as it doesn't get in the way of saving my daughter. I turn and leave the lovers to what little privacy the cattails provide. I hear Lockjaw whisper to Creon, "See, I told you he wouldn't be mad."

I kneel beside Scar and reach to tap him, but I nearly lose my footing when I see his eyes wide open. The bloodshot eyes stare intently into the distance while his body continues to sleep. I've never seen someone who sleeps with their eyes wide open.

"You twitch and talk in your sleep," Crixus whispers in my ear from behind. "You look scared when you dream."

I look up at her, the sun silhouetting her beautiful figure. "I have nightmares when I sleep."

"Are they any worse than being awake?"

Her question causes me to laugh unexpectedly. "I suppose not."

"Then maybe living is the real nightmare."

I shake Scar's shoulder and his eyes shift to examine me, not blinking once as he exits the realm of sleep. He is silent as he wakes. Doesn't yawn or stretch or pause to collect himself. Several seconds after I've woke him, he's on his feet staring at Gall sitting on the horizon. He nods at me, then thanks me silently for the chance to rest. I nod back, then turn to Crixus.

"Thank you for keeping watch. You didn't have to stay up the whole time. I wish you'd have woken me halfway through."

"It's okay. I enjoyed watching all of you sleep. You can learn much more about someone from the way they sleep than the way they compose themselves when they're awake. Can't pretend to be someone you aren't when you're asleep."

"And who do you think I am, after watching me sleep?"

"A hero haunted by his past," she whispers, smiling at me as if it's a good thing. "A troubled savior."

"And the others?"

"They each put on a tough front, but after watching them sleep, I know they are each ready to die for this mission."

"Hmm."

24

A Nightmare

It's taken the remainder of the day to finish our hike to Gall. We don't have long before nightfall. But even if I wasn't exhausted, I don't think I'd comprehend what waits for us outside the former home of Galatians. Breath catches in my throat. My wheezing lungs are rendered speechless. I blink the burning sweat out of my eyes.

"Bloody hells, they've impaled them up the arse," Creon mutters quietly.

We all are taken back by the battlements that surround the village of Gall. Wooden stakes stretch for a hundred yards in every direction surrounding the city. Each of the stakes holds upon it what looks like a decaying scarecrow, but as we draw closer I can smell the scent of death and decay that draws in carrion birds and horseflies. Some bodies are fresher than others. Some have been impaled long enough to be picked clean of their flesh. Only a few loose sinews of ligament hold the hanging skeletons from falling to the ground. Vultures and crows eye us defensively as we approach the graveyard of impaled Undead.

“Have you ever seen something like this?” Lockjaw asks to no one in particular, though I assume the question is directed at me.

“Not from humans.” I stare in amazement at the sheer quantity of dead Undead soldiers impaled upon the stakes. There must be thousands, I realize. The wooden spears are planted as far as my eye can see in either direction of the city gates. I walk up to one of the impaled bodies and stare up at it. The Undead soldier’s mouth gapes open, its fangs exposed to the light of the day. Its skin has long been disintegrated by the sunlight. It looks as if it has been burned alive at the stake. Its flesh is so charred that I’m unable to tell whether it was a male or female.

The field is filled with smoke and steam from the burnt bodies, making it difficult to see past the city’s makeshift walls. Gall was once a place of peace, Lundis taught me. But times change, and people change with them.

“I was in Gall a few years back,” Creon mumbles, equally as amazed at the display of slaughter before us. “Ya know, back before I was a wanted man. The people were so kind... It’s hard to believe they’d be capable of something like this.”

“Only one way to find out,” I say, stepping into the field of smoke. I take my raggedy shirt and cover my mouth. Within the smoke is the floating particles of a thousand slaughtered Undead. The fog created by the burned bodies makes it hard to see more than a few feet in front of me, but I let my keen eyes guide us through the wreckage. The corpses stare at us through empty sockets as we pass by, envious of the life that flows through our veins.

They call themselves the Undead, but that doesn’t mean they’re immortal, I remind myself as I look at their pitiful bodies. A wooden stake to the heart is one of many ways they can be slain. Decapitation is always a sure-fire way to make sure their soul leaves creation. But when all else fails, impaling them from arse to mouth in the open sunlight is guaranteed to get the job done.

We arrive to the village gates to find them wide open. The fog seeps into the city walls and fills its perimeter with a veil of tangible smog. Solis's light fails to penetrate the floating particles, creating a dark cloud over the village that makes it impossible to see.

"I've got a bad feeling about this," Creon mutters through his covered mouth.

I do too. My sense of smell is blocked by the overwhelming scent of death. My vision is impaired by the surrounding smoke. And all is silent in the once bustling village. My hair stands on end at the suspicion that something is drastically wrong. Either the inhabitants of Gall are all dead, or they are hiding, waiting to attack whatever enters the gates behind us.

My foot hits something on the ground and I trip, falling to my knees. Crixus rushes to my side instantly, like a mother who's just watched her son scrape his knee. "I'm okay," I assure, trying to see what it was that obstructed my path. The fog settles enough for me to see a human body lying on the ground, dead. It is a woman. Her skin is paler than the lifeless moon. Her neck is slit open, but no blood is pooled around her body. It's been drank, I conclude.

I crawl a few feet forward and find another human, this time a male, just as dead as the last. His throat is slit, his blood is drained from his body. The smoke is thinner near the ground. I drop to my belly and continue to crawl. More bodies litter the ground, the same method of death has claimed all of them. Ah, I realize quickly.

"Everyone down," I whisper.

"Huh?" Creon questions.

"Down on your stomachs, now!" I order with urgency.

Lockjaw yelps in pain. I watch her body collapse next to me, an arrow protruding from her shoulder. "Go! Go! Get into the nearest building!" I scream. The other three scramble to our left. Creon breaks down the front door of a hut with a single kick, shattering the wood to splinters. I grab hold of Lockjaw by her ankles and drag her toward shelter. I feel the wind of an arrow shoot past my face with only a few inches to spare. Its point sinks into the ground a few feet from me. Another arrow thuds into the frame of the door Creon kicked in. I quickly pick up Lockjaw's body and carry it into the hut where the others retreated and place her firmly on the kitchen table.

"Quick, search the cupboards for alcohol or matches, we need to cauterize the wound."

Creon and the others immediately tear the kitchen apart, ripping open drawers and cupboards in search of anything that can help slow the bleeding. Lockjaw has a smile on her face as I feel for the arrowhead. There wasn't enough force in the shot for it to protrude from the back of her shoulder. "This is going to hurt," I warn as I grip the shaft and push the arrowhead through the back of her shoulder. She doesn't cringe in pain, though. A giggle escapes her mouth as the tip of the arrow rips through the back of her deltoid. "If you thought that was funny, you're going to get a real kick out of this," I add, snapping the arrowhead off and ripping the shaft from the front of her shoulder.

"Easy peasy," she jokes, biting down on her opposite finger to ignore the pain that radiates through her body. My hand tingles as I grip the arrowhead. "Gods be good," I whisper, dread filling my stomach. I run to the kitchen sink that is filled with a bucket of dirty water. I submerge the arrowhead and clean the blood from it, feeling its electric current in my hands as I do so. "No no no no," I whisper to myself as I lift it from the bloody water. It's silver, I realize. I clutch the arrowhead tight in my fist and feel it split open my palm.

"I've got alcohol!" Creon cheers, pulling a bottle from a busted cupboard. He rushes over to Lockjaw, looking down at the woman he had fallen in love with a few short hours ago. “See, look LJ, it’s going to be okay, we’re going to clean you up real good and kill whoever is responsible for this.”

Her face is pale. The contact with silver is already working against her body. But damn if she isn’t still smiling up at Creon as she slowly fades away. “You going to kill them for me?” she asks, amused at the situation.

“I’ll bring you their bodies for dinner tonight, I swear it,” he promises. For a man who likes to laugh at the injustices of life, Creon isn’t finding any humor in this situation. He bites down on the bottle’s cork and rips it out with his teeth. Just as he’s about to spill the alcohol on her skin she raises a hand in protest.

“Don’t,” she whispers through her smiling teeth. “It’s over for me.”

“What nonsense is that?” Creon asks, panicked, “It’s just a little flesh wound, LJ. Nothing we haven’t experienced a dozen times before in the fighting rings. You’ll heal up in a few minutes and we will find whatever Undead bastards are responsible for this.”

“It was silver, wasn’t it?” Lockjaw looks to me with strained despair in her eyes. Creon follows her gaze to me as well. I can see the manic fire in his eyes.

“Yes,” I whisper back, numb from the pain in my heart. I was trusted to lead these people to Sygon. That implies protecting them, yet not even a whole day has passed since embarking on this journey and I’ve already let one incur a mortal wound.

“I knew it,” she laughs, unbothered by the fact that she’s dying.

“No,” Creon denies, refusing to believe what I’ve said. “No,” he repeats. “She will make it. I know she will.”

Lockjaw grips his arm faintly with her good hand, rubbing the hair on the back of his forearm. “It’s going to be okay,” she reassures. The smile on her face makes her dying even more tragic. Here is a woman who has continued to be unimpeded by the horrors of life. The sort of woman that deserves to live a full, long life. The sort of woman this world needs more of.

"You said it yourself, Creon," she whispers, her eyes getting heavy. "Any day could be our last out here."

"Don't you talk like that," he threatens, tears welling up in his eyes. Her eyes slowly glaze over as the life leaves her. But the smile, oh the beautiful smile remains on her lips as she passes on. Creon buries his face in her chest. Crixus and Scar cease their rummaging as they hear sobs pulse from Creon's diaphragm. None of us ever fathomed the day we would see the most indifferent of us all be brought to tears.

The smoke seeps into the hut from the open doorframe, but it does nothing to repel the silver light that now shines from my eyes. So much anger and resentment wells within me that I fear I might explode. My temples throb with bulging veins.

I am here, the beast within whispers to me. "Good, because I need you." I reply internally. My claws and fangs appear instantly. *My powers are yours. Avenge the she-wolf's death.*

Crixus and Scar look at my glowing eyes and see the rage.

"I will be back," I growl, dropping the bloody arrowhead to the floor.

"Where are you going?" Crixus asks.

"To kill them all," I reply.

"Syrus, don't! They have silver arrows!"

"Silver has no affect against Sylvian blood," I purr, pushing her out of my way as I walk out of the hut on a mission for blood.

25

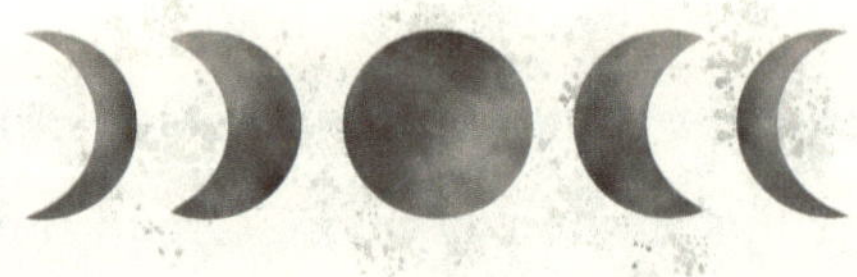

A Nightmare

The sun has set. Just this morning there was five of us. Now there are only four. Lockjaw will have to watch me avenge her from the heavens.

Darkness settles over the palpable smog that fills Gall. The Undead thrive in the dark. But so do I, and my silver eyes provide a guiding light toward vengeance.

My jaw and nose shatter and form the shape of a wolf's snout. My bones crack all along my body, taking the form of a walking wolf. Jet-black fur sprouts all along my body. The rags that cover me rip as my muscle density grows. I barely feel the pain of shifting anymore after decades of exposure to the excruciating agony. My mind is clear, and my vision doesn't begin to close around me.

For the first time in my life, I am in control of the beast I've become.

I pause in my stride, flexing my hands in front of my silver eyes. I close my padded palm into a fist, then release it. I shrug my shoulders, then lower them. My body is in my control as much as it is when I'm human. My limbs follow every action I command of them. The feeling of euphoria takes me over, intertwined with rage of vengeance.

"Thank you for this," I whisper to the beast within.

Thank me by leaving this town lifeless.

The smoke no longer bothers my senses. I can smell the sulphury scent of living Undead through the haze of mist. My glowing eyes can see past the fog. My ears twitch as they hear the draw of a bowstring. It twangs, and I watch as an arrow enters my plane of sight from an upstairs window twenty yards away. I let the arrow pierce my thigh. I want the Undead to know who the monster is that they've provoked. I tingle with joy at the feeling it produces. I rip it out and lick my blood from its point, then toss it to the side. Whoever shot it makes no noise, but I can smell their fear.

I walk slowly through the village street toward the building. There is no place they can run that will escape my wrath. I have their scent in my nose, and I'm willing to track them to the ends of the earth to avenge my pack member's death. Another bow loads, I hear the wood stretching as an arrow is drawn. This one is coming from a different shelter further down the road. "Do it," I snicker inwardly. I grit my teeth, readying for impact. The bow twangs. The arrow misses, far right. A shame.

I enter the building where the first arrow came from and climb the stairs. My vision is tunneled yet focused. I've never thought so clearly in all my life. All that matters is this single moment. Nothing else.

The Undead archer meets me at the top of the stairs, another silver arrow notched and drawn. I wonder what goes through his mind as he sees my silver eyes shining through the smoke of his companions' burned bodies. Does he see the silhouette of my monsterish form through the fog? Does he wonder how I'm able to conjure these powers? On a day where the full moon is two weeks out, no less?

Or does fear cloud his vision?

Does it drive all sanity from him?

The arrow goes straight into my abdomen and exits through my back. I hear it fall to the ground at the base of the stairs I climb. I can see the fear in his amethyst eyes as he watches me continue forward, utterly unaffected by his shot.

"But it's silver," he mumbles to himself in confusion. "Damon's sake, it's silver!" he screams at me, as if I care. He pulls another arrow free and stares at its pointed head, almost as if he doubts the ore it's made from. He stares at it long and hard, reassuring himself no doubt that it is indeed made of silver.

The wound in my abdomen heals before his eyes. A low growl sounds in the base of my throat. He attempts a third shot but fumbles the arrow while notching it. His mistake, I'm at the top of the staircase now. Just as he draws the arrow back, my paw swats the bow and arrow out of his weak hands, snapping the bow in two with a single blow.

He falls to his butt, trembling in fear before me. I tower over his cowardly figure. My silver eyes expose the fear on his face. I take a deep breath, feeding off the scent of terror in the air. I will not make this a quick death for him. I will make sure he feels the same pain that is in my heart. The gods are cruel, so I won't show his kind any kindness now.

"What are you!" he screams at me, as if I'll answer him. Doesn't he know wolves can't talk?

I am many things. I am a hero haunted by his past. I am a troubled savior. But in this moment, I am a cold-blooded killer. I dig my claws into his ankle and drag him down the stairs behind me, then out into the open street. I want his fellow archers to see his fate, so they know what awaits them. He is screaming in my grasp, helpless to defend himself.

I want him to feel what Lockjaw felt once pierced by a silver arrow. I want him to have the time to reflect on the inevitability of death.

Contrary to what their name implies, there are many ways you can kill an Undead. Wooden stakes. Daylight. Decapitation.

For this man, I will choose a more savage means.

"Help!" he screams to his fellow soldiers, who still stow themselves away behind fallible walls. Their time will come.

I hear multiple bows draw at the same time, hear the archers steady their breath, almost simultaneously. The arrows launch. I lift the Undead's body in front of me like a shield and watch a volley of a dozen arrows hit him where my heart was a moment ago. I feel a delightful chill wash over me as the impact causes my victim to grunt inaudibly. Several archers jump from their windows onto the ground before me.

This surprises me.

Normally those who choose a bow as their preferred weapon are too cowardly to fight face to face. This makes my life that much easier.

I watch the blood seep from my victim's body, pooling on the earth below me. I savor every drop that washes the dusty ground.

"Is that?" One of them asks another.

"It can't be..." The other replies.

"The Sylvians are dead." Another confirms.

"His eyes!"

"Nemour! Fly to Sygon with haste and report this to the Princess!"

"At once!" An archer replies, slinging his bow over his shoulder. He jumps off the ground to take flight but doesn't make it far. I throw the bleeding body in my grasp at him, hard. My strength is displayed in the way the corpse collides with the Undead mid-air.

Both come crashing to the ground.

I drop to all fours and pounce on the nearest archer, ripping his heart from his chest with my clawed fingers. I show it to him. It is still beating in my paw as his confused eyes register what's happened. I squeeze it until it explodes, then throw myself at the next foe. I steal the arrow in his hand and stab it into his amethyst eyeball, then slit his throat. His jugular spits blood in my face. My tongue licks it from my snout, swallowing it with delight.

Nemour is only just regaining his footing when I appear behind him, towering over him by several feet. My clawed hand wraps around his skull like it is nothing more than an orange in my grasp. I squeeze until I feel his head crack open, then squeeze some more. His headless body falls to the ground.

An arrow pierces my shoulder and I smile. When will they learn? Have they not noticed their mortal weapons cannot injure me? I cannot blame him for trying, though the attempt is in vain. He notches another and lets it fly. Through pure instinct, I snatch it from the air before it hits me. I bring the shaft to my snout and smell it. Fear.

I let it drop, then rip the protruding arrow from my shoulder like it's nothing more than a glued prop. I bring it to my snout and smell my own blood. Power.

I let it drop, then close the distance between us in two strides. The smoke of the air swirls around me from my momentum. The heavy fog dances around us like a cyclone. I hear an inaudible squeal of desperation leave his mouth. Even Lockjaw went to her death with more courage than this man.

I let his scream carry through the air. A warning to any who still watch us. His scream cuts short as I insert my claws beneath his ribcage and push upward until they're in his throat. His body is like a puppet mounted on my fist. I watch the blood pour from his mouth like a baby dripping food from its lower lip. My fur is covered in fresh blood as it pulls free from his carcass.

I spin around, reveling in my destruction, then turn to the man who ordered Nemour to flee the village. He has an aura of authority shrouding him. He is their leader. I can smell it. He lacks the same fear the others possessed. I won't kill him. He is too valuable. He knows what waits for us in Sygon. I need to question him, but that doesn't mean he needs to survive my wrath uninjured.

I walk toward him slowly, eating the arrows he fires at me. One in my chest. A second in my forearm. A third in my calf. It's almost like he isn't taking time to aim.

I don't give him time to fire a fourth.

Death is his destiny, but that destiny must wait.

I sink my fangs around his dominant hand and rip it clean from his body with a single clamp of my jaws, then grab his nondominant hand and do the same. His arms are reduced to bloody stumps. He can no longer hold a bow or arrow. I reach in his mouth and rip the fangs from the roof of his gums, then watch him swallow his own blood.

An Undead without their fangs is like a Lycan muzzled. Completely powerless.

I can see my reflection in his lilac eyes. I am fearsome. I am a horrifying demon from the pits of hell itself. I cannot be stopped. I will not be stopped.

Kill him! The beast commands.

"Not yet," I reply coldly.

Rip his head from his shoulders and pluck his eyes from his sockets!

I don't concede to the beast. I am the one in control. I will not bow to his orders.

I am a Sylvian, the master of my own body.

My muscles shrink and my fur recedes. I feel the structure of my bones return to that of a human. My height disappears as my bones snap back into place. My snout is gone, and with it, my superior sense of smell. I am now eye to eye with the gravely wounded Undead commander. My silver eyes remain, peering through the smoke at his broken body.

He does not mumble in fear like the others. He is in perfect control of his emotions. The man spits a mouthful of blood onto my skin and I laugh. "For Damon's sake, get it over with," he commands. But he fails to realize I'm not his to command. He shouts, "If you're going to kill me then just do it!"

"All in due time," I reply. I grab him by his hair and lead him toward the shelter where my pack resides, but when I turn I see each of them are standing in the city's streets observing the spectacle.

"Tie him up, he has information we need," I order, throwing the man to the ground. His arms try to catch his fall, but he forgets that he no longer has hands to aid him. The Undead thuds pathetically on the ground at Creon's feet.

The glow from my eyes disappears. My legs instantly grow weak. I can barely breathe, I realize. I can barely stand. I stagger a few steps, ready to fall. I feel hands wrap around my midsection. Crixus lowers me slowly to the ground. "Shhhh," she whispers. "I will take care of you."

I look up into her loving eyes as my vision slowly succumbs to darkness.

26

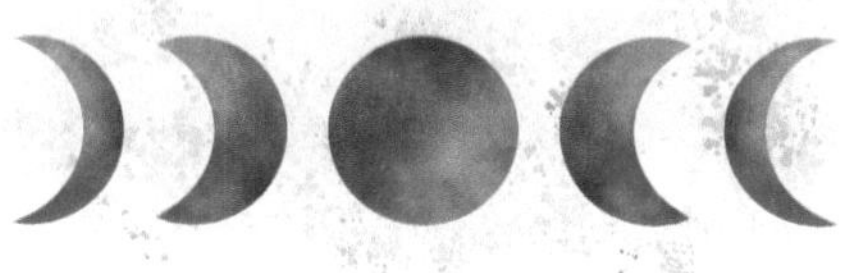

A Dream

"Dad!" Sephora screams. "Mom!"

The beast is gone. Only the destruction he's caused remains.

I wake with Vesper's lifeless body cradled in my arms. I remember nothing from the night's genocide. All I have is the desert valley to provide evidence of what I've done. Dawn shines light to expose the atrocities I've committed. Where the valley was once filled with countless chained prisoners, its ground is now littered with a legion of dead Blackbloods. Their bodies are heaped atop one another, smoldering as the sun crests the mountain peaks. Soon they will be reduced to ash. There will be no evidence of their sacrifice.

I look up from Vesper's broken body toward Sephora's voice. Though the valley is filled with the rotting scent of sulfur, I catch a whiff of her unmistakable scent. Cinnamon and cloves.

There she is, standing at the edge of the cliff where I left her yesterday. We lock eyes. "Dad!" she calls, looking around frantically for a way to climb down the mountain. Vesper must have left her in the caves as she came to my aid in the night.

"Sephora!" I call back, nearly choking on the bile in my mouth. I have to bite on my lip to hold back the tears that want to surge forward. I look down at Vesper's body. I whisper to myself, "Why did you come back? It should have been me..."

Her body has so many bite marks that I can't discern what her cause of death was. The Blackbloods have turned her flesh to swiss cheese. I bite down even harder on my lip as I see black veins rise to the surface of her pale flesh. Black blood oozes from the puncture marks that line her body. She is infected by the Blackblood virus. It will consume her blood and soon she will resurrect, another demon added to their ranks. I weep inwardly. My head is pounding. I want to scream at the injustice. I want to pummel my fist into the ground until I reach the core of the earth. My temples throb so violently I can barely see from my eyes. Tears blur everything.

"Sephora! Stay there!" I yell to her. "I will come to you! Walk into the sunlight!" I shout at her. The sun rises behind the cliff she stands on but hasn't yet illuminated where she stands. The shadows conceal her. She isn't safe.

I need to rip Vesper's heart from her body so she can rest eternally, forever.

I need to save Sephora.

But I don't want Sephora to see what I need to do.

I want the memory of her mother to be one of love, not violence.

"There is no sunlight!" she screams back at me. I examine the ridge she stands on and realize she's right. It will be another hour before the sun can reach an angle that will illuminate her. "Curse you, Solis," I whisper under my breath. The gods are cruel. Why did I expect them to be kind to me this time around?

I feel Vesper's Undead body begin to stir in my arms. It's happening.

"Dad?" I watch as a massive, shadowy silhouette appears behind Sephora.

"No!" I scream, dropping Vesper's body. The cliff is several hundred feet above me, so I'm helpless to save my child as I watch the Blackblood loom in the shadows behind her. I can't fly. Can't climb. I watch as Sephora smells the foul air around her and silently registers that she is not alone. There is no worse feeling as a parent than to see your child in peril and know you are helpless to save them.

The Blackblood wretches her neck to the side, snapping her spinal cord, then sinks his fangs into her throat, binging on the innocent stock of blood that flows through her veins. I scream violently. A chain cuts off my breath as it wraps around my neck. I clutch at the choker, looking to where the chain that lassos me leads. Another Blackblood, this one standing on a separate cliff, holds the rein. I am too weak to resist the pressure. All my energy was spent slaying their kind in the stormy night.

He pulls me in like a fish on a hook, dragging my body into the shadows. When I reach the base of the cliff, my feet leave the ground. I am suspended by my own bodyweight as I'm reeled in, my legs flailing in the open air. My vision blurs as I stare at my helpless daughter being drank from like a cup. I don't understand this world.

I sent them away so they could be safe.

I sent them away so they could live.

And in a single day, I have lost all that I have left to love in this world.

Vesper's body rises from the ground, smoke rising from her skin as the sunlight seeks to put a quick end to her resurrection. I have never heard Vesper hiss in all the years I've known her, but she does so now. Wings sprout from her back that she never possessed. They wrap around her to protect her from Solis, but the sun disintegrates the webbing of the blackened, charred wings.

I hear my daughter choking on her own blood as she loses consciousness. The Blackblood that consumes her looks up at me and smiles. The chain above me scrapes against the cliff's edge as each link brings me closer to my death.

I'm barely alive as my naked body is dragged onto the cliff. I feel something press against my mouth. The Blackblood clasps something behind my head. He's put a mask around me. No, not a mask. *A muzzle*, I realize as my vision tapers to nothingness. My daughter is dead. Vesper will soon join her. Yet I am still alive.

This isn't how it was supposed to happen.

I wish more than anything that I had the strength to leap from this cliff and hang myself by the chain around my neck. Death is the only outcome that would be preferable, but the muzzle around my mouth indicates that the Blackblood has other intentions for me.

The chain tightens around me again. The Blackblood drags me into the nearest cave like a limbless dog on a leash.

Solis disappears, replaced by the darkness of the cavernous mountain.

I suffocate from the lack of oxygen. I'm tired, so very tired. Tears fall uncontrollably from my eyes. I cannot bear the weight of living another moment. The gods are cruel. Why did I expect them to show kindness this time around?

Darkness consumes me.

27

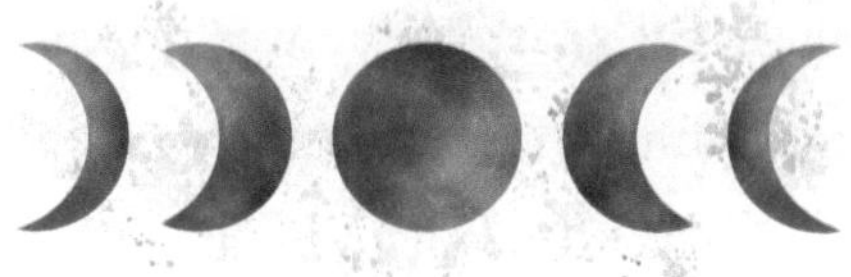

A Nightmare

I wake to the sound of my pack discussing what they've just witnessed. I don't open my eyes. I just lay on my back, staring at the sunlight of a new day on the outside of my eyelids.

"If that is what a Sylvian is capable of, I don't see why Bloodlust saw any need for us to come along on the journey," Creon spits.

"It was like something out of an old legend," Crixus replies, still astounded by what she's witnessed. "He was in perfect control of the beast the entire time. His movements and actions were calculated. He was even able to control himself as he took the Undead prisoner."

"He should have killed him with the rest."

"No," she rejects the idea. "He was right, this man can give us critical information about Sygon."

"He's responsible for Lockjaw's death!" Creon shouts. "I don't care if he can help us take Sygon over in a single fell swoop! He deserves death."

I can sense Creon's emotion. I can smell his pain. He should have never interloped with Lockjaw. The emotion clouds his vision. Blurs the purpose behind this mission.

"Besides, you may not know anything about the Sylvians, but I've heard plenty of tales of wicked things they've done throughout their lineage," Creon informs. "Even Syrus's father. He was no saint. Go to any village old enough to remember him and they'll tell you. The Undead erased the Sylvian name from the histories, but there are still those who walk this earth that remember the misdeeds the family committed."

I don't know what he is talking about. Sure, my father was no saint, but he was as chivalrous as any man I've ever met.

"We've all done things we aren't proud of," Crixus defends.

"Sure we have, but the things Syrus's father did have nothing to do with pride. Have you never heard of the Red Gates?"

"No."

"Of course you haven't. You know less history than a rock. It was before our time. The Sylvian King was only a teenager at the time. Why the kingdom thought a boy was fit to rule, I'll never know. A barge of foreign immigrants from Skaar docked at the kingdom's ports seeking entry into the kingdom. They were fleeing from the Slave King Dyran's oppression in the Isles. You hear me, Scar? These were your ancestors I'm talking about."

Scar grunts.

"They were seeking asylum. Protection. Innocent people looking to make a new life in the free world. They approached the King's gates in nothing but rags, not a single possession to their names. They were willing to work in exchange for protection. They pleaded for an audience with the teenage king. This was before the Sylvians had struck an alliance with the Undead. But there were thousands of Skaarian prisoners waiting outside the kingdom's walls.

"Instead of accepting the helpless victims with open arms, the boy saw this as an opportunity to strike a deal with a tribe of Undead known as the Celestials. The Sylvian offered the Skaarian people as a peace offering to the Celestials in return for their service in his armies. He loosed the Celestials on them in the night. By the time the sun rose, the ground outside the gates was so red with blood that the soil was forever stained crimson. To this day, the place is called the Red Gates, named after the notoriously scarlet soil that became a permanent landmark."

"You don't know what you're talking about," I say, not able to stomach another second of the man's heinous rumors. I rise, still naked from my rampage.

"Ah, if it isn't our fearless leader," Creon mocks. "Did your tutor fail to teach you this in your history lessons?"

"I wasn't taught legends that have no true origin," I spit in response. "And besides, what of your ancestors? Are their pasts white as snow? Or do you not know because they were so insignificant that no one bothered to remember their names? In fact, I'd bet that you yourself don't know past your grandfather's name."

I expect the comment to send Creon into a fury, but Crixus interrupts, "I don't even know my grandfather's name."

Creon laughs deeply, managing to murmur, "Touché..." amongst the hysteria. Scar points to himself and shakes his head, implying "him neither." The Undead prisoner stares at us in feverish delirium. The others have built a makeshift tent to keep the sunlight from hitting him, but he is not accustomed to the heat of the day. The worst is yet to come for him. I see that we are no longer in Gall. It's a few hundred yards behind us now. They must have dragged my body from its hellish smog while incapacitated.

"We buried Lockjaw while you slept," Crixus whispers as Creon continues to laugh through his pain. "What do you plan on doing with the prisoner? He cannot travel during the day, and he has lost a lot of blood from the wounds you caused. He will slow us down."

"We only need him to survive until tonight," I reply, eyeing the Undead. The sweltering heat of the day infects his mind. His eyes are squeezed as tightly shut as possible. Sweat drips profusely from his brow. His stumped hands have been cauterized by my pack members, though I never told them to do so. Yet they knew what they had to do to keep this man alive, so they did it. I'm suddenly thankful for their ability to think for themselves.

I continue, "Get as much information as we can from him today, then we will let him go."

Crixus spits on the ground. "Creon isn't going to like that. He's already tried to kill the man twice while you were out."

"Creon needs to learn there are worse things in life than death, and we are going to show them to this man." I walk away from Crixus to further examine the handless man. Scar comes to my side like a silent shadow, observing my actions.

I peel back the tent's corner until the sun abruptly hits the quivering man's arm. He screams instantly, not expecting the sudden jolt of pain. His eyes explode open, searching for the meaning of this suffering. When they do, they see me, as if everything makes sense to him at once.

I lower the tent flap so the shade returns to his entire body. "Good, now that I have your attention," I begin, "I have a few questions. Answer them, and I'll have you on your way to Sygon tonight, alive. Refuse, and I might just have to get you better acquainted with the sun. You could use a tan, after all."

The man spits at my feet and hisses, "I'll die before I tell you anything!"

"How about names? Can you tell me your name?"

He looks at me reluctantly, watches my fingers gripping the corner of the tent still. I know what he's thinking. I can read it on his face. Is his name really worth burning for? Ultimately, after a decisive juggle inside his mind, he concedes. "Wilhelm. My name is Wilhelm."

"See, was that so difficult? Where are you from, Wilhelm?"

I want to butter him up with easy questions. Get him accustomed to answering. Make him feel comfortable, like he can trust me. Then, when the harder questions come, and he chooses to burn, he will remember how easy it was to avoid the fiery pain.

"Thoren Mountains. Immortals Tribe." It's almost like he's competing with himself to see how few of words he can use to answer.

"Ah, I passed Thoren as a child. It was like paradise. The forests there are breathtaking. Much more beautiful than a sequestered swampland like Gall, I'd say. What brings you to Gall?"

His eyes furrow with suspicion. He wants to avoid burning, but he doesn't want to answer. Ultimately, he takes the easy way out.

"War."

"And why on earth would war with the Blackbloods make your kind waste time taking over a backwater town like Gall? I would have thought it was beneath Undead standards."

He spits at my feet again. So this is where he draws the line and takes his stand. No matter. I lift the tent flap and let Solis shine through with his glorious light. The Undead instantly tries to block out the sun with his hands, then remembers he has none. The sweat on his face instantly turns to steam. Pink heat blisters bubble on the surface of his flesh. He tries to scream in pain but only smoke leaves his mouth. I watch the hair atop his head coil and retreat, falling to the ground in long strands.

"Let's try that again," I say, lowering the tent. "Why Gall?"

It takes a moment for Wilhelm to compose himself. He licks his cracked lips and does the best he can to conjure saliva to his mouth once more. While he tries to catch his breath, he points at the village's walls. "Impale," he gasps. "Undead impaled..."

"You came to Gall because they were impaling your people?"

"Not Gall," he wheezes. "Galatians long dead..."

"If the Galatians are dead then who is responsible for the deaths of those thousand Undead?"

Wilhelm wheezes several more times, then manages to find the breath for a single word, "Atlas."

I glance at Scar, looking to see if the word has any meaning to him. He shrugs. I turn to face Creon and Crixus, who watch my interrogation from a distance. "Never bloody heard of it," Creon shouts.

"Me either," Crixus chimes.

"What is Atlas?" I ask, whipping the tent high in the air again. The intensity of the sun is enough to make him fall to the ground writhing in pain. An ungodly squeal leaves his mouth. It sounds as though a demon is being exorcised from his body, but really the sun is purging the darkness from him. Unfortunately for him, the darkness is the only thing that gives him life.

He is like a worm that's been stepped on, thrashing on the ground uncontrollably. A seizure causes him to convulse. His mouth foams with bloody vomit. I watch the steam lift from his skin like he is a volcano ready to erupt. "You'll have to excuse me," I scream at him, "But I'm quite irritable and impatient after losing one of my pack members, so I am going to need you to find your words faster."

I lower the tent so the shade consumes him once more. He is no longer recognizable. His flesh is withered parchment. His skin sizzles like steak over a hot fire. The moisture of his body has evaporated completely. Wilhelm's body trembles. He is on the brink of death, and all it took was a little Vitamin D.

"Not what..." he gasps, "Who!"

The Undead have such a superiority complex. They think they are stronger than humans and Lycans. They look down on us in the moonlight like we are nothing more than deplorable peasants. I live for moments like this, watching them be humbled. They are not superior. They are the inferior species. There is nothing to envy about them. They are not the elitist class they hold themselves out to be. Wilhelm is nothing more than a monster that no one will pity. No one mourns the death of his impaled companions. And no one will miss him if I choose to kill him.

"Acolytes!" he screams desperately. "Atlas..." He is sobbing the words. I've fried him past the ability to form coherent sentences. "Leader of... Acolytes!"

"Blasphemy!" I scream, threatening to lift the tent again. "The Acolytes do not exist, Wilhelm. If you're going to lie to me, I expect you to do a better job than that."

"No," he cries. A little sunlight was all it took to crack him. Minutes ago he spit at my feet, declaring he would not concede to my requests. But men are fickle once confronted with death. Undead, more so. They are raised by their elders to believe they are immortal. The first taste of mortality causes them to betray their morals. "Atlas... Acolytes... Leader... Risen..."

"Bloody hell," Creon mumbles. "Is this guy serious?"

"Keep an eye on him, he shouldn't be much trouble," I order, leaving Wilhelm behind.

"Where are you going?" Crixus asks as I walk off.

"Back to Gall. If this is true, there will be a sign somewhere from the Acolytes. If it's not, I will be back," I shout at Wilhelm. "The sun doesn't set for several hours, Wilhelm. If I find out you are lying, I will feed you to

Solis," I threaten. "Scar, come with me. You cannot talk, but I have need of your sight. Creon and Crixus, stay. And Creon," I turn to the rebellious man with anger in my eye. "If you fuck Crixus while I'm gone, I will cut off your dick and shove it down your throat. Do you understand?"

He gulps, knowing now is not the time for one of his witty remarks.

"He couldn't even if he wanted to," Crixus laughs.

28

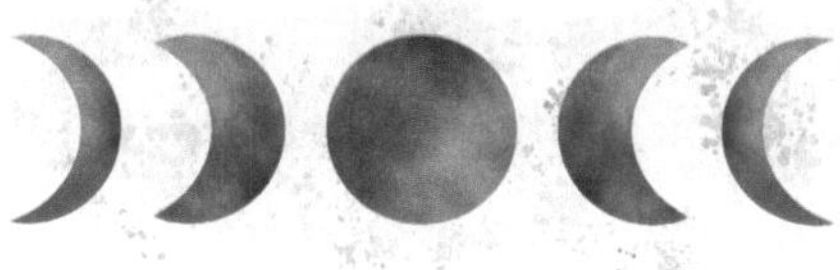

A Nightmare

It takes the best of an hour to march back to the wreckage outside of Gall. My suspicions were right that the impaled Undead stretched to the backside of the walled village.

The suspended skeletons stretch around the village like a moat around a castle. It is hard to feel sympathy for them. They have hunted me my whole life. Tarnished my family name. Hunted Lycans to the brink of extinction.

It is sights like this that make me think there could be a righteous god that exists somewhere. If I were a painter, I would set my canvas here and illustrate the beautiful scene. But I shake these feelings away. The Undead are not all evil. Vesper's tribe is the only reason I am still alive to this day. They saved me. Harbored me from those who sought to kill me, risking their own lives to do so. Some of the best people I've met in my life were Undead. How they came to be such a greedy and repulsive breed is a mystery to me. Like those not used to power, they let it corrupt them. Since the downfall of the Sylvians, they have clung to their reign of terror as tight as possible, fearing any who threaten a shift in the balance of authority.

"Have you ever befriended an Undead, Scar?" I've learned simple yes or no questions are the best way to communicate with the tongueless companion. He shakes his head.

"Do the Isles you're from have tribes of Undead?"

Again, he shakes his head.

"They're not all so bad, you know. When my father was alive, before they took over the kingdom, I actually admired their kind. Some of the wisest and most fearless people I knew were Undead."

"Mmm," he grunts.

"I don't imagine Skaar is a place suitable for their lifestyle. I hear the sun stays in the sky longer in Skaar, and the days are much hotter than here in the kingdom."

He nods.

"Do you believe in Damon and Dagon?"

"Mmm," he shrugs with indifference.

"I used to, when I was a child. The whole tale seems too far-fetched to believe nowadays though."

"Mmm."

"If Wilhelm is right, though... If the Acolytes have returned... I fear what destruction is on this kingdom's horizon... Do you Skaarians know of Holy Crusades of the olden days?"

Scar shakes his head.

"The Acolytes were humans who took up arms against Marduk and the first generation of Blackbloods. When the kingdom was paralyzed by fear to fight back, the Acolytes rushed in heroically, or so the story goes. But it has been nearly five hundred years since the last Acolyte passed from this life. Perhaps a renegade group has returned claiming to be related, but it's nearly impossible. Humans don't have access to the same histories the

Sylvians and Undead do as children. They wouldn't know the Acolyte's trademark insignia."

"Hmm?"

"The Acolytes would always leave their mark on whatever battlefield they conquered. Sort of like a calling card. A warning to any who passed by their victories. They wanted all to know who was responsible for the deaths of those the kingdom was too scared to fight. They would mark the battlefield with a cross. It was always subtle, but always noticeable enough to strike fear into the hearts of their enemies."

"Mmm."

"That's what we are looking for. If this man, Atlas, that Wilhelm speaks of, knows anything of the true Acolytes of old… He will have left their mark somewhere on the battlefield."

"Mmm."

I look at the horrendous display of dangling corpses. To see such an atrocious display of death makes me believe Wilhelm. No ordinary mortals would be capable of inflicting such an orchestration. It would take more than skill and luck. It would take strategic prowess. Brute strength. Military genius. This is more than just a few slain Undead, like what I accomplished within the village's limits. All signs point to Gall being an Undead stronghold before the Impaler came to town. Galatians litter the streets. Whatever fight they put up against the Undead, it wasn't enough.

But whoever came to save them in the aftermath left no survivors.

Scar leaves my side to enter the field of smoke that permanently stains these lands. I bury my head to the ground and do the same, searching for any indication of the one responsible for this attack.

I closely examine the stakes that hold the corpses aloft. Maybe the cross is burned into the wood, but I don't see it in any of the mounted poles around me. I search the skulls for any writing or crossed etchings. Nothing.

The smoke gets thicker the further I go. Slowly but surely it becomes harder to breathe in this hostile environment. Even the skeletons seem to struggle to find their breath, their gaping mouths searching the air from the afterlife.

I don't know why I chose to come here. I knew there would be no insignia. But I realize now I almost hoped in the back of my mind that Wilhelm's words were true. Some childish soul inside of me yearned for the Acolytes to return. I used to play with a carved figure of Xander as a child, pretending to replicate the Holy Crusades. Studying Lysander's writings were some of the only times I truly felt excited to learn in my youth. For there to be a second coming, it would be more than historic. It would be legendary.

The fog rolls so thick around my ankles that I can't even see the ground my feet touches. A cross could be drawn in the blood-soaked soil anywhere and I would miss it. Why did I think I'd be able to find the insignia with ease? The first Acolytes made it subtle enough to spot from a distance. And surely their battlefields were filled with Blackblood corpses, which means there was the same smoke from the burning bodies.

A low howl calls out through the mist of the graveyard. It is Scar. He has found something. I sprint to him, some force inside me ready to bubble over with excitement. His natural scent of coco and sandalwood is concealed by the particles of death, but I find him nonetheless.

"What have you found, brother?"

He doesn't speak.

He doesn't have to.

I pause in my tracks, instantly seeing what he does. We both stand before it, speechless. In a field filled with impaled Undead, here stands a single soldier, crucified upon a cross. Upon the skeleton's perplexed head sits a silver crown, so heavy it causes the skull to slump forward and stare down at the ground.

The body is impaled vertically and horizontally. The mounted pole enters his pelvis and holds tight to his ribcage. The horizontal stake was inserted through the nonexistent flesh of his arms and tied to the vertical pole for reinforcement. The Undead prince's skin is melted into the stakes, fused with them for an eternity.

I recognize the crown instantly. It is the one I was supposed to wear as prince of the realm when I came to the age of maturity. I used to stare at it as a child with lust in my eyes. I once fantasized about the day it would be placed upon my brow for the first time. Looking at the skeleton wearing it, I no longer envy the power it conveys upon the wearer.

It doesn't end there. The staked Undead stop in a distinct line that is walled off around the crucifixion. The crucified prince rests at a crossroads of empty space, all impaled Undead outlined around him in the shape of a cross. Each of them are angled to face their long-dead royal leader. Each of them holds the same look of agonized awe on their face.

A cross within a cross. The insignia is laid out plain and clear for all to see. Whether this was some ragged group of vagabonds, or truly the second coming of the Acolytes, they knew their history. And a rogue group of renegades would not be capable of inflicting so much destruction on such a powerful group of individuals. This Atlas, if he truly exists, is not one to be trifled with. Few mortals can stand against the Undead and live to speak of it. Here, whoever is responsible for this display of genocide, was able to slaughter thousands and live to talk of it.

Scar looks to me. Though he has spent the better part of the past year in the Muzzled fighting rings, I can tell by the look on his face he has never seen so much death.

His face says more than the gift of speech ever could. Even I, raised by the former royal family, have never seen someone crucified in all my life. To crucify another is to disgrace them not only in death, but in the afterlife. It is a form of death employed to make a statement. Where impaling one shows enemies you are a threat to their kind, crucifixion conveys immortal humiliation. It goes beyond all bounds of disrespect.

To crucify is to condemn another so publicly that their shame will never be forgotten. Or so I was taught by Lundis. He also said that real warriors do not feel the need to crucify, because regardless of their enemy's actions, crucifixion is a coward's way of killing.

It all made sense when he taught it, but this scene disproves the entire lesson. It was no coward who killed the Undead Prince. That much I'm sure of. Though I know little of the prince formerly known as Bane, I do know that he was next in line to inherit the throne once meant for me. He was not yet born by the time I went on the run, and all I know of him was learned through tales told along the road.

I'd heard it told he was an arrogant child and an even haughtier teenager. Regardless, no warrior deserves to die in this manner.

Whoever killed him didn't bother to steal the silver crown as a trophy. They wanted it to stand as a further symbol of their cause. Any onlooker will see that the Prince of the Undead stood valiantly and fought at Gall, and lost miserably.

"A cross within a cross," I mumble, loud enough for Scar to hear. "Seems Wilhelm wasn't lying after all."

"Mmm."

Scar approaches the crowned skeleton and runs his bony fingers along the steaming crown. He jumps back, startled. It is made of real silver, and Scar is not permitted to touch it. His fingertips blister from where they made contact with the crown. It's likely the first time the Skaarian has ever seen a crown molded by pure silver. The cheap dupes leaders of Skaar wear are made of brass painted to pass off as silver and gold.

"Careful there," I say. He points to the crown, then points to my head.

"No," I reply. "That is not the crown I seek."

"Mmm."

The distant squawk of a bird echoes. The violent flap of wings follow it. I look to the sky and watch as a single black raven descends on the prince's corpse. I look up at the bird, and the bird looks back at me with a curious look. I smile. It is like seeing some long-forgotten friend. A memory triggers in my mind. I quickly dismiss it, knowing now is not the time or place to entertain such nostalgia. Still though, it is queer seeing a raven this far south.

It has been many years since I've seen one. They generally stick to the northern portions of the realm. Their presence brings a message of death. Lundis always said ill tidings follow the wind passed through a raven's wings. Personally, I'm reassured to see the bird. They have never been anything more than good luck to me, though I won't allow myself to walk down memory lane now.

An idea strikes me.

Like a flash of lightning, I have the first real direction I've felt since embarking on this mission.

"I need you to do something for me," I whisper to Scar, almost as if the skeletons will hear my plotting. "I have a separate mission for you. One I need you to hold close to your chest."

"Mmm," he registers, understanding my meaning.

I bring him close and whisper to his ear the plans I've only just devised. He nods his head in understanding, then stares up at the raven. It is a quick exchange, but often the largest schemes unfold from a single order, I've learned.

"Do you understand?"

"Mmm." He nods.

"Follow the raven," I repeat.

"Mmm."

"Then go," I order. "And make haste. Our very lives may depend on your success, Scar."

He nods sympathetically, sensing the severity of the burden I've just placed on him.

"The bird will not guide you wrong," I remind. "Fourteen days from today, the moon will be full and it will be too late." He does not acknowledge my words, already knowing the truth in their validity. He is not a child. I chose him for two reasons. First, because no one will be able to discern the purpose of his travels. He cannot speak, and he cannot write. If he is caught and captured, nothing is risked in the balance. And second, because he is a lone wolf. I have seen it in his eyes since the moment we first met. Though he is a part of this pack, lone wolves are critical for missions such as this. They do not require the strength of the pack to do what needs to be done. And Scar has lived most of his life alone. His silence and solitude are his strengths.

"Then go, brother. I will see you on the other side. Or not. There are no guaranteed endings in this world."

"Mmm," he agrees.

We both turn from the disgraced prince, each of us heading in separate directions. The sun will be setting soon. I must return to the others. We embark on our journeys, and neither of us looks back at the death that looms behind us.

29

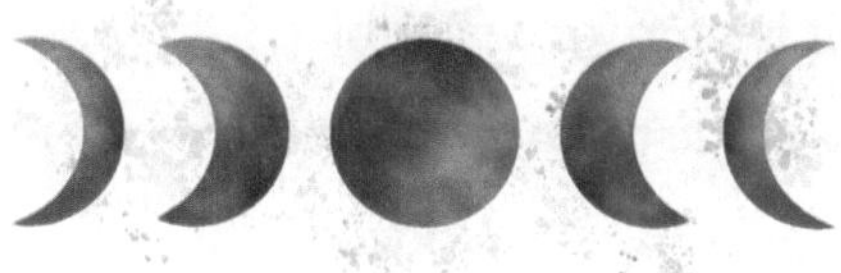

A NIGHTMARE

"Our fearless leader returns short one man!" Creon shouts from a distance. I eye Wilhelm. The prisoner still seems to be living and breathing, likely thanks to Crixus. The she-wolf eyes me uncomfortably, noticeably upset Scar doesn't return with me. I ignore both of them and walk straight to Wilhelm.

"It seems you were right," I announce. The sun sets, and soon I will enact my plan for Wilhelm. For now, the sky is filled with its brilliant yellows and oranges that clash with the blues and purples of space. Wilhelm's eyelids are so swollen from the abuse of daylight that he can barely see. I lightly slap his cheek several times to wake him up. "Hopefully you've found your voice while I was gone. I need you to tell me everything you know about these Acolytes, Wilhelm."

He shakes his head fearfully.

"You have everything to lose, Wilhelm. Answer me and I'll let you go. Don't, and you die here, and I will get the information from the next

Undead leader we find. The skeleton that was crucified, the one with the crown, was that Bane?"

Wilhelm trembles at the mention of the prince's name. He nods his head silently.

"Was it Atlas and his Acolytes that killed him, truly?"

He nods, though it is more of a tremble.

"And how did you come to know of this soldier's name?"

"My troop was assigned by the Undead Emperor to track Atlas and his followers. They've proved to be quite the nuisance throughout this war. They attack Undead and Blackbloods alike. They choose no sides, and they kill without mercy." Wilhelm's voice has changed in my absence. Getting words out is like listening to hot coals being raked over molten lava.

"And have you crossed paths with him?"

"He covers his tracks and scent well. Gall is not the first display of his defiance. He goes after Undead strongholds, since the Blackblood mountains are nearly impenetrable. So far he has successfully slaughtered our forces in Vhem, Slaavan, Thessolo, Ubat, and Hosh, in addition to Gall. I crossed paths with him in Ubat, then cut him off on his way out of Hosh."

"And?"

"I lived to tell of it. My men at the time did not."

"You ran away?"

"It is my job to survive."

"Job well done, Wilhelm."

"Your arrival was unexpected. We arrived in Gall only an hour before you. We missed the Acolyte forces by a half day. The bodies outside the gates were burned that morning. Prince Bane sent a messenger of Atlas's arrival the night before. I departed from Sygon, but even a hard night's flight was not fast enough for me to intervene."

"And what makes you so special to be the one trusted with this task?"

"I am a Black Knight."

The Black Knights, I repeat to myself. Now there's a name I haven't heard in decades. I'd almost forgotten about their existence entirely. Commissioned by Ventur for my father, the Black Knights were once heroes to my childish eyes. They were everything I wanted to be in life. Chivalrous, wise, and the deadliest warriors the realm has ever seen. They swear by the blood in their veins to protect the King, a vow so sacred its violation is punishable by death.

"Ah, so the Undead Emperor is now sending his Black Knights on mercenary missions. There was once a day they stood for something greater."

"It takes a special kind of warrior to take on Atlas in battle. You drastically underestimate what this human is capable of, Syrus Sylvian."

He says my voice menacingly, like he knows something I don't. This whole time I've refrained from my identity being revealed to him. Crixus and Creon have not said it aloud. All he has to go off of is my Lycan form in Gall paired with my silver eyes. That alone is enough for any who remember my family's powers to connect the dots.

"Underestimate him or not, it won't matter. Atlas and I share the same enemy. We stand on the same side of the battlefield."

"Your lineage protects you not, Sylvian. The First Acolytes were not friends with the Sylvians of old."

"Nor were they enemies. You forget, Wilhelm. My mother was the last descendant of Lysander the Great.""

And you forget, Sylvian. The Acolytes have never cared about lineage and bloodlines. They believe man is defined by his acts, not his ancestors."

Wilhelm has gathered what little strength he could in my absence. His flesh is irreparably scarred. The sun has scorched his identifying features. Blisters litter his face like barnacles on a crustacean's shell. Cracks in his flesh ooze puss and blood. Even his eyes are so burnt that their original color will never again be discernable. Yet he pushes through the pain stoically. He no longer gasps for air to finish his sentence or stutters over his burning tongue. The sun is setting, and the night restores him of any powers he's entitled to.

The moon won't be able to heal what I've done to his body, but he will at least live to fight another day. It's amazing what a few hours can do to fortify our minds. From tortured to valiant, Wilhelm has returned to the arrogant soldier that sought to kill my beast within.

I peer to the purple horizon. The light of the sky fades beautifully. Stars peak out in the night. Phosphorescent light soothes the atmosphere from the heat of day. The walls of the tent are barely thick enough to thwart the radiance of sunset. People think the sun is most deadly to the Undead at noon, when it crests its peak in the sky. I would argue it's even more dangerous when it rises and sets. The concentration of its light is more potent than ever. At noon, the sun scatters its light in even distribution amongst the earth. But when it hugs the horizon, its beams are laser focused. Strong enough to kill an Undead instantly.

If I was to lift the flaps of the tent now, Wilhelm would be dead in seconds. Its concentration of daylight would not merely blister his skin and boil his blood. The beautiful light would incinerate his body to ashes.

"How did you know who I am?" I ask, gazing deep into the Undead's being through his calloused eyes.

"Because," Wilhelm explains, a charred smile on his face, "Long before I was appointed to be a Black Knight by the Emperor, I was a royal guard. One of the same royal guards who discovered the aftermath of your moonlit rampage, Sylvian."

"You were there that night?"

"I was there that night, and it seems the gods have saw fit to cross our paths once more after all these years. The moment I saw your silver eyes glowing in Gall I knew who you were. And when I saw the town's mists parting before your wolfish body I knew my death was certain."

"And here you are, still alive," I remark.

"I don't fear the Sylvian," he stares coldly into my soul.

"You should," I reply.

His face twists suddenly. A look of whimsical humor takes him over. As if I've just told him a joke I can't yet understand. He chuckles, his voice the croak of rocks grinding, "You don't know, do you?"

"Know what?" I ask in return.

"Much was uncovered about the Sylvian lineage when you hid yourself away from the modern world, Syrus Sylvian. I would bet there is much you don't know."

"Then by all means, catch me up." I smile, as if I am privy to whatever joke he wields against me. "Starting with why the Undead now wage war against the Blackbloods. Why does your kind no longer fear catching the virus?"

"Your ignorance is amusing, Syrus. This is not 800 A.S. We have discovered the cure to the Blackblood virus, Sylvian. Your questions reveal how little you know, exiled prince."

He speaks to me as if I can't lift the tent flap and kill him instantly. He is past the point of fearing death. He openly welcomes it, I realize. I would too, if I were him. I've stripped him of his hands and fangs. He is a toothless wolf; a hornless thyrops. Death would be preferable to a man in his condition. But there are worse things in this life than death, I've learned.

"If there is truly a cure, why do the Blackbloods exile themselves? Why not seek healing? Why not eliminate their virus and return to being Undead?"

"Because, the very nature of the virus is to preserve itself, boy," he mocks my ignorance, talks to me like a child. "Once it has taken hold of a host it refuses to relinquish control. It would rather kill its host than be eradicated. The virus waives no white flag. And so we gladly kill its hosts in an attempt to put it to death once and for all. Those who are infected in the midst of war may seek treatment before the virus takes over their minds with delirium. Same with those we capture as prisoners of war."

"Then what is the cure, Wilhelm," I demand, grabbing hold of the tent's wall, threatening to pull it open. He doesn't flinch at my gesture. Just licks his cracked lips, almost as if he is excited at the thought of me ending his life. I have no authority over him. He wants to die.

"Put an end to this bugger, Syrus," Creon calls out. "You aren't going to get anything out of him. He's just wasting our time."

"Tell me," I demand again, doubling down on my request in vain.

He slowly lifts himself from his seated position, grunting with burning pain as he does so. His wrists and ankles are bound. He merely lingers in the shadows of the tent, staring at me with empty, glazed eyes. "You have no idea what waits for you in Sygon, Sylvian. Bloodlust has sent you to your death by sending you there. Even with your powers, it would have been more merciful for the Blackbloods to euthanize you like the rabid dog you are. You are no longer welcomed in this world, Syrus. A puzzle piece that no longer fits in the greater scheme of things. You will learn this in time, but by the time it dawns on you, it will be too late."

Wilhelm lunges at me suddenly, not hesitating to charge at me even though he poses no threat. I'm caught off guard as he throws his body into me, knocking me off balance. Wilhelm brushes past my shoulder and leaps into the open air of the ambient sunset. My body twists from the impact, turning to face him as Wilhelm dives to his knees and Solis's light incinerates his flesh. He makes no noise as his body becomes a pillar of flames. I try to catch him, but the heat of his burning body causes me to hesitate. He is already gone.

I back away as I watch smoke roll from his bones like a forest fire during a season of drought. His glazed eyes melt from his skull. His flesh is like kindling under a spark. His clothes catch fire. He is a sacrifice to a dead god. A pile of ash. Water poured on seething coals. I curse under my breath. Creon laughs. Crixus observes silently.

Within a few short minutes, there are no remains of the man once known as Wilhelm. Any plans I had at lynching information from him are ashes in the wind. Luna rises with a sick smile on her face. I clench my fists in anger. Keeping Wilhelm prisoner only raised more questions in my mind. I find no clarity from his ambiguous answers.

"Pack up, we leave at dark," I order, storming off from the scene toward Solis's parting light.

Creon's smile angers me. I want to wipe it from his face with my fist. He still fails to see the bigger picture. This mission has turned into nothing more than a chance for him to get revenge for Lockjaw. He is not in this so I can save Sephora. I'd sooner see him leave and never come back, and if it comes to it, I will let him die so I don't have to carry his dead weight any longer.

"Where are we going now?" Crixus asks, breaking down the tent for travel.

"Queensmyre is a half day's march from here. Yueltope is two. Sygon is five. We will seek refuge in Queensmyre. Eat and rest. Seek answers Wilhelm failed to provide."

"And Scar?" she asks, still perplexed by his absence.

"I've sent him on an errand," I answer, not revealing the purpose for his absence. I don't trust Creon. Can't let him in on my plan should he be taken prisoner. "Should he succeed, he will meet us in Sygon. Should he fail, he will be dead."

She nods at me with apprehension. We were once five. Then we were four. Now we are three. She asks no other questions, wise enough to know you shouldn't ask if you don't wish to know.

"I should let you know—" Creon starts.

I interrupt, "That you're a wanted man in Queensmyre as well?"

He chuckles, nodding his head.

I want to slit his throat with a silver arrow from Wilhelm's quiver. I want to leave his body for the carrion birds to devour. This man is a criminal through and through. Everywhere we go, a bounty will be on his head. He will raise eyes. Give us away. It would be easier to leave him for dead.

I bite my lip and don't respond. Having a man of his infamy has its perks. Should we find ourselves in a pinch, I can negotiate our freedom with his detainment. He is a walking, talking bargain. An ace up my sleeve. The ultimate distraction.

"Wonderful," I sigh in response, realizing my problem may soon work itself out sooner than I'd hoped.

30

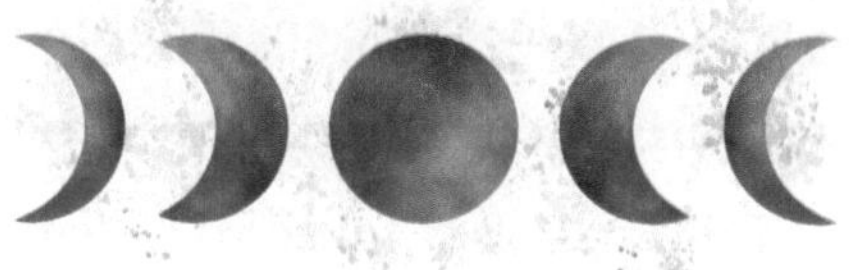

A Nightmare

There was once a poet named Alabastur. He wrote plays so captivating that people would journey several weeks to see them put on. Tragedies and comedies alike, his feathered pen had a way of making people forget about their own problems for a night. Both wealthy nobles and dirt peasants could relate to his plays the same, and they were written in a way that grew increasingly complex the more one watched them performed.

Glaring symbolism became evident after a second or third exposure to the same story. Themes as clear as the night sky were revealed, but only for those who took the time to painstakingly ponder a play's meaning.

In his old age, the poet refused for any town other than Queensmyre to be permitted the pleasure of watching his plays. Born in Queensmyre, Alabastur used his gift of writing to make his native city richer in the process. He does not leave the city, will not hire actors outside its walls, and only performs his plays in Queensmyre's renowned amphitheater. But word spread of the poet's genius, and people are naturally willing to travel for one-of-a-kind entertainment.

My father took me to see one of Alabastur's plays as a child. Selena was too young at the time to travel, so we went with Ventur and Tutor Lundis to the queer town of Queensmyre. The name of the play was *Equinox*, never performed again before or after. Historians try to attend each of the poet's plays in an attempt to transcribe their plots in written form. Alabastur only permits each story to be enacted for a single season, then burns all evidence of its existence. In truth, he is completely and utterly mad. But his madness is inextricably linked to his genius, so no one gives much thought to it.

I will never forget the telling of *Equinox*. And though I later purchased an off-hand transcription written by a historian, Tutor Lundis and I both agreed they failed spectacularly in capturing the essence of Alabastur's storytelling cadence. It was the story of Solis and Luna going to war against one another once their love faded. Also known as the anti-creation story, *Equinox* told the epic story of day and night clashing like never before. Though Solis and Luna have eclipsed many times before because of their love for one another, *Equinox* depicts their first fight as lovers, and the great destructive aftermath ensued when lovers go to war.

In its literal meaning, the equinox is the time of year when Solis and Luna take their mantle in the sky for the same duration of time. But Alabastur brought life to this occurrence with his story. Where there was previously no meaning in the celestial orbit, Alabastur told the daring story of Luna's affair with Cratos, a comet from space's outer rim. It was so compelling it almost made me confuse fiction with fact as a child.

From Cratos and Luna's sinful bond the moon bore a human by the name of Enchantress. When Solis learned of the affair, he cursed Enchantress by calling the dead to haunt her soul for all eternity. Consequently, she was shunned from the world of the living and exiled to dwell in the darkest corners of creation. In these places, the spirits of the dead found her, but instead of haunting her, they formed an alliance with her. She traveled from graveyard to graveyard as a child, calling every malignant spirit in existence to her cause. Twenty years she roamed to and fro amongst the dead, raising her army of ghosts and ghouls. She summoned them, and the air echoed with the screams of a hundred thousand mortal souls wherever she went.

Enchantress sought revenge for what Solis had done to her. Now, Solis took pride in all creation that thrived in his magnificent daylight. Plants and animals and human civilization could not survive without the sun. But everywhere Enchantress traveled, darkness followed. The grass died where she walked. The damned souls that followed her killed all that crossed her path. She could summon them with a single scream from her harpy throat.

And so Solis watched in dismay as the child he'd damned eternally returned from the darkness with an army of demons at her service. He watched from the sky as she slowly killed all creation he'd worked so hard to make prosperous. Ecosystems withered in her path. Corpses rotted. Her army of Fallen marched halfway across creation, killing all in existence. Her very being was an Equinox. She was the force of darkness that equally opposed Solis's light. And if the sun failed to stop her, she would consume the entire living world, destroying all Solis had sworn to protect during the day.

But Solis was cunning, so he struck Enchantress in the only way she could be killed—with love. Her whole life, creation had shunned her very being. No one had given her the time of day, because the day itself was opposed to her existence. Solis warned a young farmer by the name of Caspian of Enchantress's coming. Caspian, who was deeply in love with his crops and livestock, knew all he had toiled to maintain would perish if Enchantress passed over his land. His farm would be reduced to wasteland, another graveyard along the path of death Enchantress had harvested.

And so, with Solis's warning, Caspian rode on horseback to meet Enchantress in her path of destruction, carrying with him a single Thanatos rose. It was said the Thanatos rose was unable to be killed; that its very roots reached down to hell wherever it was planted. And so, when Caspian finally, after many days of travel, found Enchantress in her tidal wave of chaos, he submitted himself before her, flower outstretched in hand.

Enchantress, who had never been offered a token of peace in her entire life, didn't know what to do. When she brought herself to take the flower from the humble farmer, she saw that it did not wither in her hands. Its black petals remained, its thorny stem intact in her grip. Without a single word exchanged between the two, Enchantress was brought to tears by the exchange.

The farmer had succeeded in doing what a soldier never could—he had touched the woman's heart of darkness with a spark of light. The fallen souls that followed Enchantress tried to convince her this was a trap, but she could not see past the symbolic gesture of love the farmer had displayed. And so, at Caspian's implore, she ceased her march across creation, promising she would not step another foot forward onto the land of the living.

But Caspian purposely withheld his knowledge about the Thanatos rose's sinister nature. Like the Venus flytrap, the Thanatos rose is a species of carnivorous plant native to the Neverglade forest, the most inhospitable environment on all creation. And so, as Enchantress lay her head to sleep that night, rose clutched in hand, the plant's roots devoured her body, consuming her completely, feeding her to the earth on which she lay. By the time the morning rose, her body was no more. A tree of black bark and obsidian leaves had grown where she rested eternally. The tree—later named Summoner—grew on the Equinox line between the world of the living and the land of the damned.

When Solis rose the following morning, he smiled brightly at Enchantress's demise, and he applauded himself in his cunning scheme to bring about her downfall. But what he hadn't accounted for was, more than anything, Caspian's love that had grown toward Enchantress in the little time he'd known her.

The farmer took Summoner's seedlings and spread them, planting them in spite of Solis. The seedlings sprouted to trees overnight, and their roots spread collectively, continuing to kill all living land in their reach. It wasn't long before one night, while Caspian slept at the base of his beloved Enchantress's memorial tree, the roots, similar to those of the Thanatos rose, consumed his body in his sleep, killing him.

The next morning, when Solis rose, a white tree with bark the color of pale ash stood next to Summoner on the living side of the Equinox line, a testament to the farmer's valiant stand against the army of death. The tree—later named Blind Love—stands directly opposed to the forest of death, its white roots spreading above the ground along the Equinox line, while Summoner's roots gently caressed the roots of her former lover.

It was a lot to unpack as a child, and I'd be lying if I said I understood the story in its entirety. I remember saying to Lundis after, I could watch that play a dozen times and still come away with confusion. On the one hand, there was the story of love trumping death, but death ultimately winning in the end. On the other hand, there was this complex analogy regarding the equilibrium of light and darkness upon the face of the earth.

And the actors were phenomenal. Their performances were so captivating that I hid tears from my father when Caspian died. Ventur saw them though, and he made sure I knew it for the rest of his years.

Queensmyre was a place of wonderful color and breathtaking sights. Renowned artists were drawn from all across the kingdom to bring their creative prowess. Revolutionary sculptures lined the streets and lifelike portraits filled each home. Musicians played on every street corner and writers never went hungry. Parades once littered the streets. Confetti floated through the air. Children flew kites. Fireworks lit the night sky.

The city I look at now is not the Queensmyre I once knew.

The city I look at now is hollow and desolate.

Its once magnificent walls etched with a thousand different sculptures are now rubble.

Its vibrant gardens are long dead.

The smog we've been unable to escape since Gall fills its streets.

No music plays.

No kites fly.

The colors have faded to greys and blacks.

The streets are dead silent.

Townspeople sit along the roadway with cups outstretched for change. Homeless beggars rattle coins at me and Crixus and Creon as we slowly enter the outskirts of the city. No guards rush to prevent us from proceeding. We climb the crumbled wall and walk straight into the city's bowels. Men and women walk like zombies in the streets. Some of them beg for food, others ask if we have come to save them. Their bodies are covered with soot from head to toe. I can see the distinct puncture wounds on their necks. This city has become prime feeding grounds for the Undead.

The townsfolk are nothing more than walking bloodbags to the Undead. They stagger through the streets half delirious. Their minds likely go madder by the day as their brains become deprived of blood.

I stop and watch them for a few moments. They mindlessly shuffle through the streets, most of them too oblivious to notice our presence. Those who do notice us mumble incoherent questions and demands. It's like they are puppets orchestrated by a horrendously untalented puppet master. They move with no purpose in their steps. Most of them get up from the ashy ground, take a few steps, trip, then fall back to the ground to cuddle with the dust.

"I guess it's safe to say they won't be looking to collect on my bounty," Creon chuckles to himself.

"This war is turning the surrounding cities into graveyards," I sigh. "Over a thousand years of artistic history lost in a meaningless dispute."

The city's cobblestone streets are covered with a layer of ash thick enough to leave footprints. Embers float through the air from the dozens of fires citizens lit to keep themselves safe from the raid in the night. If I had to guess, Undead soldiers stop in Queensmyre every night looking to feed. The city lies directly between Sygon and the mountains, and there is no longer fresh blood in Gall.

Queensmyre is notorious for being built around the Pagean River. A wide canal coils through the main streets, broken boats capsized in the water now. The river was once a vibrant artery that provided life to the city. Its banks were once filled with masterfully designed wildlife. Queensmyre employed gardeners who spent their entire day tending to the beauty of the natural landscape.

The buildings are rustic townhomes pressed tightly together, balconies lining their walls for dwellers within to bask in the wreckage of the former spectacle. Chunks of the townhomes lay in the streets and fill the Pagean. The whole scene looks as though Enchantress herself has strolled through the city, bringing with her nothing but death and destruction.

War effects everything it touches.

And the magnitude of war only amplifies the turmoil a kingdom experiences.

Queensmyre will never recover from this. The former home to thousands of bureaucrats and artists who prided themselves in their peaceful nature. Other than the knights who patrolled the city streets maintaining order, weapons were not permitted within Queensmyre's limits.

Passersby and travelers could not enter with arms, and it was a free place for all species to enter. Human, Undead, Lycan, it didn't matter. They were a city of freethinking and enlightenment. Queensmyre prided itself on its superiority of ideals.

Because of their pronounced freedom of speech and expression, philosophers and intellectuals would travel from all over to take up debates on theological quandary. But war doesn't care about freedom. And though their enlightened notion of prohibiting weapons within the city walls was perceived to be superior policy, it did little more than secure their downfall when the Undead came for the Blackbloods.

Better to have a knife under your pillow than to face the darkness alone every night.

I wonder how many of these incapacitated beggars that line the streets were once genius philosophers. Artists. Inventors. Architects.

It matters little what they did in a past life. All that matters is here and now, and they are too weak to protect themselves. The Undead will continue to feed on their bodies until they dry up and drop dead. Infection will fester and plague will spread. It's a miracle they've made it this long, but they won't make it many more moons in this condition.

If I didn't know any better, I'd think a battle between the Undead and Blackbloods occurred directly over this city. The Pagean is lined with a thousand dead trees, their silhouettes in the sunrise a reminder that Solis was powerless to save them. Most trees are uprooted or cut. The earth is scarred with impact craters. Windows are sealed with soiled bedsheets. Shingled roofs lay in crumbled tatters. Any buildings previously made of thatch are now burnt down to termite-infested boards and beams. Scrap metal and rubble covers the cobblestone streets so thick that I can no longer see the direction the road leads. Our footsteps are heavy and awkward as we traverse the uneven ground.

"You there," a voice calls out, clear and coherent. I keep walking and gesture to Crixus to ignore the voice. Something irks me about the clarity of the beckoning inquiry. In a town full of half-dead corpses, this is the first person I've heard speak energetically. The voice calls out again, "I know who you are, Syrus."

The sound of my name causes me to freeze.

She continues, "And you, Creon."

The three of us turn around to face the woman. An old hag stands under a door frame that looks as though it has failed miserably at keeping the outside world shut out. All that remains attached to the door hinges are planks of splintered wood. Claw marks reap the brick walls that surround the entrance. Chunks of wall are missing throughout the building, the rocky rubble scattered on the ground around the old hag.

The hag looks as though she's just heard a bad joke. Her face is pinched with tension. Her eyes are intense. Gray bangs float above her thick, white brows. Wrinkles cover her face like they've been there longer than I've been alive. Her nose looks as though it's been broken a half dozen times and healed worse with each breaking. A rigid bump crests on its midsection like the hump on the back of a camel. Her body is shriveled, back hunched, arms short. She is an absolute crone. Death should have taken her a thousand moons ago, yet here she is.

"How do you know our names?" I ask.

"It's been a long time since I've seen you here, Prince Syrus. You were but a boy before."

I look at her with confusion. A smile lines her toothless face, raising the wrinkles around her mouth in an exhausted arc. "And you, Creon," she continues. "You are still wanted for burning down Norm's Tavern. You're lucky I'm the only one left who remembers."

Creon spits in her direction. "I've no bloody idea who you are, witch. Begone with you!"

"You may not know me, but I very much know you. In fact, I know more about you than you know about yourself. Only one I've never crossed paths with is this young she-wolf you have in your pack."

Crixus looks at me, confused, then looks back at the old hag. Even though the hag doesn't know her, she already knows Crixus is a Lycan. Lycans have no identifiable features without the light of the full moon. They are every bit human in the light of day.

"But I will know her in time. Come," the hag demands. "We have much to discuss before you depart for Sygon." With that, she ducks back into the building and retreats into the bowels of the fortress. I look at Creon with a look of perplexity. For him normally having something witty to say, he is equally as speechless. Neither of us know this woman, yet she seems to know us completely, as if she were some long lost grandmother of ours.

Creon sighs, "Bloody trip just keeps getting weirder and weirder," then disappears into the darkness of the building.

My father taught me as a child to not speak to strangers. But what do you do when you are not a stranger to them?

31

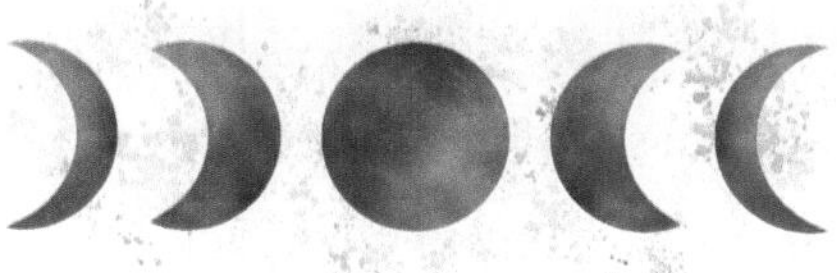

A Nightmare

The inner workings of the residence are as cryptic as the hag's mysterious nature. The only light to be found is the sporadic flickering of candle wicks. The aroma of burning sage overwhelms my senses with every turn. The walls are filled with peeling paintings and scrolls yellowed with age. It is unclear how I've gotten here. I try desperately to search my memories for any notion of who this woman is. I've only been to Queensmyre once. And though the memory is foggy and blotted by repression, I don't recall any dealings with the hag.

"Come, come," the hag calls from a removed room off to the side. I follow Creon into the small cubicle-like room. Nothing more than a single table with dusty chairs fills its presence. The hag is already seated at the table, her sunken eyes watching us like a hawk.

I instantly spot the crystal ball that sits as a centerpiece to the table. I cringe, realizing what we've gotten ourselves into. The witch is a fortune teller. A cheap crook who spews lies for a few coppers. Lundis taught me of their ways as a child. They are trained artists who draft creative generalizations over people based on their appearances. But how the hag knew our names and our business is still unknown to me. That is not information that would have been evident based on our physical features or garb.

"Bloody hell, she's just a black magic witch, Syrus," Creon moans, irritated at falling for her bait. "Let's get out of here."

"No," I counter, "Take a seat. Hear her out."

The crone smiles at my insistence. Our pack huddles around the table and claims a seat at the candlelit desk. Random cards and mementos line the tabletop. The crystal ball glows with an unknown source of light. Purple and crimson dance within the glass sphere, the light bouncing off the hag's face.

"What do you want from us?" I ask. "We have no coppers for you."

"Do I look like I want your money?" she cackles, amused by my assertion. "What would a few coppers do to help me survive the destruction of Queensmyre? Huh? Nothing. This city's fate is final, and mine with it."

"Then please tell us, what do you want with us?"

She eyes me with curiosity. Her gaze seems to look beyond my outer façade, into the pits of my being. I almost want to squeeze my eyes shut to deny her access to my soul, but I resist the urge. My vision blurs. It feels as though I am no longer in my body. It feels as though I am a spirit floating in the room, observing from a detached state of objectivity. I realize suddenly that I am in a trance. My mouth is so heavy that I don't think I could form words even if I wanted to.

"You look so much like your father," the hag whispers. "You have his stern jawline and his stoic cheekbones. It takes me back two decades to a time he sat at this very table, sitting in that exact seat, Syrus Sylvian. People don't believe in the fates, but tell me, is it mere coincidence that you chose to sit in the very seat he did?"

I cannot answer. All I can do is stare helplessly into her innocent eyes. All I can hear are her words. Crixus and Creon have disappeared from my sight. They may as well not even be in the room. My peripheral vibrates out of focus. I am stuck in a tunnel, and all I can see is the witch's face at the tunnel's opening.

"He came to me, years ago, your father did. The night he took you to see Alabastur's creation of *Equinox*. You slept in the wagon. Your tutor and Ventur watched over you while your father came to see me late in the night. He sought my counsel, unlike you, who were brought here by the fates."

Her words draw me further into the trance. I cannot feel my body. Cannot break free. I feel as though I am floating between the realm of sleep and consciousness. A helpless baby being sung a lullaby.

"My services are known to those who know how to look, and your father was one of few who had the wisdom to come seeking. I do not deal cheap fortunes. I tell the future, and the price is costly. Men pay for my prophecy by submitting themselves to its haunting consequences. To know the future is to know what Death has in store for you. There are many possible outcomes, but those who hear my oracles are gifted the ability to choose the best possible outcome, even if it means they must die as a consequence."

I want to panic. It feels like I am caught in the maw of a great predator. I cannot escape. I must stare into its eyes as it devours me completely. If I try to rip myself free from its embrace, my soul will be ripped clean from my body.

"It would do you well to know your father chose what happened willingly. His death was not your fault. This was the way he planned for things to be, for if he chose any other path, the world itself would have lost all hope. You did not kill your father, Syrus Sylvian. Hear my words. You did not kill your father, Syrus Sylvian. Trust my words. You did not kill your father, Syrus Sylvian. Your life has been a lie. Although necessary, you have deceived yourself into thinking you murdered your family. Your father sat in this very chair when I showed him all that could happen in his future. The Undead Emperor was coming for his throne, and his demise was inevitable. Your father sat in this very chair when I showed him all that could happen, and he chose the only possible outcome that would preserve the Sylvian bloodline."

I realize suddenly that my eyes are filled with tears. The hag speaks the truth I have always known but been unable to formulate. My whole life I have run from my past. My whole life I have feared the monster within. My whole life I have convinced myself that I am the reason the kingdom fell to the Undead's reign of darkness.

"I will not tell you your future, as I told your father his. Yours is shrouded in blood spattered darkness. The fates have hidden what is to come, though I know what outcomes are possible from reading your father's future. Because of his bold decisions, the Sylvian bloodline lives on in you, and in your daughter. And because of his bold decisions, there is a third. This is the way it had to be, for the Undead Empire to be defeated."

What is she talking about? A third? Does she mean a third Sylvian? It isn't possible. Selena is dead. I saw her mutilated body. How could there possibly be a third?

"Your father's greatest error in life was making an alliance with the Undead. They sought his throne, and he knew they would make a move for it in his lifetime. It was only a matter of time. And so he sought my services. Hear me, Syrus Sylvian. Your father came to me because he had nowhere else to go. I do not deal cheap fortunes. I tell the future, and the price is costly. Your father paid that price with his life, just as a tree sends off its saplings when it knows it will soon die. This was the way he planned for things to be, for if he chose any other path, the world itself would have lost all hope. Do you hear me, Syrus Sylvian? Do you believe me? His demise was inevitable. You did not kill your father, Syrus Sylvian. There is a third. This is the way things had to be."

Her eyes pierce the very fabric of my being. Reality tears at its seems. The earth trembles as the hag whispers its secrets. Fates scream as she reveals the truth. I see a vision of a blood-soaked boy holding his father's dead body in his arms. It all comes rushing back to me. I know the truth. I want to gasp. I cannot breathe. I am screaming silently. My body is convulsing. I see. I hear. I believe.

"The Undead Emperor killed your father, Syrus Sylvian. The Undead Emperor killed your mother, Syrus Sylvian. The Undead Emperor killed your sister, Syrus Sylvian. But the Undead Emperor could not kill you, Syrus Sylvian. Listen to the beast within. Trust him. Trust yourself. Search your instinct. All those years ago, on the night of your family's massacre. I will show you what happened. Close your eyes, Syrus Sylvian. Close them, and I will show you the truth of the matter. I tell the future, and the price is costly. But for you, I will tell the past, because the price is freedom. Close your eyes, Syrus Sylvian, for I will show you what actually happened. I need you to hear me, Syrus Sylvian. I need you to believe."

I look deep into the darkness of her eyes. The darkness consumes me, and suddenly I am transported to a memory I've spent a lifetime trying to forget.

32

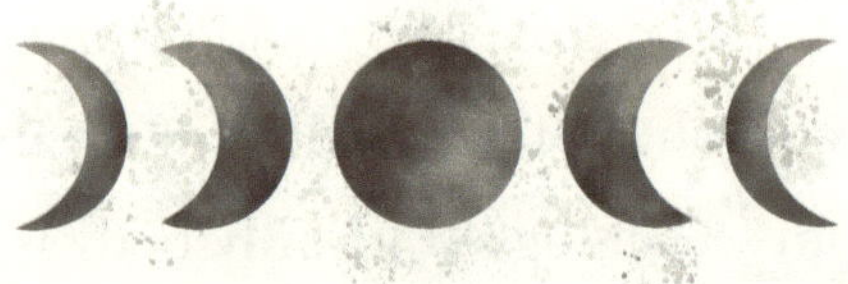

A Dream

I watch as my childish body sleeps soundly. I am a mere spirit suspended in the air, unable to control the events about to unravel. My spirit lingers in the darkest corner of the room, watching my boyish body toss and turn in bed. My eyes painfully flicker to Selena. This is the first time I've seen her in twenty years. She is every bit as beautiful and innocent as I remember her.

Wisps of dark hair cover her face while she sleeps. Her shallow breathing blows the hair enough to uncover her face. I'm forced to realize how identical she is to Sephora at that age. The two could be identical twins, though they were born in two separate ages. The light of the full moon leaves a dim light on the floor through the open doorway. The children sleep opposite the open door, the pale light revealing their innocent faces.

Hours ago, their father told them the story of Dagon and Damon and Sylvian the First. Hours ago, they smiled with glee as their father tucked them in, never to be seen alive again. I am powerless to wake them from their sleep. All I can do is watch helplessly. The only reason I've been unable to live with myself all these years is because I didn't know the events of this night. Now I'm forced to face my greatest fear head on.

A shadow blots out the moonlight from the doorway. A hooded figure now stands before the innocent children. I hear the clanking of armor behind him, then see several Black Knights emerge. The hooded figure shuffles into the room silently, seven knights entering noiselessly behind him. They file into the room and stand shoulder to shoulder, the hooded figure standing center to it all.

The knights are terrifying in their obsidian armor. Only the greatest warriors within the realm are granted the rank of Black Knight, sworn to forever protect the royal family from peril. After my exile, I learned what laymen have come to call them: The Soulless. They deal death without remorse. Though I was too young to understand their merciless disposition as a child, my travels have since educated me of the atrocities the Black Knights have committed. Cities burned. Martyrs flayed. Children tortured so parents would talk. The Soulless carry out the royal family's darkest desires while keeping the king's crown clean. They weren't always this way. Under my father, there was little need for the Black Knights, but they were a gift to him from the Undead after an alliance was formed. Since the Empire took over, the Emperor has put them to use across the kingdom.

Their armor gleams in the darkness. They are a shade darker than midnight black. The slits where their eyes should be are hollow with shadows. They stand in the room as silent as silhouettes. The hooded figure approaches the sleeping children alone, hovering over them while they dream sweet dreams. He is a demented nightmare standing over them. His hood swivels from my boyish body to Selena's. I want nothing more than to scream until the children wake. I can feel the palpable dread lingering in the room. Something bad is about to happen. Something very bad.

"Kill them," the hooded figure commands in a whisper, not wanting to wake the children from their sleep. *No!* I scream inwardly. The voice is familiar, though its growling nature disguises its identity. The Soulless silently draw obsidian blades from their scabbards. The metal slicing through empty air as they ready their weapons is like a mother shushing her children.

The Black Knights advance toward the children slowly. There is no urgency in their steps. The children will be dead soon, they walk as though there is no reason to rush it. Four surround young Syrus's bed, three circle around Selena. The hooded figure stands between our beds, peering down out our frail bodies. The moonlight once again shines on our faces. Pale and innocent, but the hooded figure doesn't care. The children are Sylvian, so they stand in his way of claiming the kingdom as his own. I know the hooded man is the future Emperor of the Undead, though his identity is concealed.

The Soulless raise their swords in unison, pointed ends hovering above Syrus and Selena, a thrust away from ending their lives. The moonlight is blotted by an emerging figure now standing in the doorframe. The absence of light causes the hooded figure to turn to face the intruder.

"I thought I smelled a traitor in the keep," father interrupts the silence. His eyes glow a menacing shade of silver. His voice is an incorruptible growl. He sounds like a mother bear who's discovered her cubs are in trouble. His arrival has caused the Black Knights to freeze in fear. Their swords hang in the air above the children, almost as if they know any further movement will mean their death. The hooded figure looks like a child caught in the act of stealing a cookie from the kitchen. He stands aloof, knowing only one will survive the fight to come.

Mother enters the doorway behind father, making no noise as she assesses the situation. Not a single gasp leaves her mouth. She is a warrior herself. Before marrying father, she fought in several of humanity's petty wars, rising to the rank of Commander. She has fought many times in her life before entering royalty, and she will do so again to protect her children. Her hand goes to the hilt at her waist and draws her iconic crimson blade. I have heard tales of the sword turning crimson before, but never seen it with my own eyes. The hilt is made of mood rock and reflects the emotion of its user. I have seen her draw the weapon few times in my own life, but it normally glows a cool shade of passive emerald. The burning crimson indicates the fury she feels within without her having to speak a single word. The glowing red light drowns out the innocence from the full moon outside the castle. Father and mother's face illuminate like rubies.

"Take your wife and flee, Silenius Sylvian. We will spare your lives for now. You can start anew on the outskirts of the realm. But your reign here is over. The time for the Undead has come," the hooded man announces, his voice unsure of the words he speaks.

"I have been prepared for this day longer than you know, Ventur," Silenius spits back. My heart skips a beat. Ventur? My father's closest confidant? This is the man that seeks to end our lives? This is the man responsible for the death of my father? My mother? My sister? The same man that rushed me to safety at the expense of his own life after I awoke from my midnight terror?

"You won't survive this, Silenius. Don't make me kill you."

"Death is the least of my concerns, brother. This kingdom is mine to protect, and I won't stand to see you destroy it all."

"Destroy it?" Ventur burst out with laughter. "You've hardly left anything to destroy! Pirates have blockaded the wharves successfully for several seasons now. Tax collectors are on strike. The Lycans have been allowed to multiply without census; they raid villages like packs of wild wolves. The land of humans slowly questions your leadership and test what they can get away with. Rumors of rebellion echo, and I hear them closing in on us. You've grown soft, Silenius. Your reign is no longer respected. It is time for new leadership. The time for the Undead to claim the throne has come."

"You have been my closest friend since I was but a boy in a crown, Ventur. It is a shame it has to end like this."

The Soulless pull their swords away from the sleeping children and immediately form a defensive arc around Ventur. My mother assumes an attacking position, bringing her blade eye-level with her elbows ready to plunge forward at the nearest soldier.

Father grows very cold in comparison. His body doubles over. His clothes stretch to the point of tearing at the seams. The silver light of his eyes disappears as he squeezes them shut from the pain. I hear the sounds of bones breaking. They grind together as they reshape into wolf-like limbs.

"Now!" Ventur screams at the Soulless, "Kill them now, while he is vulnerable!"

Mother steps in front of father defensively as he shifts into a Lycan. Unfortunately for them, it is not an instant process, but they need the Curse of Dagon if they're to succeed in winning this fight. Two against eight is no easy feat. The Black Knights waste no time in advancing toward mother. There is no fear in her eyes. The glow of her crimson blade fills the room and reflects off the obsidian armor of her attackers.

Gray hair covers father's body. His nose snaps into a snout. I stare at his mouth. Saliva drips from his drooling jowls. His fangs are white as ivory, the gumline showing as his lips lift in a snarl. Every muscle in his body has striations visible through the fur. He is several feet taller now and has to squat under the low ceiling to fit in the room.

The sound of metal clanging and vibrating in the air begins as mother parries an attempt to disembowel father. The Knights advance simultaneously. They raise their swords swiftly. Mother blindingly hacks into the exposed knee of the closest knight, then drives her shoulder into the second closest, knocking him off balance.

The swords of five fall toward father in unison. Mother swings her sword around fast enough to deflect three of the blades, but two make contact with father as he continues to shift from human to Lycan. One sword cuts clean into his shoulder at the joint, the other lodges itself in his opposite thigh. The Lycan instinctively yelps with pain, its silver eyes reemerging to shun the darkness of the room.

The Lycan is fearsome. I watch it rise, fully transformed from human, now standing on its wolfish hind legs. Half man, half wolf, the beast is something not even Alabastur could describe with words. To describe how I feel seeing the Lycan would undercut the immense dread welling in my stomach. He towers over the Black Knights. His body is laden thick with muscle. The flesh the swords pierced is a thick hide like leather. The swords barely penetrated it, and where they did, the wound now heals before their eyes. His muzzle is filled with fangs long enough to clamp down on a human's fully grown torso. Each finger sprouts an individual claw sharper than a freshly smithed sword. A salt-and-pepper gray tail swishes behind the Lycan, its bushiness reminiscent to the tail of a fox.

The yelp of pain causes Selena to spring up in bed like she's awoke from a bad nightmare, but the true nightmare is what transpires in her bedroom. Young Syrus tosses and turns in bed, stuck in a feverish nightmare as the light of the full moon covers his face. I see beads of sweat dripping from his unconscious body. The boy's face cringes with pain as something otherworldly seizes hold of him. Selena screams. The hooded man turns quickly and covers her mouth with his hand, taking hold of her body like a hostage. I hear him whisper to her over the clamor of the room, "Shhh, you'll wake the whole castle darling. No need to get them involved, this will all be over soon."

Selena's scream causes mother's blade to grow even redder, its dark crimson turning to burning lava.

I watch as the helm of a Black Knight clangs against the rocky ground, blood spurting from its headless neck. Mother's sword clashes furiously against two Soulless attackers. The Lycan takes hold of a Black Knight's neck and lifts its weightless body into the air, then pummels the knight into the ground like it is a lifeless doll. Another knight drives its sword into father's turned back, piercing his fur completely. A violent growl escapes the wolf's mouth as he grips the attacker's sword arm and rips it clean out of socket. The knight screams in agony, but the scream is cut short as a fist full of claws opens his throat, cutting through the obsidian neck guard.

Another sword enters father's hamstring and exits through the front of his leg. The knight responsible for the assault is soon dead as the Lycan squeezes his helm until it caves in on the skull within.

Mother is still tangled in combat with two attackers. She frees her fiery sword and drives it into the chest of one, causing him to drop his obsidian blade. The pierced knight grabs hold of the hilt that hugs his chest, fighting mother as she tries to pull it free from the skewered knight. The second knight descends on her with a series of lethal blows. I watch in horror as the sword punctures her lungs, then quickly slices through her neck. I watch the head roll to the corner of the room where I saw it lie as a child. Her headless body drops in defeat before the victorious knight. The crimson blade that pierces the other knight fades to darkness as it is deprived of my mother's fury. The blade returns to its normal shade of cold iron as the knight drops dead with it in his chest.

The Lycan sees the headless body of his wife and becomes lost in rage. A second string of Black Knights enter the room from the open doorway. Reinforcements that were likely on standby this entire time. I get lost in mirage of battle as the Lycan turns the attackers to mincemeat. His claws and fangs go to work against the small army of renowned warriors. Their blades continue to pierce the wolf's hide, but the Lycan seems to feel no pain as grief fills his body.

The sounds of death echo throughout the castle. The howls of the Lycan spread for all to hear. It is the perfect storm, I realize as I watch young Syrus convulse in bed. Ventur doesn't notice the boy toss and turn in his cot, and the sounds of battle drown out the sounds of the child's bones snapping as the moon calls forth the beast in his body.

The moonlight shines on Selena's flailing body and briefly exposes Ventur's concerned face within his hood. The knights continue to fall one by one as the Lycan strips their souls from their bodies. The fallen knights now live up to their name, soulless. Blood covers the Lycan's gray coat of fur. Cuts cover the wolf's hide faster than they can heal.

Five knights surround the staggering Lycan as a howl echoes throughout the room. The howl causes all in attendance to freeze, as it did not come from father's throat. The grief-stricken Lycan looks up from his massacre. Ventur's head slowly rotates to the bed beside him and sees that it is now empty. My floating spirit scans the room in an attempt to locate young Syrus. He is no longer asleep in bed, tossing and turning. A beast now lurks in the corner closest to his bed, concealed by shadows. All I can see is the boy's white fangs and venomous eyes.

I see the look of horror on Ventur's face, exposed by the powerful moonlight of Luna's fullness. Young Syrus is no longer present. His body is covered in black fur. His face is consumed with the snarl of a rabid wolf. His chest heaves with dramatic, vengeful breaths. Each exhale is a low growl filled with revenge. The Lycan cub is able to piece together what has occurred in the night and now becomes filled with rage at the sight of his mother's headless body, his flailing sister, his fatally wounded father.

There are few things more dangerous in this world than a Lycan who's witnessed the slaughter of his wolfpack.

Father's jowls lift in a smile as he registers what's happened.

Syrus slowly emerges from the darkness and leaps across his cot onto Ventur's body, teeth gnashing and claws flailing. The Undead Emperor does all he can to defend himself from the attack, shoving Selena's captive body into the thick of the fight to defend himself. The Black Knights begin slashing at father once more as he catches a second wind at the turn of the tide. Selena's frail body gets caught between the blows meant for father. The sword strikes are not meant for her but slice her innocent body open nonetheless.

I avert my eyes from Selena's bleeding body. It is too painful to watch. Father pounces on his daughter's bloodied body and hovers over her protectively, taking the blows from the swords to save her.

Syrus tears into Ventur's body, the Undead doing all he can to grab hold of the fanged muzzle that tears into him. The hood falls away from his straining face as his own blood spatters on his cheek and neck. The young Lycan tears into Ventur's body like a wolf devouring the carcass of a fallen gazelle. A silver dagger emerges in Ventur's free hand, glimmering in the silver moonlight. As a desperate, last-ditch effort to save himself, Ventur drives it into the Lycan cub's back, right where the heart rests. He buries the hilt as far as it will go, and I watch as the ferocity in the cub expires. The Sylvian affinity to silver has not yet availed itself to Syrus, so the energy from his revenge-fueled onslaught quickly fades.

The boy's attack ends as quickly as it began, and his body falls to the ground at Ventur's feet, dead.

I turn my eyes back to father, who is now a butchered mess of bloodied fur and sliced skin. There isn't an inch of fur that retains its gray markings anymore. Blood covers the Lycan's body from ear to toe. The Black

Knights don't let up. Their swords fall on the Lycan with renewed purpose. I watch as they flay the flesh from the wolf and his daughter alike.

Ventur stands from the bloodied bed he was nearly killed on, his blackened robes not dark enough to conceal the mess of wounds he's incurred. His robe is ripped to shreds, the flesh beneath opened in several dozen places. The moonlight briefly shines upon his tattered body. His hands cling to his stomach, so as to hold his entrails from falling to the ground beneath him. Ventur wheezes weakly as he staggers toward his royal guard. Two knights file into the room to help keep him from falling to his knees. He cannot talk. He is barely alive.

Father now lays dead on the ground beside Selena. Swords no longer swing. Silence fills the room, offput by the strained panting of the knights. Each of their swords are covered in blood from point to hilt. The blood pools collectively along the floor from the fallen bodies of knights and Sylvians alike. Father's body, though dead, slowly shifts back into that of a human, as does Syrus's.

I watch as the black fur retreats on the boy's body. His wolfish limbs return to that of a normal child. The silver dagger remains firmly planted in his back.

Ventur wheezes uncontrollably, coughing up blood as he orders, "Dispose of... all evidence..." before the knights drag his crippled body from the room.

I stare in horror at the scene before me.

I see my father's body first. It is motionless. I've never seen a being so dead as he currently is. It is so dead it could convince an onlooker that it never possessed life in the first place. I'm shaking, unable to process what's happened. The parts of his face that aren't torn open or covered in blood are ghastly pale. His eyes do not glow silver anymore. His mouth gawks open. Blood trickles from the corner of his lips.

I do not cry. I'm too confused to conjure tears. My head throbs like war drums pounding while an army marches.

My mother's head lies several feet away from her body, staring at it like a snail stares at a shell that used to be its home. I may be too dazed and confused to know much, but I do know that heads are not supposed to be so unattached from their bodies. Her face stares with a look of horror at the bloody mess her body has become.

Selena lays not far from mother. Her limbs are a tangled mess of dislocated sockets. Selena's body caught the brunt of the damage. Her frail frame was defenseless against the assault. Selena lost the fight before it began. Little flesh remains on her body, though chunks of it are scattered throughout our shared bedroom. Her bed is soaked in blood, as if the killer started their attack while she was sleeping. It looks as though someone has used her sheepskin mattress to mop up the blood on the floor. Its entire surface is smeared red.

I watch as one of the Soulless wretches the silver dagger from Syrus's back, kicking his naked body to ensure he is fully dead.

Satisfied with the lifeless response, the knight leaves the boy lying in a puddle of his own blood.

33

A Nightmare

I wake as though I am still that fear-filled boy of ten years. My body is soaked with sweat. My heart races like the gallop of a horse. I gasp for air as though any breath will be my last. Sweat drips in my eyes, blurring my sight. It stings. I squeeze my eyelids shut tight. I listen to the sound of my heart vibrating up the side of my neck.

A tender hand grips my shoulder. I take in Crixus's familiar scent of tea olive and eucalyptus without opening my eyes. "It's okay," she whispers. "We all were forced to face our past." Her hand gently rubs my back, the touch reminding me of Vesper's comforting nature. My mind is lost between space and time. I have entered into the haunting abyss of my past and I have emerged unscathed.

Everything has changed, I realize now, reflecting on what I now know.

Ventur is not dead.

He is the Emperor.

He killed my family.

How he survived, I have no idea.

Though I shifted that night, I had no part in my family's downfall.

My entire life has been a lie.

Ventur thought I was dead.

When he returned to the room later that morning to find me alive, he had to think fast.

Ventur framed me, I realize now. He framed me, then did the only thing he could with hundreds of eyes watching from inside the keep. He exiled me and made me believe it was my own fault.

He expected to find my body lifeless on the floor when he returned to announce the death of my family to the castle. And though I have spent all these years thinking he sacrificed his life for my own, I know now he survived the light of the sun somehow. It matters little how he did it. All that matters is that I know now.

Ventur is the Undead Emperor.

He usurped my father from the throne and took over all of Areopagus, from the Scorpos desert to the Thoren Mountains. His son, Bane, born after my exile, is now dead, slain by Atlas and his Acolytes. Now all that is left is his daughter, Saunter. If I had to bet on it, she will be the one commanding forces in Sygon.

Though she was born after my exile, I've heard plenty about her throughout the years. She is every bit clever and cunning as Bane was arrogant and haughty. Word traveled fast to the corners of the kingdom that the Empress was pregnant with child soon after I was but a distant memory. Ventur probably thought his son would be safe commanding a backwater stronghold like Gall. When word of his son's death reaches him, his wrath will be felt throughout the kingdom. He will divert the war efforts to Atlas and his Acolytes. The Blackbloods will take a backseat to the Emperor's vengeance.

Saunter will be in Sygon, that much I know. I will start my path to vengeance with killing her. She will pay for the sins of her father. I will kill Ventur's whole family, and then I will put an end to his life. I no longer care about Bloodlust and the twenty-four moons I spent being tortured. Though the Blackblood leader was my greatest enemy a day ago, confronting my past has shifted my priorities. I want the entire Undead Empire to feel my pain. I am only one man, but like my father before me, I will die for this.

My breathing slows. Calmness passes over me as Crixus continues to rub her fingers along my back soothingly. We are no longer in the witch's abode. I am sitting outside where the hag confronted us, the building we entered to talk with her in front of us. The building is vacant. There are no signs of life. No candles flicker inside its halls. Cobwebs fill the splintered doorframe.

For a moment I look around. I try to convince myself that what I just saw wasn't a dream. I take in my surroundings. We are still in Queensmyre. The hag took us in the building, but now we lay outside its premise as if we never entered in the first place. Creon sulks silently with his back against a nearby wall. For once, he is silent. His brows are furrowed deep in contemplations. His mind seems heavy with thought.

"Where is the hag?"

Crixus replies, "We don't know. We all woke up outside the building. Me and Creon don't remember how. Did she show you your past as well?"

"Yeah," I whisper, the scene still heavy on my mind.

"Somehow she showed us each separate visions. She made me face my past, and Creon has been acting queer since he awoke, so I'm guessing he's bothered by whatever she showed him."

"Building is empty. Crystal ball, candles, scrolls. It's like no one ever lived there in the first place," Creon mumbles to himself.

"We need to get out of here," I say, looking to the sky. We've been asleep most of the day. The sun slowly descends in the distance. "This town is feeding ground for the Undead at night. If they intercept us, it won't be good."

"Queensmyre is several miles long," Creon spits, "Sun will only be up for another half hour, and you don't strike me as a sprinter."

I look around frantically. The same ruined streets I previously analyzed stretch in every direction. Creon is right, though I hate to admit it. We would need the speed of the beast to escape this town in time. It is at least another five miles before we reach the nearest gate, and ten to the other side of the city. Damn witch. Her black magic wasted away the entire day.

I don't have time to sit here and think about the past.

Instincts kick in, washing away the vision the hag showed me. I force all thoughts of Ventur's betrayal out of my mind. Adrenaline alone gives me the power to stand. A pit grows in my stomach as I realize there are only so many things we can do to save ourselves. I like each idea that pops in my head less than the previous. I don't have time to meditate on what's right and what's wrong. When the sun goes down, a force of Undead and Blackbloods will converge on this town like nothing we've ever seen before.

This is the direct middle point between Sygon and the Blackbood mountainous siege. The two armies will collide in the airspace above us. They will engage in combat all throughout these city streets. They will feed on all they find with fresh blood in their veins.

We will be too outnumbered to fight back if we are forced to make a stand. I stare at the city of ruin that stretches before me, knowing what I must do. Queensmyre was once a place of freedom. The pursuit of happiness once filled these streets. People came to chase their dreams. Actors and artists and musicians alike made this great city a place of acceptance and peace.

But acceptance and peace are antagonistic to survival. This city fell for lack of putting up a fight. My fate will not be the same. My pack's fate will not be the same. We will survive, I think to myself as I pull flint and steel from my bag.

"What are you planning to do with that? Light a campfire so the Undead can find us easier?" Creon asks.

I look at him dead in the eye, intensity in my face. He gulps, seeing the magnitude of what I'm about to say before I say it. "We are going to light the entire city on fire."

Creon and Crixus stare at me blankly. I walk off, too tired and hungry to explain myself. With or without their help, Queensmyre burns tonight.

34

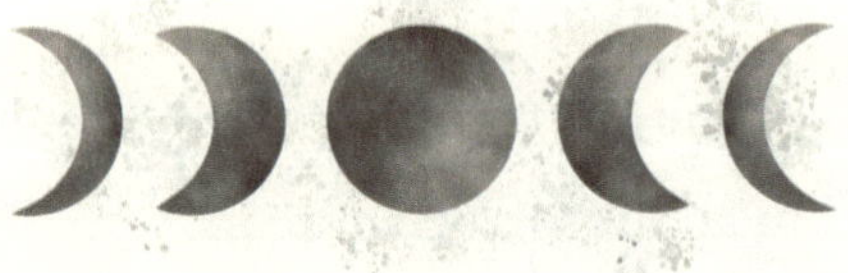

A Nightmare

The funny thing about fire is that it never shows up in a timely fashion. Half the time it seems if you want to start a fire, you're out of luck. Sparks won't catch, and coals refuse to burn. You spend what seems like an eternity blowing on kindling and breaking small sticks in the hopes of getting flames big enough to keep you warm. Then even when you get a fire going, the Creator puts it out with rain.

The other half the time, if you want nothing to do with fire, it burns down your house while you're running errands or burns your hand or devours an entire forest in a period of drought.

I was hoping the fire I lit tonight would be more like the latter of the two, but as I furiously strike sparks against kindling like a pyromaniac, I quickly realize it will be the former.

My plan seemed perfect on paper. The world-renowned amphitheater that drew in tourists from across the kingdoms is the perfect place for my arson to start. The tree-hugging architects responsible for the amphitheater's construction so wisely built the entire building from recycled materials. They wanted it to be a testament to the world that resources can be reused in beautiful ways, if one has the creative prowess to envision it. For some idiotic reason, the epicenter was constructed from recycled wood beams and topped with a thatch roof. The amphitheater is the epitome of someone devising a way to build a monument that could double as a future pyre in the right conditions.

And to add insult to injury, the management team kept a tall stack of lumber behind the magnificent stage to use for prop construction for each of Alabastur's plays. I hunch before the lumber pile, cursing at my inability to light a small pile of wood shavings. I light sparks, watch them catch, then watch them disappear. I light sparks, blow on the burning shavings, then watch them disappear.

You'd think I've never lit a fire in my entire life, though I have spent the past twenty years on the run, preserving my warmth at night through campfires of my own construction.

We have just fifteen minutes before dark, and another half hour before the Blackbloods and Undead will arrive.

With each failed spark I curse, a madman engrossed in his distorted mania. Creon and Crixus watch from a distance, both of them sitting on the edge of the stage that once displayed history's most famous artistry. The stage is empty and hollow now. The theater is filled with darkness. The seats are vacant of spectators. The integrity of the theater resembles the rest of Queensmyre, decrepit and destroyed. Beams have collapsed. The walls are filled with holes. The roof has caved in several places. Black mold crawls along the walls and floors like ink on a map. This is not the same theater I witnessed as a child. The music has died, and along with it, so too has the joy these walls once held.

My fingers shake as I bite my lip and continue to shoot sparks hopelessly. The kindling catches. Several beads of sweat drip from my brow and extinguish the small flames. “Fuck!” I yell, throwing the flint at the pile of lumber so I can wipe the perspiration on my face. I stand and pace, holding my sweaty-soaked head in my clammy palms.

Creon advances and grabs the flint and steel I’ve tirelessly toiled over. Without a word, he crouches low and pulls a single spark. I secretly watch through my spread fingers as the flame catches the kindling and Creon adds several woodchips from the sawdust to it. The fire grows as it consumes the sticks, then sears the underside of logs from the lumber pile.

By the time Creon stands, the flames are beginning to lick at the base of the dry lumber. Soon, it will devour the entire pile and grow to a flame large enough to light the roof aflame like the wick of a candle. The surrounding buildings will succumb to the firestorm and spread throughout the city. Within a few hours, all of Queensmyre will burn because of the flame Creon has ignited. There are no townspeople left to put it out in time. The destruction is now inevitable, I think to myself as I stare at the pile of lumber.

“Thank you,” I sigh toward Creon as he leaves the flames alone to do what they do best.

“It won’t be the first building I’ve burned down in this shitty town,” Creon exhales, claiming his spot at the edge of the stage again. I’m reminded of the old hag’s words. *You are still wanted for burning down Norm’s Tavern. You’re lucky I’m the only one left who remembers.*

I join the two at the edge of the stage and take a seat beside Creon. “Why did you burn down that tavern the last time you were here?”

Creon doesn’t look up from his twiddling thumbs. His mind has been lost in thought since the moment I woke from the nightmare of my past. He’s barely talked, though I previously thought talking was his favorite thing to do. “What’s it matter to you?” Creon asks in return.

I reply, "Pretty soon this entire city will be aflame and all we'll be able to do with our lungs is fight against the smoke. Hell, this might be the last conversation we have together. Why not end it with a funny story?"

Creon peers up at me finally. "Is that all my delinquency is to you? Humor?"

The man who previously couldn't take a single situation seriously now puts his foot down. His face is strained. Filled with pain. Something has broken behind his eyes. Something deep in his mind. His eyes are bloodshot. The fire building behind him illuminates the agony on his face.

Creon's remark catches me off guard. The man I've only ever known to laugh in the face of pain now stares at his palms like he's committed murder.

"What the hell did that hag show you?" I ask.

His gaze is long and drawn out. He conducts himself in a way contrary to the idiot I've deemed him to be. I've heaped judgment on him in my own mind this entire journey. Wrote him off as a fool that has done nothing but slow me down. But perhaps I was wrong.

"Not all of us were born to be heroes like you," Creon whispers softly, staring at his hands like they're a mirror into the past. Creon slowly turns his body and points at the fire. "My whole life has been nothing more than destroying everything I touch. Every goddamned moon. I've killed more people than that bloody fire will after consuming the whole city."

Crixus whispers, rubbing his back, "We've all done things we aren't proud of. Whatever past the woman showed you doesn't define you."

"Past?" Creon questions, looking up at her. "The witch didn't show me my past, she-wolf. She showed me my future." Creon turns to lock eyes with me. I see something lurking inside him. A hatred ready to boil over, but it isn't directed at me. It is an unfathomable self-loathing that not even I can comprehend. I briefly glance at Crixus. Her face is etched with concern. Neither of us had expected this. Since waking, we'd both assumed the hag had shone Creon his past, the same as she did with us.

"And what did your future hold?"

After a few moments of silent reflection, Creon builds the courage to respond. "I kill you, Sylvian." We both fall silent as the sound of crackling wood consumed by fire grows behind us. I can feel the heat building in the room as the tension rises. Creon continues, "I want you to know that I was sincere in my intentions on this mission. Though I joke and jest, I seriously thought I could change my trajectory in life in finally doing a single noble thing. My entire life has amounted to nothing but death and destructions, but the gods saw fit to bring our paths together, and I almost began to hope I could rise above the sins of my past. But the old hag..." Creon still stares at his palms like they are smeared with the blood of someone he loves. "The hag showed me the truth of things. Showed me how I will soon betray you. Showed me how I will die the villain of this story."

I have no words for the man who just told me he will soon kill me. I don't feel anger or betrayal in my stomach. I almost pity Creon. All we can do as mortals is try to be better than our past selves, and all we have control of is our present and future. But the hag has stripped even hope of a better future away from the man who has nothing.

A man with no hope is more dangerous than any mortal man provoked by wrath. But I remember what the hag said to me before I fell prey to her trance. *There are many possible outcomes, but those who hear my oracles are gifted the ability to choose the best possible outcome, even if it means they must die as a consequence.*

"The future is a fickle thing, Creon," I say to him, my voice calm and fatherly. "The premonition could have been a warning more than the true events of what's to come. There is no way of knowing. The slightest action can change the entire outcome of things."

"No," Creon interrupts. "It felt real. Like dejavu... Like I'd lived through it before. I could feel the dagger in my hand as I drove it straight through your heart. The emperor—Ventur—he made me. I had no choice."

The fire now climbs the surrounding walls and spreads to the roof. Within a few short minutes, the building has turned to a chamber of hell. The first bead of sweat squeezes free from my pores.

The fire catches hold of the moldy seats that once held thousands of spectators at once. We need to go. There is little holding this palace together. It is minutes away from capsizing on its compromised structural integrity.

An idea strikes me. Chills run down my sweaty neck. I stand and retreat to the back of the stage. There are shelves that span from ceiling to floor.

The shelves were built to store the thousands of petty props used for the plays put on. The fire feeds on the wooden shelves like a man dying of thirst finding a basin of water. Smoke rolls along the floor of the stage like a thick carpet. Soon it will rise and attack our lungs. We need to go. I spot what I'm looking for. Fire consumes the shelf it sits on, yet it sparkles silver nonetheless. Its glimmer catches my eye. I grab it and throw it onto the ground, stamping the flames that consume it. I grab the silver-painted prop. The metal burns into my hand from the heat of the flames.

I walk over to Creon and hold it out for him. "If you are to stab me with a dagger in the heart, let it be done with this dagger," I say to him. He looks up at me with confusion, then eyes the blade once more. I continue, "It is a prop." I grab the hilt and raise the blade over my head. I drive it down fast toward Creon's thigh. Crixus gasps. Creon flinches. The dagger sinks into the man's leg to the hilt, but no yelp of pain leaves Creon's throat. When Creon ceases his flinching, he stares down at his unwounded leg as I pull the dagger from it. Crixus eyes the man's pants for blood but there is none to be found.

"It's a false blade used for plays," I explain. Creon eyes me and smiles. "So if the gods are going to force you to kill me, I'd prefer you do it with this blade." I watch as a wave of relief washes over the man. He did not expect me to take his premonition so lightly. He takes the dagger from my hand and turns it over in his own.

"Bloody brilliant," he whispers to himself, then hands the dagger back to me to stash in my bag. I watch as the man's anxiety and unspoken troubles wash away. He continues, "They were selling children for sex."

"Huh?" I look at him in confusion, completely caught off guard by the statement.

Creon eyes Crixus, then looks back at me. "Norm's Tavern, the place I sent up in flames. They had a habit of selling children for sex, so I burnt the bloody place down to the ground." We connect eyes. For the first time since meeting Creon, it's like I see something behind the mask he presents to the world. A soul of sorts. There is a deep darkness behind his eyes, countered with an eternal flame to vanquish the abyss. I understand now that there is more to him than I'll ever know.

"Let's not let our fate be the same as theirs," I reply, my throat already affected from the rising heat. A beam collapses on the stage, bringing with it a larch chunk of the thatch roof. I look through the hole and see that the sun has fully set. The smoke rises to escape the hole toward the star-filled night sky. Together, we jump from the stage and walk down the central aisle between the fiery gallery of seats. Flames swell around us, crawling up the walls and ceiling, devouring all they can. Soon, the amphitheater won't be enough. Soon, the fire will search for more fuel. Soon, the fire will devour all of Queensmyre.

35

A Nightmare

It is hard to remember why my thought process perceived burning an entire city to the ground would give us greater odds of survival than trying to hide from the converging armies. We run through the city's streets as fast as the fire will allow us. We don't leave its veil of light, knowing anything could lurk in the darkness of night. We cannot see whether or not war wages above us. Smog fogs the air above us, making us blind to what happens in the clouds. Nor can we hear anything. Fire itself may be silent, but all that it burns creates a tremendous cacophony. The fire creeps slowly from building to building, illuminating the city streets as we creep down the road.

The Undead and Blackbloods won't risk landing in the ring of fire we've created. Though it does not burn them instantly like daylight will, Undead and Blackblood still dislike heat. Their bodies were born to adapt to the coolness of night. It would be like putting an arctic bear into the desert. I have lived with the Undead long enough to know they do not need campfires to stay warm at night. They are cold-blooded creatures. The very fire that threatens to melt our flesh is currently our greatest ally to survive the night.

We stumble across several disoriented citizens of Queensmyre. They pour from their fiery homes like ants whose hill has been stepped on. They look down the street of fire in confusion, looking for an explanation for the destruction. They stumble into the city streets half asleep and coughing from the billows of smoke.

I don't stop to save them. If they want to survive, they will know they must leave this city at once. There is nothing here for them anymore. They should have left months ago. The Undead have fed on them like humans feed on cattle. And they've remained, allowing it to happen because they were too ignorant to leave their fallen city behind.

They are like sheep. They don't know what is good for them, nor do they sense a threat when it presents itself. As a child, Lundis took me to a farm to learn about livestock. It was one of the better days of learning I experienced, though I'll never forget how stupid the sheep were. I distinctly remember one being tethered to a pole with a rope leashed around its neck. The sheep would walk circles around the pole, wrapping its rope tighter around the post. The rope grew shorter with each circle the sheep walked. Within an hour, the sheep had run out of loose rope and its neck was pressed into the pole from the lack of slack in its leash. The stupid animal would call out for help, too dumb to know all it had to do was walk in the opposite direction to free itself. It would thrash and buck and fight for freedom from the pole that choked it, but was too dumb to know its own efforts were the ones that suffocated it.

The farmer would hear the sheep's desperate cries for help and eventually free it, untangling the rope it choked itself with. Then, when the farmer left, the sheep would begin circling the post again, as it did before, slowly shortening its lead until it reeled itself in closer to the post once more.

Such is the case with most humans. They know not that they bring about their own suffering. They are too stubborn and stupid to see the error of their ways. People of Queensmyre committed themselves to peace, then refused to adapt when war came to consume them. They'd rather give themselves up to being prey of the Undead and Blackbloods before picking up weapons and fighting to save their lives.

The fire forges a clear path toward the opposite side of Queensmyre. Ash and smoke make it difficult to see which way we travel, but the fire is a guiding light through the chaos of destruction. We stray to the opposite side of the main road that dissects Queensmyre. The heat of the fire is too much to bear. Feels as though it burns our flesh by heating the air around us. Singes our hair and clothes. Several times I run my hands through my sweaty mane and beard to make sure it is not aflame.

I hear a desperate cry sound from behind us. "My baby is in there! Someone! My baby!"

My ear perks as my gut drops. I don't have to turn to know what's happened. The very fire I'm responsible for has caught a parent by surprise. As their instincts convinced them to flee a burning building, they forgot to retrieve their child on the way out. I pause in my stride, unsure of what to do. I turn to face the helpless woman, ash and soot covering her face like war paint. She is young. Her face looks no older than sixteen. She is a child herself, swaddled in ash-covered silk pajamas. Tears cut through the soot on her face as she stares up at her flaming house. Fire shoots from the windows like Wilhelm's eyes melting from his sockets.

A knot grows in my stomach.

This is my fault.

Before I can decide what to do, I'm shoved out of the way by Crixus. I stumble a few steps and stand, embarrassed by my selfishness as I watch the she-wolf storm into the hellstorm. Crixus barges into the burning building without hesitation. The fiery door welcomes her.

The mother cries with joy and relief, "Oh gods be good, thank you! Thank you kind stranger! Gods be good! Please save my baby!"

My heart flutters with anxiety as all noise ceases. I watch the flaming building with desperate anticipation. If Crixus dies, it will be my fault alone. Another person who inadvertently died from trusting me.

The mother mutters prayers furiously beneath her breath. Her lips whisper indistinguishable words to deaf gods. It is not the gods who will save her child. It is not even the Fates. It is Crixus. But the mother will fail to see that, if Crixus manages to be successful. Years from now, the mother will tell her friends the story of the horrible fire that burned Queensmyre to the ground, and she will tell them how the gods were good enough to send a savior for her baby. She likely won't even ask Crixus her name. She will sing her praise for saving her child but will see the act as some divine intervention from the Creator.

A loud crash sounds from inside the building. The wall breaks open on the second story of the house and Crixus emerges from behind the rubble. The she-wolf jumps from the second story and lands gracefully. Flames outline her body. She rolls on the ground like a dog trying to get the scent of earth on their fur after a bath. The flames extinguish after a few belabored moments of toil. Smoke rises from Crixus's body like a hog roasting above a barbecue pit.

My jaw drops as I see her rise, a toddler cradled safely in her arms. Her skin remains unburnt from what I can tell at a brief glimpse. Her hair, though, is now singed in an uneven bob that cuts off right above her petite collarbones. She has a motherly look in her eyes as she stares down at the unharmed child, rocking it gently in her arms. Her clothes are covered with burn holes. The smoke accentuates her caramel skin. She looks as an angel would after plummeting through the atmosphere. She is like a goddess I'm unworthy to dream of. A heroine that even the noblest knights could not impress. Her delicate, dark eyes look up from the baby and lock gaze with me. A thin smile grows on her face, revealing her white teeth.

I startle when she looks at me. I force myself to shut my mouth, realizing I'm more aroused than I should be. But damn if she isn't one of the most beautiful things I've ever seen. The street around her is filled with flames. The smoke parts around her just to reveal her beauty to the world.

Here stands a woman whom the world has failed over and over again, yet her compassion has remained intact through it all. For a moment, time slows for me as I'm lost in her dark eyes. The firelight glows all around us, but I forget about its destructive nature. I want to be closer to her than I should. I want to feel her body pressed up against me. I want to run my hands down her tender skin from her face to her thighs and everything in between.

I want to devour her like I'm a starving man and she is an oasis in the desert.

The bereaved mother steps into the picture and breaks my trance of lust. I rub my eyes and curse inwardly. I've let the sight of another cause me to forget my entire mission. This is about Sephora, I remind myself. My daughter is the only girl who can be important to me. I cannot let another distract me with looks. I breathe as deep as I can, acknowledging that there is smoke all around me. My heart still flutters with lust and love. I need a distraction. I need to keep moving.

The mother sings her praise to Crixus, reclaiming her child and covering its delicate body with kisses and tears. How Crixus was able to jump from a two-story burning building and keep the child safe, I'll never know.

"What is your name?" the mother asks, proving me wrong.

"Crixus," she replies, a concerned smile on her face. "You need to leave. This fire will spread throughout the whole city."

"But where am I to go?" the mother implores. "This city is all I've ever known, and all my belongings were in that house!"

"Follow us!" I call out, my dry throat barely loud enough to be heard above the destruction. "We will lead you to freedom, but we must go now!"

The sweltering heat leeches the moisture from our bodies relentlessly. The air between us grows so hot it becomes visible in distorted waves. Embers fall around us like snowflakes in a blizzard. All that can be heard for miles is the sound of crackling flames and collapsing buildings. If the Undead and Blackbloods go to war outside this hellstorm, we would have no way of knowing. We are equal parts safe as we are in danger.

The same fire that protects us is the one that could put an end to us.

But the Undead and Blackbloods will not risk drawing near to the burning city. Fire is their enemy, and the enemy of my enemy is my friend.

I trudge through the smoking city like an animal escaping the burning wilderness. There is no time for paused reflection. Every step I rely on instinct. I remove my sweat-soaked shirt to cover my mouth. The heat burns every inch of my body. It feels as though I'm being seared in a cast iron pan. A lobster placed in a vat of boiling oil. With every twist and turn of the winding cobblestone road I check to make sure Creon and Crixus and the mother still follow. A few dozen civilians wander after us, assuming we know the way to safety.

We don't.

All we have to guide us through the fiery storm is the outskirts of darkness the fire has yet to reach. The only certainty I have is that if we keep moving, eventually we will reach the other side of the city. It may take hours, it may take all night, but anything is preferable to facing the war that wages outside the storm.

This is not like a hurricane. There is no central point of safety. The only option is burn alive or fall prey to exsanguination. Neither is preferable, but humans have a primordial drive to survive, so the dazed citizens of Queensmyre follow us to freedom. Though they have remained in their queer town this entire time, the fire forces them to move on. Sometimes you must burn your past in order to seek a brighter future. And sometimes, if you are too stubborn to adapt to the circumstances, you will die as a consequence.

I run when I can, and walk when my lungs burn. Coughing possesses us all. It scrapes the inside of my throat like a scalding razor. The smoke dries my eyes like grapes shriveling to raisins in the summer sun.

There is no time to question my decision. If I doubt the destruction I've enacted, those who follow me will fall prey to doubt. The night is dangerous. There were only so many things I could have done, so I made the best decision I could with the time I had. I will have to live with the consequences.

If the things Creon said about my father's decision now called the Red Gate are true, I silently acknowledge that this will be my life's Red Gate. I came to this city as a child, optimistic and innocent. The boy who watched Alabastur's *Equinox* would have never believed that he would burn this city to the ground two decades later. This is an Equinox it its own right. The sun does not remain in the sky, so we turned Queensmyre into a second sun. The light repels the darkness, and the light has never been so deadly.

This city will burn for days, and all will speak for years to come of the great glory it once was. As I run through the streets watching the beauty burn, I picture Sephora's face to make me feel at ease. As I watch the world burn, all I think about is her. This is all for her. People will tell the story of how it was a father's love that destroyed an entire city, just as Caspian was willing to lay down his life for Enchantress. Love makes us do terrible things, but we justify our actions nonetheless.

So many lives will be lost so I can save Sephora.

I feel no regret.

From the moment I held her fragile body in my arms for the first time, I vowed I would do anything to protect her.

It was a selfish vow, but one that remains true to this day.

I already lived twenty-four moons believing I was the reason my daughter died.

My conscience refuses to bear this burden again.

The lives of many sacrificed to save the one I love.

I am no savior, as Ophy once said. I am the reaper, culling all who stand in my way at redeeming what little I have left in this world.

All saviors must befriend the reaper. They must be okay with death. They must embrace it in their soul, so that they are its chief executioner. It is the very nature of saving someone that guarantees death. Saving implies killing. Every victim has a captor, and every captor must yield or die as a result of their oppression.

I don't care what it takes to reclaim my throne and save Sephora. The Emperor will die, and I will grant the death of any who choose to follow him to his reaping. Bloodlust will die, and I will purge the Blackblood virus from the face of the earth soon after. If Atlas refuses to yield, the Acolytes will perish.

In life, we are who we follow. Follow the wrong person, the wrong cause, and you will suffer the consequences of where the path leads.

My wolfpack is now baptized by fire. Where I go, they go, and I will not lead them astray.

Fire leaps from building to building, from tree to tree, from hayrick to hayrick. It is a glutton devouring all in its sight. It will not end its binge until all has been consumed. I pray my feet don't fail me as I force them to continue running. Each step brings me closer to freedom.

The smoke fades as I spot the city walls on the horizon. My nostrils smell no Undead in close proximity, but I can't rely on my sense of smell after the fiery assault. The only scent I'll smell until dawn is charcoal and ash.

We leave the fire behind us and sprint through the darkness. If the gods are good, the Undead and Blackbloods will steer clear of Queensmyre altogether. There soon won't be a single inch of shadow left to spare within the city's streets.

I'm delirious. I've just run five miles through smoke-filled streets while using a tidal wave of fire as protection from the monsters of the night. I can't tell left from right. I want to dive into an arctic lake and let the ice freeze over me. My skin blisters like an Undead in midday heat. My mouth feels as though someone has stuck a scalding branding iron in it. I want to cry but my tear ducts have been evaporated for good. My eyes don't have the liquid to spare a single blink. Ash falls from my hair like dandruff from a dry scalp.

My heart drops as I see purple eyes glowing through the darkness near the city's gate. I slow from a sprint to a run, then to a walk, then freeze altogether. There is no hiding ourselves in the night. We pant from the exhaustion and cough the ash from our lungs. I turn to face those who follow me. Behind Creon and Crixus are several dozen citizens of Queensmyre who have followed us this whole way. Sixty humans, maybe more. As a group, we are incredibly loud. Even if the Undead weren't lined up before us, they would be able to hear us from a mile away.

The fire has destroyed our ability to see in the night. I'm forced to look at the gate and count the amethyst eyes that shine through the dark.

We are like wolves backed into a corner. We can bite the hand that tries to harm us, or we can submit ourselves into its control. Fight or flight, and flight is not an option in this case, unless we want to dive back into the fiery storm behind us.

Fight it is, then.

I cannot see the pale faces that stand between us and freedom. My sight glows orange from the hours of fire surrounding me. But luckily for us, we have one thing in our favor. The fire is still behind us, protecting our backside from the Undead flanking us unaware. There are no more buildings between the outskirts of the city and the walls that protect it from outside threats. No buildings means the fire has no more fuel to consume. The blizzard of flames will stretch no further in our favor.

All we have to do is protect our frontside, and though we are temporarily blind in the night, we outnumber them five to one. From what I can tell, there is only a dozen or so Undead before us. I count the purple eyes to confirm once more, then divide by two. Make that thirteen Undead, matched against our sixty or so.

We need any advantage we can get. Our group is not made up of warriors. We are three Lycans and several dozen homeless artists. I force my brain to focus and think. How can we survive this? We can barely stand. The smoke blots out the moon's light from lending us any power at all.

They will try to sink their fangs into our necks and drain us of every last drop of blood. After running through the fire, we are like a medium rare steak that has grown legs and presented itself to them for a pre-dawn dinner. But they don't know a Sylvian is in their midst. That itself is another advantage.

A Sylvian who still struggles to control the beast within, I curse inwardly.

A Sylvian who cannot control his inner beast is like a dog with no teeth, a snake with no fangs, a bear with no claws.

Creon grips me from behind and whispers in my ear, "Now's the time when you do the silver eye thing and save us from dying again."

I grunt through my teeth in return, "I'm working on it."

I feel like a man with erectile dysfunction trying to get a hard on. These powers are not mine to control. Channeling them seems to be subject entirely to the beast within offering itself up to my service, and if I have to wait for an offer of help, we could be here a while. Something tells me the Undead won't be patient enough for me to pull out a miracle in time.

"Citizens of the great Queensmyre!" a voice calls out from the dark like the ringing of a dinner bell. He continues, "You've nowhere left to run it seems! Your city is ash and ember! It seems we can benefit each other, though. You humans are no good to us dead. Your bodies produce that which sustains our lives. Submit yourselves into our service and we will only take from your veins what we need. We can provide you with lodging and food, so long as you continue to feed our desires. We will not treat you as slaves. We can replace all that has been taken from you in this great fire. Our cities have need for great artists such as yourselves! And it is often humans who say artists must bleed for their art." He snickers at the double entendre.

My cheeks flush with anger. I grind my molars and clench my burnt fists. This is what the Undead do. I'm instantly brought back to the valley of death. I can see the chained humans like it was yesterday. Humans are nothing more than livestock to these creatures. He dresses his offer up like it is an honor for us to be fed upon. None of us reply to the offer. None of us can. Our throats are entirely too dry to form words. Our lips are cracked like canyons between mountain peaks. But I can read the minds of the Queensmyre citizens without turning to face them. They consider this offer a great mercy. They will throw themselves at the feet of the Undead without hesitation. They have not had to fight a single day of their lives for the freedom they've been entitled to. They've forgotten the bloodshed that was paid for them to preach peace. For most of them, this is the first real adversity they've ever faced.

But they wait behind me, watching my every move. Like a King of sixty people, I lead a nation of vagabonds. My body is the only thing standing between them and slavery. If I kneel now, so too will they.

"I do not have all night to wait for an answer," the Undead leader announces. "My mercy only knows so much patience. We have no need for living prisoners. We have all the humans we need to survive the war that wages outside these walls. But the Undead Emperor is a merciful leader, so I extend this offer merely as a formality. Kneel before me now, or die."

Even if we manage to kill these thirteen soldiers, there is no telling what waits for us outside these city gates. The night is long, and several hours remain before dawn. We cannot trudge back into the fire to save ourselves. Our bodies have endured enough smoke for a lifetime.

I don't know enough to make an informed decision. I have more to think about than just myself. The entire mission is at stake now. Not only is my daughter's life in the balance, but now there are dozens of humans whose lives depend on me making the right decision.

Damn the gods. They are cruel beings, so I won't show his kind any kindness now.

My body shakes with anger as I lower myself to my stiff knee.

"What are you doing?" Creon shouts. "Get back to your feet and fight, Syrus!"

I turn to look over my shoulder at him whisper, "It is over, friend. We have done all we can."

"The hell we have!" He spits at me but his mouth is too dry to conjure saliva. I watch as Crixus places her hand on his shoulder to comfort the broken man. She whispers something delicately in his ear. He looks at her with sadness in his eyes, then concedes. They kneel together, and those who follow us lower themselves to the ground in submission.

"Very good," the Undead calls out to us. "Your species is smarter than I thought. Do not be embarrassed by this defeat. Life is all about survival of the fittest, and now you shall live on to survive another night."

The thirteen sets of amethyst eyes march toward us silently, their pale faces slowly exposed by the glow of the fire behind us. I watch closely as they enter into our view, no longer concealed by the shadows of the city's wall. Their faces are hard and lean. They are each battle hardened by the war that has been waged for many moons now.

Six of them are female, seven are male. They are each dressed in black, distressed tunics. Black leather gloves cover their hands and hoods conceal the details of their faces. Each of their lips are a bright shade of supple red, like polished apples. Lethal fangs lurk within their closed mouths. Fangs that will bend us to their will and feed off our souls.

The leader approaches me and I gaze straight into his Undead eyes. His silver hair is long and falls from his hood on both sides of his face. He has the complexion of an albino, which tells me his lineage hails from the Celestials. His genetic structure is identical to the Undead I once knew within the Areopagus's city limits. This man, along with his followers, are purebred Celestials. It is the only tribe of Undead I know who have silver locks to compliment their violent, violet eyes. He eyes me with a smirk as he approaches me like a pig sent to the slaughter block.

I twist my head to the side to expose my bare neck. The man looms over me a moment, staring down in superiority at my subordinance. Though he has offered us a chance to live, it is likely most of the Undead will feed on us until we are too weak to stand. After they've used us for our blood, they will leave us here to die. The fire will roast our corpses by the morning, and the carrion birds will strip our bodies of the cooked meat when the sun rises.

I hear several humans let out desperate moans as the other Undead sink their fangs into them. The man who looms over me smiles at the sight of it. We are nothing more than rats caught in a trap to him. His to abuse until he no longer has a use for us. If we survive this, we likely won't survive the journey to whatever lodging the Undead spoke of. Each of us will slowly drop dead from blood deprivation along the road.

Finally, the Undead looks down at me. He slowly lowers his face to my neck. I hear his nostrils taking in my scent. He is a wolf smelling the carcass of hunted prey before taking its first bite. I hear his lips part open. The clear sound of his tongue running over his fangs with hunger. He gulps back the saliva that builds after beholding a fresh feast.

Are you ready? A voice rings clearly in my ears. I resist the urge to flinch after hearing the voice growl within my mind. The beast senses a threat and suddenly wakes from its slumber to save me once again.

"I thought you'd never ask," I whisper under my breath.

"Huh?" the Undead man grunts before sinking his fangs into my neck, caught off guard by my comment. A strength unknown to mortal men takes hold of my body and my hands shoot out without thinking. I snap my captor's neck with my bare hands before he has time to sense the danger he is in. He drops dead to the ground with a look of shock in his eyes. His tongue hangs from his mouth, forever unable to lick his fangs again.

The death was silent, and the rest of the Undead are currently caught up in their feasting. They don't notice me rise behind them. They do not see the silver that shines in my eyes. I am a god once again, sent to save my people from their afflictions.

But saving and reaping go hand in hand, and so the Undead must meet their deaths. They brought this upon themselves. They could have let us pass and we would have let them live. But the Undead are incapable of passing up a chance to feed. Their existence is contrary to human life. It is hard to feel sympathy for those who arrogantly bring about their own downfall.

A female Undead soldier has her fangs in Crixus's neck. Creon eyes me with a look of wild triumph on his face, swallowing his urge to shout with joy. He knows how important the element of surprise is in this moment, so he instantly averts his eyes from me and looks down at the ground. I grip the woman's shoulder and pull her away from Crixus. A spurt of blood shoots into the air as her fangs leave the she-wolf's neck. The Undead's body hits the ground before Crixus's blood. Two down, eleven to go. Crixus smiles up at me approvingly, unaffected by her spilled blood.

I do not shift to my Lycan form. Though I would be able to draw from more power if I let the beast come out for a moondance, it takes too much time and makes me too vulnerable for a situation like this. I have to kill these eleven as a human. No matter, death is death regardless of the means.

I scan the crowd of kneeling bait. The baby Crixus saved from the fire is currently safe in its mother's arms. This child will be raised in a world of death and destruction, but it is up to me to ensure the child survives this night alone. Crixus's heroism will not be in vain.

I grab the two nearest Undead soldiers by the collar of their tunics. They are too lost in their own bloodlust to register what's happening to them. I drag them to the nearest flames and shove them into the fire's deadly caress. They open their mouths to scream but the smoke of their burning bodies fills their lungs before they can make a peep. Their bodies combust instantly like an ancient scroll turning to dust at the sight of sunlight.

Nine left.

I cut open the throat of one and snap the neck of another. The sliced throat gushes blood on the Undead's victim, spurting in the face of the innocent human. They look up at me as the Undead body drops dead before them. My silver eyes reflect in their irises. Their face is equally horrified and awestruck.

Seven left.

One lifts her head from her prey and sees me with enough time to alarm the others. The firelight dances around us as the others form a defensive semicircle around me. It reminds me of the Black Knights positioning to attack my mother and father. Just like the Soulless, so too will these fighters die for their retaliation.

They lunge at me in perfect harmony, blood dripping from their chins from their interrupted meals. I move with blinding speed—their immortality is no match for my primal force. My claws cause a flash of severed limbs and bleeding bodies. I take one soldier and force its fangs into the neck of another. A guttural growl exits my throat, "You want to feed, feed on him." I hold her mouth clamped on his neck until she chokes to death on his blood.

I grab hold of another and he headbutts me violently, cracking his own skull open from the force. I hear his temple snap. I press my thumb into the fracture until it breaks completely. His skin goes soft from the lack of bone and my thumb causes him to go brain dead.

Only two are standing now, one of which only has a single arm left on her body. "I will cauterize that for you," I growl, planting my heel in her sternum and kicking off. Her body tumbles into the flames and disappears among the ash.

I go to kill the final male but watch as a set of nails slash open his throat from behind. The body drops to the ground, revealing Crixus standing with bloody claws. She licks the blood from her fingers like someone licking the salt from their fingertips after a feast. Only we remain. The thirteen foes have met their end faithfully, as I knew they would. My silver vision fades, and I remain conscious as the feelings of euphoria disappear.

The crowd of humans looks up at me in horror. They have never seen someone kill so masterfully. I am not a savior in their eyes. I am a monster. I am eviler than any of their creative minds could have imagined. And they've only seen a fraction of a fraction. Imagine if they could see all the death I've caused since the first moon long ago. They would die from fear if they knew who I truly am. What I'm truly capable of. They would be dead without me, but they look at me as if that would be preferable to owing their souls to a demon.

Crixus and Creon are the only ones who don't stare at me with condemnation written on their faces. They smile at me instead, relieved to have survived the threat of slavery. The humans, on the other hand, remain motionless where they kneeled previously. They avoid eye contact with me. They're still, as if they've convinced themselves that if they don't move I won't see them.

"What did you say to Creon?" I ask Crixus in a whisper, thinking back to her ability to calm him enough to kneel in subordination.

"I told him you would soon shift," she replies, wiping the blood from her neck from where the Undead punctured her skin.

"How did you know? Not even I knew when my powers would return..." I stutter, confused by the occurrence of events.

"My beast could sense yours stirring within," she replies calmly. Crixus possesses something I do not. She is confident in her relationship with the beast within. Though I don't know it for certain, it is almost as if she is in constant communication with it. Tamed it. Formed a bond that cannot be broken.

I dismiss the idea. It is nonsense to think a Lycan can make friends with the beast within. Only Sylvians possess that power, and not even I have scratched the surface of this ability.

Still, though. It is queer to hear Crixus speak as if she could sense my beast when not even I can.

"Burn the bodies," I command, scanning the bloody mess I've made. An audible wave of gasps and mumbling erupts from the crowd. I don't turn to analyze their faces. I do not care what they think of me. If they'd prefer to give these predators a noble burial, they can dig the graves themselves.

Just as soon as I've said the words, the sound of chains rattling echoes louder than the noise of a city burning. The rusted chains screech as the city gates behind me open slowly and methodically, swinging outward toward the outside world. Creon and Crixus freeze. I turn to meet our newly arrived guests, my nostrils still too burnt to catch their scent on the ashy wind.

The gates take their sweet time opening. It takes all I have to not shake with fatigue as I search for a potential enemy. My heart drops as I see an entire army of purple eyes shining through the darkness.

The forces march silently within the city walls, pausing to take in the sight of the ruined city. They wade in the shadows of the city walls, examining the scene before them. The dead bodies of their fallen comrades still lay at our feet. Blood puddles around us and evaporates into crimson smoke from the heat. The female Undead who I forced to feed upon another of her own kind still lays at my feet, her fangs still penetrating the corpse of another Undead.

There are at least a thousand warriors before us. There is no fighting our way out of this one.

"Bloody hell," Creon whispers under his breath.

First daylight is still hours away. Our fate is sealed. If they do not kill us, they will take us for prey and feed on us until we are of no use to them. Same deal as before. I curse inwardly. Still I ask myself, why did I expect the gods to show kindness this time around?

A single warrior advances from their ranks, her face concealed by a hood filled with darkness. Her silver hair flows from the hood down to her breasts. Her black tunic is battle-worn. Holes litter her sleeves and bodice. Blood seeps from wounds across her body. But she walks as one who has never felt pain. She does not limp or stumble toward us. She has graceful control over every step she takes. If she is tired from a night of fighting, she does not put it on display for us to see.

She stares at us thoroughly before speaking, though we cannot lock eyes through the darkness of her robe. Surely she knows what has happened. Surely she sees my body covered with the blood of her soldiers. Surely she will repay me for what I have reaped.

"Bind them and bring them with us. We will lodge in Yueltope, then make for Sygon on the morrow," she commands, her voice filled with authoritative majesty.

"At once, Princess Saunter," a soldier echoes, a party of Undead advancing toward us.

I hide the look of epiphany I feel within at the echo of her name.

Before us stands Princess Saunter, sister of the deceased Prince Bane, daughter to the royal Undead Emperor himself.

I hold out my hands freely and willingly as her followers bind me with rope I could easily snap. I have unintentionally fallen into the belly of the beast, which makes it much simpler than cutting my way into its stomach.

This makes things much more interesting.

36

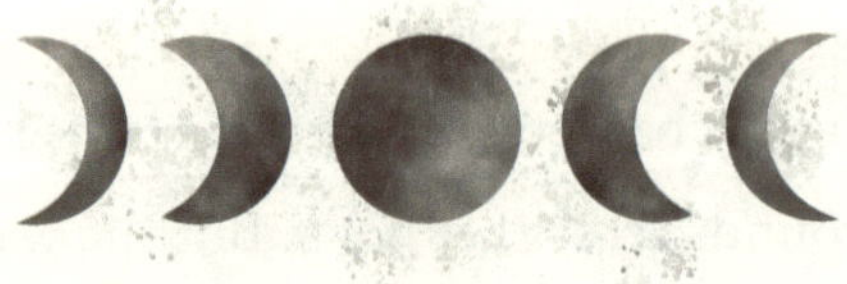

A Nightmare

They didn't even check the contents of the bag slung over my shoulder. If they had, they would have seen the silver dagger I stole from the amphitheater, and they definitely would have seen the vial of black blood potent enough to infect their entire army. They tied us up like lamb for the slaughter and ordered us to follow.

There was no mention of the soldiers I massacred. They did not ask who was responsible for the death of their companions. They shrugged at the sight of mutilated bodies and carried on with their mission. I expected to pay for the damage I caused. Death for death, or at least a firm beating.

But Saunter didn't breathe a word about the blood that covers my body nor the fact that it belonged to members of her own race. After giving her orders, her hood stared at me for a brief moment, then she turned and disappeared into the army's ranks without another word.

We prisoners huddle together in a tight group surrounded by the marching Undead. They surround us like herding shepherds around a flock of sheep. Every step hurts at this point, but the Undead have long whips to persuade our feet to keep moving.

My skin is charred and peeling from the exposure to fire. My crotch burns from sweat battling chafe from long days of travel. My skin can barely breathe from the thick coat of mud and ash and soot that covers me—like layer upon layer of makeup on an actress. The soles of the boots I stole days ago are falling off. I often trip over the torn laces and peeling toe cap. My ragged shirt and pants are barely holding on at this point. They were cheap to begin with, but not even royal seams were designed to withstand this volume of travel.

My mind runs as I mindlessly shuffle along with the Undead army. I try to ascertain the meaning behind keeping us alive. What use could Saunter have for sixty half-dead, half-burnt prisoners. We are a tumorous dead weight on them. The Undead could be in Yueltope by now if they flew there. Instead, we march, because humans cannot fly.

It doesn't make any sense to my overthinking mind.

Surely they have all the humans they need to sustain their hunger in Sygon. It is the largest western city on the coast. Nationally, only the Areopagus has a population larger than Sygon. Why preserve our lives? Why risk traveling with Solis's rise a few hours away?

Creon and Crixus stick close by. We stay in the middle of the humans to avoid being whipped by the surrounding lashes. We do our best to avoid drawing attention, but it is hard when we three are the only ones covered in blood belonging to the Undead. None of us talk. We look down at the ground and watch our feet as we march.

Some humans drop dead along the journey. Heat exhaustion from the fire and dehydration are a deadly combination. Luckily for my pack, we have been trained to go without water in miserable conditions before. Twenty-four moons I suffered from dehydration. Twenty-four moons I toiled with internal agony. I've learned how to suppress my misery. Taught my mind to not entertain the feeling of suffering.

The privileged humans, though, have no mental fortitude to endure this journey. They give in to their weakness and drop dead like flies in a rainstorm. We walk over their bodies and pay no attention to the injustice of it all.

Despite the situation we find ourselves in, I'm more optimistic than ever on this mission. We have been swallowed whole by the predator we hunt. Being prisoner to Saunter's ranks gives us a one-way ticket into Sygon if we can survive. Not only does this get us in without raising suspicion, it gives us a military escort the entire way.

But still, the thought nags in the back of my head that it would be easier for them to kill us and leave us for the buzzards than take the trouble to preserve our lives.

Whatever game Saunter is playing, I don't trust her. She is her father's daughter. My back aches from where Ventur drove a dagger into my heart as a boy. His treachery is in Saunter's blood. They are a family of conniving miscreants. I will kill them both in due time.

Unlike Queensmyre, Yueltope is nothing someone would write home to their mother about. For every Queensmyre, there must be a town equally as committed to lawlessness and destruction. In the West, Yueltope is that place. We are so far from the Areopagus that the Emperor's laws make little difference out here. Before war broke out, Yueltope was led and managed by whoever was strong and cruel enough to take it. Outlaws and criminals used the town as refuge. It is a town of anarchy that Lundis taught wasn't worth the fight to reclaim. With Sygon to the North and Queensmyre to the South, Yueltope did its best to be a nuisance to travelers seeking passage to the renowned cities. Pickpockets and knife-throwers and drug-slingers made their livings in Yueltope and call the place their home.

There was once a saying that if you want twenty years shaved off your life, go to Yueltope. Father addressed the town by building a major road around it, far enough from threat of bandits that passersby could safely avoid the city altogether. It adds a few days onto the total time of travel, but when the only other option is being robbed, beaten, and left for dead, most travelers take the detour.

Yueltope is one of the few cities that has no bordering wall protecting it. After all, half the mercenaries for hire throughout the kingdom live there, so why bother putting up a wall when your population is made up of entirely warriors?

Its geography is one-of-a-kind, though. It is perfectly defensible without building walls or posting defenses. The entire city is almost completely surrounded by quicksand—a mix of waterlogged clay and sand that will grab hold of your body and suck you into the earth until you are buried alive. Natives know their way in and out of the city by avoiding the potential landmines, but most forces have remained deterred from attacking Yueltope out of fear they will be devoured by the sands.

The risk of traveling to Yueltope is far greater than the reward, but it does not surprise me the Undead has taken it as a military stronghold. The only way for the Blackbloods to enter the city is by the sky, and like Bloodlust said, the Undead have more than enough archers to prevent an attack by air.

Like in Gall, remnants of the Pagean River are responsible for the quicksand and wetlands we slosh through on our way to Yueltope. The massive river opens its mouth and divides into several forks after crossing through Queensmyre. Though the Pagean twists and heads Northeast, it creates deltas outside Yueltope that eat away at the callous of our feet.

The mud sucks at my boots and rips away the sole that has been fighting to stay on this entire time.

"Undead!" Saunter screams from several leagues away. "We take to the air! Bring the prisoners!" I watch as the bodies around us levitate effortlessly. Water and mud drip from their boots onto our grounded bodies. Several of the humans around me are lifted by their armpits like a newborn baby being held awkwardly by its parent for the first time. If I had to guess, there are only forty of us left after the several hour march. I recall stepping over at least a dozen bodies, and I'd guess there was at least another half dozen I didn't have to step over.

An Undead soldier grabs me from behind and lifts me into the air. The mud fights them, suctioning tight to my shoes. The wetland pops and gives way. My bare feet lift into the air, my tattered boots remaining forever to be buried on the outskirts of Yueltope.

I stare down as the ground grows distant below us. I cannot see who grips me in their arms, and my nose still only smells ash and ember. Their silver hair whips in the air around us. I must be lightweight, having been a victim of starvation for twenty-four moons. No doubt an Undead child could likely lift me with ease. I am a skeleton of the man I once was.

The city of Yueltope is beautiful from afar, as any city would be in the early dawn of the day. The stars now sing their last goodbyes as they make their exit from the sky. Solis's yawn can be heard from several worlds away.

But as we get closer, the city's devilish details expose themselves so that any onlooker can steer clear from the nightmarish hellhole.

I'd like to say there isn't much that surprises me anymore, but what I see at the edge of Yueltope manages to make my hair stand.

"What do you think?" The Undead who holds my body chuckles in my ear as we descend toward the mess. "Do you like what you see?"

All I see is bodies hanging from their broken necks in every direction. Yueltope has no bordering wall, but there is no shortage of rooftops for nooses to hang from. The ropes are nailed to the walls of buildings and the hanging bodies are crowded shoulder to shoulder along the makeshift gallows. The sun hasn't risen yet, but my night vision is adept enough to see every building as far as my eye can see is covered with bodies like paintings in a gallery.

Some are old and rotted, most are fresh and decaying. The sound of horseflies doing what horseflies do best echoes throughout the city limits. The smell is pungent enough to displace the scent of ash in my nose. It smells as if I am buried alive in a casket with a deteriorating body pressed up against me. The putrid scent surrounds me like a feces and flea-covered blanket, invading my personal space with its filth.

The wave of stench gets stronger as we approach. Lowering ourselves from the atmosphere is like peeling an onion. The stink permeates the closer we get. Nausea overcomes me. The difference between the sight before me and Gall is the bodies. Outside of Gall, the staked victims were all Undead. Their bodies burned away their impurities before the carrions could attack their flesh. These bodies, though, are human. The sun does nothing to save their flesh and blood from the circle of life. It only makes the death worse.

Their heads are inflated like purple balloons ready to pop. I suspect the drop wasn't enough to break most of their necks. Most of them died from oxygen deprivation. Suffocation. The hanging I witnessed in the Areopagus as a child was nothing like this. It was as civil as death could be. Those sentenced to death were dropped with cinder blocks tied to their feet, to ensure their bodies were heavy enough to snap their necks. The executioners took no joy in their job. There was order the whole way through. The sentenced felt no pain as they went to the afterlife.

This was no hanging.

This was a lynching.

No legal trial. No order. No justice.

Just barbaric restitution.

"Caught the Acolytes with their pants down night before last," the Undead shouts in my ear as the wind whips across our faces. "Couldn't stake them up the ass like they did to us back in Gall since the ground is half quicksand here, but we found a way to improvise." His laugh is perverted, as though the smell of death is sweet as honeysuckle in his nose.

With a final chuckle to end the flight, my captor drops me for fun before landing. My body lands like a sack of rocks. I try my best to mitigate the impact, but a jolt of pain shoots up my shins and knocks the breath from my lungs as I thud ungracefully. The muddy banks of Yueltope accept me like an offering, but we are safely inside the ring of quicksand now, so they do nothing more than dirty my ash-covered body further.

I feel pathetic. Once again I find myself a prisoner to a group of people I wish I had the energy to kill. My life at this point ebbs and flows between points of euphoric godliness and depressive imprisonment.

As my mouth fills with shit-colored water I find myself wondering once again what my father would do in a situation like this. My whole life, I never saw Silenius Sylvian face oppression. He would not have stood to be restrained and beaten like I have. He was a King, for Dagon's sake. When Ventur came for his throne, he looked his enemy in the eye and fought to the death. I wonder what he would think of me, if he could see me now. Would he say I'm a coward? A disappointment? An utter embarrassment of the Sylvian name?

When Bloodlust gave his orders, did I really think it would be so simple as walking straight into Sygon and opening the gates for the Blackbloods?

I knew it was a suicide mission, but as I pull myself up from the mud and stare directly at the hanging bodies before me, I feel a tinge of fear. It dawns on me like the morning that Princess Saunter did not save us from Queensmyre out of mercy. She saved us because death by fire was too merciful a death.

37

A Nightmare

The sun rises and the Undead army retreats into Yueltope's several hundred buildings. Bars and inns and long-abandoned homes. They leave the few remaining prisoners from Queensmyre out in the sun without saying a word. We are left to contemplate our fate, because the fear of dying is worse than dying itself.

There is nowhere for us to go, unless we want to be sucked into the earth in an attempt at escape. We are rats in a maze, except the maze is the mental torture of wondering why our lives were preserved. I try to put the pieces together the best I can, but there is only so much to go off of. If the Undead's words can be trusted, these naked men and women that hang from the town's buildings were once Acolytes.

Going off that, this massacre was obviously a revenge mission to pay the knights back for the genocide outside Gall. That much makes sense to me. But why bring us here? Why take the time to trap us in a backwater town of decomposing corpses while hibernating the daylight away? What possible explanation could exist for our continued lives?

I stare at the corpses in deep contemplation. The early morning sun bounces off the Pagean's delta waters and creates a blinding glare. The town is hot and humid. Mosquitoes the size of small rats buzz relentlessly. They too, like the Undead, search for blood wherever they can find it, feeding off the generously left corpses like pigs at a slop trough.

"Help! Oh gods help me!" a voice screams, breaking my fixation on the gallery of death before me. "It's got me! Someone help me!"

I turn toward the desperate plea, scanning the delta's waters for signs of life. Dagon's sake, I curse inwardly as I spot the woman's sinking body a hundred yards away. "I hit my head when they dropped me! I passed out!" she continues, her voice filled with hysteria. "Oh gods be good, please someone help!"

The woman's body is submerged to her torso in quicksand. It slowly consumes her the more she flails for help. For every attempt she makes at freeing herself from the earth's suction, the ground pulls her closer to its subterranean embrace.

I leap into action, scanning for anyone nearby who can help. The only body I see from the night's march lays face down in the water a few dozen feet away. His neck is bent in an unnatural angle and gives no signs of life. Likely broke his neck on the drop from the sky. "Fuck," I whisper under my breath as I sprint toward her panicked body.

"Stop moving!" I shout at her. "Stop! Now!"

I catch her attention and a wave of relief washes over her. "Oh gods be good, you have to save me! Please! I passed out when we fell from the sky! I woke up stuck in the mud! It's sucking me down!"

"It isn't mud!" I interrupt, my feet sloshing through the delta's perimeter as fast as I can. I need to be careful. There is no telling where the firm ground gives way to the bottomless pit of suctioning mud. "It's quicksand, so stop your thrashing! The more you move the faster you'll sink!"

My logic doesn't seem to penetrate her fight-or-flight instincts because she continues to fight the hold the earth has on her. She puts her hands against the ground to push herself up, so the sands consume her arms as well. She is now nothing more than an upright reed swaying violently back and forth. "Listen to me!" I continue to plead with her. "If you don't stop moving, you're going to kill yourself!"

I take another step and feel the ground give way below me. My bare foot sinks a few inches and I instantly throw myself back, freeing myself from the hold the earth has over me. I land on my butt and scramble to freedom, then assess the situation. Now I know where the ground gives way, but I am still a dozen or so yards away from the trapped woman. "Please save me, I'm begging you!"

"Shut up!" I scream back at her. Her disposition changes immediately. She instantly becomes offended, but I prefer her look of dumbstruck confusion over her lunatic flailing. "I need to think," I continue. Think damnit, think.

I look around for something to throw to her. No trees surround us. No stray branches litter the ground. I scan the buildings for a ladder or plank of wood. Nothing. Think damnit, think!

"Please," she sobs. "I don't want to die, I don't want to die!"

I breathe deeply in an attempt to slow my heart rate. Lundis once taught me you can't make rational decisions when emotion controls your mind. Easier said than done.

"I'll do anything! Don't let me die!"

Curse the damned gods for putting me in this situation. Everywhere I go is surrounded by death, whether it is my own doing or someone else's. I am the Enchantress, killing everything I touch despite my efforts to do good while on this earth.

"Please, just swim out and pull me free!"

"It's quicksand, dumbass!" I shout, "I'll get stuck too! Then we will both die! Is that what you want?"

I continue to scan. It is a simple problem to solve. She is stuck and I need to pull her free. All I am missing is the tool to pull her out. Find the tool, find the solution. I need a ladder or a plank or a rope...

A rope.

I look eerily at the hanging bodies that paint the walls around me. My feet thrash through the water before I have time to question my decision.

"No! Please don't leave me! I don't want to die!"

She is like a parrot that only knows how to say different combinations of the same twenty words. I go to my bag that floats in the shallows of the delta where my body landed. I rummage through its contents and see the vial of black blood has not cracked and thank the gods under my breath. At least one thing has gone my way. I push it to the side. A bushel of wolfsbane, now soaked with water, is in the way of what I seek. I locate the silver dagger I grabbed from the props inside the Queensmyre amphitheater and pull it free from the bag. I run my finger along its edge. It is dull, as I figured it would be, but still sharp enough to do the job. It may be a prop when it comes to stabbing, but the edge is still good for cutting. I run to the closest building and, without thinking, grab hold of the legs of a dangling man. I use his body like a ladder and pull myself up, hugging him like a koala hugs a tree it climbs. I curse as the scent of his dying flesh fills my nose, then hold my breath to push back the nausea.

I try to not think about what I'm doing and pray silently the man's neck doesn't snap under the weight of my ascent. We sway together as my climb jostles his long motionless body. I grab hold of his shoulders and lift myself up, dagger blade in my mouth. I feel and hear his neck snap under the pressure, but before his body has time to rip free from his bulbous head, I grab hold of the rope, climbing quickly to the top of the building. I count the rope's length as I scale it hand over hand. It is approximately twenty feet long, give or take. I look over my shoulder at the ground below me as I reach the building's roof. It is a long drop, but don't allow myself the luxury of overthinking the pain that awaits. I saw through its thick girth with my free hand and watch as the strings unravel. Soon, it is only a few threads that hold on. I grit my teeth when I hear it snap, then plummet toward the earth once again.

The dead body cushions my fall, but the man's inflated head explodes as my body's weight gives it the final push it needed to be freed from its discomfort. Blood spatters all over my body and a chunk of mushy brain flies into my open mouth. I spit the blood from my mouth and gasp for air, looking at the pancaked man beneath me. If it wasn't for him, I likely would have broken my leg in the fall. He is now twice dead, but I silently thank him for his sacrifice.

I loosen the noose from his decapitated neck and run back toward the screaming woman. The mud is now risen to her chest. I don't have much time. I need to act fast and efficiently. My adrenaline drowns out her desperate pleading for a savior. The outside world fades away. I no longer notice the mosquitoes that dive bomb my flesh or the vultures that circle her flailing body in the sky above.

I loosen the noose into a lasso. It has been two decades since Lundis taught me to wrangle a cow or pig, but I pray the muscle memory hasn't faded. I twirl the rope above my head and throw it in the woman's direction. It flies wildly to the left of her, missing by several feet. I curse, then pull the rope back in. I twirl it again and let it fly. This time it goes directly at her but flies over her head. Too much power. I curse and reel it back in. I am learning on the fly, wiping away the rust slowly but surely with every throw.

I twirl and throw the lasso again. It falls a foot short of her head. I curse. She is muttering something indistinguishable to me. I don't have time to listen to her ramblings. I lift the rope again, closing my eyes for a moment as it twirls above me. I feel the noose's weight swirling in the air, then open my eyes and aim directly at her. I let the lasso go and watch as its weight carries it toward her. I watch as it lands loosely around her neck and breathe a sigh of relief.

"Oh thank the gods!" she screams with joy. "My savior! I owe you my life! Please, now pull me in! Pull me in, I beg you!"

I sit on my butt and slowly pull the rope toward me, watching as the noose tightens around her neck as the rope grows taut. The pressure cuts off her breath so she can no longer scream at me. I thank the gods for the silence and continue to pull. This is the hard part. I cannot pull too hard or I'll snap her neck from the pressure, but I cannot pull too slow or she will suffocate to death. I slowly pull one hand in toward my body, then another. I watch as the sands give way to my strength. Her body slowly rises inch after inch. Her chest is now free from the earth's cruel embrace.

The woman's face is drowned red with panic. She is starting to suffocate as the blood is cut off from running to her head. If she could, she would probably thrash like a fish on a hook. But the mud prevents any excess movement in her body. I pull one hand toward my body, then another. Slowly, her torso begins to lift from the sands. I just need to pull a little longer and her hands will be free, then she can grab the rope and release the pressure from her neck.

Three more pulls and her arms should be released from the mud. I pull and watch as her face turns as purple as the eggrew leaf. I pull again and watch as her wrists rise from the ground. One more pull, I tell myself in a frantic panic. I put my back into it and pull with all my might. I grit my teeth and squint my eyes to avoid the burning sweat that drips from my brow.

A loud snap sounds and the rope loosens. I instantly let go, my heart skipping a beat. The woman's body is now lifeless, her head bent at an unnatural angle where the noose grips her. She no longer thrashes for freedom. She doesn't scream for help. She doesn't plead desperately for a savior.

She is dead, and I am her killer. I let go of the rope and watch as her body slowly sinks into the sands once more, this time slower than before, since she doesn't fight its grip any longer. I sit, motionless and in shock at what's just happened. I've never seen something turn so wrong so fast. All I wanted to do was help her. All I wanted to do was save her.

I am Enchantress.

Everything I touch, dies.

The woman's voice echoes in my mind.

I don't want to die, I don't want to die!

Even when my heart is in the right place, no one is safe in my presence.

Please, just swim out and pull me free!

All saviors must befriend the reaper.

I'll do anything! Don't let me die!

They must be okay with death.

My savior! I owe you my life!

Saving implies killing.

Please, now pull me in! Pull me in, I beg you!

Every victim has a captor.

Please don't leave me! I don't want to die!

But sometimes the captor will take the victim's life in the process of saving them.

I don't move as I watch the rope slowly be suctioned into the ground once the woman's head disappears beneath the waters. My breath is shallow and shaky. After all, I've just killed an innocent human.

Despite my best intentions, another person who put their trust in me has died at my own hands. Foot after foot, the rope disappears into the ground, and with it goes any hope I had of being the hero of this journey.

38

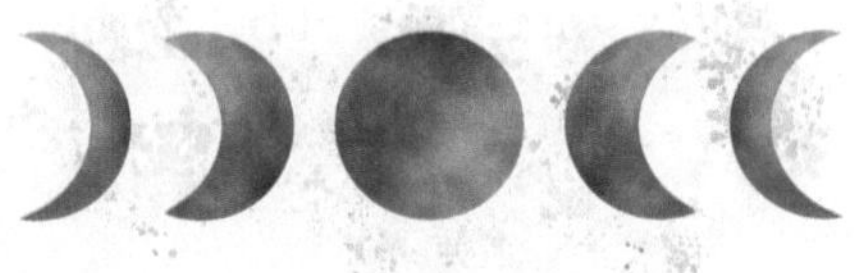

A Nightmare

"Damn pussies wanna drop us from the sky, I say we light this city on fire too," Creon shouts from a distance, his voice breaking me from my trance. I still sit in the delta's brown waters, staring at the spot the woman's body previously was. The rope has long disappeared, and all evidence of the accident is erased by Mother Nature. But it will scar my mind for the rest of my life.

"They wanna trap us here, we'll burn ever last goddamn building down like we did in Queensmyre. Burn them up while they sleep the day away. I know what you're thinking, you're thinking then we will be trapped in a burning city we can't escape. And to that I say, better to die by fire than let these blood sucking bitches get another meal," Creon jeers, "Besides, I'm no dumbass myself. I know why they brought us here. Even the common peasant is smart enough to know why they brought us here."

This makes me turn my head in his direction finally. If Creon has been able to solve the reason for our confinement on this island before I have, I may as well walk into the quicksands and let them devour me now. He is walking with the mother we saved from Queensmyre, though her arms no longer carry the baby Crixus saved. Her eyes are puffy and rimmed in red. I may not know why we are here, but I am smart enough to know her child did not survive the trip to Yueltope. Whether it died along the march or didn't survive the drop, the mother wears her grief on her face like a mask. She shrugs Creon's conviction off. The two are perfect for each other. Creon needs someone to ramble to and the mother simply needs to be in another's company to dilute her mourning.

Others begin to file toward the banks where I sit, though there is still no sight of Crixus. The citizens of Queensmyre crowd around me as if I am their unelected leader. I can barely make out the incoherent babbling as they all chatter amongst themselves what's to be done. My mind is still in shock from the death on my hands. I barely register the people surrounding me. None of them have witnessed what I just did. This pain in my heart is solely mine. I can't afford the luxury of wearing it on my sleeve as the grieving mother does.

I must be strong.

That is the only way we will survive whatever comes.

The ringing in my ear fades and I take in the incessant talking of the crowd. There are only forty or so who remain after the trip here. They go back and forth with each other arguing over anything and everything. They want a clear path of freedom laid out before them. Some inkling of hope they can cling to. I cannot provide that for them, though they look to me for guidance. It isn't that simple.

"Syrus?" Creon's voice breaks through my dazed trance. "Whaddya say? You with me buddy?"

"Huh?" I mumble, trying to regain composure. I can still feel the innocent woman's neck snapping in my hands through the rope.

"I *said* we should start breaking into the buildings one by one so you can go ape shit on these bastards. Are you with me?"

"No."

"And why the hell not?"

"It isn't that simple."

"It seems pretty damn simple to me."

"Where's Crixus?"

"Who cares? I'm sure she's around here somewhere. She's probably scoped the entire town by now. She's a cold-hearted bitch, and I mean that in a good way, if ya know what I mean."

"We need to find her. We don't leave a wolf behind."

"Since when? Last time I checked, we left Lockjaw behind, and *you* left Scar in no man's land outside of Gall, and I'm still not even convinced you didn't kill him while the two of you were alone out there."

"What are we going to do?" Another voice breaks in from the crowd. What sounds like a thousand others begin asking the same question. Something doesn't feel right. I can't shake the feeling. This town is more than what it seems. I smell something in the air. My ears are still human, but they twitch as if they were a wolf's. My previously dry mouth now oozes saliva. What's happening? I sense something.

"I'm telling you," Creon continues, "There's probably a maximum of twenty in each building. You do the silver eye thing, shift to the beast, and barge in while they're hibernating. They won't know what hit them. They won't be expecting it. They think we are all human. Besides, most of them will die peacefully in their sleep."

"Do you hear yourself right now?" I ask, glaring into his eyes like he's a neanderthal.

"You're asking me to take on an army of a thousand by myself with powers I don't even know how to control yet. And the only time I have wielded them has been a total of a few minutes, max. Then, after exhausting whatever inside me is responsible for controlling the beast, I pass out. Why don't I just kick a nest of wasps and let them come sting me while I'm at it?"

"It's daylight," Creon quips, "They can't come after you like wasps."

"No, not now, but where the hell will I run off to before the sun sets? If you didn't notice, the whole goddamned town is surrounded with quicksand. Dagon, do you ever use your brain? Any of you?" I spit, looking at the crowd with wrath in my eyes. These people let their panic and delirium influence their decision making. They are no better than directionless children. They want everything to be done for them, instead of pitching in and helping to find a real solution.

"Then what the bloody hell are we going to do?" Creon asks. My ear twitches as I hear a rope snap in the distance. Creon continues, "We can't just sit here and wait for the moon to—"

"Shut up," I interrupt, trusting my instincts. "Everyone shut up!" I whisper loud enough, raising my index finger to my lips. I face Creon and point to my ear. "Listen."

I hear sawing, then another rope snaps. Sawing, then another rope snaps. I hear bodies fall to the ground, but they do not thud awkwardly. I can hear feet landing gracefully. Sawing, snap, thud. Sawing, snap, thud. The humans around us look at me and Creon with confusion, none of them possessing the ability to hear like a Lycan. But Creon hears it. I can see the shift in his face. We stare at one another as the bodies in the distance continue to fall.

Is it Crixus?

Is the she-wolf cutting the hanging bodies down?

With what blade?

And for what reason?

It doesn't make sense, but the sawing continues, and the ropes continue to break in the distance. The bodies fall silently, and suddenly the sawing grows in volume. There are multiple ropes being cut at the same time now. More than one cutter. Bodies fall simultaneously. I stare at the walls that face us. None of the bodies move. They are all varying levels of dead and rotted.

Saw, snap, thud.

Saw, snap, thud.

Now it is loud enough for the humans to hear. There are at least five cutters now, which leads to five bodies dropping at the same time. The crowd gathered around me grows eerily silent. I can sense the shift in their dispositions as their demeanor shrinks in fear. Their shoulders hunch slightly. I can smell the newfound hormones of fear in the air around us.

I can hear footfall now. Whatever walks toward us surely isn't Crixus. There are dozens of bare feet smacking against the city's asphalt street. They're walking toward us, that much I'm sure of. I can hear their march growing louder and more numerous. The cutting continues to grow in volume. The bodies continue to march. The marching becomes thunder in my sensitive ears.

Where the hell is Crixus? I don't feel confident without her by my side, I realize, though I would never say it aloud. What if something has happened to her? What if they dropped her in the quicksand? What if she broke her neck when they dropped her?

I grind my teeth as the crowd around me slowly shuffles behind me, inadvertently pushing me between themselves and the oncoming threat. Creon remains by my side. His nose lifts to the air and silently sniffs like a bloodhound. He whispers, "It isn't Undead. All I smell is humans and decay."

"As do I," I grumble under my breath, frustrated by my inability to understand what's happening. Whoever it is, they've covered their scent well enough to throw my senses off. I spread my feet defensively. I left the prop dagger at the base of the building, so all I have to make myself look intimidating is my clenched fists.

I don't like our positioning. We are vulnerable with our backs facing the quicksand. If the marching army storms us, we will be pushed back into the gluttonous earth. But our only other option is to storm them first, and something tells me the cowardly artists of Queensmyre will not be willing to lay down their lives to save themselves from a potential enemy.

That leaves only one option.

I wait for the threat to arrive and hope the beast within wakes in time to protect us all.

The gore-covered humans enter the main street and march straight toward us like an army of resurrected, mummified remains. I watch as they walk five abreast through the city's street, the individuals on either end of the line climbing the buildings' walls to cut the ropes from several hanging bodies. Or at least, I thought they were hanging. What I see now is that the bodies being cut down were never truly dead. Their heels dig into crevices in chiseled cracks of the clay buildings, saving the weight of their body from being fully suspended.

"Dagon's mercy, they have been hiding in plain sight this entire time," I whisper loud enough for Creon to hear. The living men and women are mixed in between the countless victims who will never walk again. But as I watch the forces cut down their living comrades, I realize quickly what we are up against. They are naked and covered with bloody tissue that resembles decomposition. If I had to guess, none of it belongs to them, but was smeared on cosmetically to cover their scent and sell their deaths. Even now that I know several of these bodies still hanging are actually alive, their acting skills make it impossible to tell which are dead and which are breathing.

"Is that who I think it is?" Creon asks. I instantly know who he is talking about. The man that leads the zombified army stands at the front of the pack as his soldiers continue to cut down the hanging bodies. Though he is covered from head to toe in bloodied gore that makes it look as though his body has been torn apart by vultures, I can see clearly the man behind the makeup. He is everything I'm not, after twenty-four moons of starvation.

Tall and muscular. His arms are lean and etched in stone. They are the sort of arms that look as though they've swung a sword since he was old enough to hold a stick in his hand. Striations of muscle flex in his quads with every step he takes. His shoulders and chest are wide but his waist is thin, shaped in a v. Long, shaggy, red hair flows just above his collar bones. It is uneven, as though it was recently cut with a dagger. Veins flow across the surface of his naked skin like a Blackblood, only his skin is tan and healthy in the places it isn't covered in gore.

His face is one of a military commander. Chiseled jawline, stone-clad cheekbones, stormy blue eyes. A scar covers his face from temple to chin, curving around his left eye. Though I can tell the blood that covers his body is fake, I know with certainty there is no faking a scar like that. He looks dead at me, and suddenly I feel as though I'm the one naked, even though my ragged clothes still cover most of my body. His stare is like a bolt of lightning hitting the ground in front of me.

He has the walk of one who refuses to die. The soldiers that follow him mimic his confidence. Shoulders back, chests out, chins raised. They drop from their suspended ropes and free themselves of the nooses around their necks, then fall in line with the marching army. Somehow, though I don't know their scheme, they have snuck into Yueltope while the Undead were away fighting their war and hid themselves among their slaughtered brethren.

I don't have to reply to Creon. He knows it as well as I do. Though I have only heard stories of him, and though I have never seen him face to face, I know the man who marches toward us.

Atlas and his Acolytes are here, and I can tell by the determination in their eyes that they've come for revenge.

39

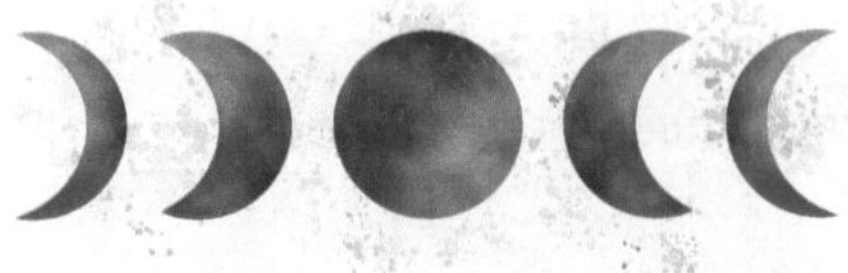

A Nightmare

After the brief exchange of eye contact, Atlas disregards us altogether. He and his followers are on a mission. They've faked their own deaths to make it this far, and a small crowd of forty prisoners from Queensmyre won't distract them. The small army of naked men and women storm the banks of the delta and begin digging with their hands in the mud without a word said. Whatever plan they've devised, they hold it close to their chest.

Atlas himself gets on his hands and knees to dig. He does not stand by as most military leaders would, micromanaging his ranks, commanding them to do a million different things. He crouches low and muddies his hands, scraping through the clay for some long-lost treasure. I eye Creon. He is just as confused as I am. Neither of us know what to do. We are like unwelcome dinner guests.

All I know is that when I look at the Acolytes' leader, I feel inferior. He is everything I should be. He leads with action. His charisma is unspoken. Everything about him seems to be stoic. He is the sort of man my father would look at and admire. I am the kind of man my father would look at and disregard.

I find myself wanting to submit myself to his leadership by just watching his small movements. He moves with purpose. He knows where he's going, what he's doing. He has direction. These are all things I lack. I am not a man with a plan. I am a man who figures out where to step after my last stride is complete. He is a man who thinks miles ahead.

You can read a man by his body language. But even more, you can read a man by the shape of his body. Fat is a symbol of wealth, but muscle is a symbol of determination. Muscle is the only thing that cannot be bought in this world. It is earned, Lundis taught me early on. You can tell the warriors from the wannabes from body composition. Those who've swung a sword for ten thousand hours will show signs in their appearance. Those who have shot ten thousand arrows will show it in their back and biceps. And those who have done nothing but eat and drink their days away will show it with their gut.

I can see Atlas's wisdom in his eyes. I can see the warrior within by his muscles. This is the sort of man who can take on a thousand Undead and live to tell the tale. The sort of man who will stake a thousand Undead up the ass to leave a message to the world.

Atlas is everything I have wanted to be since I was a child.

I have never resented anyone more than I do him.

I hate this man, though we've never exchanged a single word.

I watch as he pulls metal from the ground, washing it off in the still water of the delta bank. His soldiers do the same, and I see now they've buried their swords and shields and armor. I realize moments ago I was standing on an entire cache of weapons without even knowing it. Whenever they buried it all, enough time has passed for the delta's waters to erase all signs of digging.

How long have these men and women been hanging from the walls of Yueltope?

How long have they been awaiting the return of the Undead army?

The Undead who flew me in said they killed the Acolytes the night before last. That means these soldiers could have been waiting nearly two days for their chance at revenge. This goes beyond levels of determination I've ever seen. It is like something out of a history book on the Holy Crusades. Like Lysander or Xander, Atlas possesses the patience and ferocity of a lion to reach his goals, and any who stand in his way will face the consequences.

The soldiers dress themselves in armor without a single word spoken. This plan has been communicated and rehearsed well in advance. Metal rattles as they fasten the plates along their limbs and torsos. The army is ready for war.

Atlas pulls his sword from the mud and washes it delicately in the water, exposing its familiar shape and appearance to me. I watch as his bare palm wraps around the stone hilt. The metal blade glows under the water as he washes it. The black blade slowly turns blue, then purple, then crimson red. An aura from the shining metal glows beneath the waters, feeding off the anger that radiates from Atlas's palm.

It can't be.

I must be hallucinating.

I squeeze my eyes shut, then open them once more.

The sword still shines a violent shade of red.

I would know that sword if I saw it in the furthest corners of earth. I spent countless hours staring at it in my childhood. I used to fantasize about grabbing hold of it as I rushed into some made-up battle. The vision from the old hag flashes before my eyes. The memory of my mother gripping the same iconic blade is seared in my mind as she faced the seven Black Knights. A cold chill seizes my sweaty body.

I am not hallucinating.

There, in Atlas's palm, is my mother's mood sword.

A thousand questions enter my head along with a thousand emotions. I am confused at how he has come in possession of the sword meant for me by right of succession. I am angry how he washes the mud from it as if it is his own. I am jealous of the fact that he truly is everything I am not. I am lustful for the chance to hold the blade myself. I am enraged by the Fate's decision to make him everything I am not.

I want to kill this man.

I want to steal the blade and drive it into his heart.

Envy is a deceitful devil, but I want to cave to its desires and strike Atlas down and force the Acolytes to follow me, the rightful heir to the Areopagus Throne. I am supposed to be the leader. I am supposed to wield my mother's sword. I am supposed to lead this army. I am—

I catch myself mid-thought. What am I doing?

Everything this man has, everything he has become, has been earned. These people do not follow him because he forced them into submission. They follow him because he is a leader worth following. Killing him and taking the sword would do nothing more than prove I am the inferior of us both. He is better than me in every way. So what?

Caving in to the feelings of bitter resentment won't do anything but dig my grave deeper. This is the sort of man I need by my side, not as my enemy. If I'm going to retake my kingdom, earning this man's trust will be the first step I can take in the right direction.

"Who are you people?" I ask coyly, acting as though I am as confused as the others regarding the turn of events.

The Acolytes turn to face me, almost as if they've only just noticed the crowd of prisoners for the first time and registered their presence. They look at each other in turn, wondering what to say to us, if anything at all.

Atlas is the only one who doesn't bother turning to face us. He is wrestling with the leather strap that fastens a vambrace to his forearm. Without turning, Atlas speaks on behalf of his soldiers, "I'm sorry you have been dragged into this war, citizens of Queensmyre. The Undead have taken you all as bait to draw us in, not knowing we already hid in plain sight. They have been taking humans hostage this entire war in an attempt to expose us."

Finally, Atlas spins to face us, now fully covered from neck to toe in war-battered armor. The metal that covers his body is sleek and lean. It hugs his body like a glove. It has several exposure points along his joints, allowing for increased flexibility and speed. That is the pitfall with all armor. The wearer must choose between protection and agility. It serves little purpose to be fully protected if it turns a knight into an immobile tank. On the flip side, too little coverage to gain speed and the wearer is exposed to deadly injury. Atlas's armor is the perfect medium between the two absolutes.

Atlas continues, "We are the Acolytes, and we are here to put an end to the Undead." His voice is more stoic than even my father's was. It is the perfect balance between humility and pride, wisdom and stupidity, experience and lethargy. His face is etched in exhaustion. He is a man driven purely by purpose. The scar along the side of his face makes him appear dangerous, yet his voice is a blanket of comfort to the ears. Atlas is a demigod. A warrior that only belongs in story books and fables from times long forgotten. His birth was a product of necessity. The gods foresaw the coming war and bred him strictly for the purpose of instilling order.

"For many months we have went to war against the Undead and Blackbloods in order to save humanity from their tyranny," Atlas continues, assuming the citizens of Queensmyre know nothing about the Acolytes' origins. "You are safe for the time being. We have come to slay your captors and enact revenge for what they've done to the men and women who hang before you."

"But the quicksand... How did you get pass the quicksand? I mean, I don't see any boats," I stutter convincingly. It isn't hard to sell myself short. Fear is one of the easiest emotions to replicate because I have an eternal storage to pull from. I can only imagine what Atlas sees when he speaks to me. I am likely nothing more than a starving, uneducated peasant covered in soot and mud and blood. I want him to underestimate me more than he's ever underestimated a person. I want him to think I am stupid and weak and unworthy of his leadership. Moments like this aren't survived with conjured bravado. Moments like this are about manipulating the strong to do your own dirty work. And standing before me is a prime candidate to kill every last Undead soldier in this godforsaken hellhole.

Atlas answers, "The same way the outlaws of Yueltope came and went for centuries. If you can't go through it and you can't go over it, you have to go under it."

Tunnels! Suddenly I'm reminded of Lundis's geography lesson on this region, though the memory is foggy and covered with dust. But Atlas's words are the spark that light the fire in my mind. Yueltope has a tunneling system beneath its infrastructure to travel outside the city. It remains the reason why the criminals of Yueltope were able to remain safe from law and order for so many years. All they had to do was protect their underground passages from intruders. The only people who could enter the town elsewhere were the Undead who could fly into city limits, but the Undead wanted nothing to do with the miscreants that lived in Yueltope.

"Commander," a soldier interrupts, "We must begin. Daylight will not last forever."

"Patience, Percival. The Undead are not going anywhere. Addressing the concerns these humans have is the least we can do, seeing the Undead brought them here to lure us in," Atlas replies. The uneasy looking man named Percival concedes and lowers his eyes to the ground.

"Why would they use us to lure you in?" I ask. "After all, we have no stake in this war. We are just artists and thespians from Queensmyre."

"Have you ever hunted, thespian?" Atlas asks. I have hunted more times than Atlas could fathom. Any meat I've eaten over the last twenty years has been killed with my own hands. I would not be alive without my ability to live off the fat of the land.

"Never," I reply, confused by his question.

"It matters little for you to understand my message. It is common practice as a hunter to catch a fawn when it has wandered off from its mother. Catch a fawn and use it as bait. The child will call out desperately for its parents, screaming in terror at its captivity. After the calling starts, it won't be long before a buck comes to find its lost child. Hunting is made easy when you can make the prey come to you instead of having to hunt for the prey. In this case, you are the fawn, and we are the buck. The Undead knew we were not far away from Yueltope after killing our brothers and sisters, and catching you to use as bait would ensure we came to save you."

He talks to me like I'm stupid, which makes it hard to hide my smile.

"Are you going to kill them all?"

"Every last one of them."

I stare at the intensity in his eyes and it spreads to my body. My mother's sword glows fierier than the sun above. There are only two ways this war will end. With Atlas dead, or the Undead and their infected counterparts purged from the face of the earth.

"Is there anything us people of Queensmyre can do to help?" I stutter, earning my role as thespian. "We are not much for violence, but—I don't know—we could help cook and entertain your soldiers." The offer is a mere formality. These soldiers plan to save us so it is only courtesy for us to offer a form of repayment. Besides, I know Atlas's hubris is too mighty to accept a peasant's offer.

"You're far too kind, sir," Atlas exchanges, "But we have no need for such services. After we finish what needs to be done, we will show you the tunnels and lead you to freedom. You are free to return to Queensmyre after that."

"We can't!" a woman calls out from behind me. "It has burned down! See! There! On the horizon! That billow of smoke is all that remains of our city!"

Another cries out, "We have nowhere to go!"

Others join in, "We need your protection!"

"We won't make it on our own!"

"...food and water!"

"If we return..."

"...nowhere to go!"

Shockingly, not a single one of them mentions what they saw me do near the Queensmyre gate. My claws, my silver eyes, my fangs, nothing. Every person here knows I am some sort of Lycan, but they do not give away my identity or tell Atlas the fear they feel toward me. None try to correct me as I pretend to be something I'm not. They all see how my demeanor has shifted from a leader to a meager peasant in Atlas's presence. The smart ones know I am up to something, but they don't say it aloud. I somehow doubt it's because they trust me. Fear is a fantastic silencer.

"Silence!" Atlas booms, commanding the crowd with a single word. "We will talk later about where you may go. You may return to Queensmyre to help rebuild it from the ashes, or you may embrace Yueltope as your new home and turn it into a destination of true beauty. It matters little! We Acolytes will take no part in either journey, and it is up for you to decide amongst yourselves what you wish to do. Now please, remain here on the delta as we go wake the Undead. It is for your safety."

Before we can say another word, Atlas turns his back to us once more and marches off to the city. His entire army is now fully clothed head to toe in armor. They move in silence, each and every one of them focused on what needs to be done.

A half hour ago, Creon proposed we do exactly what the Acolytes intend. He told me to go from house to house, killing the Undead within like the angel of death passing over the city. I dismissed his idea as ludicrous. I made him feel a fool for thinking such a thing could be accomplished.

Why don't I just kick a nest of wasps and let them come sting me while I'm at it?

Now Atlas and his soldiers will do exactly what Creon proposed, and the idea no longer seems impractical. After looking eye to eye with the Acolyte leader, I know there won't be a single life spared in the massacre to come. He will kill all of them. Even the princess herself. His soldiers will drag them by their hair into the daylight and watch them burn alive.

The man before me will easily enact Creon's plans I previously criticized. He does not scoff at the idea of taking the Undead on head-to-head. He does not concern himself with caution. He does not rely on supernatural blessings to deal with his foes. He does not silently pray for the beast within to save him from peril. He has no beast within. Atlas is his own beast, and it is better to be your own beast in this world than to rely on one you cannot control.

I watch the soldiers walk off in perfect synchronization. Their formation is perfectly rehearsed. Every link in their chain knows where to be and when to be there. No commands are uttered. They are a well-oiled machine that has drilled this scenario countless times. Having grown up in the Areopagus, I know how painstakingly difficult it is to get a unit to move as these men and women do. As a boy, I watched my father's army practice these formations day and night. It takes more than discipline. It takes strategic prowess. Every soldier must understand the purpose behind their positioning.

I hate myself for admiring the Acolytes to the degree I do. Envy boils beneath my skin like grease atop a fire. I know there is nothing to be envious of, yet it doesn't stop the feelings of jealousy from growing. Atlas earned every second of this. The human has stolen nothing from me. He had no hand in my family's downfall. He hunts the same Emperor who ruined my life. We are unknowingly united in our cause, yet that doesn't stop me from hating him for his success.

I turn to Creon and whisper under my breath, "We must leave now, but first we need to find Crixus."

"What are you in a rush for?" he asks, staring at the magnificent army as they re-enter the city's main street. I stare down at the craters in the earth where the Acolytes buried their armor. The Undead likely expected them to arrive by nightfall, drawn in to enact their revenge. Saunter must've thought her army would have time to sleep the daylight away comfortably, regrouping their strength for the coming battle. She was wrong, and her army will soon pay dearly for her error.

"Where do you think Atlas plans to travel after this?" I ask Creon rhetorically, hoping he is smart enough to put the pieces together. I continue, "The Acolytes have successfully overtaken the Undead in Vhem, Slaavan, Thessolo, Ubat, and Hosh, Gall, and now Yueltope. Their crusade makes a westerly path straight for Sygon, and if we don't beat them there, they will claim the city for themselves."

"So what?" Creon asks, "Bloodlust only said we need to make the city fall. He didn't say we need to do it ourselves. I say we wait it out and let these blokes do it for us. Ride on their coattails and let them fight the good fight while we sit back and watch. Then, when Sygon falls from their destruction, we kill their main man and take the show over."

"No," I dismiss the idea completely. "We will claim the city with our own hands. I refuse to rely on human intervention."

"Swallow your pride, Syrus. There is no shame in letting others do your dirty work for you. Look at you. You can barely stand. You need food. Sleep, for Dagon's sake. If you storm Sygon yourself, there won't be anything left of you by the time you take it over. What's the sense in earning your daughter's freedom if you die in the process?"

"That's the whole point," I snap violently. I stare at him with venom in my eyes. "Do you think I signed up for this mission with the intention of returning alive? I am beyond the point of fighting to survive. The throne I fight to retake is not meant for me. But it isn't too late for my daughter. All of this is for her."

"Then you are a coward," Creon spits on the ground.

"Excuse me?"

"We both know I have no room to talk, but when are you going to stop running Sylvian? Bollocks, you run from every opportunity that comes across your path. You have the wisdom to lead. You have the strength to endure. You have the power to overcome. All of this, and you still run toward your death like an arrowless archer. Dying is easy, man. Way too easy. Any coward can die. It takes a real man to face living. But you'd rather your daughter do your living for you. When are you going to take a stand? When are you going to say enough is enough? Where are your balls? I know the Blackbloods didn't neuter you, but you walk around like a mutt in a world of purebreds. It's a damn shame if you ask me."

Nothing Creon says is disputable. He reads me like an open book, and this is a man who probably can't even read a picture book. To stand here and argue with him would be a waste of time and breath. He says the things

I already know. He shines light on my inner demons like no one before. But this is a man who has never been one for formalities. He says it how he sees it. No beating around the bush.

His speech is profound, but it does nothing to dissuade me from my intentions. I won't let Atlas take Sygon for me. Call it pride, call it envy, call it whatever it is. I have let others fight my battles for me my whole life. As he said so pointedly, I have run from every adversity I've faced. I won't run from what awaits in Sygon. I will not back down from what Bloodlust has ordered. Saunter is here, which means Sygon is mine for the taking.

"Stay here then, it makes no difference to me. Sygon's downfall will be my own doing, no one else's. The moon will be full by the time the Acolytes arrive. If you'd like them to learn who you really are, follow them. But be warned, they hate Lycans just as much as they do Undead."

I walk off, saying nothing. After all, there is nothing more to be said. I'm done presenting people the option to follow me or leave. Creon is a grown damn man. He can decide for himself what he wants.

"Where the snot are you going, bugger?" Creon calls after me. My ear twitches as I hear the Acolytes break open the first door in the distance. I can hear their fists tightening on their hilts. Another door breaks open, then another. They are dividing and conquering. This town will soon be filled with more death than any band of outlaws could have previously enacted. Swords tear into flesh. Chills run down my spine. Creon hears it too, though the citizens of Queensmyre are spared the ability to pick up on the massacre.

"I told you. To find Crixus," I say, not turning to face him.

"And if she's dead?" he calls after me, running to catch up.

I turn to face him, looking at him with a queer smile. "A she-wolf like that does not die that easily."

40

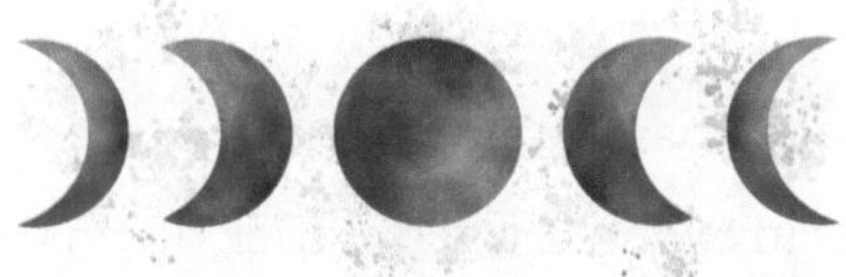

A Nightmare

First I walk, then I run. The longer I go without seeing evidence of Crixus alive the faster I fall prey to panic. Yueltope only has a circumference of one and a half kilometers, but that gives more ground to cover than I have time for. I can't explore the city streets for her body. The Acolytes have spread like plaque in an artery as they go from building to building. Though Creon and I stick to the outskirts of the city, we can hear the atrocities occurring within.

The Undead don't go to their deaths silently, and they put up the best fight they can. For all intents and purposes, the Undead are the first army I've ever seen be ambushed on a trap they baited themselves. Surely they left us prisoners from Queensmyre on Yueltope's delta with assurance they had plenty of time to rest before the Acolytes came. They likely blocked off the underground tunnels and anticipated Atlas's soldiers would have to come by riverboat. I cannot blame them for thinking they were safe enough to sleep. But Atlas's presence in the city was never anticipated by those who go to their death screaming.

And there is nothing the Undead can do to protect themselves other than bar the doors of the buildings they reside in. They cannot take the fight to the city streets in order to gain space for open combat. The sun is crested in the sky and would do Atlas's work for him if they were idiotic enough to do that.

I run along Yueltope's jagged coast line. It really is a strange city. Its foundation is just raised enough to not be flooded by the Pagean's delta, yet the delta wraps around the entire city like a moat. It is the sort of stronghold military commanders of olden times would dream for. Unless you are commanding an army within a hollow mountain such as Bloodlust and his Blackbloods, this is as defensible a city you can stumble upon.

The city itself is an utter dump. The outlawed citizens that resided here previously did nothing to liven the place up. They have no natural landfill to dispose of trash. Piles of garbage litter the outskirts of the town. Broken glass and soiled toilet paper and human sewage. The trash floats along the delta moat, refusing to dissolve, turning its water a perverse shade of shit-brown.

Hanging bodies are put on display throughout the entire outskirts of the city. Though it would take a day to census the lynched men and women, I would guess there are several thousand. In the places where the walls aren't covered by corpses I can see the painted graffiti that lines the walls. Skulls and crossbones, warnings, mediocre art, and surprisingly enough, a few beautiful murals every now and then.

The further I go, the more I start to lose hope. There are so many places she could be. Whoever flew her in could have dropped her in the middle of the city or on a rooftop or in the quicksand or in the Pagean itself. Could it be possible she is dead? Could it be possible she isn't even in this city?

Surely she would have sought us out after waking from the drop. Maybe she wasn't knocked unconscious in the first place. There are so many uncertain variables. So many things that make my search for her futile. I can feel Creon losing hope even faster than me. He doesn't see the point searching for a ghost. We've run for almost two miles along Yueltope's manure coastline. There is only so far we can go before we circle back to where we started, and then I know there will be no convincing Creon to continue the search.

I don't turn to look at his judgmental face. If it was up to him, we'd be following the Acolytes instead of wasting time with this manhunt.

"You know what's most messed up about this," Creon calls after me. I don't answer, partially because I don't want to, but mostly because I'm too out of breath. My body barely has the strength to stand, let alone walk, let alone run. My joints burn with pain. It isn't the discomfort that is tolerable. My hips and knees scream with pain I've never experienced. A human body was not designed to do so much while fueled by so little. I am past the point of hunger gnawing at my stomach. The hunger spreads to my every limb and burns my throat with bile.

Creon continues, "If it was me that went missing, I doubt you'd be out here searching this hard. You've been looking for a chance to get rid of me ever since you first woke up outside that mountain."

He is right. Creon is many things, but dumb isn't one of them. Above all, he knows how to read a situation. It's likely his ability to do such that has allowed him to survive all these years. Degeneracy is not an easy lifestyle to endure. The Fates have a way of killing off miscreants who don't contribute to society. But here is a prime example of a man who has been able to thrive as a degenerate. Hopping from town to town murdering people, burning down buildings, robbing banks. And if that's while the moon has been silent, I'd hate to see what his beast within has been responsible for after all these years.

A silent part of me wishes he had left when I gave him the chance to, days ago. Another part of me is glad he is still by my side. I've seen parts of him I didn't think existed in watching him closely. He is more complex than first impressions revealed. But regardless, I know he is right. I would not sprint around the coast in search of him if the tables were turned. At the end of the day, Crixus is a greater ally to me than Creon. Her loyalty has spoken for itself. Her dedication to the cause is unquestionable. I know she would lay down her life for my own, and I would do the same in return.

It is the way of wolves to protect one another. The strength of the wolf is the pack, and I am only as strong as my weakest member. Because of this, I need Crixus more than Creon. Creon is out only for himself. He is a wild card. I can trust my life in his hands no more than I can trust a baby to speak intelligently.

Yet I can't fight the nagging thought that he is still here. He has not betrayed me in the slightest, and he has actually contributed toward the completion of this journey more than he has harmed its progress. Should I feel bad that I put Crixus on a higher pedestal in my mind than I do Creon? Should I—

I pause in my tracks, my mind wiped clean of whatever trail of thoughts it was on. My nose twitches.

"Do you smell that?" I ask, closing my eyes and pulling from my senses. Though my soot-filled nose still struggles to smell more than ash, I sift through the wavering scent of sewage from Yueltope and smell a familiar fragrance through the smog. Tea olive and eucalyptus, I note inwardly. She is near.

My strides quicken. Excitement bubbles beneath my flesh. I knew she was alive, but having confirmation in place of doubt sets me over the edge. It takes another few minutes of silent running to find her, and when I do, my mind is instantly set at ease.

Crixus stands in the shallows of the delta's murky waters. Floating at her ankles is a makeshift raft made from human bodies, gallows ropes, and deconstructed roofing. I can see the bodies tied together in bundles of four like buoys off the coast. On top of the human buoys is the raft's platform. It is constructed from—from what I can tell—spare roofing shingles and rotted drywood. I'm somewhat speechless. I could have never thought to construct such an ingenious means of escape. Yet this woman has survival skills unparalleled by anyone on this quicksand island.

"Forget everything I said," Creon chuckles, panting from the sprint. "We need this she-wolf more than Solis needed Caspian."

I see Crixus catch our scent. Her petite nose scrunches and lifts to the air. She turns to face us and wipes her sweaty bangs behind her ear. Emotions stir deep in me when I see her flash a smile my direction. Her white teeth sparkle in the sunlight. Beads of sweat collect on her caramel skin. Her stained shirt is soaked in sweat and the delta's water. It sticks to her skin like a glove, exposing her breasts and nipples in a way that makes it hard to not stare. The only way to describe her is beautiful, yet she doesn't act like she knows it. Her thin waist is offset by her wide hips. She's rolled her pants up above her tone calves. My fingers itch to hold her body. I want to kiss every inch of her from her forehead to her toes.

I breathe a sigh of relief to see her alive. I don't know what part of me caused a panic at the thought of her dying. I've only known her a few days. There's no rational explanation for why I feel the way I do about her. Yet a primal force deep inside of me has imprinted on my heart. I feel emotions toward her I've never felt toward anyone other than Vesper.

"I see someone's been busy!" I call to her.

She laughs, staring at her raft. "I can't swim, remember?"

"This bloke wouldn't have left you behind regardless," Creon calls out. "We've been on a manhunt for the infamous Crixus for the past hour. He was going to find you whether you were dead or alive."

My face blushes and I'm suddenly glad my face is covered in soot and mud. Her smile makes me weak in the knees. Her eyes open me up like a patient under the blade of a surgeon. My stomach flips upside down from the fluttering it feels when we lock gaze.

I shove the feelings deep inside me and move forward. "We need to leave now," I command, returning to my role as leader of this pack. "I will catch you up when we get past the tides of the Pagean. There is a small river called the Tyber that branches from the Pagean. It will take us to Lake Askamyre. Sygon is only a few miles hike from Askamyre. We aren't safe here. Do you have oars?"

Crixus's smile disappears at my seriousness and she shoves whatever emotions she feels deep inside herself. She nods slightly. I've ruined the moment, but people like us are used to positive emotions expiring too soon.

"Here," she says, pulling two hastily made oars from a compartment in the raft. One looks like a rake handle with a plank of wood tied to the end; the other looks like a broken leg from a kitchen table with a wide chunk of shingle at the end for paddling.

Creon laughs, grabbing them from her. "These look about as useful as a fishnet condom."

Crixus isn't offended in the slightest, joining him in his laughter. It makes me happy to see her smile again. I shouldn't have rushed away her joy moments ago. There are only so many moments we truly feel happy in this world. We should linger in them when they come. There's no guarantee we will ever feel another.

I join the two in pushing the raft further out into the delta, then when I feel my foot stick in the mud I jump onto its platform, pulling Crixus up after me, then Creon. I can no longer hear the sound of Acolytes slaughtering the Undead inside of Yueltope. We are on the other side of the city. It will take them hours to march their way from building to building. But by the time the sun sets, there won't be a single Undead left.

Saunter, like her brother Bane, will soon be dead. Sygon will be left without a leader, ripe for our reaping. The moon grows fuller with every night. I shove my hand into my side bag and grab hold of the black blood vial to make sure it's still there. I release it and grab hold of a bushel of wolfsbane, ripping the bud from its stem. Elsewhere in the bag is a pipe carved from elderwood. I remove the bud, the pipe, and a small box of matches while Creon dutifully rows the poorly shaped oars in a motion close to unison.

I stare at the wolfsbane intently before packing it into the pipe. Known for its ability to kill a Lycan, wolfsbane is one of the most potent toxins to our kind on the face of the earth. But, like with all poisons, I learned long ago from Lundis that if a Lycan microdoses by consuming small amounts consistently, they can teach their body to tolerate larger dosages without a lethal effect.

After fleeing the Areopagus as a child, I was taken in by an indigenous tribe of Lycans known as the Lupus Cruor, which roughly translates to Wolf's Blood. These people did dozens of things to minimize the effect of the beast within when the moon grew full, and I absorbed their knowledge and wisdom for several years. Located in the foothills of the Thoren Mountains, the tribal people of Wolf's Blood took me in and taught me how to control my beast to the best of my abilities. Without them, I would be dead. And because of me, now they are dead.

The wolfsbane bud before me is white, though the most common strain I'm accustomed to smoking is a dark shade of purple, like the eyes of an Undead. Legend goes that when Damon sent the meteor known as Phobos to earth, the Undead mined silver from its ore. But later, after sitting dormant for many moons, the meteor began to sprout life from its rocky surface. From the crater where it landed and all along the meteor grew wolfsbane, a flower unknown to creation until Phobos's arrival. And just like silver, the flower proved to have a deadly effect on all Sons of Dagon. The Undead would lace their blades with it and poison the drinking water of Lycan camps. When it enters a wolf's bloodstream, it sours a Lycan's blood and eats away at their heart. Thousands of our kind were killed by the toxin before learning how to properly microdose. Yet the same deadly bud responsible for the death of so many wolves has no effect on humans and Undead who consume it.

One of the most horrific wars in the Before Sylvian period took place between the Undead and the Lycans. The Undead had planted an entire field of wolfsbane but concealed its scent with the blood of slaughtered Lycans. When the full moon came, the wolves came to the field to seek revenge for their fallen brethren, but by the time they entered the battlefield it was too late. They dropped dead by the dozens, not knowing the flowers covered in their species' blood was the same flower toxic enough to kill them through airborne contact.

The sons of Dagon exiled themselves, marching to the outermost corners of the earth to evade capture by the Undead. The historic phenomenon became famously known as the Walk of Wolves, Lundis taught me. Before Sylvian was born and called the wolves back from exile, uniting them under his cause, they spent many years hiding in darkness, slaves to the beasts within.

I pack the wolfsbane tightly into the pipe and light a match. I breathe the fire into the open end of the pipe, watching the white buds succumb to the flames. Smoke billows up the mouth of the pipe and enters my throat. I inhale deeply, holding back a cough that builds at the bottom of my lungs. The fragrant smoke burns terribly along my throat. My head gets light. My vision gets blurry. My body feels weightless. The world spins around me. I bring the pipe back to my mouth and inhale once more. I can no longer move, paralyzed by the toxin's trance. My senses become dull. My skin itches horribly, then burns, then becomes consumed by chills. I feel the smoke cloud inside my skull. It feels as though a fire burns under my brain. If this is what death feels like, I welcome it gladly.

I lay back against the raft and close my eyes. The raft bobs up and down along the delta. I silently thank the gods for the dead bodies that hold us afloat. Their sacrifice was not in vain, for they will carry us to Sygon to finish what they started. I fall asleep to the sound of water lapping against the raft's sides and Creon's grunts as he fights against the tides with his makeshift oars. By the time I wake, we will be in the Tyber. I must gather my strength. When the sun sets next, there will be no telling when I'll be able to sleep again.

41

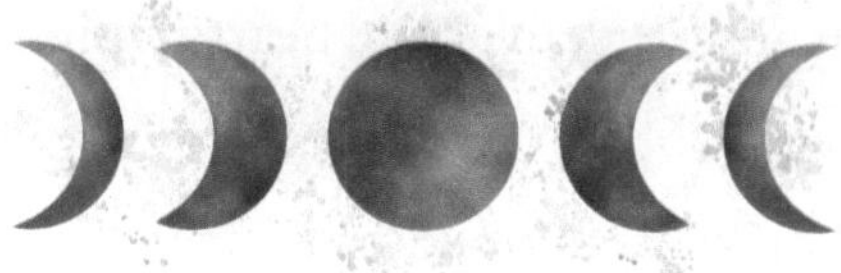

A Dream

I tuck Sephora in with the knitted blanket. Vesper made it herself in the hours of daylight she doesn't sleep. There isn't much for her to do while she waits the day away, so she knits and cooks and studies subjects with Sephora. I never understood the concept of a knitted blanket. It is covered with a million holes in the space between stitches. The elastic yarn itself is warm but leaves plenty of room for cold air to penetrate the blanket.

Good thing Vesper has knitted more than one. I grab a second blanket and place it on top of Sephora. Winter nights are merciless. Without proper warmth, people die in temperatures like these. It doesn't help that the little insulation our hut has seems to be ineffective. The clay walls seem to let in the cold like immigrants into a wall-less kingdom. But it is only temporary.

We move lodging with every few moons, never getting comfortable enough in a town to stay a whole season. Threats are everywhere we go, and people are always nosy about our past. Go to a big city and guards will soon catch suspicion. Go to a small town and it's the townspeople that will give you queer looks and refuse to assimilate to your arrival.

Regardless of where we go, the only work I am offered is barely enough to feed a single stomach, let alone three. Vesper hunts wild game in the night to satisfy her bloodlust, but Sephora and I must live off a human's diet. We require meat and vegetables and hearty fruit. Dairy and bread and starchy potatoes.

The few coppers I make from building and farming and cutting lumber aren't enough to feed us, but Vesper brings home the game she kills so we rarely go to bed with an empty stomach. Being raised in a castle, the past decade of my life has taught me how the other side lives. Chefs used to cook three meals a day for us and cater to our room if we were too busy to join a party in the dining hall. As a child, I did not question where the food came from or how much it cost or how long it took to prepare. I greedily ate without questioning how little others had to eat or how many people died annually from starvation.

Sephora's childhood is the opposite of my own.

She knows nothing of the luxurious lifestyle I was raised in.

And though she knows she comes from the Sylvian bloodline and I've told her of our past reign before the Undead Empire, her childish mind cannot fathom what it was like living in the Areopagus's castle. All she can do is let her imagination run wild and ask me childish questions as she contemplates a life as a princess.

As her father, I try to set realistic expectations for her. Although I tell her stories of the past, I try to make sure she understands we will never return to the throne. I let her have her optimism, but at the end of the day I know none of us will ever wear a crown. The only life left for us is one hopping from town to town, avoiding any attention we can in order to fly under the radar. The only reason I'm still alive is because I've mastered the art of hiding in plain sight. It has been many years since the Undead Emperor's soldiers have come searching for me. The Undead Empire has given up wasting time and resources on hunting a fallen prince. Their efforts have been focused on asserting control over the rest of the kingdom. Fine by me. The sooner they forget I exist the easier it will be to live in peace.

I walk away from Sephora after tightly tucking the blankets around her tiny body. The cot she sleeps in is barely big enough to accommodate a toddler of her size. It is so small that if she were to roll over in the middle of the night, I fear she would fall off completely. But it will do for a few more months. When we move again, I will look to build her a bigger one. That is the problem with children her age. By the time you finish building a bigger bed, they've already outgrown the one you just built. Sephora has grown like a weed the past year, and it will only get worse from here.

"Daddy," she calls out to me. I turn to her, watching as she clings tightly to the stuffed thyrops I gave her as a baby. It's humorous to me how us humans take such dangerous animals and turn them to harmless stuffed creatures fit for a baby in a cradle. The amount of times I've heard of a thyrops mauling an innocent bystander to death with its horn is incalculable, yet Sephora clings to the stitched plush like it is her best friend.

"Yes, Seph?"

"Can you tell me the story of Sylvian again?" she whispers, smiling through the darkness. I look down at the flickering candle in my hand as a wave of déjà vu washes over me. How many years has it been since I pleaded with my own father to tell me the same story?

"I beg you, father, tell us the story of Dagon and Damon!" I cry.

"Please, father!" Selena echoes.

The man laughs stoically. He's denied this request dozens of times by now, but he finds our persistence to be comical. "You already know my answer to that, children. You aren't old enough. The story will give you nightmares."

It's the same response he's given us for years.

"Can't you just skip over the scary parts?" Selena begs. I don't agree with her logic. Half the reason why I want to know the story in the first place is so I can hear the scary parts. But beggars can't be choosers, so I will take what I can get.

"My father made me wait to hear that story until I was twice as old as you are now. Besides, it is too scary. It will give you nightmares. How about I tell you another story? I can tell you the one about the fox and the chicken again? Or a new one? Perhaps you'd like to hear the tale of the field mouse and the lion?"

"I don't want to hear more kiddie stories!" she exclaims. "I want to hear how Sylvian conquered Damon and Dagon! I won't get scared, I promise I won't!"

I look at her from the doorway, as my father once looked at me. I spent the better part of several months trying to get my dad to tell me the story of Sylvian. He always refused, trying to preserve my innocence and hide the horrifying truths of life from me. He thought he was doing me a service by sparing me from the gory details of real life. I asked him every night to tell me the story of Sylvian the First, and Silenius Sylvian died before getting around to tell the full story. I've since learned tomorrow is not promised.

I can die any day, living a life on the run.

I won't treat Sephora like my father treated me.

I won't do her the disservice of hiding the evil of the world from her.

Because tomorrow is not promised, and I don't want to leave her behind to be shocked by what our ancestor did to gain the throne eons ago.

Because my father died without telling me the truth about Sylvian, I was forced to hear it secondhand from others. As I stare at Sephora's innocent face lying comfortably in bed, I know deep down I want her to hear the story from me, not someone else should I pass on from this life. It's true, she is likely too young to hear about Sylvian's rise to power and the genocide he caused to claim the throne, but if I refuse to tell her tonight, I may never get around to telling her the truth.

I will tell her, and unlike my father, I won't skip over the scary parts.

This world is a cold, miserable place.

I need Sephora to be prepared to face it.

"Where did we leave off when I told you about Damon and Dagon?" I ask, my voice low so Vesper does not hear me.

Sephora scrambles to sit upright in bed, clinging to her thyrops tight, excitement in her eyes. "Luna and Solis created Sylvian the First during their third eclipse! You said they created him to best the Creator, who cursed Damon and Dagon, said Sylvian's powers cancelled out their curses so he could both walk in the daylight and control the beast!" she whispers eagerly. I return to her bedside and set the candle down on the dresser beside her. I take a seat next to her and kiss her forehead.

"I will tell you, but you can't tell mom, okay? Do we have a deal?"

Sephora nods quietly. I can tell from the look in her eye that she didn't think I would give into her demands so easily.

"Okay, where should I start?" I think to myself, scanning my memory to tell the story in as succinct a manner possible. "Well, as you know, Damon and Dagon wreaked havoc along the face of the earth. They infected others with their curses and multiplied their offspring in order to conquer the globe. Damon and Dagon turned against one another, realizing only one of them could hold a position of power, since neither of them was willing to submit themselves to the other. From Damon came the Undead, who despised Dagon's Lycan breed for their inability to control the beast within. The Undead consider Lycans to be the most sinful creation on all the earth. To the Undead, a Lycan's inability to control their beast makes them an abomination in the eyes of the Creator. To the Lycans, an

Undead's unwillingness to set limits on their bloodlust is the highest form of treachery a creature can commit. The two species stood at odds with one another, and each species sought to destroy the other.

"Now, the Undead had the advantage of the two. Undead can call on their supernatural powers at any time, while Dagon and his disciples could only shift to their wolfish form when the moon was full. And even when they could draw from their powers, the Lycans had no means of controlling the chaos their beastly forms craved. There was no unity in their movements. They were just as likely to attack one another for hierarchical power as they were to go after the Undead. Because of this, the Lycans would attack the Undead during the day while they slept, and the Undead would barrage the Lycans on all nights the moon wasn't full. Humanity often got caught in the crossfire between the two species, and many died for many years in a struggle for power over the globe.

"The war became known to historians as the War of Flesh and Fang, and hundreds of thousands died before Sylvian came of age to take control. Sylvian the First was born into the thick of it, and grew up watching the atrocities Damon and Dagon committed to gain power over the realm. But unlike Damon, Sylvian could walk in the light of day. And unlike Dagon, he could call on the beast's powers any given night, not just when the moon was full. Sylvian spent the first eighteen years of his life learning how to control his powers. His existence was unknown to Damon and Dagon. Like your father, Sephora, Sylvian was raised by detached, exiled tribes of Undead and Lycan alike, drawing from their wisdom to learn how to turn the curses into strengths. Sylvian walked with the wolves and followed the Undead, traversing the entire globe in search of answers."

Sephora interrupts, as I did when I was a child, "How did he get his silver eyes, daddy? Why don't we have our silver eyes yet, if we are Sylvian?"

I wish I had an answer for her. I've spent my whole life asking the same question. I am twenty-five-years-old and have still been unable to access the powers Sylvian the First called upon. The curse of Dagon claimed me as a boy before the curse of Damon could, so I've fallen prey to every full moon since I was ten-years-old. Father told me as a boy that either curse claims a Sylvian's body depending what the Fates see fit, and they are forced to deal with a single curse until they unlock the powers of Sylvian. It was a flip of the coin chance for me to age into an Undead as it was for me to turn Lycan. It was merely coincidental that Dagon took possession of my body before Damon could, and so I've dealt with the beast within my entire life, praying for the day when I am gifted the ability to control the monster that dwells within me.

"The powers come at a different time for every Sylvian," I tell her, repeating what my father once told me. "For my father, your grandfather, he received the powers at a young age. For me, the gods have not seen me as fit to wield the powers of the Sylvian name as of yet. And I am just as in the dark on when I will be instilled with them as you are."

"Will I have to wait as long as you have, dad?"

God I hope not, I think to myself. Neither Dagon's Curse nor Damon's has laid claim to Sephora's body yet. She is still an innocent human, and I pray she will remain that way for as long as possible. If I got to choose for her, I'd hope she is claimed by Damon's Curse. At least then Vesper will be able to raise her as Undead until she receives Sylvian's power. If Dagon seizes hold of her first, though, there will be little I can do as a teacher to help her control the beast within.

"There's no way to tell, sweetheart," I answer, not wanting to give her a sense of false hope. The greatest disservice I could do would be to tell her she will receive Sylvian's powers sooner than I have, that way she doesn't spend her life dealing with the frustrations I have. I add, "But whatever time the powers come to you will be the right time. The Fates have a way of crafting the perfect timing in all things." I wish I could believe those words myself, but hopefully Sephora believes them.

"But regardless of which curse claims you first, your mother and I will be able to help you adapt to your new abilities. Don't worry about it, baby," I whisper comfortingly, rubbing the back of her hand. I backpedal, "Now, back to Sylvian..."

"Yes, what happened next daddy!" Her mind suddenly forgets about the uncertainty of our powers and becomes engrossed in the story once more.

"The War of Flesh and Fang raged on for many years, but by the time Sylvian the First was old enough to take action, Dagon and his Lycans had initially exiled themselves into the Neverglade Forest and the surrounding foothills of the Thoren Mountains. But after some time, the tribes of Dagon's descendants became fractured and spread across the globe, distancing themselves in different regions because of the animosity they held toward one another. Now—"

"Daddy, what does animosity mean?" Sephora interrupts.

I laugh at myself, realizing I've become so caught up in this story that I've forgotten I'm speaking to a child. "It means they hated each other, Seph."

"Why did they hate each other? They needed to rely on each other if they wanted to win the war against the Undead!" she squeals, waving her thyrops around.

"But it is hard to stay united with one another when their beasts sowed discord amongst themselves every full moon."

"What does discord mean?"

I sigh inwardly. When Vesper told me she was pregnant, I had no idea the hardest part of being a father would be learning how to talk like a child again. You would think I would have learned to dumb myself down in the five years Sephora has been alive, but instead I've taught her to catch up with me. Her mother is responsible for teaching her math and sciences, but language and history lessons come from her father.

"It means conflict between two groups. Disunion is another way to say it," I add. "So because of their beasts within, they were constantly fighting with one another, and because of the fighting, they broke into separate tribes. Some wolves traveled to the arctic, others went off to the desert. Some remained in the Neverglades, and some took a chance at city life, though living in populous areas presents another danger altogether.

"When Sylvian turned eighteen, he inserted himself into Damon's armies inconspicuously—that means secretly—and used his powers to hide his Lycan side. He tricked the Undead into thinking he was one of them. He avoided the daylight, concealed his silver eyes, and consumed blood like the rest of them. He marched with them, trained with them, and quickly rose in their ranks as they witnessed his abilities. Within a few years, Sylvian became Damon's right hand man, and Damon gave his firstborn daughter to Sylvian to take as his wife. Sylvian became Damon's closest confidant, and he revealed to Sylvian his plans to put an end to Dagon's Lycans once and for all.

"But Sylvian the First had other plans. He knew that the only way to save the Lycan race was to put an end to Damon and Dagon and assume the throne himself, uniting both species to coexist peacefully. So in secret, Sylvian began traveling to the farthest corners of the globe to meet with the Lycan chiefs, hiding his amethyst eyes to show the Lycans he was one of them. He earned each of their trust, and asked for their alliance in a plot to usurp Damon's control over the kingdoms. His journey brought him to the Neverglades, and he challenged Dagon himself for an audience. The two fought under the full moon for an audience of thousands. To this day, it is known as the Blood Moon, because Luna herself bled the night she watched her two children fight to the death. The Lycans fought ferociously all night long. It is said the gnashing of their teeth could be heard all throughout the world, and their yelps of pain caused the moon to turn red in the sky. But both warriors were too skilled to best one another, and neither could serve the killing blow on the other. Their moondance stretched until dawn, and when Solis rose the following day, the two shifted back to their human appearance, both of them gravely injured from their beastly forms hashing it out all night.

"The fight ended with Dagon embracing Sylvian in a brotherly hug, their bleeding bodies collapsing in exhaustion. Sylvian the First had earned Dagon's admiration by his abilities, and because of this, he gave his firstborn daughter to Sylvian to take as his wife."

"But you said Sylvian was already married to Damon's daughter!" Sephora cries.

"He was, but Dagon did not know Sylvian was working for Damon, so he accepted Dagon's daughter as a symbol of their alliance."

"But wasn't he technically an uncle to both of these girls?"

"Times were different in those days, Sephora. You did not marry for love. You married as a sign of status, and Sylvian took both of his wives as a strategic advantage to earn Dagon and Damon's trust."

"Did you marry mom for status?" Sephora asks innocently. I laugh at the question. Oh what I would give to be five-years-old again.

"No, I married your mother for love, and whoever I allow to marry you will be only if you love them in return," I answer, rubbing the back of her hand again. "But like I said, Sylvian wanted to unify the Undead and the Lycans, so accepting wives from both of these clans was a pivotal moment for making progress in the right direction. So he took Dagon's daughter to be his second wife, and quickly became Dagon's closest confidant, like he had to Damon. Dagon had no idea Sylvian was actually his youngest brother, and he had no idea Sylvian planned to betray him. And so, using

Dagon's trust against him, Sylvian plotted with Dagon to usurp Damon from his throne at Cardone, the central kingdom in the middle of all other kingdoms. The two knew they needed to control this throne if they were to bring the Lycan race back to its former glory. For whoever controls Cardone controls the entire world. It was the place Damon himself had taken as a place for his throne.

"It is said the sun itself stood still in the sky for Sylvian and Dagon as they made their march toward the city, and Sylvian's howl called forth the exiled Lycan tribes from across the globe. And by the time they arrived, Solis refused to set, knowing what needed to be done. The sun stood still as Lycans invaded Cardone from all directions. The Undead were helpless to leave their castles to defend themselves.

"When Damon watched Sylvian walking by Dagon's side from his throne room window, he knew the end had come. The moon and the sun hung in the sky for the duration of the war, observing from opposite sides of the horizon. Luna's appearance in the sky allowed the Lycans the ability to shift freely while fighting in full daylight. Damon and Dagon were pitted against one another while the Lycans and Undead wreaked havoc within the city's many castles.

"It was the first time the brothers had faced one another since the Walk of Wolves, and not even the Creator himself could prevent the death tolled in their battle with one another. But the Creator smiled to see Luna and Solis punished for their adultery as their children of the eclipse sent one another to their deaths. Sylvian and his two wives watched from the outskirts of Cardone as the city was diminished to rubble in the two days it took for the battle to commence. His wives pleaded for him to intervene and spare their fathers' lives, but Sylvian distracted them by commencing in an—" I pause mid-speech. The next part is not appropriate for a five-year-old to hear. I cannot tell Sephora what a threesome is, nor do I want to explain what sex is to her at this young age.

"Sylvian got both of his wives pregnant, to ensure he would have children to succeed him whenever he died. By the time they were pregnant, the war was over, and Cardone was Sylvian's to control. It is said Dagon and Damon both died in each other's arms, the same way they had been born as twin protectors of the eclipse. And when they died, their armies were leaderless, and the fighting ceased. Sylvian was able to march right into the destroyed city and take it as his own, declaring he was next in line to rule the throne on both sides of the battle. The Lycans and Undead bowed before his leadership and submitted themselves to his authority, finally forced to be at peace with one another. And that, my daughter, is the story of how Sylvian single-handedly took control of the kingdom."

She stares at me with awe in her eyes, not fear. I wish silently I could have shared this moment with my own father. Though there are a million different ways I've heard the story told over the years, this is the version I've accepted as truth. Now it is up to Sephora to pick and choose what she believes to be historically accurate.

"Dad?" she asks quietly.

"Yes?"

"If Sylvian got both of his wives pregnant, which wife do me and you come from?"

It's funny how similar we think, since that was one of the first questions that came to my mind the first time I heard the story. "Well, your grandfather once told me our lineage can be traced back to Stoic Sylvian, who traced his origin back to Sylvian the First. I pulled the histories myself before you were born, and Stoic's notes indicate we descended from Sylvian's first wife, Damon's daughter."

"Then what about his second wife? Is there a separate family out there just like us?"

"I doubt it, Seph. The histories don't tell what happened to Dagon's firstborn daughter, and if they do, no one has discovered record of it. Dagon's line probably died out at some point down the line. I wouldn't worry about it, though. If there were other Sylvians out there, we would know about it."

"But what if they have hidden themselves like you have?"

"Okay, it's obviously time for bed, you curious Cathy. If I sit here and answer all your questions we will be up all night," I say, retrieving my candle from her bedside once more. I lean down and give her forehead a kiss, then retreat from her room once more.

"Daddy?" she calls after me.

"Yes, sweetheart?"

"I love you," she whispers.

I turn to face her, my candlelight just strong enough to reach her beautiful face. She is the light of my world, one of the only things I am proud of in this life. "I love you too, Sephora." I wish I could live in this moment forever. I wish the sun and the moon would pause in the sky for me like they did for Sylvian the First so I never have to leave this memory. But time waits for no man, and like my father before me, I leave Sephora to her dreams, and I will be left to my nightmares.

42

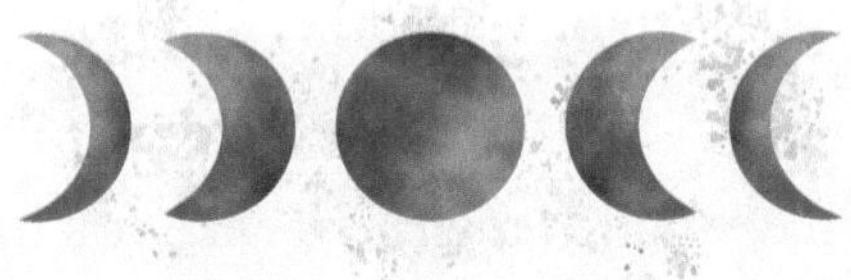

A NIGHTMARE

Reality distends as I come down from my high.

The only time I'm truly happy is when I'm alive in memories of the past with Sephora and Vesper in my life.

It takes a few minutes for me to register where I am in real time. I rub my temples to massage the migraine that builds behind my eyes. Coming down from a wolfsbane high is never pleasant. After all, I have just poisoned my body. My muscles ache, my chest burns, my head pounds, my lungs wheeze. But I will be made stronger for inhaling the wolfsbane bud.

And who knows, maybe now that I have unlocked the Sylvian powers, one day I will no longer need to microdose to save myself from dying. Perhaps like my recent affinity from silver, wolfsbane will soon have no effect.

The sun is setting. Luna stretches in the distance. Crixus rows the raft now, and I'm amazed to see we are still perfectly afloat. I half suspected the rapids of the Tyber would have washed over us and drowned us in the riptide. From what I can tell, we are now past the roughest waters of the Tyber and passively embraced by the estuary of Lake Askamyre. I have slept through the entire journey, though I doubt I've missed much.

"Sleeping beauty, good to see you," Creon calls after me. "We saved you some food. Freshwater bass. You should have seen Crixus catch it. Snatched it from the water with her bare hands! Now that's what I call a woman!"

I swivel my drug-laced body to face my two companions, seeing the spread of butchered, raw fish before me. My stomach does somersaults at the sight of food. Crixus looks over her shoulder to see me awake, flashing a quick smile before returning to her rowing. The oars look like they've held up for the most part.

Without a word, I grab hold of the raw fish and bring it to my mouth, ripping chunks of flesh from its carcass. Its meat is chewy and filled with water. When was the last time I had something to eat? I remember drinking bone broth and crackers before Gall, and Crixus gave me a chunk of bread and hunk of dehydrated venison jerky on our trip to Queensmyre. Regardless, my body accepts this food like it is the first thing it's eaten in years.

The fish's juices run down my chin, hydrating my cracked, parted lips. I put my face into the fish like a child cleaning a rind of watermelon or cobb of corn. I close my eyes and move the fish left to right, then right to left, my teeth going to work to clean it of all remaining meat. By the time I'm done with it, not even the fish's organs will remain. I'll eat all that isn't bone, even the eyes, and even when I feel the crunch of bone in my mouth I don't slow my progress to spit.

My hunger grows the more I eat. I accidentally bite my own fingers several times throughout the frenzy. I am like a virgin fucking for the first time. My hands shake violently with excitement. I lose sight of what I'm doing. Reason goes out the window. I am a bottomless pit. A void capable of consuming every fish this estuary has to offer without satisfaction.

The food is gone all too soon, and I'm left feeling hungrier than I was when I woke. I lock eyes with Crixus. She stares at me sympathetically. I'm sure I look like a deranged lunatic at this point in the journey. My flesh is covered in mud and blood and ash, and in the places it is exposed it is seared by the fire from Queensmyre. My hair and beard are matted like a barbarian. Not even the sharpest sword in all the kingdom could cut through the mess I've become to reveal the prince beneath.

Without another word spoken, I leap into the Tyber's fresh waters. The raft is floating lazily at this point. I have no concern about losing it from my sight. Everything should be smooth sailing until we reach Lake Askamyre.

The water washes over me. At first, it stings like hell in all the spots I've been burned. The flesh is likely fighting a million and one infections at the moment, so I grit my teeth tightly and let the water's bacteria join in on the fun. Fresh minerals will do the wounds some good. I remain motionless for the better part of a minute, eyes closed. I can see the waning sunlight pierce the water's surface through my eyelids. It feels so peaceful to float in complete bliss. After a short while, the pain of my wounds dulls to a low throb.

I wonder briefly if this is what death feels like, and silently hope for my family's sake it is. Selena deserves eternal peace. Anything but the constant suffering of living. I hope they cannot see me, wherever they are. I don't want them feeling sorrow over my afflictions. But then again, I hope whenever I die, I am able to keep tabs on Sephora. It's a selfish wish, but there's no knowing what death is like until I meet it head-on.

I can feel my lungs aching as the oxygen evaporates from my mouth in the form of beautiful bubbles. I force them to wait a little longer. They have already endured the smoke of a burning city, there is no reason they cannot allow me to lay in peace a moment longer. If we got to choose our own death in life, I would choose this moment. Right here, right now. Take me before the pain becomes too great to bear. Reunite me and Sephora with Vesper in paradise.

I can picture the scene now on the inside of my eyelids. All three of us hugging for the first time in over twenty-four moons. My tears dripping from my cheek onto their resurrected faces. All three of our bodies floating peacefully in the tranquil waters. My eyelids slowly turn white as light beams on my face. I am submerged in water, but I don't have the energy to return to the surface. I want the river's algae to drag me down to the cold, dark depths. I want the fish to feed on my flesh and organs like I just did theirs, a mutual end to the circle of life.

A hand smacks my face, ripping me out of my afterlife delusion. The force from the blow drives the remaining oxygen out of my mouth and stirs enough bubbles to blur my vision. I return to the surface, gasping for new life. The air feels good on my drenched face. A calm breeze washes over the back of my neck. Water drips from my bushy eyebrows like a waterfall. I wipe the droplets away so I can see.

Creon stands on the raft looking down at me with amusement. He's pointing at something below me in the water. "I told her now was a better time than ever to learn how to swim," Creon calls. "But I didn't know she would sink like a knight in full armor." He laughs while I panic. Crixus jumped in after me knowing fully well she cannot swim.

I throw myself back down into the water to find her. She is a half dozen yards beneath me already. Dagon's sake, she sinks like there is an anchor wrapped around her ankle. I have never seen someone defy physics as she currently does. I don't think I could sink as fast as she does if I purposely tried.

I dive into the depths after her, chasing the trail of bubbles her mouth leaves for me to follow. The image of a woman sinking in quicksand flashes in my mind. The feeling of a taut rope snapping in my arms. Watching her corpse disappear beneath the surface.

Watching a mother call out in the night as her baby burns in a fire I started. My idle feet with no intention to come to her aid. Crixus seeing the injustice in the situation and springing into action before the thought has time to cross my mind.

Lockjaw's body going lifeless after I pull the silver arrow from her.

The dead man's body in my prison cell.

Sephora's snapped neck.

Vesper's mutilated body.

Mom's decapitated neck.

Dad's final stand.

Selena's untapped potential.

Dagger in my back.

No more.

I grab hold of Crixus's flailing hand tighter than Solis grabbing Luna the night of an eclipse. All momentum of her descent to the river floor ceases as my body refuses to let the depths steal her from me. I kick against the current like a bull in a rodeo. The Creator has taken everything from me, I won't let him have Crixus. She is mine, I think selfishly. Not even the fates could pry her from my hands.

I rip her violently into the open air and grab hold of the raft. She doesn't breathe or move. The water has likely invaded her lungs. I need to act fast. The reaper seeks to claim her soul, but he will need to deal with me first. I pull Crixus onto the raft and instantly begin compressions on her sternum. I tilt her head back to clear her airway and lower my lips to hers, blowing air into her lungs in an attempt to purge the water from her system. Her lips on my own is like lightning coursing through my body.

The only thing holding back arousal is the urgency-driven adrenaline. Her mouth tastes like home after a long voyage. Their supple texture pulls me in for more. Suddenly, it is me who can't breathe, my body unfamiliar with this feeling of entrapment. Her lips are like a warm funeral pyre and I am her corpse. I can't pull away. Water surges up her throat and her body suddenly seizes. The water shoots into my mouth and I swallow it gratefully, enchanted by the fact that it has been in her body previously.

I wrap my hands around her back and neck as she coughs violently. I don't remove my lips from hers for a second. I let her cough into my mouth. Her resurrected eyes look into mine with intensity as she fights for air. But her hands don't push me off her. They wrap around my head as she inserts her tongue into my mouth. Her eyes devour mine with their ferocity. I feel her hips press themselves into mine. I push back, my hardened member pressing into the space between her legs. Our clothes hold us back, but that doesn't stop us from pulsing our waists into each other.

I bite her tongue and she spits in my mouth. I swallow her gift sanctimoniously. I feel her claws dig into my neck and it drives me crazy. It has been many moons since I've felt the touch of a woman. I want to rip her clothes off and go into her hard enough to break the raft beneath us. I want to pummel into her until she screams she can take no more. I want the warmth between her legs to fill the void in my heart. I want to lay on my back and watch her mount my hips until I twitch with pleasure. She is a feral wolf and I want her to unleash her savagery on me until she is domesticated. I want—

"Dagon's sake, I'm literally right here!" Creon shouts, breaking me from my trance. We both look up at him with embarrassed grins, water dripping from our bodies like shipwrecked pirates. I clear my throat and remove myself from Crixus's body, sitting on the opposite side of the raft. I can't stand without unveiling my hardness, so I sit quietly while the two of us catch our breath. We both avoid each other's eye contact. We are a slave to our own unfinished business, both hungry for each other like rabid rabbits.

Creon laughs at our awkward dispositions, then continues, "Perhaps you can fuck each other *after* we've conquered Sygon. I hear there are plenty of private rooms there. Hmm? Capeesh?"

I clear my throat once more and do my best to erase the lust from my mind, but there is no suppressing the feelings I hold for the she-wolf. "And why, exactly, did you think now was a good opportunity to learn how to swim?" I ask, turning to Crixus.

She smiles at me infectiously, "You made it look much easier than it was."

"It is remarkably easy for those of us who don't have the density of a rock," I joke, wiping the water from my eyes. The water has washed the layers of mud and ash from my face. I slick my hair back from my eyes, my bangs long enough to hold onto the back of my ears.

"Maybe when this is all over you can teach me in a more appropriate setting?" she jokes back.

"Oh brother," Creon groans, sensing her flirtatious tone. "Let me grab the oars again so I can get myself out of here faster."

Creon turns his back toward us and resumes paddling, leaving the two of us to stare at each other from a distance. I can still feel her claws in my neck. My fingers still remember the feeling of her body in my arms. My tongue still burns with her saliva. My hips yearn for hers. And as I stare into her eyes, I sense she won't be forgetting this feeling until we have time to finish what we started.

43

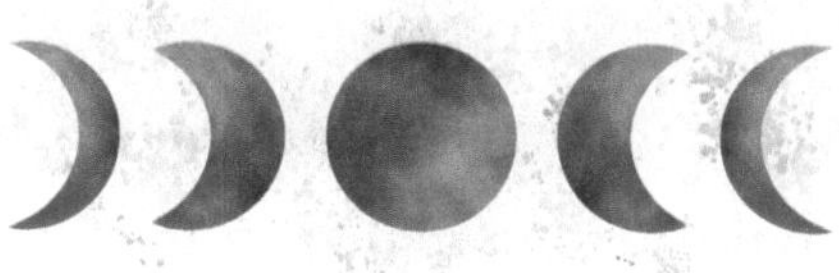

A Nightmare

I have never seen Lake Askamyre in real life. The rising sun of a new day illuminates the captivating landscape. I have been many places in this world, but views like this never get old.

Though father has taken me to Sygon before, back when we originally journeyed to Queensmyre, Askamyre has too awkward a geography to visit for mere pleasure. However, its beauty is renowned for those who take it upon themselves to visit. Askamyre is the connecting body of water between the Pagean's overflow and the estuaries flowing from the Dead Sea.

As we approach its wide mouth, I stare in awe at the cascading waterfall that shatters the still waters like glass under a hammer. The green saltwater of the coastal ocean clashes with the blue freshwater from the Pagean. They swirl around each other like yin and yang in the middle of the lake, separated like oil and water mixed in a dish.

Now that I've laid eyes on Askamyre, I can see why few have journeyed to visit its beauty. The surrounding landscape is inhospitable. Around the water's edge is red-rimmed water covered in salty crust. Lundis taught me about the phenomena. Salt-loving bacteria known as medusian flow into the lake from the ocean's waterfall. They sit stagnant in Askamyre, feeding off the Dead Sea's constant stream of saltwater. When accumulated in such large potency without natural predators, the bacteria cause the water to glow red as lava.

They cause the alkalinity of the lake to become extreme. The surrounding air reeks of ammonia, and it is said the waters are dangerous enough to turn flesh to stone. Though I'd never believe such a thing without proof, Lundis once explained that the theoretical science behind it was that medusian create a scaling effect once exposed to flesh. They burrow into the skin, feeding off its salt, and enter the bloodstream, feeding off a body's sodium until the human turns to calcified rock. Most travelers steer clear of Askamyre for that reason alone. That is what gives us the strategic advantage. The Acolytes and Undead will not bother us here, day or night.

There are enough superstitions surrounding Askamyre to keep it as vacant as Cardone. Though few have risked it to see the beautiful clash of nature, the reward of seeing the red waters that surround the blues and greens of the Dead Sea and Pagean are not enough for most to put their life on the line.

The salty crust cracks as our raft enters the lake. The smell of ammonia is nearly too much to bear. It stings at my senses as we become surrounded by the lava-like waters. The white crust breaks before our voyage and we leave a trail of crimson behind us like a snail whose slime is red. It is truly the strangest enigma I have ever seen in nature, and I have traveled all over the world.

Crixus bends over to naively touch the red waters. I lunge after her and pull her away from the side of the raft, thankful for any excuse I can find to touch her skin once more. She jumps in surprise as I yank her away from the water.

"Don't," I command. "It will turn you to stone."

She laughs at my warning, then slowly becomes serious as she sees my lack of humor. She looks over my shoulder at Creon, searching for someone to contradict what I've said.

"Allegedly," Creon adds to my sentence, shrugging his shoulders. "But I'm not going to be the bloke who tests that theory out."

She looks back at me and nods her head. I can tell she doesn't understand how water could do that. I am not a good enough teacher to explain it, so I won't try. All I have to go off of is Lundis's word, and I can barely remember the lesson from childhood. Regardless, it is best not to risk it.

"They say it burns your skin and eyes, then turns your flesh to stone," I elaborate.

"The further we go, the more I realize how little I know about the world," Crixus mumbles to herself.

"That's kind of the point," I laugh. "At the end of the day, we are only ants."

When I turn to face Creon, I see he is now standing at the edge of the raft peering over the edge. Panicked, he shouts, "We have a problem!"

"What now," I groan, staring at Creon.

"The rumors are true," Creon shouts, standing and looking around for an avenue of escape. "These waters turn flesh to stone!" He quickly grabs the oars and paddles furiously toward the nearest bank.

"We are safe up here Creon, what is the problem?"

"Moron! The she-wolf put the raft's platform on human bodies! They turn into rock at this very moment! We are sinking!"

Dagon's sake, I curse. I completely forgot the reason we are able to float. The bundles of humans that hold the raft above water are subject to the water's calcification. Soon they will lose their buoyancy and turn to rock. When that happens, the raft will sink, and we will go with it. I look over the edge as Creon mantically rows the raft. I see the chemical reaction the water has on the corpses that carry us. Bubbles fizz as bacteria consume any salt the bodies have left to give. I notice now that the water has risen along the side of the raft. We have already sunk a few inches, and there is no telling how long we have before we are submerged completely.

I look to Askamyre's coast and my stomach drops. It is a quarter mile away. We won't make it. And even if Creon and I can swim to safety before our bodies are consumed by medusian, Crixus will sink to the lake's floor and never be seen again.

This journey could not be any more imperfect if we tried. It feels like every turn we take is filled with more unanticipated perils than we can comprehend. Just when I feel comfortable and relaxed, my mind is faced with solving another life-threatening dilemma.

How could I be so stupid to let us travel into Askamyre's waters?

We should have docked on the Tyber's riverside banks hours ago and hiked the remaining difference. Part of my decision to boat in was sheer ignorance. I never believed the rumors about Askamyre's lethal properties. It didn't make sense for there to be a bacteria capable of turning the human body to stone. Even Lundis greatly disbelieved in such a thing when he taught me the lesson. After all, I visited Cardone as a child, and the rumors of it being possessed by ghosts and demons simply wasn't true.

But as I watch our raft sink rapidly as the bodies that hold us afloat turn to rocky anchors, I realize I have put all three of our lives on the line because of stubbornness. Why hike when we could boat? My thought process seemed simple. Keep us off our feet longer so we can continue to rest. Let the water go to work in our favor.

I am an idiot for putting us in senseless danger. We have come all this way to die on the doorstep of Sygon. We have done the impossible. Traversed Gall, Queensmyre, Yueltope, and everything in between, for nothing! I want to scream. I want to—

Fly, a voice whispers to me in a low growl, cutting off my raging inner monologue.

What? I don't know how to.

You've done so once before. Do it again, or we will all die.

It isn't that easy, beast. I don't know how to control these powers.

Now seems a better time to learn than any other. The water now laps over the edges of the raft. I can hear Creon grunting with exhaustion with every row of the oars. Crixus simply stares at the waters with silent fear. She remembers the feeling of drowning. The pull of the riptide. The inability to swim to safety.

Close your eyes, Sylvian.

I can feel the water touching my bare toes and heels as I let the threat of dying drive me to dialed focus. I close my eyes and feel something shift inside. It is as if I remember a part of myself that has been available to me this entire time. A sense of power and confidence washes over me that makes me wonder why I ever panicked in the first place. The stress I felt moments ago melts away. Gods don't die from pathetic bacteria. Gods walk on water, they part it down the middle, they bend it to their will. Gods do not drown. Gods fly.

I can feel my eyeballs warm as a light comes over them I cannot control. I look down at the water that pools around my feet and see only the glimmer of silver from my eyes staring back in my reflection. The gleaming light turns the salty red waters around us to silver. Creon notices the light in the waters around him and looks over his shoulder at me.

"Oh hell yes," he sighs with relief, dropping the oars from his hands. The look of fear melts from Crixus's face. After a life spent letting people down who needed saving, it feels weird to see people thank the gods for my presence alone. I can no longer remember my past faults. Gods do not dwell on their previous mortal sins. Gods make deals with their demons so they can continue to live in the light.

I feel my feet lift from the water below me. The raft no longer supports my weight as it capsizes. The air bends to my will. It carries me without me needing to think. Moments ago, I had no idea how to fly. Now it feels as instinctual to me as breathing and walking. It feels as though I have been able to fly my entire life, as if I have been able to carry my weight through the atmosphere since I was a toddler taking my first steps.

I see now why the Undead view themselves as superior to humanity. As I stare at Creon and Crixus clinging to the sinking vessel helplessly below me, unable to save themselves from their afflictions, I feel as the Undead do. Humans and Lycans cannot do what I can. The Undead see them as inferior because they are inferior. Even if they possessed the ability to access the beast within, such a power would be useless in a situation like this. But to make matters worse, they have no control over their beastly instincts. They are prey to their inner demons. I watch them raise their hands in the air for me to grab hold of, and for a moment, I can't remember why I need their support in the first place.

Gods do not need mortals to aid in their affairs.

In this condition, I am perfectly capable of taking Sygon myself.

I no longer feel lust for Crixus.

I no longer feel loyalty for Creon.

They are chains holding me back from my true potential.

I am a Sylvian.

I am a God.

I can watch Crixus drown from this position.

I can watch Creon turn to stone as he swims toward Askamyre's shore.

I am under no obligation to save them.

I don't need them.

Moreover, I don't need my daughter. In this state, Sephora means nothing to me. Is this how Ventur feels? Is this why it was so easy for him to betray my father? Did he feel any grief at all at the news his son Bane was dead?

I can't remember why I allowed myself to be commanded by Bloodlust in the first place. I don't need Bloodlust's allegiance to retake my kingdom. I don't need the Blackblood's backing to force the Undead Empire into my service. The world is mine for the taking. Sygon will be mine. The Areopagus will belong to me. The Acolytes will kneel before me or die.

Creon and Crixus call out for my help but I cannot hear their desperate cries. Now I know why gods cannot hear the prayers of mortals. It is not because they are deaf. It is because they don't care.

This must be how Sylvian the First felt as he watched Cardone fall. Utter disregard for the lives of mortals.

Bastard! The beast within growls at me, *If you want to condemn mortals, I will show you mortality!*

My body feels heavy suddenly. The air beneath my feet starts to slip. The silver disappears from my eyes. The hunger and lust and exhaustion of mortality returns instantly. I submerge into the bloody red waters beneath me. Instantly, my skin begins to burn as the bacteria burrows into my salty skin. I writhe in pain while Crixus and Creon stare down at me from the sinking raft. They are like gods peering down at me while I suffer in agony. The bacteria enters the wounds that litter my body. The blood in my veins burns instantly. I force my eyes to remain shut, fearful that even the slightest crack will open an opportunity for my eyeballs to be turned to stone. I want to scream but my sense of survival tells me to keep my mouth shut to the infected waters.

I feel instantaneous guilt from my enlightened thinking. I am no god. I am as fickle as a newborn babe. I am a slave to the flesh that wraps around my bones. These powers are not mine to control, I'm painfully reminded. I am the same miserable human that has caused the death of all who love me.

I feel something grab hold of my shirt. I gasp for air as something pulls me out of the waters and lays me onto the sinking raft. My eyes sting as I stare up at Creon holding me. "What the hell happened, man?" he shouts. My ears are ringing. The burning doesn't stop. It feels as though my entire body is covered with poison ivy. It itches and burns and oozes uncontrollably. I have never felt so uncomfortable in my own skin as I do now. There is no escaping this agony.

Creon slaps my face, hard, breaking me free from the feelings of misery. Now all I can feel is the sting of my throbbing cheek. "Snap out of it, Sylvian. Get us the fuck out of here!"

My eyes turn silver again and the feelings of flesh disappear. Before I have time to reflect on the feeling of power taking over my body again, I grab each of their hands and lift us into the air. The raft turns on its side and disappears beneath the red waters. Creon and Crixus dangle helplessly in my grasp. I am not willing to risk tangling with the Fates should these powers disappear again. I waste no time in flying us to the nearby shore. The wind dries my skin as we soar over the salty beaches. We reach the lake's banks in seconds, but I don't stop there. I will exhaust these powers as long as they are mine to control.

I become lost in a trance of focus. Like the Undead who flew us into Yueltope, I fly us toward Sygon. I can barely feel Creon and Crixus squirming in my grasp. Their bodies feel weightless in my renewed strength. My vision is blurry, but just focused enough to know we are soaring through the sky like eagles. Rational thought leaves my mind. I pay little attention on whether or not people can see us from the ground. We are now several hundred yards in the air. It is pure instinct that controls my body. I just know that the further I fly us now, the less we need to walk. But thoughts of Atlas and his Acolytes keep me going. The faster I go, the more time we have ahead of them, the more distance I put between us.

I can see Sygon on the horizon now.

Its impossibly high walls loom in the distance. The miles of farms that stretch outside its control are now below us. Its unparalleled beauty is all I can focus on. The clouds part before me as I am drawn toward the city like a moth toward light. I am a god again. I can land on the steps of the kingdom's castle if I please.

I can take control while the Undead sleep the daylight away. Nothing can stop me. I will mount Ventur and Bloodlust's head upon my throne. I will command the globe as my father before me once did. I will kill any who oppose my rule.

I am too lost in my daydream to notice my body is descending, falling through the air now. I do not notice how heavy Crixus and Creon suddenly feel.

All I can think about is how I will restore peace to the kingdoms. Any who defy me will be crushed like ants beneath my heel. How dare the Undead think they can allow me to live and not think I will return to take what is mine. I will show them, and I will make them pay for what they've done to me. I am a vengeful god. I do not forgive easily. I will make this entire kingdom bleed if that's what it takes to force healing.

"Syrus!"

"Watch out!"

Crixus and Creon scream in the distance but I don't register their words. The walls grow bigger as we draw closer. The ground grows closer as we fall faster.

"What are you doing! You're going to kill us!"

I am a god, I remind myself.

I am in control.

I forge my own fate.

I have run my whole life.

The Undead thought they could hunt the Sylvians into extinction.

They have no idea what's coming for them.

I will kill every last one of them for what they've done.

"Dagon's sake, brace for impact!" Creon screams.

I am a god, I remind myself.

I feel the ground swallow me hole as I crash from flight.

Everything goes black.

Darkness consumes me.

44

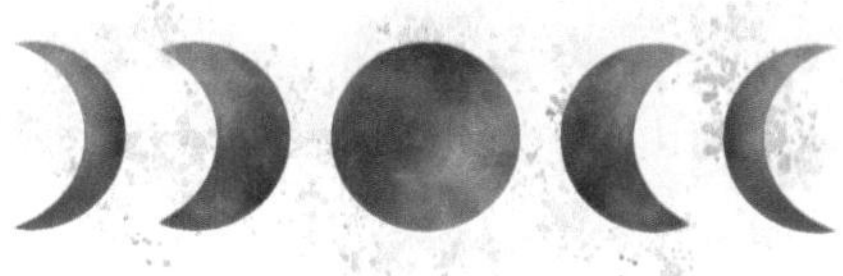

A Dream

"Not good enough," Mordecai sighs. "The Undead aren't going to have mercy on you when, not if, they catch you, Syrus. You need to move faster. You need to be stronger. More agile. Lighter on your feet. You're like a bull romping through a potter's shop. Loud and clumsy and awkward. We've been at this for weeks, when will you evolve? Again," he commands, no sympathy in his voice. "Run it again."

"But—" I gasp, my lungs on fire from the incessant drilling and lack of breaks.

"No buts," Mordecai cuts me off. "Are there any buts on the battlefield, Ziva?"

"Only the ones with a pike wedged between them," she laughs. "On your feet, young cub. You will learn with repetition, as we all did at your age."

I can hardly see straight. My vision is blurred with exhaustion. My sweat-soaked bangs dangle over my eyes. I can't think straight. My brain burns from oxygen deprivation. I've lost count of how many times I've run the course since dawn. The more I do it, the worse I perform. Mordecai wants me to run faster but my endurance left me long ago. And the anticipation of when I'll be done is killing me. What if they have me running until sunset? What if I pass out from heat exhaustion or dehydration?

Lundis never made me drill this hard.

We always took breaks from our workouts to rehydrate and allow our muscles rest.

Mordecai has never heard of breaks it seems. I doubt if I took the time to explain the scientific benefits of recovery it would sway his mind any. He seems set in his ways, so I do my best to huff and puff all the air I can as I walk back toward the starting line.

"Running is what wolves do, cub. We are only as fast as the slowest pack member. Do you want to be the reason we all die?" Mordecai asks. I grunt audibly so he can hear it. I find it hard to believe he has made all the pack members endure this level of physical torture. I have only just turned eleven and he has me running more miles than a continental messenger.

"Even wolves take time to catch their breath," I grunt in response, struggling to stay on my two feet.

"Not when they are on the hunt."

"I see no prey around. Besides, what's the point of all of this anyway?"

"The point, stubborn cub, is that you are a Lycan living in a world where the Undead would happily mount your head on their wall as decoration. So, you either learn discipline and control over your beast, or you will remain a liability and endanger our entire tribe."

"But we are in the Neverglades," I rebut, "No one comes here. No one will ever find us, not even the Undead."

"Don't be so sure, cub. Now quit stalling with your questions and run the course."

"Well hold on," I continue, disappointed he's seen through my tactic so quickly. Mordecai is not one to entertain shenanigans. "How exactly is this going to help me control my beast?"

"I have already answered that a half dozen times, so you're either stalling or stupid, and I highly doubt it to be the latter of the two. But if the reason for this drill fails to come to your mind, I'll jog your memory when you finish another lap," he answers, a smile of satisfaction on his lips.

"How about this," Ziva says, jumping down from the tree stump she sits on. "If you can catch me this time around, you can be done for the day."

I eyeball her suspiciously, sizing her up. She does not have a sprinter's figure. She is short and her legs are thinner than mine. There is nothing about her that makes her seem noteworthy at first glance. Her features are plain and the wildest thing about her is her unkempt hair. Though she is five years older than myself, I am already taller than her. If there is any member of the pack I feel confident I could beat in a leg race, it is Ziva. I—

"See you at the finish line!" she screams, taking off.

A second wind rushes over me as adrenaline takes over my body. If what Ziva says is true, all I have to do is beat her to the finish line and I won't have to run another damn lap around the course today. Finally, I can lay it all on the line. I know I can beat her. I just need to give it my all. A few more minutes of pure misery for the chance to be done for the day.

I take off into the forest's undergrowth. The trail is carved like a winding snake through the middle of the Neverglade forest, where mortal men don't dare to travel. The Neverglades are home to the world's most dangerous species of both animal and plant. Its humid climate makes the perfect condition for reptiles and other cold-blooded creatures, as well as tropical trees with a carnivorous nature. It is the sort of place no one would dream of living, unless you're a species that's been exiled by the Undead Empire.

Large elephant leaves whip against my face and ferns attempt to trip my every step. I have run this trail so many times that my feet have memorized the best route by memory. Ziva may have had a head start, but there are plenty of places along the racing track where I can gain the advantage.

I pick up speed as I know in the back of my mind the chasm is approaching. I eye the same vine I've swung on each time today. It hasn't broken beneath my weight yet, no need to switch tune now. I watch as Ziva approaches the chasm several dozen yards ahead of me, watching to see her method in scaling the gap of open air. It is not a jump to take lightly. A single misstep and the consequence is a hundred foot plummet into rocky darkness. There's no telling how many long-forgotten bones lurk at the chasm's floor.

Ziva leaps, not grabbing hold of the swaying vines. She dives through the air like a leopard pouncing on prey. A knot builds in the pit of my stomach as I watch her clear the chasm in a single leap, rolling over her shoulder and onto her feet on the other side gracefully. It is the most fluid movement I've ever seen. The sheer athleticism she displays with ease is not something I possess. I grit my teeth together as I approach the chasm's edge and leap, grabbing hold of the dangling vine so I can swing to the other side. I let my body's momentum carry me through the open air, not daring to look down at the darkness below.

Ziva's body disappears into the forest once more as I land clumsily, almost tripping over my feet as I attempt to land as gracefully as her. She runs like a doe and I stagger after her like a freshly born fawn. I throw myself into the forest head first, convincing myself I will run faster the further forward I lean. I vault over a fallen tree, then slide under the next. I can barely see Ziva now. Her scent is fresh in the air—dandelions and sourgum. It covers the path like a constant reminder I'm losing this race.

Next up is the white-water river.

"Wolves must not fear water, for it gives them life," Mordecai taught when I first laid eyes on it. This river, though, is to be feared greatly. Its waters roar with enough power to suck a child of my size under its current and pin them under the riptide. And if you manage to fight to stay afloat, the crocodiles won't be far from your scent. Piranhas and other carnivorous fish fill these waters, constantly searching for fresh prey to sink their teeth into.

There is a path of spaced-out rocks Mordecai taught me to jump on, followed by a short distance swim to the other side of the riverbank. Though the river first struck the fear of gods into me, I have swam across it enough times today to wash away my fears. It is no more than a creek to me now. If the waters were going to kill me, they would have twice over by now. I jump onto the first boulder that protrudes from the white-water, staggering my feet wide on its slick surface. The wet moss that covers its surface is slippery. It feeds the unsuspecting jumper to the rapid waters below. Jump too fast and you will surely fall. Go too slow and you will face the wrath of Mordecai.

I waste no time jumping several feet to the next boulder, grabbing hold of its craggy surface with my hands while my feet slip upon impact. I steady myself, then leap to the next outcrop of rocks, repeating the process to secure my balance. I jump again, only this time my feet slip as I launch myself, not giving me the momentum I need to clear the space between. I flail desperately and manage to grab the next boulder's peak, my feet dangling beneath me helplessly. My chest thuds square into the rock. The wind leaves my lungs with a grunt. My fingers manage to cling onto the rock by the grace of the gods, though they cut straight into my flesh.

I look over my shoulder at the raging waters below and allow the fear of falling to motivate me. I pull myself up and, without any air in my lungs, leap again. All my mind can think about is how far ahead of me Ziva is.

The course is nearly a mile long, and the fastest I've managed to finish it in is nine minutes and some change. I'm running out of time.

I must risk it all if I'm to win this one.

I land on the last boulder and immediately jump into the roaring waters. The river consumes me violently. Whiplash attacks my body. The current rolls me uncontrollably in several somersaults. I had no air to begin with, but now I'm surely drowning. My limbs fight back against the current and drag my useless body toward the surface. I claw tooth and nail against the riptide. My strokes are manic and frenzied. I fight the waters as though they are my own worst enemy. Thoughts seep into my mind about whatever monsters lurk below and around me. Fear pierces my brain. I swim faster, pummeling the waves one after the other. I'll have time to breathe later, all I have the energy for now is survival.

My hand makes contact with the river's shore and I pull myself out of the water like a man being chased by a demon. I am waterlogged and utterly defeated. I can't help but picture what Ziva will look like at the finish line. I might as well save my energy for when Mordecai inevitably makes me run the course a dozen more times after losing to the she-wolf. It is not a matter of losing the race at this point, but by how badly I lose. I must carry on.

I throw myself back into the wilderness. Immediately I'm tackled by some force unknown to me. My feet leave the ground and the little oxygen I've managed to gather since my swim is once again knocked from my lungs. A body lands on top of me, pinning my hands and legs to the ground. I wheeze as my body sucks for any air available to it.

"Shhhh," a voice whispers to me. I smell the dandelions and sourgum before I can make out Ziva's face. Her hand covers my mouth so I can't make any more noise than I already have. I don't have the energy to fight her off of me. In all honesty, I am thankful for the opportunity to be pinned forcefully to my back. This is the first time since waking this morning I've been granted the opportunity to rest. I could fall asleep in this very spot with Ziva on top of me.

But when I open my eyes I can suddenly see the worry written on her face. I can sense the panic radiating from her body. I can smell the fear in her pheromones.

We are lying in a bed of tall ferns that blocks my view from seeing what she hides from. I don't try to talk. I can understand from the circumstances we are in grave danger. We are wolves, and wolves can sense when the pack is in trouble.

We both pant in silence from the race. She clings tight to me to reduce the size of our bodies. I try desperately to lift my nose toward the air. Anything I can do to catch a scent on the stale wind of what danger awaits us. All I can smell is Ziva's sweaty palm that covers my mouth. That, and dandelions. I want to whisper to her, but I'm afraid the slightest noise will give away our position. The anticipation is killing me. Are we going to die? Have the Undead found us? What could possibly strike so much fear into a she-wolf who has never shown any signs of fear since I've known her?

She makes very little movement. We lie as flat and still as a decaying log. Our breaths synchronize. I can feel her heart beating through her ribcage. I've never been pressed so tight to a girl before. She clings to me like a koala clings to a tree. There's no telling how long we will be here or if we will make it out alive. Part of me is glad I don't know what threat lurks nearby. I may not be able to be as calm as Ziva if I did. The other part of me wants to know what we are up against, though that is a much smaller part of me.

I wonder what Mordecai would think if he saw us here. Surely he is going to have one hell of a scolding when we get back. Our race time will be worse than any of my previous performances today. There's no way he will let me stop training for the day. Will he believe Ziva when she tells him we had to lie and wait?

No. He will say wolves don't hide and wait. He will turn the danger into a life lesson. I can hear his voice now, "Wolves attack their dangers head on. They don't run and hide like prey."

He won't understand. The man has little sympathy for anything. I watched one of the cubs come up to him to show a deep gash along their heel, begging for a few days of rest from training. "Looks like you'll learn how to run with a limp today," he laughed at them, not accepting their puppy-like eyes as a means of persuasion.

I came to the Neverglades to escape my past but found Mordecai instead. This tribe of Lycans has been peacefully living here for centuries. They call themselves Lupus Cruor. *Wolf's Blood*. They have learned the way of the forest and made it home. In my delusional mind, this was the only place I could run to after my family's death that would protect me from the Undead. Scouts were on my heels every day before I entered the Neverglades. But there are even some places the Undead fear to go on this earth, and this forest is one of them.

I had no intention or knowledge of finding Lycans here. But they found me and took me in all the same, even though I was not born into their folds. They train me like a cub, though most cubs graduate that title at the age of six. Most others my age in the tribe have since advanced to teen-wolf. But Mordecai made himself clear the first day I would not graduate from cub until I proved I was capable of more than a cub. Hence the endless days of training and my current affliction. Why Mordecai thinks this forest is safe enough for an eleven-year-old to run through alone is the core issue; all other issues stem forward from that.

A wave of tiredness washes over me, though I know I need to be awake and alert. The circumstances combine to lull me to sleep. The warm, humid air above. Ziva's rhythmic heartbeat. Her tight embrace. The smell of dandelions. Her body is like a blanket smothering me to sleep.

I hear the decaying leaves crunch on the forest floor near us. That alone is enough to wake me back to this nightmarish reality. I feel Ziva's body shiver as she senses the danger looming closer. I'm forced to stare up at the sky as a shadow descends over us like a veil. A strand of saliva longer than a shoelace stretches through the air above us. It cascades through the air like a spider lowering itself on a single web. I cringe with utter fear as the saliva drips onto my forehead and slowly pools down each side of my face. I squint my eyes to prevent it from burning my vision, though this makes it that much harder to see our predator.

We are quieter and stiller than we've ever been in our lives. Ziva and I could fool an onlooker into thinking we've been dead for centuries with how little we move. We both hold our breath, terrified that even the slightest movement of our ribcage will give away our position. I can smell the predator now, even though I cannot see it. It smells of saltwater and rust mixed with infected gums and festering scales.

I can hear its nostrils smelling the air above us, catching our scent before it sees us. It follows the scent down through the air toward the ground, but doesn't attack as its eyes look directly at us. The sun above blots out my ability to fully see what we are up against. All I can see is its talons in the ferns beside us. The creature is four-legged like a dog but is covered in grey scales that look like the armor of an alligator. But this is no alligator. Its belly is not close to the ground like a serpent. Its haunches are elevated several feet above the ground like an elephant. I can tell from the exasperated breaths it takes that it is the size of a behemoth. Its legs are like tree trunks. Even the small shifting its feet make on the forest floor are like pounding earthquakes.

If it moves another step forward, the weight of its body will crush our childish bones. Our continued existence is a miracle. The fact that it has yet to find us is the work of gods guarding us. I woke today thinking I would see the sunset. I realize now my life may set before the sun does. But for some strange reason, I feel peace instead of fear at the thought. Though I can feel Ziva's body tremble, I am still with serenity. Maybe it is the exhaustion that causes the delusion. Or maybe it's the fact that I may see my mother's face again today.

I hear a low snarl build in the monster's voice as its face comes closer. Ziva's hair blows in the gust of wind its nostrils create. At least we won't die alone. In this moment, we have each other. And though we were only strangers months ago, Ziva has grown to be the older sister I never had. She has looked after me. Cared for me. Given me a second family in one of the darkest regions in the world, in one of the darkest chapters of my life. If we both die, we will wake in the heavens together.

The behemoth nudges our bodies with its tusk with enough power to nearly roll us over. I hear the caw of a raven in the distance but the sound is diluted by the blood pumping in my eardrums. My heart is so loud now I fear it may pop in my chest like a balloon. The mighty beast above us scrapes the forest floor with its scaled paw like it is ready to charge. It lowers its nostrils once more in our direction. From its nose sprouts a single, massive, ivory tusk sharp and long enough to pierce through both our bodies.

Slowly, as the nose moves to nudge us again, its tusk presses into Ziva's side. I feel her fingers dig into my back as she winces in pain. The monster doesn't stop there. I can feel as the tusk penetrates her flesh. Ziva bites into my neck to keep herself from crying out. My hand can feel the tusk continue to penetrate her, digging more than a few inches into her stomach. Her teeth feel as though she is going to bite a chunk of my neck off. I feel her shudder with pain. She cannot take much more. If the monster is going to relent and leave us alone, it needs to be now. But the gods have never been kind to those who love me. Why did I expect them to now?

The behemoth nudges us with its tusk in Ziva's body and she lets out a desperate cry of pain loud enough to shake the leaves overhead, giving away our position immediately. The scream catches the beast off guard, startling it, as it digs its tusk into Ziva completely, bucking its head back defensively and lifting her off me and into the air. I watch in horror as her body levitates, spurting blood from the entry and exit wounds the horn has carved into her body. She manages a faint scream, "Syrus... Run!"

It is the last words I ever heard her speak. I stare up as the fully grown thyrops lifts her pierced body into the air. She flails desperately to escape the tusk, but her body has already slid down the mighty horn to the beast's nose. Blood drips from her mouth onto my forehead, covering the pool of saliva the thyrops created. I am paralyzed by fear as the thyrops bucks onto its hind legs.

It lets out a roar gut-wrenching enough to shatter glass. A dozen ravens scatter throughout the trees above at the beast's mighty squeal. I see its razor-sharp teeth as its scaly maw opens wide enough to taste the droplets of blood that flow from Ziva's body down its tusk. Its slitted tongue licks its upper lip with delight. And now I can see its full body in completion. It is the size of a rhino with the aggression of a crocodile. Its entire body is covered with thick, grey scales except for the obsidian tusk that sprouts from its skull. Its eyes are dark and blind, as Lundis once taught me.

The common thyrops hunts by scent and sound, not sight. That is why Ziva made us freeze along the forest floor. It was an attempt to let the predator pass without incurring harm. But our sweating, panting bodies were likely what drew the creature in with the scent of ammonia and exhaustion.

There is nowhere for me to run. The river is not an option; the thyrops can swim as fast as it can run. Sprinting away into the forest will bleed my scent into the air and lead it back to the tribe. I am damned if I do run and I'm damned if I don't.

I stare up at Ziva's lifeless body curled around the blood-soaked horn. She no longer fights to free herself from its grasp. Her limbs dangle in the air like a limp puppet. I wipe the saliva and blood from my eyes as I scramble away from the bucking thyrops. The monster slings Ziva's body off its horn and into a nearby tree. She collapses to the ground, fully dead, and all I can do is stare in horror at the scene before me. Several ravens descend from the forest canopy to defend her body as the thyrops approaches to feed off her. The birds caw violently at the creature, not fearing its massive figure or the fact that it could swallow them hole in a single snap of its jaws.

Black feathers ruffle. Their wings protrude to either side to make their bodies look more intimidating. Their black beaks look as if they are ready to strike the thyrops at any second. And the longer the thyrops stares at them, the more they accumulate. At first there was only a dozen, but now there are hundreds of the black birds that fly to Ziva's aid. The thyrops cannot see them, but it can surely smell and hear them. The ravens create a great cacophony that echoes their squawks throughout the forest, presenting them to be a bigger danger to the thyrops than they actually are. They fly around its scaled body like a tornado of floating black feathers.

The thyrops's nose can smell their scent surrounding it. It looks around in confusion, not able to discern what is happening. I realize now what is happening. The ravens are distracting the mighty beast. *Syrus... Run!*

Ziva's words play over in my head.

I stand to my feet and watch as the gods send down so many ravens from the heavens that their black feathers make it seem as if it's night. The birds dive into the beast's armored body, plucking at its scales one after the other. The thyrops whips around to protect itself but it is too big to match the speed of the ravens. The predator likely wonders how it could have been turned from a hunter into prey so fast.

Syrus... Run!

I won't run, I tell myself as I stare at Ziva's dead body. I will get revenge for my fallen sister. I can hear Mordecai's teachings in the back of my head, "Wolves do not run. Wolves do not feel fear."

But how do I kill a beast whose entire body is covered with armor?

I have no sword or spear to pierce it.

I have nothing but my bare hands and the forest around me. The ravens continue to dive toward the thyrops and pluck away at its scales to no avail. Their beaks are not sharp enough to penetrate its body. Though they make a magnificent distraction, their attack is nothing more than bought time for me to think.

When dealing with hand-to-hand combat, you focus on your opponent's weaknesses, not strengths, Lundis taught me. So instead of looking at the beast's impenetrable armor or its horn protected razor-sharp teeth, I look instead at its dull, squinty eyes. I watch as the thyrops is basically blind to protect itself from the onslaught of pecking ravens. Further, its sense of smell and hearing are preoccupied by the obnoxious stench and squall of the ravenous birds. For all intents and purposes, this animal is a lethal tank with no eyes or ears to defend itself. "Find your opponent's weakness, find your victory," Lundis always said as he taught me how to grapple against children much larger than myself.

Size is a weakness in and of itself. Though it provides the beast greater strength, it slows it tremendously. I snatch a raven from its flight, quickly twisting its neck before it has time to attack my fingers with its beak. I feel its head snap from its shoulders and the bird instantly ceases all movement. I poke its beak with the tip of my finger to test its sharpness. Blood pools along my fingertip when I pull it away. I smile as I suck the blood and realize

I have a chance at winning this fight. This raven's sacrifice will not be in vain. If the thyrops is not totally blind already, it will be soon.

I charge the great beast before my mind has time to cower. No retreat. Wolves do not retreat. They do not feel fear. They face their challengers head-on. I am not the hunted. I am the hunter. And although it is too late to save Ziva, she will watch from the heavens as I claim this thyrops's soul as penance for her life.

I leap like a monkey onto the thyrops's back, driving the raven's beak directly into the monster's eye. I feel the beak gouge directly into the beast's eye socket, and when I pull my arm back, my hand is covered with blood. Wolves don't retreat. I thrust the beak downward once more as the pain registers in the beast's mind from the initial strike. I'm thrown from the bronco-like back as the thyrops bucks in agony, roaring to the heavens from the feeling of its eye being lost.

I tumble to the ground in a tangle of limbs, rolling to cushion the violent momentum.

Wolves do not run. I pick myself up and throw myself back at the monster's body, my childish fist balled up small enough to fit into its eye socket. I thrust my arm into the demon's skull through its gouged eye. My feet lift off the ground as its confused body attempts to fight off the attacker it cannot see. My body dangles as it stands to its hind legs and claws at me with its front paws. I feel its talons dig into my back and cut open my flesh from shoulder to hip. I bite down on my tongue to keep myself from allowing it the pleasure of hearing me scream.

Wolves do not fear. I drive my fist deeper into its brain and swirl the organ around like batter in a mixing bowl. I grab hold of any guts I can and mush them between my fingers as the claws continue to dig into my back. I know I won't make it out of this fight alive, but I'll be damned if I don't drag this creature to hell with me. It is pure rage and adrenaline that keeps me going as I crush the brain in my closed fist.

Instantly, I feel the life leave the defenseless body as the thyrops tumbles forward. We fall together, my fist still stuck in its skull. The tremendous body lands on top of me, bending my arm in an awkward angle with enough pressure to snap my forearm in half. This time I scream, satisfied that the thyrops is no longer alive to hear the pain it's caused me. The blunt side of its mighty horn pins me to the ground, my legs crushed beneath the weight of its massive head. The ravens continue to attack the beast's carcass. They too will not retreat, nor will they fear. Blood pools around me from my sliced open back. My head grows faint as the pain of my broken arm radiates like electricity up to my shoulder joint. My legs go numb from the monster's body lying atop them. My vision grows blurrier by the second. I can't think of many better ways to die than this.

I did not run.

I did not retreat.

I did not fear.

I died a wolf's death.

And though the gods were not kind this time around, I've sent their reaper back to them with my bloody fingerprints on his carcass.

45

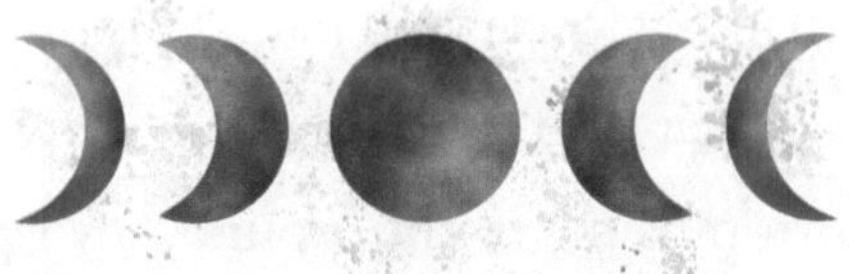

A Dream

The greatest lesson you learn in life is that it goes on.

I stare down at the splint fastened around my forearm and try to ignore the pain that burrows through my arm like worms in feces.

"Take the feverfew," Kateri demands. "It will help with the pain and reduce the inflammation."

I stare at the crumpled feverfew flowers in my hand. They look like dandelions, which only causes my mind to fixate on Ziva's absence. I shove them into my mouth and instantly regret it. They are more bitter than tart bark and cause my tongue to go numb. I cringe as I fight to chew through the petals and stems. The flowers quickly turn to mush between my molars and I nearly choke as I force myself to swallow.

I stare around the healer's tent. There are clay jars scattered around the multiple desks, each one containing a multitude of mixed herbs and salves. Dried lavender burns next to the cot they've laid me on. It fills the air with its potent aroma, lulling me to sleep after the near-death experience. The ashwagandha salve spread over my stitched back burns like fire, fighting the infection that seeks to devour my body.

"Here, take this, it will help delay the fever," Kateri orders, handing me a cup of hot water with mixed herbs. I take it with my unbroken arm and bring it to my lips gratefully. I haven't had water to drink all day, not counting the mouthfuls of water the river forced down my throat from the course's repeated drilling. The hot water washes down the bitter taste of the feverfew with its sweet taste of honey and chamomile. Though it is scalding hot, I let it burn the inside of my throat as I drink the entire cup in three large gulps. Steam leaves my mouth as I exhale.

I don't remember how I got here. By the time I woke my arm was already splinted and my back was already stitched. How the tribe found me, I'm not sure. Shock overwhelms my body and prevents my mind from asking any questions. All I have the energy to do is stare at my arm and feel the excruciating pain wash over me in waves. When I close my eyes all I can see is Ziva's body dangling in the air by the thyrops horn. When I keep my eyes open all I can see is the empty cot next to me where Ziva's body would be if she was still alive.

"There were ravens," I murmur under my breath, more so to myself, recalling the anomaly. In the moment, I was too panicked to question their arrival. Now that I'm removed from the encounter, all I can do is think about the tornado of black birds that came to our aid to distract the thyrops. There was something supernatural about it. Like nothing I've ever heard of in all my years learning from Lundis. Since when do birds randomly attack apex predators to protect humans?

"The raven is the Lycan's best friend," Kateri says, bustling around the hut as she continues to mix herbs into another salve. She jumps from pot to pot, adding pinches of each ingredient into a big clay cauldron. "Has Mordecai not taught you yet about wolves and ravens?"

I look up at her slowly, shaking my head. I keep my words limited because I feel one sentence away from breaking down and crying. Wolves don't cry though, so I force the emotions back behind invisible floodgates.

"Ah," she sighs, peering up at me from her constant bustling. "Probably a lesson better left for Mordecai to tell you. I'm no good at storytelling like him. Best for me to stick to healing and leave the teaching to him."

"No," I respond, anger bubbling up inside of me at the mention of Mordecai's name. None of this would have happened if it wasn't for his stubbornness. Ziva would still be here if he hadn't forced me to drill for hours on end. My endless laps around the course were likely what drew the thyrops in. Hours upon hours of noise in the wilderness and my constant stench signaling to predators miles away. This is all his fault. Ziva's death, my injury. All of it. I never want to see Mordecai again. He may be a teacher, but he is not wise. He is reckless. Irresponsible. A leader not fit to be guiding cubs of this tribe. I don't care what mercies he showed me by accepting me into his pack, I refuse to listen to anything he has to say from here on out. "I want you to tell me," I continue, "Not Mordecai."

Kateri looks up from the mixing cauldron with a whimsical look on her face. It is clear no one has ever given her the time of day to do anything more than tend to her herbs and healing medicines. Everyone in this tribe has their place, I've learned. The men hunt and the women gather. The women cook and the men protect. Both men and women are expected to keep their fighting skills sharp and duel several hours out of the day. They are a clan of warriors and operate with little deviation. This way of life has helped them survive several eons so they stick to what's worked and shun new perspectives like the plague.

For this very reason I can tell Kateri is hesitant to tell the meaning behind the ravens. But I implore her for more with my eyes. Like a puppy looking to its master for scraps I pull her forward from her cocoon of normalcy.

"Fine," she breaks, "But Mordecai mustn't know."

"He won't," I promise, not wanting to tell her I have no plans on speaking with him again.

"So be it," she sighs, though I can tell she is happy to take a break from the herbs and salves for a chance to be a storyteller. "Wolves and ravens have had a symbiotic relationship since Dagon's reign. The earliest Lycans formed an unnatural friendship with the birds, the stories tell, and that friendship never ceased. Nowhere else in the animal cycle has two other species formed such mutual welfare through teamwork. The bond between wolves and ravens has, over thousands of years, remained unspoken and unexplained. The raven, once known as the messenger of death, observed the way of the wolf from the air without its knowledge. It watched as packs hunted together, strategically tracking down its prey and working together to feed each other. The cunning raven, seeing an opportunity that the wolf wouldn't refuse, realized it could spot unsuspecting prey from the sky miles away from the wolf's detection. With this ability, ravens knew they could bring something to the table that could enhance a wolfpack's ability to hunt more efficiently. Ravens began leading wolfpacks to the prey they spotted from the sky, letting the carnivores complete the kill for them. Then, the wolves were wise enough to know that if they wanted the raven's help again, they would let the raven partake in the hunt's feast.

"Over hundreds of years, the animals evolved together, building a trust deeper than primordial instinct. Ravens learned how to scout more efficiently and developed ways to communicate with wolves. The wolves were eternally grateful for the raven's keen eye and unwavering loyalty. Together, neither species succumbed to starvation, even in the worst of winters.

"Then, after the birth of Dagon and his eventual curse, the ravens saw there was a new breed of wolves. The ravens watched as Lycans formed tribes in the earliest generations of mankind. They saw how, similar to the average wolfpack, Lycans hunted in order to survive. The wolfmen were exiled from humanity after the war of Flesh and Fangs, and that is when the ravens spotted a new opportunity to extend their friendship. Like their alliance with wolves, the ravens offered their scouting services to Lycan tribes, and the Lycan tribes gratefully accepted the raven's keen abilities, as the wolves had thousands of years before.

"We Lycans have few in this world we call our friend, but the raven has been there for us since our inception. They show us where to hunt. They warn us when danger comes. And, as in your case, they come to our aid when we are in peril. You are only a cub, so you have yet to learn how ravens can be of use while on the hunt. But today, for the first time in your life, you have seen firsthand how the raven will lay down its life to protect our kind. The messenger of death is never far away, no matter how dark life may get. You would be wise to remember that, because if it was not for the raven, you would be dead right now."

Kateri stares at me with sincerity in her eyes, like a mother who knows her child has lost his innocence on this very day. But death is no stranger to me. I have been facing it for the better part of an entire year. My palms are still stained with the blood of my slain family. And Ziva's lifeless body will haunt me the rest of my life.

The tent's front flap opens, revealing Mordecai's body. The leader of the tribe enters the hut and doesn't spare me a single glance. "How is he?" Mordecai asks Kateri, still refusing to look at me.

"He will heal in time. When the full moon comes, the beast within will mend his bones and erase the scars along his back. But until then, he will need to rest. Luckily the break on his arm was clean. There is no need to reset it. Until the full moon, we just need to make sure his back does not get infected."

Mordecai nods, and only then does he look up at me. The look in his eyes is different than before. He used to look at me like I was nothing more than a childish cub incapable of anything more than failure. But now he knows what I am capable of. I, a mere cub, have killed a grown thyrops with my bare hands. I have looked death in the face and defied it. Like the raven, I am the messenger of death.

Mordecai's eyes are filled with a tinge of admiration and respect. I am no longer a cub to him. I doubt even the adult Lycans would be able to do what I accomplished today and live to tell of it. I doubt Mordecai himself would have been able to pull off such a feat.

"The moon is coming," Mordecai whispers tenderly. He speaks to me like a father now. It is the first time I've heard him speak in such a caring tone. "We will continue your training after the moon heals your wounds."

Suddenly all resolve I had to never talk to him again melts away. Seeing the sincerity in his eyes makes me realize I misjudged him. It wasn't that he didn't care about me before, it was that he wasn't willing to let himself expose that side of him. Especially not to a cub who entered the tribe a few short months ago.

"But Ziva..." I stutter, seeing her dead body when I blink to hold back tears. "She... I... Her... Dead..."

Mordecai approaches and sits on the side of my cot. His face is completely different from how I once knew him. It was as if he took off a mask to reveal his true self. The man before me is selfless and caring, not brash and cruel. The man before me is the kind of man I trust just by peering deeply into his eyes. He speaks to me in a low, sympathetic tone, "What happened to Ziva is not your fault, Syrus."

"But—"

"That girl took you in like a long-lost little brother. She loved you, Syrus. She was willing to die for you. There is no greater love in this world than what Ziva put on display for you. But if you cease your training—if you let fear infect your mind—your life will amount to nothing, and Ziva's soul will wish she had never spared you in the first place. Don't take that the wrong way, child. You now have a guardian angel watching over you. But don't let her sacrifice be in vain."

I nod. The urge to let my tears roll forth builds inside my diaphragm with uncontainable pressure. But wolves don't cry. And so I will stay strong for Ziva, and I will let my life be a testament that her sacrifice was not a mistake.

"Someday it will be time for you to choose a mate for life, Syrus. Let Ziva's sacrifice set the expectation for what you need in a she-wolf. In the wild, a she-wolf is the one responsible for raising their offspring, protecting her partner, remaining loyal in all seasons, and guarding the pack when the alpha male is away. You want a she-wolf who will protect your neck when another attempts to slash it open. Whoever you choose to be your she-wolf, they will play the most pivotal role in your life of any other person you ever meet. Ziva is the she-wolf I would have matched you with when you reached adulthood. But now you must go out into the world to find another. But do not settle for any less than one who would lay down their life for you. Do you understand? Any less would be a betrayal to the sacrifice Ziva made."

I nod, a single tear slipping free from a crack in my façade.

"Good," he whispers, patting my leg. "Now rest. The moon is coming soon. Your training will resume, teen wolf."

The title catches me off guard.

He no longer calls me cub.

I am now referred to as a teen wolf.

I have passed all the testing required of a cub.

I killed a thyrops with my bare hands, after all.

Fear fills my stomach at the replaying of Mordecai's words in my head.

The moon is coming soon.

The moon is coming.

The moon.

The words echo inside my mind like the echo of a war horn warning of something dangerous coming.

The beast within may heal my arm and back, but what other destruction will it cause when it comes forward for a moondance?

46

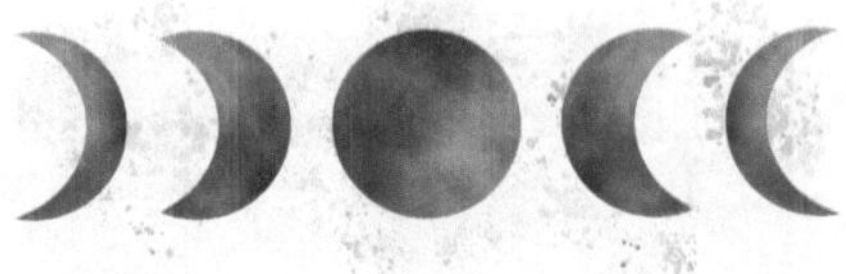

A Nightmare

The moon is coming soon.

The moon is coming.

The moon.

"The moon is coming soon, Crixus, and we can't bloody well let him sleep through it!" Creon exclaims through the darkness of my sleep from a world away.

"Look at him, Creon! Does he look like he is in any shape to storm Sygon? Dagon's sake, let the man rest another day..."

"He has slept an entire week away!"

"The healer says he is in some sort of coma," Crixus defends. "He said there is no telling how long the sleep will possess his body. All we can do is sit by and wait. It could kill him if we wake him too early."

"And it could kill *us* if he doesn't wake at all!" Creon snaps, "Or did you forget we have a deadline to carry out Bloodlust's orders? Just because you're in love with the bloke doesn't mean I have to die for your love affair!"

"Are you dumb or are you just stupid?" Crixus laughs, "If you want to storm Sygon lone-wolf style, be my guest. But the last time I checked, Syrus has more power in the tip of his pinky than you do in your entire body. I'd put money on it that the Undead would strike you dead before you even entered the city's streets. Trust me, I'm just as anxious to get this mission over as you are, but I'd rather have a fully recovered Syrus on our side than a walking zombie."

"And have you given the slightest thought what's going to happen if he sleeps through the full moon? Sylvian's sake, our beasts will ravage his unconscious body where he sleeps, Crixus! We can't risk staying here this close to the full moon. Neither you or I have the power to control our beasts like Syrus does."

"He will wake before the full moon, I know it."

"So I'm just supposed to trust a gut feeling?"

"What other choice do you have?"

"Hiking back and finding the Acolytes, for one. Besides, any distance we put between ourselves and them by flying to the outskirts of Sygon is made useless since Syrus has slept nearly a week away! I'd bet money the Acolytes are readying their attack on the city the same as we are. We could just join forces or—"

"Why do you constantly insist they will be so accepting of us trying to join them. You speak as if they don't already have their minds made up! You saw their army, I didn't, but I'd assume they made no offer for vagabonds to join their ranks," Crixus argues.

"They would have if they saw how well I can handle a blade and shield," Creon rebuts. "But our genius leader over there insisted we pretend on being poor actors from Queensmyre to avoid suspicion, so my dumbass trusted him."

"Then go! If you want to get out of here so damn bad, nothing is stopping you!" Crixus shouts.

"Fine! I will!" Creon screams, slamming objects around. "But I want one thing to be clear here. I am not betraying this wolfpack. I am doing this solely so I can claim Sygon before Bloodlust's deadline. I'm doing this for Syrus's daughter, not for myself. Will you at least do me the service of telling him that if he wakes before the moon? I won't let this be like the vision the hag showed me. I will not betray him. That's not who I am anymore. I am doing this for him, not in spite of him."

"Justify it however helps you sleep at night. The strength of the wolf is the pack, and you are abandoning yours."

"I need you to promise me you'll tell him, damnit! I don't need him thinking I betrayed him. Not after I've seen what he's capable of. I am just as loyal to him as you are."

"Then stay and wait for him to wake!"

"And let his daughter die? Crixus, don't you see? Has this journey blinded you? The only reason we are here is to get that little girl back. The only reason *Syrus* is here is to save his daughter. At all costs. I will prove my loyalty to him by finishing what he started, not by sitting idly by waiting for his miraculous awakening. So please, I beg you, tell him..."

There is a steady silence throughout that comes from the room where Crixus and Creon hash out their differences. I am forced to listen as Creon whispers, "If I don't see you again—if I don't make it out of this alive—let him know it has been an honor serving him. Okay?"

I hear the door open and shut, and suddenly there are only two of us left. Just me and Crixus. The way I wished things had been this entire trip. But my mind floods with panic at the realization I've been in a coma for the better part of a week. The full moon is likely a few short days away, though I'll need to see its fullness tonight to confirm my suspicion.

I open my eyes and slowly sit up on the edge of my cot. I can feel every inch of exhaustion that infects my body. From my fingers to my toes, there isn't an ounce of me that isn't sore and achy. This is the cost of expending such tremendous energy to fly from Askamyre to the outskirts of Sygon, I realize. I wonder if it will ever get any easier. Surely it must. The Undead take flight like it is no more difficult than going for a walk. If they can do it with such ease, so can I. I just need my body to grow used to the strain it requires until I can no longer feel it. I take the few moments of silence to rest my head in my hands.

My arm is no longer broken in half from the thyrops encounter but the memories of my past are still fresh in my head. I can still feel Ziva's trembling body embracing my own. The crack of my arm. The swirl of ravens in the air. The look in Mordecai's sympathetic eyes.

The boy who sat in that cot healing wouldn't recognize the man I've grown to be. If we passed one another on an empty street he wouldn't think twice about who I am, a stranger. So much has happened since Kateri taught me of ravens and wolves. I finally met a she-wolf who lived up to Ziva's expectations, only she wasn't a she-wolf. Vesper's image crosses my mind. My heart sinks as I remember her.

But now you must go out into the world to find another. But do not settle for any less than one who would lay down their life for you. Do you understand?

Vesper was that woman for me. She bore me Sephora, and gods save whoever tried to threaten our family. Not only was she willing to lay down her life for me—she did. Like Ziva, I would not be here if it wasn't for Vesper. The Blackbloods would have overtaken me if it wasn't for her coming to my aid. Even though I told her to, she did not abandon me. And now I am condemned to walk this earth without her love and affection.

All I have left of her is Sephora, and I will give my life to save her.

I make no move to call to Crixus in the other room. I don't want her to know I'm awake. I don't want her to call Creon back. His resolve is true, and his plan is better than the one I've devised. If there is anyone tough enough to join the Acolytes, it is him. Whether or not Atlas entertains his request is to be determined, but at least I know now he is truly on my side. Whether he storms Sygon by my side or Atlas's, I know he does it for Sephora at the end of the day.

But now you must go out into the world to find another.

"You're—you're awake!" Crixus stutters in amazement as she appears in the doorway.

You want a she-wolf who will protect your neck when another attempts to slash it open.

I look up at Crixus and take in her image. Like Vesper, this is the sort of she-wolf Mordecai once spoke of. She has every quality Ziva and Vesper had. She is beautiful in the dull glow of the hut we reside. I can see the concern on her face as she rushes forward to hug me. Her arms wrap around my back and she buries her head into my shoulder. My body aches as she squeezes me tight, but it is the best ache I've ever felt.

We don't speak. There are no words to describe the moment we share.

Whoever you choose to be your she-wolf, they will play the most pivotal role in your life of any other person you ever meet.

I cannot let this woman fall in love with me, I realize.

Every person I've let into my life and shared my love with has died. And this time, I realize I love Crixus too much to let such a fate befall her. I am done letting people die for me. If I truly love her, I will send her away, permanently. I won't let her take another step following me on this folly mission. I can't stand to watch another person I love die.

But as I feel Crixus's nails dig into my back and her tears soak my neck, I know she is too stubborn to leave me, even if I demand it.

But do not settle for any less than one who would lay down their life for you.

I cannot follow Mordecai's advice any longer. The woman who now holds me is all that tethers me to my inner emotion. I was dead inside before she came into my life. And for the first time in a long time, I feel a spark within bright enough to set my body on fire.

I want to hold onto her forever.

I want to live in this moment until the day I die.

But Sephora's safety comes first before all other people I love, and so I must put her life before Crixus's. An eternal conflict wages war within me as my past and my future clash. I love Sephora, but I also love this woman. But it is likely that only one will survive the battle to come, and so I must choose my daughter over Crixus. That epiphany alone is enough to shatter my heart.

47

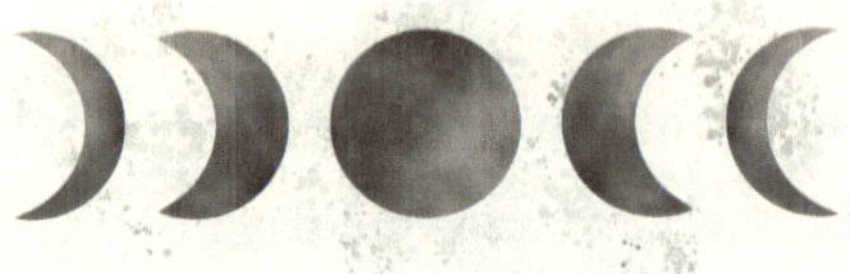

A Nightmare

"How can something so beautiful cause so much pain and suffering?" Crixus whispers over the crackling of the fire. We sit next to one another staring up at the nearly full moon. Its fullness pulls at us like a magnet to metal. I can feel a force inside myself waking as I bask in the moonlight. After tonight, we will only have one more night before the moon is full. Then there will be no stopping Crixus from shifting and causing incalculable damage to Sygon.

Our two-week journey has expired. I spent the majority of it unconscious, resting my body for what's to come in a comatose state. When we arrive in Sygon, there will be no time to infiltrate the enemy from within.

But until then, we spend the night feasting. Crixus has filled me in on what happened after escaping the Askamyre. I apparently managed to fly both her and Creon all the way to the outskirts of Sygon, which is several miles.

Sygon's layout is ingenious. It has three separate walled portions, one within another within another, each getting progressively smaller. Outside the outer most wall is nothing but sprawling farmland for miles. This is where farmers raise crops for sale inside the first wall. Inside the first wall is more farmland, only it is dedicated exclusively for raising livestock. Whoever designed the city's socioeconomic positioning wanted the farmers inside the first wall to raise their livestock free from having to deal with predators. Because of this, the outermost wall is the weakest of the three and designed strong enough to keep out predators, but not strong enough to ward against enemy advances.

The first portion of Sygon is called Vygon. It is farmers who have enough money to afford the protection of living inside the outer wall, but the section is still filled with destitute poverty. It doesn't take much to be wealthy enough to live in Vygon, and most of those born there will die there. Farmers are typically only good at one thing in life—farming. Still though, the production of food is an essential prerequisite to a city's flourishing, so the largest plots of land surrounding Sygon and within Vygon are dedicated solely to this purpose.

The middle portion of Sygon is called Lygon. It is where the middle class and lower nobility ranks live. Most merchants and tradesmen dwell there, and those rich enough to evade the poverty-stricken streets of Vygon try to make their living in Lygon. The middle wall is much more fortified than the outer. It is several feet thick and higher than any mortal man can climb. Still though, it is only made of rock, and if push came to shove, a catapult would easily turn it to rubble.

Sygon itself is the third section, where only the richest can afford to live. Back before the war, the king of Sygon himself would dwell in the elevated castle visible for miles around. And the wall that guards Sygon was smelted and forged by some of the greatest blacksmiths of the Iron Era. The wall, as Bloodlust suggested, is impenetrable. It is patrolled by guards all hours of day and night. Archers line its walkways always searching for looming threats with their hawk-like eyes. Lundis described it as the land of milk and honey. Those who live there will never want for anything a day of their life. Its inhabitants are the descendants of old money, and they've devised a lifestyle where they will remain the richest of the rich and the poor will never be able to raise themselves from the mud.

It is an essential part of a hierarchical society, Lundis taught. There must be many who hate their lives so a few can enjoy the rich pleasures of the world. The Areopagus has no walls separating its noble class from the poor. The streets are free to roam and intermingle between all citizens, keeping in mind that a city is only as strong as its populace.

Crixus told me that by the time I lost consciousness and crashed, we had made it as far as the farmland directly outside of Vygon. However, the war has left no signs of life in the land dedicated to raising crops. When the Blackbloods first stormed the city, any farmers outside Vygon's walls likely died or managed to escape into Vygon.

That left the current farm house where I've been incapacitated uninhabited. A lone healer wandered by in search of refuge within Lygon. Luckily for me, he was hospitable enough to issue treatment upon Crixus's request. If not for him, I may still be prisoner to an unending dream state.

Crixus and Creon spent the past several days gathering food for when I woke, and now my stomach is full with the toiled harvest of farmers long forgotten. Crixus and I filled our bellies with roast corn and mashed yams. Spotty potatoes boiled with cloves of garlic. Homemade pasta with mashed tomato sauce. Charred bread and stalks of broccoli. It is perhaps the most random meal I've ever consumed all at once, but my starving stomach was impartial to the mouthwatering feast.

Now we lay beside each other curled up by the fire pit, staring up at the stars in the sky. No war wages on above us. Crixus says the night has been devoid of fighting these past few nights. I reckon Bloodlust is saving his soldiers for the night of the full moon, so the Undead inside the city walls are left to patrol anxiously every night, awaiting the arrival of winged demons.

How can something so beautiful cause so much pain and suffering? Crixus asked, referring to the moon.

I am left to ponder the question.

It seems all things in life that are truly beautiful are the cause of pain and suffering. Every positive emotion we experience can be turned to pain. Loss accompanies love. Betrayal follows loyalty. Envy counters every generosity. There is no escaping the horrors this life presents. We are all malleable clay in the hands of a spiteful sculptor. The same moonlight that stirs my feelings of romanticism toward Crixus will soon be our undoing.

Her hand fondles my thigh. She rubs her thumb up and down my leg, arousing feelings I haven't felt in what feels like a lifetime. It takes every inch of willpower to not fold into her caress and show her body how I truly feel. I can still remember the feeling of her lips on mine. Heaven is in her mouth but she's got a hell of a tongue. I want to cave to the desire I feel toward her. This night will be the last opportunity for me to make love to her. Acknowledging that to myself is nauseating. The same woman I've grown to love may soon be dead, and that is what holds me back from losing all composure.

There is an invisible boundary between us, and once I cross that line there will be no going back. I can't afford to love her any more than I currently do. Allowing my body to communicate its love to hers will only blur the lines and make us both susceptible to the danger we will soon face. I would be a fool to let my desires take over. But her hand on my thigh makes me think being called a fool isn't such a bad thing after all.

Oh how painful life can be when the thing you want most will lead to your own downfall. There is an unspoken connection binding us together.

I can feel the tension between our bodies. I can feel the pent-up pressure in her fingers. She wants me as bad as I want her. But we've both built up walls around our vulnerability, so neither is willing to make the first move. We are each like Sygon. Walls within walls within walls. A complex interworking of emotional infrastructure built to dam the pain in our hearts and prevent ourselves from feeling true happiness.

I reach down and place my hand on top of hers.

The hairs on my arms stand as my skin touches hers.

It is too cliché to say butterflies flutter in my stomach. Instead I feel a tornado's whirlwind. Lust and love mixing like cold and heat fronts in the atmosphere to create a hurricane. We are perfectly imperfect together. Our many flaws do not matter to one another in the moonlight. Our pasts dissolve when we are in each other's presence.

"How can so much pain and suffering exist in the presence of something so beautiful?" I ask, flipping her question. "I can't help but think life is supposed to be simpler than this. All the fighting and killing. Humanity's constant sinful nature. Where does all this evil come from? Do you ever stare at the stars and think about that?"

She laughs. "I stopped thinking like that a long time ago. Figured I'd save myself the headache. If life was supposed to be simple, I think we'd have discovered world peace a long time ago. But instead, we invented war, because our problems are too complex to solve over simple conversation."

"Then what would you do, if you could rule the kingdoms?" I ask her as our fingers interlace. "I mean really? What would Queen Crixus do to help her sovereign citizens?"

"That's quite the loaded question, don't you think? Asking a common whore from Varne what she would do if she was important enough to wear a crown..."

"A common whore?" I laugh out loud, "Even Queens enjoy their fair share of promiscuity. How many men you've fucked isn't the least bit indicative of how pure your heart is. No, put your past aside. Truly, I want to know how you would rule a kingdom in a way that would lead to peace."

"I think people are so evil because they are all searching for something that isn't out there," Crixus whispers. "They all think there is some universal answer waiting for their discovery. They do anything and everything they can to claw themselves closer. They turn themselves from men into monsters. When they realize this is all meaningless, they give in to their fleshly desires. They rape and murder and steal to fill the void inside. Convince themselves that they must fuck the world before the world fucks them. I guess I'd start there. Build a society where people don't need to be bad in order to feel good."

"Ah, so you'd become a philosopher then?"

"The first ever philosopher who doesn't know how to read, mind you," she laughs.

"One doesn't need to know how to read in order to be wise. I'd like to think the true answers to life are intrinsic. Written on our hearts, so to say. Even the smallest child can discern the difference between right and wrong, after all. So what would your kingdom look like, to accommodate such epiphanies in its people?"

"I think I'd want it to be more of a community than a kingdom... You know? Like a place where everyone feels equal. Selective, of course, to weed out those with ill intent. With no vices, like wine or sniffing powders. No money, strictly bartering, that way the farmers are just as important as the leaders. No fighting, just negotiating. And everyone would be required to learn fighting, to further deter fighting. I figure a place where you can get punched in the mouth for speaking is less prone to be filled with gossip. Everyone would be accountable for their actions. No good deed would go unrewarded, no crime would go unpunished. I don't know, it would be simple. No more guarded egos or elevated prides."

"It sounds like utopia," I sigh, knowing such a community could never exist. Human nature prevents it. For some crippling reason, people can never seem to let peace thrive in this world. At the slightest hint of perfection on earth, someone feels called to go and introduce chaos.

"What do you plan on doing, after all of this is over?" Crixus asks. "Do you really intend on taking back your father's throne?" I sense a tone of prying in her voice. It is like she is probing to know if I intend to keep her in my life after Sygon has fallen, though it is implied in her ambiguous question. Still though, I can sense it, the same as I can sense the tension between us.

"I have no idea," I answer truthfully. "I've lived my whole life from day to day. The ability to plan for the future has never been a luxury I could afford. All I know is that once Sephora is back by my side, my world will be set right. Until then, all I can do is focus on getting her back."

"I admire the love you have for your daughter," Crixus sighs. "If my father loved me a fraction of how you care for Sephora, I would not have become the monster I am today."

I turn my head to face her and realize she's been looking at me this whole time. Her eyes sparkle in the moonlight. Her face radiates with love and loyalty. It is hard to believe this is the same woman who has killed dozens of Lycans in the fighting pit. She is a rose covered with thorns, and I want my hand to be left bleeding with how hard I hold her. I whisper, "I have never seen a monster so beautiful as you."

She is taken back by the comment, as if she is Enchantress being handed a Thanatos rose. Being called beautiful is not something she's accustomed to. I scoot my head closer to her. She leans in to kiss me, but neither of us closes the gap. We lay here, centimeters away from completing the kiss, our hot breath bathing each other's face with the desires that boil within us. Our eyes can't leave the trance we've entered into. My face is flush with a warmth I've never felt. We are driven breathless by the exhaustion it requires to hold up our walls. We are like virgins who don't know what to do with our hands. My spine tingles for her touch.

I pull myself away from her, gasping for air. "I'm sorry, but I can't..."

"No," she comforts me, "Don't apologize. I understand... You have your daughter to think about. She is the only girl your heart has space for at the moment."

We let go of each other's hands, raising our walls back to a height that hurts our hearts. We are both warriors first, and we both know how fatal going into battle with distractions will be.

"Do you think... After this..." she begins.

"Yes," I complete her question before she can ask it. "If we both survive. Yes."

"Good," she says, breathing a sigh of relief.

"We owe ourselves that," I conclude, mostly so I can justify the notion in my own mind.

"I agree. Then do your best to not die on me," she laughs.

"No matter how hard I try, the Fates won't let me."

"Then the Fates must be on our side," she whispers, moving her hand back to grab mine. I let her, and soon my walls fall back down.

We fall asleep under the stars, warmed by the glowing embers of firelight.

48

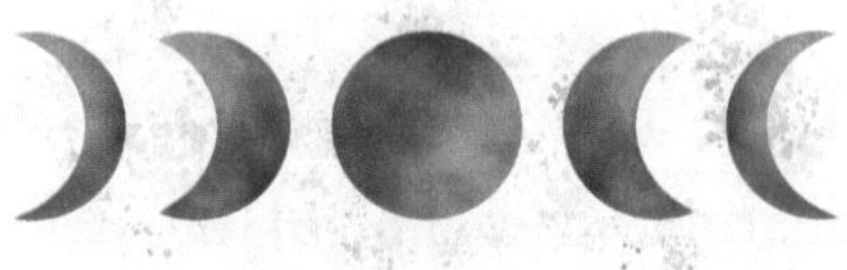

A Dream

You'd think the pain of loss gets easier to bare the more you endure.

It doesn't.

I cradle Mordecai's slain body in my arms and finally the tears I've held back after years of repression burst forth.

Wolves do not cry, but if a wolf cries alone no one will be there to see it.

And once again, I am truly alone.

Five long years I've called this tribe my family.

They took me in and raised me as their own.

They alone are responsible for the man I am today.

And now their bodies litter the ground around me. Their hearts no longer beat. Their lungs no longer breathe.

Never again will Mordecai scold me for my mistakes. Never again will Kateri tell me stories of the world in secret. Never again will Gondor grapple with me, nor will Kistka tell her silly jokes, nor will Ruth shoot archery by my side, nor will Ryle race me through the Neverglades. For the second time in sixteen years, I've lost my family, and I can't help but feel as though it is my fault.

Dead ravens litter the ground in the space between the dead bodies.

If silence could kill, I would be among them.

The same forest village I've called my home for years no longer has laughing cubs running around or playful parents chasing after them. No banter is exchanged, no songs are being sang. Everything is quiet. Everything except the echoes of my sobs and the choking of my snot. Maybe, just maybe, I could have saved them if I was here. I stare at the dead boar I dragged back to camp. Maybe if I had been faster in hunting the wild animal I would have been back in time to fight. Maybe if I hadn't been so stubborn and brought Ryle with me, I would have killed the boar days ago instead of turning the hunt into a wild goose chase. But I let my pride get to me, and I got lost in the forest. Only minutes ago I carried its carcass over my shoulder, anticipating the tribe's enthusiasm upon my return. We haven't had a kill this bountiful in weeks. The people would have sung my name with praise as we roasted its body over the fire tonight.

But then I smelled bloodshed, and then I saw bodies.

I can still smell the perpetrators responsible for this massacre. Their scent lingers in our village like smoke on fabric. But even if I had never met the Undead before, the puncture wounds on the victims' necks are enough for me to put the pieces together.

Five years I've gone without encountering the Undead, but somehow they found me. In the darkest of all forests, in the most remote, isolated sanctuary on planet earth, they tracked me down. Did they kill my tribe because of me? Or was it a meaningless, coincidental attack?

For them to catch Mordecai by surprise and overwhelm our fighting forces, they must have been savages. Brutal barbarians out for blood. But they have no idea what they've started. There is nothing more dangerous in this world than a man with nothing to lose, and I've just lost everything I've grown to care about in this world. I may be only sixteen, but they've messed with the wrong teen wolf. I am the child who killed the thyrops with bare hands. I am the boy who murdered the Sylvian family. I am the one person in this world who is not to be messed with. I am cursed by the gods, but today I vow to make that curse somebody else's problem.

I let go of Mordecai's lifeless body and stand to take in the scene around me. I memorize the sight of my loved ones pale and motionless on the ground, their bodies drained of their lifeblood. This is what I will picture when I close my eyes. I will not let go of this feeling of revenge until I've plunged my dagger into the heart of those responsible. I will tie the Undead tribe leader up and make him watch me slaughter all he loves. I will drag them into the daylight one by one. I will look them in the eyes as their bodies burn alive. I will make sure they know the grave error they made by interfering with my family. And then, only when they are all dead, will I feed on the leader while he is alive, devouring him limb by limb until he passes away from the excruciating pain.

"Syrus! Syrus!" A voice squawks from overhead. I know the voice like the back of my hand. I hear the fluttering of wings as the raven lands on my shoulder.

"Wolfsram," I growl, welcoming the messenger of death. Ravens are not stupid. The bird knows what happened as much as I do. Like me, Wolfsram was too consumed by our boar hunt to be present for the massacre. The raven has taken to me like a best friend. He is the sole bird that accompanies me on all my hunts, and I reward him generously for his loyalty. But now I force Wolfsram to take in the sight of his fallen brethren. Hundreds of ravens litter the ground like fallen leaves. I can sense the bird's emotions flaring as he reacts at the scene before us.

"Undead! Undead!" he squawks.

"I know," I reply, "I can smell them."

"Revenge! Avenge them!"

"Can you lead me to their killers?" I ask, my voice a low growl in my throat.

"Follow! Follow!" Wolfsram screams, taking flight into the air. Though we have only just returned, it is time to go on the hunt once more. But this time it is personal. This time I don't intend on bringing any prey back with me. When I return to bury my loved ones, I will return with news that their killers burn in hell.

49

A Dream

I wait outside the cave with the most violent patience a mortal has ever felt. Three days I've stalked the assailants to learn their ways. The Undead brutes hide away by day in a cave in the foothills of the Thoren Mountains, ten miles north of the Neverglade's edge. They trekked a considerable distance to kill my tribe. I will surpass their efforts tenfold to show them the pain they've caused me.

I won't rush this mission.

This is personal. I want to know them on an individual basis. I want to know their children by name before I kill them for what they've done. I watch their every move. I know when their scouts patrol the area as the sun first sets. I know when their women go to fetch water. I watch their children go to play in the bordering creek, or when they climb trees and practice flight through the air like baby birds stretching their wings for the first time.

My body is covered in mud to hide my scent. I chew wolfsbane like Kateri taught me to calm my senses. My blood is cold. My eyes are rimmed with red. I haven't eaten anything more than wild berries and eggrew leaves since staking out my enemy.

Wolfsram sticks close, perching in the branches of a Sequoia nearby. He is just as committed to my cause, and even more excited for blood to be shed.

The tribe's leader goes by the name Ragnar. He is every bit as savage and barbaric as my tribe's massacre suggested. His body is well over seven feet and his body is covered with enough fat to suffocate a skeleton. He carries with him a studded mace everywhere he walks that looks big enough to have been a tree branch in a former life. The man looks as though his father was a wildebeest and his mother was a troll. His forehead is so blunt and thick it looks as though he could headbutt a tree and send it crashing to the ground. He has no neck, as if some witch doctor sewed his head directly onto his shoulders. His fat nipples are larger than thick slices of pepperoni and his tits jiggle with every step he takes.

The other members of the tribe are no better. They all look inbred, the result of several generations of brothers fucking their sisters. Their eyes are too close and their underbites are extreme enough to leave their lower fangs exposed at all times. Their skin is covered with warts and moles. Their fingers are like fat sausages and their limbs look like the pale piping bags of custard bakers use to ice a cake.

The more I watch them the more I become enraged at their continued existence. Screams echo from inside their caves, indicating to me there is living prey they've trapped to continually feed their needs. Their men and women sneak off into the distance every night to fuck, moaning like wild boars in heat.

They are the most perverted and perverse iteration of Undead I've ever laid eyes on. An abomination in the sight of the gods. It feels as though Damon himself has led me to their encampment to put an end to their being. It is the first time I've ever taken joy at complying with the god's wishes for my life.

I will gladly be Damon's vessel, and by the time I am done with these monsters they will be wishing they'd never been born.

I have tallied a census and gathered there are approximately fifty in all, give or take a few stragglers who may remain in the caves. The only heavy hitters I need to concern myself with are Ragnar and his dozen closest men. Each of them is tall as a giant and thick as a bull. I'll need to catch each of them unaware and deal with them in silence if I'm to stand any chance. I may only be sixteen, but these men are nothing compared to the thyrops.

They are totally unaware of my presence. I lurk around them like a shadow, using the techniques Mordecai taught me to stealthily observe. This is the night I will strike. Once Ragnar and his men have been dealt with, the rest will be easy picking in the daylight.

During yesterday's daylight I set traps for the tribe's biggest warriors. Work smarter, not harder. Each of the traps is enough to maim them, but not enough to kill them. I want to be the one who watches the life leave their eyes. They have not earned a swift death. I want them to suffer before I discharge them to the afterlife, and I want them to know the reason why they've lost my permission to live.

I look up at Wolfsram and nod at him as the moon rises in the distance. The bird acknowledges me, then leaps into action. Wolfsram takes flight and lands directly outside the cave's mouth. Nothing is visible beyond the veil of darkness that conceals the home of the troglodytes. But I know them better than any hunter knows his prey. They will stumble into the open world looking for opportunities to cause mischief. Their neanderthal nature can't resist a call to cause trouble.

Wolfsram squawks loudly into the cave's echoing darkness. "Ragnar!" the bird calls aloud, just as I instructed him to do. It is a thing of beauty how intelligent these birds are.

I lean over and pick up my makeshift bow I've carved in my free time. I examine it closely. It is by no means a work of art, but Ruth would be proud nonetheless of what I've managed to construct in such little time. Regardless, I have spent countless hours perfecting my aim with it while the Undead sleep the day away. Every bow is different and requires tuned muscle memory to get the perfect shot. Each arrow flies different. The shooter must learn exactly how every arrow will glide through the air and adjust each shot accordingly. I have spared no expense in mastering this bow. My back aches with muscle memory I've drilled into it these past three days. Anything less than the perfect shot at this point is on me.

Ragnar stumbles forward into the night with a single grunt loud enough to send chills of joy down my spine. His massive figure looms over Wolfsram with confusion in his eyes. He looks down at the bird and scratches his head, then releases a belch strong enough to be smelled from a mile away. I scrunch my nose as the odor hits me, then draw the arrow back to my face. There is no turning back now. All I can do is trust in my preparation and hope it's enough to see me through to the end.

Just as a smile curls on Ragnar's blunt face I release the arrow, aiming directly for his eye. If there is anything the thyrops taught me, it's that an opponent that's bigger than me loses any advantage in battle when they've lost their ability to see. The arrow flies just as I taught it to, and the countless hours of drilling pay off. I watch as the arrowhead stabs directly into Ragnar's left eye with enough force to blind him, but not enough to penetrate his brain.

There is a reason I didn't aim for the dolt's throat, and that reason is what happens next. After the millisecond it takes for the moron to realize he's been shot, the pain registers in his miniscule brain and he unleashes a howl of pain loud enough to shake the ground below me. Wolfsram takes flight and retreats to his Sequoia tree in the distance, knowing his job here is complete.

The scream lasts long and its echoes last longer as the giant stumbles foolishly into the minefield of traps I've set. Ten men barge forward from the cave's mouth to learn the reason behind their master's girlish howl. None of them comprehend the danger they could be in, and none of them step cautiously into the field that borders their home. I watch as their heavy, thunderous footsteps set off my traps in tandem, each one of them meeting their end before they can comprehend what's happening.

It is all too easy, I sigh inwardly, watching the giants sign their own deaths. The first four walk straight into the ditch I've covered with leaves and branches, plummeting down the ten-foot drop to land on sharpened spears I've staked at the bottom. The other six are at least smart enough to take note of their fallen brethren and cease all movement before falling over the edge. I listen to the yelps of pain as the spears pierce their arses and enter their bowels. I will deal with them later.

I pick up another arrow, the one that has a rope tied around its feathered end, and draw it back, aiming directly at who I presume to be the next most dangerous target. It is a man who is slightly smaller than Ragnar in size but twice as feisty. His mind seems to be catching on quicker than his companions, which means his intelligence level is equal to that of at least a five-year-old. I don't give him time to think and send the arrow his direction, watching the rope dance in the air as the shaft penetrates the Undead's forearm. I was aiming for his bicep, but the forearm is close enough.

Instinctively, the man yanks at the rope. The miscreant cannot help himself. He is like a mouse that sees cheese and must bite down on it, not sensing the trap attached to it. As he pulls the rope, the lever attached to the other side of it activates. A log the length of three men and the width of Ragnar's fat torso swings into action, spears tightly fastened to its base, each protruding outward to penetrate anything and everything that gets in the way of its momentum. I watch in fascination as the log rams into all six of the standing men and three of the spears find targets. It is like I am learning physics from Lundis once more and I've just watched an unstoppable force collide with six unmovable objects.

It takes a moment for the three unbloodied men to gather their footing after the assault. I can hear their breath wheezing from behind their broken ribs. Meanwhile Ragnar spins in circles, blood squirting from between his fingers as he tries to apply pressure to his shish-kebabbed eyeball. He still screams as if the sound of his voice will be able to heal his wound.

The final two men emerge from the cave now to join their wounded comrades. They both emerge into the darkness of night in utter confusion of what's happened. They see the arrow in Ragnar's eye, the four men who fell in the ditch impaled up the ass, three men skewered by the log, and the other three sucking wind as if they mean to start a tornado. None of the wounded have the mental capacity to understand what's happened, and certainly none of them have the mental capacity to explain what's happened.

Now it is time for the grand finale.

I scramble over to another rope that's been concealed by the tall grass that borders the foothills. I grab it firmly and pull with all my might. It grows taut, then begins to tip the upright boulder I've set in place in front of another cave's opening. The neanderthals watch in dismay as the boulder falls over to uncover the hidden cave mouth. A sound emerges from the darkness of the cave. They do not know what to do, nor do they know what I've trapped inside the cave in their absence.

Idiots! I laugh inwardly.

I watch as the fully grown thyrops emerges from the cave's opening, its nostrils lifting to the air to identify the nearby odor of targets. Immediately, the beast smells the blood in the air and paralyzing fear associated with its presence. These are prime conditions for a thyrops to hunt. It does not need to rely on its poor eyesight in darkness like this. The strong odor of the Undead tribe's poor hygiene is enough to knock a buzzard off a shit wagon. The thyrops would be able to locate these men if they were hiding on the moon with how terrible they smell.

I hear the cry of the thyrops's child echo inside the cave. It is the same thyrops cub I kidnapped in order to lure the thyrops into the cave and trap them both there. What most don't know is that the thyrops is one of the most protective parental beasts in existence. Few teach this because those who learn that lesson rarely live to tell of it. I watch as the thyrops scrapes its paw against the ground, rearing backward as it prepares to charge the survivors.

The Undead brace themselves but the fight is over before it began. I watch as the thyrops charges into them like calvary colliding with lifeless scarecrows. Though the Undead are monsters among men, their bulky frames do nothing more than make them bigger targets for the thyrops. I watch as the beast's horn penetrates one of the men and lifts him off his feet, then shrugs him off and tosses him aside like leftover dough at a baker's shop. The thyrops goes on a blind rampage as it tramples over one Undead to get to another. Its horn thrusts into another's body and sends blood splattering against the nearby cave wall like paint against a canvas. The noise of my tribe's killers screaming in agony and confusion is beautiful to my ears. They deserve every second of this, and I have never watched people die with such little remorse in my heart before.

The remaining two Undead that have yet to be harmed attempt to jump on the thyrops's back to restrain it. Big mistake. A thyrops is not the same a bull. It is not something that can be wrangled and bound up like a cowboy taming a stallion. This is a wild, vicious animal, and it reacts accordingly. The thyrops bucks both men off and soon adds them to its list of carnage. I watch in amusement as Ragnar's staggering, half-blind body stumbles in the way of the thyrops and is knocked off balance. The idiot falls over the ledge to join his four companions that fell earlier, screaming aloud as the stakes impale various spots along his broadside.

I still have three arrows left and nothing to do with them. I notch them and aim at whichever men seem the least injured, releasing them for the fun of it, but making sure I am hitting them in places that won't kill them instantly. Maimed, not dead, I remind myself.

I sit down and let the thyrops have its revenge, the beast no doubt thinking these men are the ones responsible for stealing its child. All I need is a bowl of popcorn or a leg of mutton to enjoy the spectacle.

The especially stupid members of the tribe emerge from the cave to see what's happening and instantly regret choosing to do so. The thyrops makes short work of those whose footfall sounds like thunder.

The bigger they are, the harder they fall. Wolfsram descends from his perch to watch the thyrops enter into a feeding frenzy from the comfort of my shoulder. The raven likely relishes the sight of bloodshed more than myself. This is why he follows me, after all. To feed off the death I reap. Soon enough, there will be enough corpses to feed an entire army of ravens, though only Wolfsram remains from his flock.

It takes the better part of an hour for the thyrops to be content with the damage it's caused. I watch as the beast slowly lumbers off with its child walking between its legs for protection. It was a miracle I was able to find the child while its mother was unaware. I made sure to leave its scent along the trees and ferns that led to the cave where I tied it up and trapped it. The hardest part in truth was moving a boulder big enough to contain a fully-grown thyrops. It took the better part of two days to devise a pulley system strong enough, and the Undead were entirely too stupid to notice the rock I'd moved ever so slowly day by day.

I realize how lucky I am to be dealing with Undead who lack the mental acuity to know they're being stalked. The majority of their species possesses intelligence far beyond what my childish mind can discern. I would have never been able to pull such a feat off if I was dealing with Celestials or another tribe of pure-blooded Undead.

With Wolfsram still perched on my shoulder, I slowly approach the pit of death where Ragnar and his men rest. They've ceased their screaming for help for quite some time, realizing their writhing does nothing more than make them bleed out faster.

I carefully avoid the concealed traps that the Undead didn't make it far enough to set off. It's a shame I didn't get to see my full plan flesh out, but I am grateful my first two traps were powerful enough to maim all twelve of them.

I stare over the edge of the pit. Ragnar stares back up at me with his good eye. Three separate spears protrude from his body. One in the gut, another in the shoulder, a third in his thigh. He has since pulled the arrow out of his skull, ripping his own eyeball out of its socket in the process. Blood pools around the victims. I can smell the iron rising in the warm air that lifts from the trench.

"Who... who are you?" the leader of the barbarians calls up to me.

I smile back at him as I lick my lips. "I am the hellhound the devil has sent to collect your soul," I reply coldly.

50

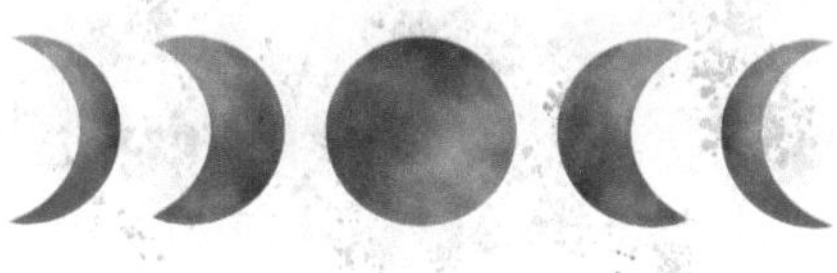

A Dream

I have nothing more than two sharpened dagger-length sticks in either hand, ready to thrust them into anything and everything that moves. I walk with swift caution as I enter the cave. The only inhabitants left in the tribe are the women and children. It will be easy to make mincemeat of them. By the time the sun rises, there won't be a single member of this Undead tribe left alive.

I hear chains rattling in the distance. I can smell the collection of feces and urine. The cave reeks of festering wounds. "Who goes there?" a voice calls out in the darkness, concern and fear laced in its tone. It is not the perverted voice of one of the tribesmen. As I turn the twisting bend of the cave expecting to come face to face with more monsters, I'm met by innocent eyes instead. I see no sign of the trolls who dwell inside this cavernous fortress. Though I can smell their presence, they have likely retreated far into the maze of tunnels that run into the Thoren Mountains. Left behind are their shackled prisoners, whom I come face to face with now.

"If you are here to kill us, just get it over with," the same voice calls to me. It comes from a man who looks as though he's already been killed twice but refused to die. He is missing half his left arm, the limb chewed up to the elbow. I can see the bone and ligaments hanging where the sawed flesh gives way. He spits blood at my feet and smiles up at me with a row of broken teeth.

"I have no quarrel with you, prisoner. I am here to kill the Undead who've captured you. Tell me where they've gone and I will free you from your chains." I try to sound as heroic as possible, but my voice shakes as the adrenaline begins to dissipate.

"They've retreated into their tunnels, boy. You will never find them now."

I look over the prisoners each in turn. Most are human, but some are Undead themselves. Their bodies are naked, though some still have a few rags clinging to their skin. I spot a set of purple eyes peering at me in the darkness. It is a young girl my age, chained to a wall, anger in her eyes like amethyst set on fire. She does not belong to this group of neanderthals. The wounds and bruising along her body are enough to gather that.

"Say boy," the man calls out. "That raven on your shoulder... Are you Lycan?"

I look back at him, still processing the anger that boils under my skin at the fact that the Undead have escaped my grasp. If I chase them into the mountains I will get lost. These tunnels are their home, and they have the homefield advantage to defend themselves. What this man tells me is that I'm better off thanking my lucky stars I was able to kill as many of them as I did.

"Me and my wife here are Lycan too," he stutters, probing me to answer his question. "Our tribe uses ravens for hunting too... What tribe do you hail from?"

I stare at him in silence, then pick up a nearby rock. I bash it into the chains that restrain the man, then break his wife's. His demeanor changes as he stares up at me like I'm some savior. I did not come here to rescue prisoners, but I may as well accomplish some form of good to pay back the universe for the deaths I've caused.

I stare at him with little sympathy. He looks just as capable of breaking the chains that have held him hostage. There is no excuse why he could not have freed himself from this bondage and saved his wife. Even with one arm chewed off, if I was in this man's shoes I would have cut my own leg off to save my body.

"Gods be good," his wife moans, staring at the broken chains. "You've saved us!"

"We owe you our lives!" her husband calls out.

I turn my eyes to focus back on the Undead female that still stares at me. "You there," I call out to her. "What is your name?"

She stares at me violently. I can feel the tension in the air between us. "Vesper," she whispers, her soothing voice causing my heart to skip a beat. A name as beautiful as she is. I can see through the soot and grime that covers her body. I know this girl is an angel in disguise. The chained bodies around her are all dead, their bodies consumed to the point where their souls were forced to leave this world in search of another.

"Do you know these tunnels, Vesper?" I ask.

She nods her head. "My tribe lives in the Thoren Mountains. These people abducted me while I was fetching water for my family."

"Could you help me find them?"

She smiles for the first time since seeing me, realizing that I am on her side. I am an avenging angel, and she is the cavernous raven that can lead me to what I seek.

"So long as you promise to kill every last one of them for what they've done to me," she replies. I match her smile with my own. A woman after my own heart. I drop the rock and approach her, picking up her chains in my hands and ripping them from the rocky wall they're nailed into. She stands as her broken chains drop. We stand eye to eye for a brief moment. I can feel electricity in the vibrating space between us. It is like the Fates predestined this moment. We are two sides to the same coin. Me, Lycan, and her, Undead. Automatically bonded through our trauma. Instantly united in our revenge.

I quickly free the remaining prisoners that line the cave walls. None of them speak to me. None of them have the energy to muster their verbal gratitude, but I can see it in their eyes, and that alone is thanks enough.

"Please," the Lycan male calls to me, "Is there anything we can do to repay you? I will not descend into these caves further, but we have a tribe! A whole group of Lycans who can take you in! Do you need a home? Our kind is stronger in packs... We have need of warriors like you!"

I turn to face him. "Can you take my raven?" I ask him, my heart breaking as I know it is time to part ways with Wolfsram. The bird on my shoulder instantly squawks in protest, as I knew he would. We have been bonded these past five years. Basically inseparable. Best friends in the most meaningful way. But where I am going is no place for a bird of his nature. If these Lycans are telling me the truth and they have a tribe with their own flock of ravens, Wolfsram will have a much better life in their company.

"Of course we can!" the man replies, "But what about you? Where will you go?"

"To finish what I started," I reply coldly.

"Surely you can't expect to find them all? They know these tunnels like the back of their hands! They took off the second they heard their leader scream in pain. They have a several hour head start over you."

"Then I better get moving," I respond.

The man nods, knowing there is nothing he can say or do to convince me otherwise.

He raises the one hand that remains intact for me to shake. "My name is Urriah, son of Umbast, member of the ancient Fang Clan that descended from Dagon himself. I owe you a blood debt for saving my life, and the life of my wife. I will never forget the great deed you've done today. I will return to my tribe and give news that a teen wolf took on an entire group of Undead and lived to tell the tale. Should you *ever* need help, follow the ravens to the outskirts of the eastern edge of the Neverglades. There I will remain, waiting to repay you for the kindness you've shown me today."

"No!" Wolfsram squawks, refusing to leave my side. I grab the bird by his feet and make him face me.

"I will come back for you, Wolfsram, but these mountains are no place for a raven. I am not asking you to go with this man. I am ordering you. The day will come when we are reunited. I promise you that."

Urriah carefully grabs Wolfsram from my hands as the bird attempts to take flight in protest. His midnight wings thrash against the air violently like a pup squealing as it's removed from its mother's tit.

I turn to face Vesper, who watches me with adoration in her eyes. "Are you ready?"

She nods in response. We take off together. I don't turn around, knowing it will be too painful for my heart to see Wolfsram fighting to be back by my side. I listen as he calls out for me. "Syrus! Syrus! No! Syrus!" His selective vocabulary confines him to repeating my name over and over again. The further I move away from him, the more I hear my name echo off these dark walls. My heart shatters with every step I take away from him.

I will see him again.

I know I will.

It may not be tomorrow, it may not be this year even, but I vow to return to him.

I make the promise to myself, hoping I will survive to keep it.

But I have another promise I must keep to myself that requires finding the remaining members of the Undead tribe that killed my family.

I follow Vesper's slender, pale body into the dark, leaving behind my best friend in order to sever all that tethers me to my past.

"Syrus!" the echoes call.

"Syrus!" the walls moan.

"Syrus!" the ground shakes.

I shed a single tear as the voice drowns out in the distance.

51

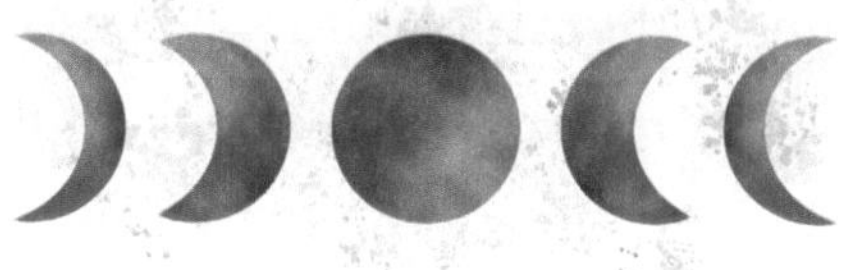

A Nightmare

There are signs in Vygon that the Acolytes have already arrived. When we enter the unmanned gates of the outer wall, we are met with nothing but trampled mud of a party larger than several hundred. Horse hooves and armored boots leave their trace straight through the city's unguarded farmland.

It does not seem they are concerned with covering their tracks. They've carved their path violently through the landscape well enough for a blind man to follow. When they got here, I have no idea. It could have been days ago. But one thing's for sure. I hear no fighting from the elevated city of Sygon.

As we stare at it in the distance, it is like a beacon on a hill. It sits perched far above Lygon, several miles from where we currently stand. Vygon itself is laid to waste. The crops were lit on fire long ago and stamped into the mud. The livestock either escaped or was eaten. A few stray sheep and cows scatter the desolate space inside the walls, each of their coats dirty enough to make them look like clay sculptures.

I hear the familiar flapping of wings overhead. It causes some instinct in me to ignite. I stare up at the sky and watch as a single raven lands on the outer wall, watching me and Crixus's entry with intrigue. I smile up at the bird. It is like seeing an old friend. I smile for more than nostalgia's sake. If it is any indication of the Fates, my plan is coming to fruition.

"Why are you smiling at the carrion bird?" Crixus asks, stopping alongside me. "Don't you know they are bad omens?"

"Bad omens? Ravens?" I ask in return, not moving my eyes from the black bird's analytic gaze. "No, I've always considered them to be somewhat a product of good fortune."

Crixus looks at me with confusion. Obviously she has not spent time learning what this species of bird has to offer our kind. Most Lycans haven't. Ravens do not ally themselves with rogue wolves. It wasn't until after the death of Mordecai that I learned it is not common for Lycans to band together in the wild. Most are too concerned with hiding themselves away so their beast is not discovered. Since the control of the Undead Empire, evidence of being a Lycanthrope is punishable by death.

"You obviously haven't been told many horror stories by the campfire then," Crixus chuckles.

"No," I admit, "I'm too busy living a nightmare to concern myself with fake scary stories. But trust me, the bird's presence is good luck for our venture."

"Good, I was beginning to think it meant we were going to die," Crixus laughs. Just as she finishes the sentence, a second raven descends from the clouds and perches next to the original one, squawking to acknowledge its brother. Both stare down at us like twin messengers of death. But it is not our deaths they foretell. It is the death of those who wait for us above.

It takes the better part of the morning to trek through Vygon. It is the widest ring of the three-tiered city, and the landscape is difficult to navigate after the war's pillaging. While farmland is a great place to be in times of peace, its fertile soil turns to filth when all signs of life have been eradicated. There are no more plants to slow the erosion. The fires and floods have turned the soil to an uninhabitable patch of loamy mush. It seems like all we've done since we arrived at Gall is fight to free our feet from mud. Swamp, delta, quicksand, now this. It makes me miss the firm ground of the easterly Areopagus and bordering cities. Hell, I'd take a walk through the Scorpos desert over hiking through mud any day.

But signs of life begin to appear the closer we get to Lygon. Local farmers that haven't succumb to death batten down their hatches outside the middle section. Their makeshift huts are constructed directly outside of the middle wall, close to the protection of archers that patrol Lygon's middle class. What little livestock is left is found in poorly constructed pens. Pigs rolling around in slop. Cows covered in their own manure. Free range chickens looking as though they've just returned from battle. Tethered goats staring up at us with wearier eyes than the farmers.

The ground slowly is restored with signs of new life. Pastures of grass that haven't yet been ripped apart by hooves. Fields of wheat and barley fresh for reaping. It sways in the afternoon sun with a golden glow. There are patches of field dedicated to growing viny vegetables. Eggplants and squash and pumpkins. I can see the spurts of growth where underground vegetables burrow—onions and carrots and potatoes. The farmers go about their business as if the war is a thing of the past—bustling along the fields as if they are unconcerned about anything other than providing food for their bellies.

Not a single one raises their thatch hat to examine me and Crixus as we move onward.

They are not paid to ask questions. See no evil, hear no evil, speak no evil. So we press forward, and in the back of my mind I'm conscious as I see the dozens of ravens lining Lygon's stone wall. The patrols that walk along its barrier shoo the birds away, but the stubborn carrions simply circle around and land elsewhere.

As I expected, we are met with resistance as we come to Lygon's closed gate. A battalion of human soldiers stand ready, each of them cooking in their armor beneath the summer sun.

"What business do you have here?" one of them calls out to us. I have been crafting this narrative since we left the mountains. There is no one more skeptical than a lowly knight in a time of war.

"We are actors from the city of Queensmyre!" I shout out. "Our city has been burned to the ground. We seek asylum! We have traveled many days to get here with little food or water. We fear for our lives and seek refuge in Lygon's hospitable rule!"

The knights look at one another with mistrust. They've likely heard every story there is to hear since the war began. They are human no doubt, which makes them particularly gullible to sympathy.

"Actors from Queensmyre?" he repeats, almost as if he has never heard of an 'actor' or 'Queensmyre' before. "We have no need for your kind here, nor the food and resources for two more groveling citizens. Your journey was a waste, turn back now and seek refuge in Yueltope!"

"Yueltope?" I spit back at him. "You'd have us go to a city of anarchy to be robbed and killed? Everyone knows Yueltope is a city of criminals and outlaws!"

"Not any longer," the knight dismisses the idea completely. "New rumors come bringing news of Yueltope's reform. A few dozen citizens of Queensmyre have already settled there and claimed it as their own. They seek to make it a new town dedicated to peace and this 'acting' you speak of. You would both be better suited there. I tell you this for your own good. Sygon is home of the Undead now. You two would be nothing more than blood bags if I let you inside these gates. Turn away now, while you still can. Go to Yueltope, it is the safest place within a hundred miles for you."

This is going to be harder than I thought. It is time to switch up. If entry isn't permitted by innocence and ignorance, time to act like this city has something I need. I press on, "But I have heard rumors the Acolytes marched through these very gates most recently. Met a man in a roadside tavern that said they put an end to the Undead a few nights back. I figured we would be safest in whatever city they lodged in and was told they were coming here. Is that not their tracks left in the mud that we followed through Vygon all this time?"

I see my words strike a nerve with the lead knight. He bites his tongue and considers his words carefully. It seems as though my knowledge of the Acolytes' presence in Sygon is not something I should know, nor should it be common knowledge to anyone who lives outside these walls.

"Whoever told you such a thing was mistaken. There is no one here who goes by the name Acolyte. But I can tell you that if you were caught asking such a thing inside these walls, Princess Saunter would have your tongue for blasphemy or hang you for heresy, depending on her mood."

Princess Saunter?

Does this knight not know that she is dead?

Atlas and his Acolytes took her and her army by surprise in Yueltope. Surely the fact that she hasn't returned for over a week is enough to indicate to these men that she is dead. But perhaps news of her demise is not information awarded to knights of their low status. This is, after all, Lygon's outer wall. Any knights privileged to be trusted with that information would be guarding Sygon itself, not its less fortunate brother.

But still, it worries me to see the look of nervousness that washed over the knight's face when I mentioned the Acolytes. Clearly he is hiding something I don't know about. It is time to stop playing coy. There is only one way this troupe will let us into the kingdom's gates, and that's if I show them my cards.

I walk up to the lead knight, leaving Crixus to watch from behind. The man's face is covered with a sheen of sweat. His armor looks as though it hasn't been polished in years. The other knights press closer to their leader as I march toward him courageously. I watch as their hands close around the hilts on their belts. Why they feel intimidated by an actor from Queensmyre, I'm unsure. But maybe it's because they see something in me that doesn't line up with my narrative. Maybe it's the way I walk, or the venom in my eyes.

As I walk up to the knight's leader my head is looking straight down at the ground. But as I get only inches away from his face, I raise my head to reveal gleaming silver eyes that cut into his soul. The light between our faces radiates from the silver aura. The unpolished armor sparkles anew. A look of pure horror possesses the man's face as he nearly falls backward, but the gate he guards prevents him from retreating. I hear swords draw from sheathes all around me.

But they won't attack without command from their leader. All I need to do is win over his heart. He alone has authority to let me inside this gate, and he alone can tell his men to stand down. Anything else will result in a bloodbath, and I will still gain entry into Lygon's walls if I have to step over a few dead bodies to do so.

"Do you have children?" I ask earnestly, my stoic voice not matching with my look of intimidation.

The knight nods his head fearfully. He has a second chin of fat that bounces as his head shakes.

"Then do them a favor and make sure they don't become fatherless today," I threaten through my smile. If he is going to make me be the villain, I'll be the villain. But the man's loyalty to Lygon is thinner than thread. I don't have to explain who I am or why I come bearing threats. The man complies without another word spoken, and none of his subordinates question his actions.

That is the silver lining with humans—they can detect when a fight is not worth dying over. The knights pull the rusted gate open, its hinges the only thing screaming in protest, and Crixus and I enter Lygon without a moment of hesitation.

My silver eyes disappear, and once again we are nothing more than actors from Queensmyre.

The archers that walk the wall above us are too preoccupied shooing ravens to see the interaction between me and the gatekeeper. We fall into Lygon's streets and become lost among the crowds. For the first time since departing from the Blackbloods, we enter the first truly populous city. Lygon's streets are jam-packed with humans going about their business. There is hardly enough space to walk shoulder to shoulder by Crixus.

I am suddenly reminded why I hate city life.

Too many people, too much noise, too little peace.

I pause to take it all in, holding Crixus's hand in my own to prevent us from being separated. Tens of thousands of humans navigate the streets like bees crawling along a tremendous hive. They go about their business, none of them knowing the names of the others they pass. Each of them seems to be on their own mission. So many people with so many plans. It's funny, how self-important each of these people view their lives to be. When they woke this morning, they did so with the intention of going back to bed tonight.

None of them have any idea what destruction is about to befall their great city. Like the ravens that crowd the surrounding walls, I bring only death with me.

Like all metropolises, this place built too many dwellings without expanding the road infrastructure. They crammed inns and apartments and homes so tightly packed that a piece of paper can't fit between the buildings. Yet the roads look as though they are constructed to support two wagons abreast, if that. So the people flock like corralled sheep in a pen three times too small for them. Bodies press into one another. Strange, repugnant odors fill the air from lack of hygiene.

It's a wonder some rogue pandemic hasn't brought these people closer to death already. To die from the plague would be a much more merciful death than what awaits them. It is hard for me to feel sympathy for any of them, really. These people haven't experienced an inkling of the tragedy I've faced in life.

I watch the merchants and bureaucrats shout at passersby. Degenerate priests occupy every street corner preaching about the end times. Fire and brimstone and things of that nature. No one stops to listen to their manic ramblings. Why would anyone waste their time filling their head with such nonsense, after all?

But the priests might be the only ones who have the simplest clue of what is coming for this town. Only it won't be fire and brimstone that brings wrath upon this city. Darkness and bloodshed are the only things that linger on the horizon. Darkness and bloodshed, and the silence that follows.

Like the slain tribe of Lycans who took me in as a child, soon this city will be haunted by the silence that follows massacre. Silence is the shadow that clings to the reaper's heels. But unlike with Mordecai and my fellow deceased Lycans, there will be no one left to avenge these peoples' deaths. Because unlike the Undead who killed my family, I won't leave anyone behind to be filled with righteous vengeance burning in their heart.

Crixus squeezes my hand, pulling me from my intrusive thoughts. I look to her, then lean close to her ear.

"Do you remember the plan?"

She nods, "Follow the ravens."

"Good. We have one more night before the moon is full. Let's not leave this up to Dagon's Curse. Sygon falls tonight," I declare, releasing her hand. She smiles up at me briefly, then disappears into the crowd to carry out the dark deeds I've assigned her.

I pray to the gods silently it won't be the last time I see her smile. But the gods have never been kind to me, so I won't expect them to be this time.

I watch as she disappears like a shadow, and then I am alone in a street filled with thousands.

At first we were five.

Now I am utterly alone.

But I am better off being left to my own devices.

Tonight I will be in hell, and I won't be dragging my loved ones with me.

52

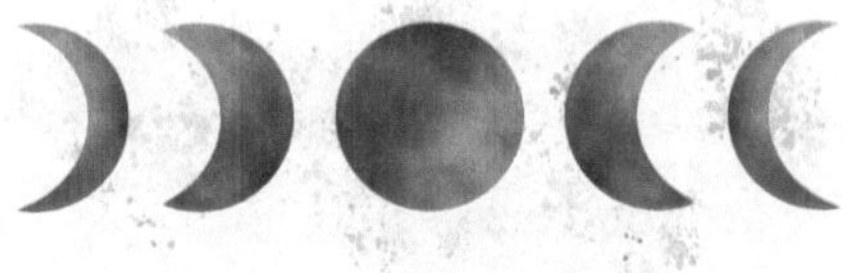

A Nightmare

I stare down at the bodies shackled in chains.

Their consciences float between life and death every wavering moment.

They are each trapped in purgatory, but I'll make sure their sacrifice is worth the hell the Undead have put them through.

I stare down at the vial of black blood in my left hand, then at the dagger in my right. I dip the blade inside the glass tube. How it has made it this far without shattering is miraculous. It must be built from the same glass my soul is made of. Unbreakable. Resilient. Volatile.

I don't have long before the sun sets. It took the majority of the day to find where the Undead store their blood bags. Though Saunter and her army are dead, I suspect this city to still be filled with Undead miscreants. They sleep the day away, but surely they will feast when the daylight fades.

Saunter was never my concern in the beginning anyway. It is her archers that prevent Bloodlust's forces from entering the city. Just because Atlas put an end to her reign doesn't dilute the Undead's resolve in the slightest. This city is still Ventur's stronghold on the west coast. And to win back my daughter, I must assure this place is defenseless when he arrives on the morrow. Account for all contingencies. Leave no Undead behind.

I look at the warehouse of shackled slaves. Like the valley of death that led to my captivity, these humans provide an invaluable service to the Undead—food.

There are thousands of Lygonian citizens. How these unfortunate souls were the ones chosen to sustain the Undead Empire's bloodlust will remain a mystery. Each of them won the unluckiest lottery a human can win. The luck of the draw, only these people drew the death card.

They are like flesh-covered skeletons. The floor around them is covered with their own urine and feces. Sadly enough, I can relate to how they feel after my time spent in Bloodlust's custody. Each of them have puncture wounds covering their bodies from head to toe. Most of the lacerations are infected and leaking puss.

It is hard to not feel bad for what I'm going to do to them. But their lives have been wasted anyway. Regardless of what happens tonight, their lives are already forfeit. Better to make their deaths heroic than for them to add to the toll of meaningless deaths the Fates enact.

I pull the blackened dagger from the vial, staring at it in the low light. The black blood has no effect on mankind, but a drop of it in their bloodstream will be enough to infect the Undead who feed on them. I grab the arm of a naked girl closest to me. Her skin is hot with fever. Her will has been broken by the countless nights of being fed upon. She doesn't protest my grip. She has learned to not fight back when contact is made with her skin.

I hover the blade over one of her many puncture wounds and slowly let the black blood on the blade gather along the tip. I watch as a single drip pools, then drops directly onto the cut. For a moment it does nothing. The bead of black blood just sits on her cut like a puddle on the ground, but within seconds I watch as it disappears beneath the skin's surface. The Blackblood virus is good at surviving, even in human hosts. It will enter this woman's bloodstream and multiply. Red blood is the perfect breeding ground for the spore to breed. The human's body possesses the antibodies to fight it off eventually, unlike the Undead, but it will take days for the virus to be purged from her body. By the time she is cured, her body will be long dead and Sygon will have fallen.

I repeat this process with as many of the slaves as I can. I have no guarantee which bodies will serve as food for the Undead when they wake from their slumber, so I need to leave nothing to chance. A single drop can go a long way. I have enough black blood in the vial to infect all of them.

The warehouse is long and dark and the bodies are many. I count the number of slaves I infect as I go, not sparing more than a single droplet of black blood per person. Like the Undead, these humans sleep the day away, fearing what will come for them in the night. The sores that are infected thankfully accept the black blood into their bodies.

Though I feel bad for doing this dark deed, it makes it easier on my soul that they do not oppose me. This would be a much more strenuous task if each of the slaves protested my mission. But they are each like livestock beaten into submission, the teeth marks along their bodies like branding on a bull to identify who they belong to.

How the rest of Lygon's citizens shuffle through the city streets going about their own business while such horrible things happen in the night to their fellow humans is beyond me. Ignorance is bliss, and as long as it isn't happening to them they don't give a damn.

My father would have never permitted anything like this to happen. Though the Undead occupied the Areopagus, he had passed strict blood consumption laws to regulate the Undead from creating an atrocity such as this. If you were a blood bag in the Areopagus you were treated with the dignity of nobility. Whichever Undead possessed you was responsible for paying you for your services. Some of the richest humans I knew were blood bags. The Undead were forced to pay them handsomely for their services, and any who couldn't afford to feed on human blood were forced to feed on animals.

Their species acts like feeding on animal blood is a burden, but Vesper did it the entire time I knew her. Any time she was sick or feeling weak, I would lend her my own neck, but she never took more from my body than what she needed.

But without Sylvian control to hold the Undead accountable, they feed on humans like sex addicts at an orgy. Animal populations flourish while humanity suffers gravely. They are apex hunters in a world where they have no natural predators.

But now I have returned to be that predator.

I have seen what this world was like before Ventur took control, and I plan to restore it to what it was before.

I wipe the sweat from my head as I drop the last bead of black blood into the final slave in this warehouse. I've counted as many as two thousand, seven hundred and twenty-three blood bags. I'm sure this is not the only warehouse that holds their prey, but it is enough to turn the lot of them into Blackbloods tonight.

And this is only Lygon. Whichever Undead soldiers occupy this town were not noble enough to be permitted entry into Sygon's fortress, but the Undead archers will be taken by surprise tonight when thousands of their own kind turn into Blackbloods and storm Sygon's gates. It will be my free ticket into the city's capital. Once the rampage begins, it will be too late to stop the destruction that will ensue. The Undead will be forced to go to war with their own brethren in their own city.

When the archers take their patrol tonight, they will look to the horizon for invaders, not knowing the monsters have already breeched Lygon's gates.

Still, doubts circulate in the back of my mind.

I can still picture Wilhelm's whimsical face when he learned I didn't know there was a cure to the Blackblood virus. Hopefully whatever cure he spoke of was not enough to prevent the virus from claiming over two thousand Undead.

But on top of that, throughout all my searching today, I've yet to see a single sign of the Acolytes' presence in this town. There were several hundred of their troops in Yueltope, and their footprints left in Vygon indicated most of them made it to this city alive. Where they disappeared to, and why no one is mentioning their name in the city streets remains a mystery.

It's likely they've marched straight into Sygon, but I have no idea what purpose they have there if it wasn't to take control over the city. I pray whatever conniving plot they've schemed hasn't endangered Creon.

But like all wars, I must fight one battle at a time.

If I concern myself with the potential of losing the final battle when the war has only just begun, Sephora's life will be forfeit.

One battle at a time, I repeat inwardly.

I stare at the enslaved zombies before me, then down at the empty vial of black blood. I wipe my dagger against my sleeve and tuck it back into my bag. By the time I leave the warehouse, the sunset pierces my dull eyes with a reminder that night is coming.

I stare up at the beautiful sky and smile when I see several ravens soaring overhead.

On their wings rides a reminder of death.
On their wings flutters a promise of vengeance.

53

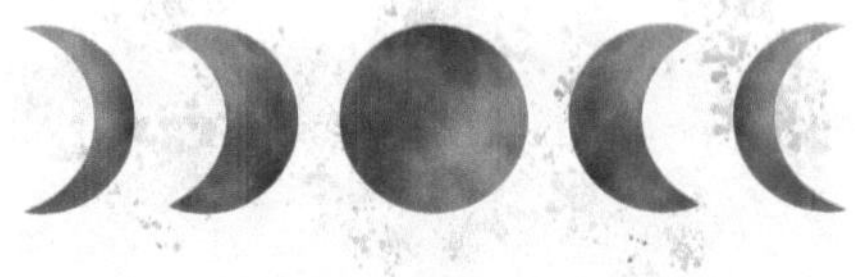

A Nightmare

There is no longer darkness in the distance.

It envelops me.

Spreads through the city streets like smog. Enters my body and pierces my soul. As the sun set, so too went any mercy I may feel. I am dead inside, standing in the darkness of the city square, waiting for human eyes to sleep and purple eyes to wake.

The moon is so full it could convince an onlooker to beware of Lycans. The ravens sing it midnight praises. I can feel it pulling at the beast within.

Before I grew to possess Sylvian's power, the night before the moon was normally more terrifying than the full moon itself. Its potency was enough to make me feverish as a child. It gives Lycans heightened abilities. Our sense of smell and sense of hearing is enough to make a mortal go mad. I'd often go to sleep cradling my head to drown out the noises. Overstimulation is a hell of a demon. We Lycans are weakest and most frightened when the storm brews on the horizon. But Mordecai taught me how to train these fears into strengths. Make my demons fight for me. And so an eerie sense of calmness washes over me as I see figures take to the sky.

Their eyes are like purple shooting stars as they fly into the night, analyzing their own perverted sense of morning. While mortals pray by their bedsides before going to sleep, the Undead wake to greet another bloody day. They float in the sky like false gods, surveying the dark horizon with pure bliss.

When I was a child I was afraid of the dark. When all the candles throughout the Areopagus castle were blown out and the darkness settled, I would lay in bed staring at the shadows. When a limb would slip from the side of my bed I would panic, fearing some unknown monster lurking beneath my bed would snatch me.

But as I grew older I learned that the real monsters come from the sky above, not the ground below. Demons are real, and their eyes are purple. Some, like Vesper, are better than others. But most, as demons are prone to do, commit themselves to their wanton ways. They are a depraved species. When my eyes turn silver, I too feel the power that corrupts their bodies. I know what it is like to feel as though I am a god wrapped in mortal flesh.

But perhaps the greatest power a Sylvian possesses isn't the ability to be both Lycan and Undead, but instead the ability to return to their mortality whenever they please. Like an anchor tying me to reality, it is my humanity that keeps me from being corrupted absolutely. This is not something the Undead possess. They are stuck in their preconceived notions that they are the superior race. They are dissociated from their own proclivity to die. They perceive themselves to be invincible.

I will show them tonight how weak they truly are.

The figures floating in the night descend upon the warehouse for breakfast. I reach in my bag and pull a bud of wolfsbane off the stalk and place it between my molars, calmly chewing it while I wait for the demons to foolishly infect themselves with the same virus they wage war against. The bitter taste of the wolfsbane calms me further, repressing the ill effects I feel from the moon waning in the distance. Unlike inhaling the toxin, chewing it and absorbing its bitter juices through my gums sets me at ease. In the same way alcohol is a poison to a mortal's system, so too is wolfsbane to a Lycan. But not all poisons feel like an intoxicant once consumed. Some poisons, ironically, feel like heaven. So I kick my feet up and wait for bloodthirsty monsters to arise from the warehouse the Undead entered.

I can see in the distance an entire unit of archers patrolling Sygon's impenetrable wall. They will soon have their work cut out for them. There is no sign of Bloodlust's army in the distance, and my sense of sight is heightened enough to see miles away. I doubt the stalemate in the war will end tonight. It is much more likely Bloodlust will stroll into town tomorrow once his enemy has been slain from within.

In the center of Lygon's city square is an erected statue of the Undead Emperor, his face covered with his trademark robe. I always thought the Emperor wore the robe to conceal his identity, to further shroud himself in mysticism. After learning the Emperor is Ventur, though, it makes sense. I now realize he hides his face from the public to hide the hideous scars that remain from the day he nearly burned alive.

Still the question remains...

Why did he save me all those years ago?

If he was going to go through the effort of murdering my family, why not put an end to me after escorting me from the castle.

Was he afraid someone would see and catch on to the fact that it was him who betrayed my father?

Or was there some ulterior motive?

It is a question I'll be sure to get the answer to before I cleave the man's head from his shoulders.

I stand silently, mostly out of boredom, and approach the statue. The Emperor is chiseled in such stoic admiration. One arm is raised, his finger pointing north. His other hand holds a scroll. Etched around his waist is a mighty sword big enough to cut a human in two with a single swing. From the ground, he looks like some sort of philosopher king. All wise, all knowing, all powerful.

"Be careful who you call a god," Lundis taught me as a child. "False idols bring nothing more than fake prophecies."

I feel the urge to tip the statue over, but I resist the childish behavior. By the time the morning rises, the rampage that fills the street will likely accomplish that for me.

I am the only one that walks these streets. The many homes and inns around are locked and boarded for the night. The thousands of inhabitants that bustled around earlier have long since returned home. Now that I'm not surrounded by a cesspool of people, I can almost appreciate the city life. Chimneys spit smoke into the night sky. Oil lamps glitter from behind boarded windows.

It is nice to be alone once again, but in all honesty, I miss Crixus already. Her companionship is something I've taken for granted along this journey. It is nice to have someone in my presence, even if not a single word is exchanged to fill the silence. I sit back down and wait, still chewing the wolfsbane until my mouth goes numb. My face tingles from its effects. The beast within will sleep good tonight, knowing tomorrow is his day to reign supreme.

I hope to the gods it doesn't come to that, but I've planned for every contingency possible. Now all there is to do is wait and let my enemies go to war for me.

I gently nod off, my head resting against Ventur's marble-etched feet.

I don't wake for quite some time, but when I do, I wake to the shout of the archers nearby.

"There! In the distance! Blackbloods!"

Another screams, "Ready your arrows men!"

"Draw!"

"Aim!"

"Fire!"

I jump back onto my feet, excited to see the show like I'm sitting in the front row of an Alabastur play. My vision is fully adjusted to the darkness and can see the winged demons rising from the warehouse in a riot. My plan worked! The beasts take to the sky like bats beneath the moon. I watch as they pour from the building like a beehive that's been kicked. The warehouse is busting at the seams. The doors fly open, the roof breaks, the walls crumble as the infrastructure fails to hold in the virus-infected soldiers.

It doesn't take long for the virus to reach their brains. I know that from personal experience. I can still see Vesper's infected body when I close my eyes. But when I open my eyes, I'm proud to see the monstrosities I've created taking flight. They are like my resurrected children going to war on my behalf, only I don't care in the slightest whether they live or die.

I watch the panic enter the amethyst eyes that guard Sygon's metallic walls. Volley after volley of arrows fire into the sky at the descending demons who look for a chance to spread their newfound virus.

The archers engage in brutal warfare as the Blackbloods in the sky become so numerous that they blot out the moon above. I hear Sygon's city gates open as armed calvary comes riding into Lygon on horseback. War chants sound. Blackbloods hiss. It is a wonderful storm to my neutral ears. And as the war escalates exponentially, I take to the sky.

My silver eyes gleam brighter than the moon above as my feet leave the ground and the wind carries me upward. I have no wings so the archers likely won't mistake me for a Blackblood. Still, I am weary of stray arrows and do my best to fly past Sygon's walls in an area where there are no archers below.

Nobody below even notices me as I fly past the frontlines and drift among the clouds into Sygon. I don't land among the city streets. I can see the castle on the horizon, elevated on a hill to separate it from the rest of the population. I look down as Sygon comes alive with action. The streets here are as busy as Lygon's were during the daytime. This is where the majority of the Undead's nobility lives. Knights and commanders and generals. They rush forward into war like hyenas rushing toward a pride of lions.

Pride rushes to my head as angelic powers take over my body. All fatigue fades, all doubt disappears. Suddenly it feels as though I've already won this war. Once I land on the front steps of the castle and open the doors, the throne will be mine. I will watch the war wage through the night from the throne room's balcony. There will be no fire, but Sygon will burn worse than Queensmyre tonight.

By the time the sun rises, whoever remains will be severely weakened by the night of rampage. Then I will hunt the survivors down and send them to their deaths until only humans remain as inhabitants. I can't believe I doubted my capabilities to take this city over. If I knew it would be this easy, I would have taken flight straight from Gall and left Creon and Crixus and Scar behind days ago.

But I didn't have control of these powers then like I do now. The ability to fly is starting to feel like second nature to me. I am more comfortable channeling my silver eyes, too. The only thing I can't account for is the energy it requires to sustain these powers. When I flew from Askamyre to Sygon it made me unconscious for a week. I can't afford to strain my body like that again. I need to be fully awake and aware for what happens tonight.

Because of that, I won't fly anywhere unnecessarily. I slowly lower myself through the air to the castle's front gate. Though the majority of the city's army has fled to join the battle, Black Knights remain at the castle's entrance, and if I had to bet on it, a few probably patrol the inside of the castle itself. Though Wilhelm claimed to be a Black Knight, I haven't seen Black Knights donning their full armor since the old hag's vision from my father's final stand.

Those awarded the honor to guard the royal family are among the world's greatest warriors. The knights stare down at me from the top of the entrance stairs with condemnation written on their helms. Their midnight armor is the perfect camouflage for the night.

The castle itself is much smaller than the Areopagus. I suppose the royal family on this coast keeps a much smaller circle of confidants. The building is beautiful from an architectural standpoint. Its main body consists of three cylindrical pillars topped with pointy spires. Gargoyles line the balconies like dark guardian angels peering down at me. Delicate ivy vines cascade down the black stone walls, most of them in bloom with crimson red flowers. The walls have etched alcoves where outer facing rooms open onto several balconies. Archers stand at the ready on each ledge, arrows notched and ready for the first sign of a disturbance.

I clench my fists as I stare at the Black Knights. So many have already died for my cause. Two more bodies added to the pile makes little difference to me.

"Syrus Sylvian," one of the knights calls out into the night. "The Princess has been expecting you." Together, the two knights grab hold of the golden gates and pull them open, each standing aside for me to enter the castle freely.

Princess Saunter?

Expecting me?

How do they know my name?

Better yet, how is the princess still alive?

None of this makes any sense. I expected the throne room to be empty, or worst-case scenario, occupied by Atlas. But I've still yet to see a single instance of the Acolytes in any degree other than their tracks leading up to Vygon.

This whole time I saw myself as five steps ahead of my enemy. But what if they are the ones who have conspired far enough in advance to undermine me?

No, that can't be possible.

I proceed up the stairs without hesitation. I don't want my enemy to detect the simplest sign of caution on my end. Even though their request catches me by surprise, I won't let my face reveal it.

I walk into the castle like I own the place. Confidence is the only thing that separates me from being victim to these circumstances. The Black Knights close the castle gates behind me and lead me toward the main staircase. Their armor is as horrifying as I remember it from the hag's vision. Their helms don't reveal an inch of their face. Their black capes swirl behind their feet like a bride walking toward the altar. Their breastplates gleam in the flickering candlelight that lines the grand marble staircase. They are like hell's reapers sent forth to collect souls for Saunter's devilish quota. They each hold an obsidian spear in one hand and strike it against the marble floor like a walking stick.

Their metallic boots and thunderous spears are the only noise that echoes throughout the cavernous interior. To either side of us are separate spiral staircases. I can see the silhouette of archers at the top floor peering down at us, waiting for me to step out of line. I will let these soldiers think they have the upper hand, but I still remember what happened in Gall. The beast is mine to control, and the second things become chaotic, I will allow him to negotiate on my behalf.

The Black Knights lead me to another set of thick, oak doors at the top of the staircase. This is the throne room no doubt. I have frequented enough castles to know their layout is basically the same in all kingdoms. One throne room, one kitchen, one dining hall, and several dozen rooms for lodging, more or less. Whatever scheme the enemy is up to will await me on the other side of these doors.

Soon I will have my answers.

Soon I will take this kingdom to be my own.

The knights grip the door handles and pull them open, each standing to the side so I may enter.

My breath catches in my throat at what waits for me.

Within a split second, everything changes.

My face grows flush as it takes a moment for me to register what's happening.

"Good evening, Prince Syrus. I have been awaiting your arrival," Princess Saunter calls to me from across the throne room.

I step into the vast, cathedral-like amphitheater and the knights close the doors shut behind me, neither one of them entering. I hear the lock click in place as the knights twist a set of keys outside the door. I am locked in. There is no turning back.

"Syrus," a voice moans from beside Saunter's stone-carved throne. "It's a trap! It's a trap!" Creon screams. My eyes twitch as they see my fellow wolf crucified upon a cross next to the throne. The man's body is beaten and bruised. His eyelids are so swollen and bruised he can barely open them more than a squint. Nails pierce each of his hands into the wooden cross. A single nail penetrates both of his ankles into the splintered wood he hangs upon. Creon is naked and bloody. His skin is covered in puncture wounds from where an Undead—presumably Saunter—has fed on his blood.

A whip lashes out to silence Creon. The whip cracks against his cheek and slices his jaw open with a new wound. I watch the blood splatter through the air. I trace the whip to the person that holds its handle.

There, standing stoically several feet from the cross, is Atlas, the same man I met face to face in Yueltope.

My heart drops. Creon is right. This is a trap, only it's worse than I thought.

There, chained to the base of the throne with thick, impenetrable links, is my daughter. Her unconscious body is splayed on the ground in front of Saunter. I can hardly smell her distinguishable scent anymore. Her stomach rises and falls in shallow breaths. Bruises litter her pale flesh. Her soul barely clings to her frail frame.

I'm filled with inconsolable rage as I realize I've been played this entire time. The only way Saunter could have gained possession of Sephora is if she defeated Bloodlust or Bloodlust cut a deal. Either way, I realize now I've been a pawn in this game the entire time.

My heart is racing. My vision grows blurry. I have never felt so equally foolish and stupid in my entire life. Ten minutes ago I waltzed into this castle thinking I held the upper hand. I see now Saunter has had an ace up her sleeve this entire time, waiting to call my bluff and submit me to her authority.

I don't speak, it would only be a waste of my breath. I charge forward irrationally, losing control of my emotional turmoil. All I can focus on is my daughter's broken body. My sweet child, exposed to the world after the years I've spent trying to hide away her innocence. She pays for the sins of her father, and knowing that is too much to bear.

I am the reason she is here. I knew the danger I was putting on her shoulders when I brought her into this world. I knew the risks I was subjecting her to when I raised her as my own. I spent years trying to run from my past but my demons ran faster. This moment, right here, is the amalgamation of the consequences I must face for refusing to face responsibility.

Wolves do not run.

Wolves do not fear.

Wolves do not retreat.

I drop down on my knees at my daughter's side, cradling her body. Saunter and Atlas make no move to prevent me from being reconciled. I wrap my arms around her comatose body. She is freezing cold to the touch, as she was when I hugged her in Bloodlust's mountainous dungeon. She is not the warm toddler I once let sleep next to me after waking from nightmares. Now her nightmares are a reality, and not even my fatherly comfort can cure her fears anymore.

I have failed.

In life.

As a husband.

As a father.

As a Sylvian.

Every decision I've ever made has led to this moment.

I am not fit to live a second longer.

I would sacrifice my own soul right now if it meant I could save her life.

My emotions well inside my chest like a fire far more destructive than the one that burned down Queensmyre. My whole body shakes with rage. I can see Saunter's spry smile out of the corner of my eye. A pressure builds in my stomach. An urge I can resist. It wells into chest and burrows into my lungs. I lift my head to scream, but it is not a scream that exits my throat.

Instead, I howl.

Like never before in my life, the beast within lets loose and howls toward the moon in gut-wrenching agony for the injustice that's occurred. The ear-splitting howl shakes the entire chamber and bounces off the walls. The wolfish shriek is loud enough to make Luna's ears bleed. The sound of a thousand ravens squawking in disturbance echoes in the distance, replying to their master's cry for help.

Silver eyes pierce the darkness as tears stream down my face. The smile on Saunter's face only grows wider. Creon moans in pain as he confronts his own failure in the situation. There was no way for him to know Atlas was in league with Saunter this entire time. But now that I see them next to one another, it all makes sense.

Of course Saunter survived Yueltope, and of course Atlas knew how to catch the Undead by surprise. The Acolytes' attack was coordinated not by Atlas's military genius, but by a lead from an informant. It only makes sense that this lead was the military commander of the Undead army that led them like lamb to the slaughter in Yueltope.

I may be an outcast, but I studied military strategy from Ventur himself as a child. The enemy of my enemy is my friend, and these two are the best goddamned friends that exist. The leader of the Undead and the symbolic savior of humanity, united in their causes to annihilate one another.

Saunter scratches his back, he scratches hers. It all makes sense as I think about Bane's crucified corpse outside of Gall. Saunter had her younger brother killed to get rid of any who may threaten her line of succession. In secret, she has used Atlas to be her white knight for hire, and in return, she has tossed him a few thousand unsuspecting Undead to further his cause.

They are like the wolf and the raven, each benefiting the other in their own form of mutual gain.

They may have fooled the entire world into thinking they are at each other's throats, but I know the truth now. These two are using this war to make their own move on the throne. I can see it written on Saunter's grin and Atlas's stone-cold eyes. And Sephora's bondage only means they've gained Bloodlust's favor in the process. With the military might of the Undead, the Blackbloods, and all of humanity behind their cause, I will be the only one who stands in their way from usurping the crown and taking it for themselves.

In the blink of an eye, a dozen mysteries are solved, and a million more begin. Only now do I realize the war that wages outside is useless. Though the Undead and Blackbloods may not know they are truly on the same side, their leaders have been in cahoots this entire time. Whatever bloodshed is spilled on this night will not lead to any decisive victory on my end. All it will lead to is more dead bodies in the streets.

The questions flood my mind while my howl continues to vibrate from my diaphragm up my throat.

What did Bloodlust get in return?

Why are they working together?

Does Ventur know about their treason?

Was Creon crucified just to send me a message?

The more the questions invade my mind the faster my howl turns from one of grief to one of wrath. The veins in my neck bulge. My throat is burning like hot coals. Blood pounds behind my temples like war drums. Spit flies from my fang-filled mouth as my eyes scorch silver. I can feel claws digging into my palms.

I demand answers for the atrocities these two have committed, and I won't be leaving this throne room until they are dead or I am satisfied with their answers, whichever comes first. Slowly, my howl fades into nothing more than bouncing echoes off the walls of the acoustic cathedral. The powers of Sylvian dull the throbbing pain in my heart and still my racing mind. As I stand, I stand with the power of a god coursing through my veins.

"Now that's more like it," Saunter whispers under her breath as she stands from her throne of deception. I watch in horror as Atlas and Saunter walk side by side toward me, both of their eyes igniting the darkness with their own separate hues of silver.

Gods be good, I pray. The old hag was right. I am not the only Sylvian left. Atlas's eyes beam violently at me. Saunter's eyes burn holes into my soul. Somehow... Someway, they are both descendants of Sylvian.

My father's words from a lifetime ago echo in my mind.

But family trees and namesakes do not matter, young ones, he told my sister and I. *For on the darkest of all nights, you need only to see the glow of your silver eyes to know you are a Sylvian. 'Twas a gift from Luna to Sylvian, to light his way on the darkest of nights. Only Sylvians bear silver eyes, and only Sylvians can control the beast within.*

The old hag's words ring in my mind like a bloody memory, *Your father sat in this very chair when I showed him all that could happen, and he chose the only possible outcome that would preserve the Sylvian bloodline.*

Her warning was clear as the full moon in the night sky. *Because of his bold decisions, the Sylvian bloodline lives on in you, and in your daughter. And because of his bold decisions, there is a third. This is the way it had to be, for the Undead Empire to be defeated.*

It was all in front of me this entire time but I didn't have the ability to see the bigger picture. This is what the fortune teller spoke of. All those years ago when my father visited her, this is what he saw. This path, right here, is what had to happen to save our bloodline.

What the hell did you do, dad?

Now Sephora is not the only one who will pay for the sins of the father.

"I knew it was you the second I laid eyes on you in Queensmyre," Saunter laughs. "A dozen of my own men dead at your feet and you thought I wouldn't know who you were? Granted, your escape from Yueltope was unexpected, but I knew you would come right back to me. The Fates have preordained this moment in history, Syrus. Our paths are intertwined. There is no running from death this time."

"Bloodlust delivered you into our hands to seal our alliance," Atlas growls. "He did not send you here to kill us, Syrus Sylvian. He sent you here to *be killed*."

54

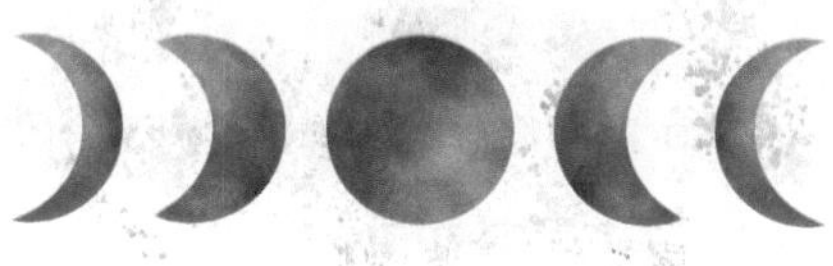

A Nightmare

"How?" I stutter, my confidence leaving me with every step they take toward me. "Your silver eyes! How? Are you truly both Sylvians?"

"Tsk tsk, you didn't think you were the only one, did you?" Saunter chuckles. "There is a lot you have missed out on these past twenty years of exile, Syrus Sylvian. While you've been playing hide and seek, the powers that be have been using your absence to their advantage."

"But Ventur is your father..." It is hard for me to get the words out of my mouth when I instinctively know they are not true.

"Surely you don't actually believe that, do you? You were taught by the great Lundis himself! Surely you are smarter than that."

"Then who?" I walk backwards as Saunter and Atlas converge on me.

"Isn't it obvious?" Saunter's silver eyes devour me whole with their stare. "Your father knew Ventur was making a move for his throne. The man knew his death was inevitable, so he did the only logical thing he could to preserve the Sylvian bloodline... He fucked Ventur's wife without the Emperor knowing."

My heart sinks into my bowels. "You... You... We..."

"Are siblings," she finishes the sentence.

And because of his bold decisions, there is a third.

There is a third.

Everything I've come to accept as truth that makes up my worldview falls apart. Like a well-constructed sandcastle on the beach's shore, Saunter is the immature child that comes along to kick it into smithereens. My whole life is a lie. The man I viewed my father to be is not the man he truly was. And now, before me is this woman who I've planned to kill without remorse, telling me she is my half-sister and sporting the silver eyes to prove it.

I am distraught. The very fabric of my reality is tearing at the seams. Did Bloodlust know this whole time Saunter is my sister? Did he send me on this mission to kill her because he actually thought I could, or was I merely a sacrificial offering to her to unify their forces?

And then there's Atlas.

The very man I despise for being everything I am not, and now I come to find he is a descendant from Sylvian the First as much as me. It finally makes sense how he is better than me in every way. The only reassurance I had to give myself was that with my powers, I am more powerful than he can comprehend. I realize now that even if I fought him one on one, he could even best me in combat. I turn to face him and stare at his intimidating posture. It is only when I look at him that I realize I am the false god. The man who stands before me is perfect in every aspect. He is bigger than me. Stronger than me. Faster than me. In better control of his powers than I am. I am like an ant challenging an elephant. There is no contest between the two of us.

"Though we are descendants from Damon's daughter that wedded Sylvian the First, Atlas here is the product of Dagon's ancestral line after Dagon pledged his daughter to wed Sylvian. He is something of a cousin," Saunter laughs, then adds, "And a spectacular candidate for a husband, so long as he has your blessing, older brother?"

Saunter leans on her tiptoes and plants a kiss on Atlas's scarred cheek. His indifferent glare doesn't leave me for a second. The two have imprinted on one another. Chosen each other as mates to further strengthen their claim to the Sylvian Throne.

This woman taunts me with every chance she gets. It is like she has planned this intervention for years. She is nearly half my age yet already possesses the ability to access Sylvian's powers. Unlike me, Damon's Curse possessed her body first, signaled by her amethyst eyes. I have no idea how long she's had access to these powers, but I'm guessing she has a wholly better mastering of them than I do. I still can't tap into them for more than ten minutes without passing out. And now these two tap into their silver eyes like there is nothing abnormal about accessing the powers, as though it is not exhausting for them to do so in the slightest.

Saunter pauses and grips Atlas, asking him to cease all movement. She raises her finger in the air like she's just had some brilliant idea. "Ah, Atlas sweetie, I've only just realized this is our first time with all Sylvians being in the same room together. It is like our own little family reunion! It is such a shame Syrus must die at such a symbolic event!"

"His time has come, darling," Atlas replies, not removing his eyes from me for a second. "But we will raise his daughter as our own. We will keep her safer than this coward ever could."

I pause.

Atlas's words echo in my mind.

He has crossed a line that cannot be mended.

Suddenly, all anxiety flees my body. Suddenly, I am no longer the man who has been on the run for twenty years. Instantly, I remember who I am. I am no coward. I am the child who killed an entire brigade of Black Knights who dared to harm my family. I am the boy that killed a thyrops with his bare hands. I am the one who hunted down and slaughtered an entire tribe of Undead for massacring my Lycan family. I am the man who stood alone to face the endless spawn of Blackblood demons and woke from my bloodlust victorious.

Saunter and Atlas don't threaten my life because they have no need for me in their plan to usurp the throne. These two don't wish to kill me simply to put me out of my misery. I am not some minor nuisance to their overall scheme. I am not some hiccup in their plan. I realize now they seek to kill me because they are afraid of me. They have unilaterally went out of their way to devise this entire intervention for the sole purpose of ensuring I don't screw up their claim to the throne.

They could have let me live in peace. That's all I wanted. They could have given me Sephora and let me be on my way. I would have promised to never stand in their way as they ascend the Areopagus Throne. But power-hungry people such as these sniveling brats do not leave behind those who are an essential threat to their plans. They must tie off all loose ends.

They have made a grave error making me their enemy.

And now they will die for their mistakes.

Coward? The beast within repeats the word as it bounces off the inside of my skull. *They call us a coward?* I can sense the rage in his voice. My confidence returns as I realize I am not alone. They may think they have me outnumbered two to one, but I have made friends with my demon within. *Do they have any idea who they are talking to?* The beast growls. He is my mirror image, and he will not let the wrath I feel go unpunished. The full moon may be tomorrow, but they will have to answer to my beast a night early.

The sound of wings flapping distracts the two of them. Both their heads turn as a single raven enters the throne room through the open balcony off to the side. The black wings flutter violently to control the bird's descent. Screaming echoes from outside the throne room's doors. Atlas and Saunter's heads swivel back and forth in confusion. They are no longer in control of the situation, a feeling that, unlike me, they've never had to experience before.

But I am the master of finding control in moments of chaos. I have planned for the contingencies chaos brings. Atlas and Saunter have not.

"Syrus! Syrus!" the raven squawks as it lands atop Sephora's defenseless body. When I blink, I can still see the host of ravens landing on Ziva to protect her from the thyrops. I smile, then reply, "Wolfsram. I told you I would see you again." The bird peers at me through the darkness. The years, like me, have made him old and weathered. But he is still the same bird that accompanied me through some of the darkest times of my life. And now, he will see me through to the bitter end.

The throne room's doors crash open violently. The bodies of the two Black Knights that escorted me fly through the air. They each thud to the ground before my feet, lifeless. I look up from their bodies to watch as their attackers strut into the throne room. I am met by Crixus's loving eyes. Beside her is Scar, his stoic silence causing a chill to wash over all in attendance. I see now the mission I sent Scar on has been successful, though I knew that the presence of ravens along the city gates was a premonition of such. Beside Scar is a man I haven't seen in many years. The one-armed man has changed since I saw him last. Urriah is accompanied by his wife, the same woman I freed from the Undead's imprisonment when I was a mere child of sixteen. Both are ready to make good on the life debt they owe me. The two stare up at me like they are ghosts from my past ready to haunt those who threaten my future. Behind Crixus and Scar and Urriah stands an entire host of men and women that I can only assume to be the Lycan clan famously known as Fang.

Descendant from Dagon's ancient clan, these Lycans are like something out of a history book. Famously known for taking in Sylvian the First and witnessing his battle with Dagon, the Fang clan has remained exiled since the battle that destroyed Cardone, but they have not forgiven the sins of the Undead and humanity for exiling their people. Tonight they return to the limelight to reclaim what has been stolen from them, and I am the one who will lead them to newfound freedom.

"We heard your howl," Crixus says, "Didn't want to leave you to have all the fun without us."

"You two are in bloody trouble now," Creon calls out from his cross, spitting blood in Atlas's direction. "You morons must be stupider than most if you thought Syrus Sylvian would show up to claim his throne without an army of his own."

"Revenge!" Wolfsram squawks from my daughter's half-alive body. "Revenge!"

"Please excuse my bird, it has been quite some time since he's last been able to feed off one of my kills," I laugh crazily as I step toward Atlas and Saunter.

"What are you doing, idiot! Call your Acolytes!" Saunter yells at Atlas, "Don't just stand there!"

Atlas doesn't budge, nor does he look intimidated. He stares at me with dead eyes that tell me he's ready to die before he calls for backup.

"I think your boyfriend wants to hear what I have to say before crying wolf, sister," I say, not pulling my eyes away from Atlas's glare. "After all, he seems to be a man who can respect when he's been outsmarted."

Saunter looks like she is about to have a mental breakdown at the thought of having to bend the knee to me. Her head frantically searches the vast room for answers to her dilemma, but all she sees are shadows, and I am the master of these shadows. My Lycan army spreads around the perimeter to surround our foe. Several of them block the exit doors and open balconies so no one can make a run for it. Though I've never met the majority of these wolves, they come to my aid like I've been a member of their pack my whole life.

I watch as Crixus instantly rushes to Sephora's side and several other Lycans slowly lower the cross onto its back so Creon's weight is no longer rested on his impaled wrists and ankles. I hear Creon groan, "But I can't see the action from here!"

I speak calmly, "You said it yourself, I was taught by the great Lundis, and my military knowledge comes from the father who raised you. Don't you find it funny how it is only Sylvians who stand opposed to one another in this throne room? Neither Bloodlust nor Ventur is present, don't you find that odd?"

Saunter doesn't comment, but I can see on her face that she's following my train of logic.

"It's eerily reminiscent of the destruction of Cardone, don't you think? The historic battle of brothers... Only now the tables have been flipped, sister. Eons ago, it was our forefather that deceived Dagon and Damon into killing one another. The twin kings of night and darkness brought together in one place for only a single victor to remain. Only, neither one of them remained alive after the destruction they wrought on one another. In fact, the only person who truly won was Sylvian the First, for he didn't have to lift a single finger and yet he gained control over an entire kingdom. Brilliant, don't you think?"

Saunter replies, "Bloodlust wouldn't—"

"Do you know that for sure? Last time I checked, I was the one who was tutored by him personally as a child, not you. The man really was a genius, which is why my father paid him to be my tutor in all things. But the Blackblood virus didn't make him any stupider, Princess Saunter. Face it, he has single-handedly moved each one of us into this very room. Every last Sylvian left alive, including my own daughter. He has given each of us sufficient motivation to carry out his deeds. He has leveraged my love as a father to get me to come here and kill you, and he has leveraged your thirst for power to get you to put me out of my misery. The only person here who doesn't have a solid alibi is..." I look from Saunter to Atlas. "You." I stare at him accusingly. "What has Bloodlust promised you that you've hidden from your own partner in crime?"

Saunter stares at Atlas now, suddenly believing me as my words start to make more sense. The look of fear on Saunter's face tells me there is something she doesn't know.

"If I had to guess, Bloodlust is the only reason why you are standing here," I continue. "And if I had to guess, you have cut your own separate deal with him before falling into alliance with the gullible Princess Saunter."

Atlas smiles as I put the puzzle pieces together, dissecting him in the open and revealing his true nature that he has hidden from the light.

Atlas replies, his composure not failing for a single moment, "You have earned my respect, Syrus Sylvian. You are quite the formidable opponent. I heavily doubted Bloodlust when he told me to not underestimate you... Now I see the caution he heeded was well-measured."

Atlas separates himself from Saunter and his demeanor changes completely. Like myself in Queensmyre, he too has been an actor this entire time. To the Acolytes he is one person, to Saunter he is another, but none of these masks he wears are truly representative of the monster that hides behind his face.

He continues, "The wolf skull Bloodlust wears as a helm of protection belongs to me. Bloodlust and his demons murdered my whole tribe when I was a child, and I watched him cleave my father's Lycan head from his wolfish body as he tried to protect me from the evil. Since then, he has worn my father's head as a mockery to me to remind me I am his slave. Bloodlust took me in and raised me, turning me into his soldier so that I could convince humanity to follow him when he sits on the throne. When I was but a mere child, he said to me I won't receive my father's skull until I've won him the crown."

Saunter looks at the man she loves as if she doesn't know him. It is evident to me that she knows nothing of his past, or that he fed her lies about where he comes from. Surely she is smart enough to know that if he fights for Bloodlust to sit upon the Areopagus Throne that makes his cause directly opposed to hers. Now all three of us are equal in the animosity we feel for each other. Saunter staggers several steps away from Atlas in disbelief. The shadows of the night dance off Atlas's pale face. His silver eyes grow brighter by the moment while Saunter's nearly disappear completely.

Saunter shouts, "You said you'd never met Bloodlust!"

"I lied," Atlas chuckles, "And you bought it."

My work here is done. I have sown perfect discord between the two of them. Saunter was too stupid to see the bigger picture, but like all big brothers, it is my job to guard her heart.

"So what will it be, Atlas? Are we going to join the same team, or must we put on a show for your puppet master?" I ask.

Saunter continues backing away, tears building in her eyes at the realization she's been betrayed by the man she thought she loved.

Atlas raises his arms to unclasp his breastplate from his shoulders, letting it drop to the ground with a loud thud. He unbuckles the belt around his waist. I watch as my mother's sheathed sword thuds to the ground at his feet. "Jest all you want, but my job is already complete. All I had to do was keep the Princess preoccupied from returning home to the Areopagus before the full moon. Right now, Bloodlust advances all his forces toward Ventur's kingdom to make a move for the throne. By the time the moon is full tomorrow night, it will be too late. The Undead Emperor will be dead, and the reign of Bloodlust will begin."

"No!" Saunter screams at the man who's fooled her into loving him. "Traitor! I trusted you!"

I am ignorant as to how Saunter feels at the news that the man who raised her will soon be dead. Does she still love Ventur though she knows he is not her biological father? Surely she doesn't if she previously planned to come for his throne. But I can see the hurt written plain on her face. All of this was completely unexpected. She must feel foolish, knowing that I was able to put the pieces together with only a fraction of the information she had at her disposal.

Atlas laughs, "Trust is cheap. I have a whole army of idiots who trust me. Only it was even easier deceiving you into helping me." I watch as Atlas continues to unbuckle his vambraces and leg guards. Slowly, he sheds the black tunic he wears beneath the armor until he is as naked as the day I first met him. I'm confronted with his chiseled muscle once again. Every inch of his body is etched in stone. Knowing now that he was raised by Bloodlust as an artificial father, I know I am up against the most dangerous man on the face of the earth. And now he stands before me, totally naked, ready to fight to the death. "Let's settle this like Dagon and Sylvian did," Atlas announces. "It seems only fit since you've employed the ancient Fang Clan to witness this fight, as they did thousands of years ago when our forefathers clashed claws. No weapons, no backup, no retreat. Just my beast versus yours. What do you say, Syrus Sylvian?"

"Are you sure you really want all these people around to watch you lose?" I joke, signaling to the countless Lycans that surround us. Atlas doesn't shed so much as a smile at my humor. He looks at me without any emotion written on his face. It is almost as if the man he acted to be in Yueltope was just that—an act. I now see his true colors. This is not a human. This is a demon in human skin. Whatever Bloodlust did to the boy he took in has turned Atlas into a monster.

There is a crazy look in the man's silver eyes. It is the look of a man with nothing to lose. These past twenty-four moons have taken everything from me. But now, I stare at my daughter lying helpless on the ground and realize I do have something to lose, and Atlas is standing in my way of getting to her.

I guess I was wrong. The most dangerous thing in the world isn't a man with nothing to lose. And now I realize how the thyrops I trapped when I was sixteen felt when the boulder came tumbling down. It would do anything to protect the child I stole. Like the thyrops, I will kill anyone who stands in the way of me getting my daughter back. This ends tonight.

I speak clearly as I feel my bones start to break, "Historians will write for eons to come how two Sylvians went head-to-head..." I can feel my skull snapping and rearranging into the head of a wolf. Unlike Atlas, I don't remove the torn rags that cover my body. They fall on their own as my massive size begins to stretch them apart. I feel whiskers sprout from my cheeks. Black fur grows exponentially to cover my nakedness.

"... A battle like this has not occurred since Dagon and Damon slew one another. Only this time only one will die, and all will remember my name as the one who rose victorious."

As my silver eyes raise to meet Atlas once more, I stare into the eyes of his Lycan form. Standing before me in all red fur is Atlas, leader of the Acolytes, adopted son of Bloodlust, descendant of Sylvian the First, and traitor of mankind.

In our human flesh, he is stronger and more superior than me in every way.

But as beasts, I am the one with the advantage.

55

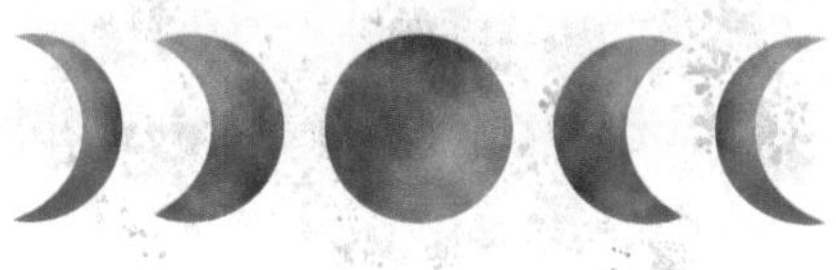

A Nightmare

An entire hour we've fought and neither of us will budge.

I stare down at my midnight black fur and see that I'm covered in spattered blood. I've lost track of how many wounds Atlas has inflicted on me. I can only guess how many times I've injured him. Every time one of us lands a devastating strike it is healed within seconds. Our bodies heal and regenerate our wounds almost as soon as we gain them.

I have never fought an adversary who matched my every move. I curse. It is like I am fighting myself in a mirror. The only thing giving me hope is that he, too, is covered in scarlet blood from head to toe. He may act like he is a god, but gods do not bleed. And gods do not take this long to deal with their devils.

Both our maws drip each other's blood. Our claws look like we've just gutted a pig from how red they are. But this fight will not be won by who can land the most strikes, I realize, but by who can go the distance longer.

We are each other's equals. Like long-lost brothers separated at birth. Twin flames destined to burn separately against one another.

I block Atlas's strike and sink my fangs into his bicep. He buries his opposite elbow into the back of my head to get me to release. I bury my shoulder into his torso and pick him off the ground. I see the throne behind him and pile drive his body into its rocky structure. If he wants to sit on the throne so bad, I will bury him in it. The stone chair cracks under our momentum and breaks to pieces as I drive Atlas's Lycan body into it with enough force to move the earth upon impact.

I see Sephora's chain still lying on the base of the throne. Crixus has long freed my child and removed her safely from this room. I made sure of that before engaging in battle.

I grab the loose chain and wrap it around Atlas's struggling physique. His hands are buried in the rubble of the throne's collapse. I sling the chain around his neck and pull, thinking of the woman I tried to save in Yueltope from drowning in quicksand. I can still feel the way the rope went slack as her neck snapped. I pull against Atlas's neck with enough strength to break fifty mortal necks.

I hear a snap and the chain goes loose, but not because Atlas's spine has snapped. I look down and realize the chain has broken in two from the pressure I exerted on it. Atlas picks himself up from the mess with a chunk of boulder in his paws. I'm blinded as he thrusts it into my temple. I stagger backward and he throws another chunk directly at my head. I feel the crunch of rock breaking against my skull. It turns to dust around me and enters my snout as I try to catch my breath.

Blood drips in my eyes from where the rock split open my forehead. I can already feel the cut closing as it heals itself, but the blood blurs my vision. I feel my feet leave the ground as Atlas picks me up and throws me through the air. My back collides against the wall closest to the balcony but doesn't stop there. The stone wall gives way at the impact of my collision and breaks. Suddenly my body tumbles through the open air and crashes into the ground hard enough to create a crater. Pain jolts through my entire body as several bones break.

I gnash my fangs as I feel the bones instantly snap back into place.

I stare up at the hole in the castle wall as the red wolfman peers down at me from its makeshift ledge. He leaps through the open air and plummets to the earth toward me, his fist ready to drive through my skull and bury my brains in the ground below me. I jerk myself to the side and avoid the assault by a split second, rolling to my feet and throwing myself back into him as he lands. I catch him off balance and we both roll over the other exchanging blows however we can. His claws dig into my chest, my jaw latches onto his neck. He pushes me off him and my teeth rip a chunk of his throat off. We both stand and I watch as blood spurts from his torn jugular, then watch as his flesh seals itself over the wound.

We are surrounded by Blackbloods and Undead going to battle around us. The winged demons and amethyst warriors collide in the air and on the ground. Atlas and I have stumbled into the battlefield of an ongoing war. I watch as a dueling Blackblood and Undead make the mistake of stumbling between us. Atlas decapitates the Blackblood with a single swipe of his claws and then drives his claws into the Undead's chest, ripping out the man's still beating heart. The red Lycan takes a bite of the heart and throws it to the side, licking his blood-drenched snout with his wolfish tongue.

If wolves could smile, Atlas's grin would be unmistakable.

We aren't that different, me and Atlas. But I am the lesser of two evils. My whole life has led to this very moment. My training under Lundis and Ventur. My drilling from Mordecai. The teachings from Vesper's father, Vespian. The twenty years that taught me how to survive. The countless people I've killed to make sure I've lived. The twenty-four moons Bloodlust forced my beast to fend for itself. All of it has led to this single fight. The Fates have forced me to feel immeasurable pain all so I don't back down from Atlas's tyranny.

I look up at the moon above us. Does Luna cry tonight as her children commit themselves to killing one another? Has she picked a side in this fight? Is the victor already written on her heart? The gods have never showed me kindness, but maybe that's because they needed me to show Atlas how unfair life can be.

Ravens fly above us, their swarm great enough to blot out the moon's light. Screams and hisses from Undead and Blackbloods echo all throughout this fallen kingdom. Buildings burn and break as the soldiers come crashing down to the earth like fallen angels.

Atlas and I throw ourselves at each other once more. We become an indistinguishable tangle of flesh, fur, and fangs. Claws lash out faster than our vision can register. I feel my body become torn open in several spots as I unleash a series of devastating cuts along Atlas's body. Enough blood flies from our body to feed an army of Undead.

I see the statue of the Undead Emperor still standing in the distance behind Atlas. Shame, I thought the war would reduce it to smithereens by now. I will fix that, I think to myself. I plant my heel in Atlas's chest and push off, kicking him backward until he stumbles several strides in front of Ventur's all-wise caricature. Perfect!

I sprint at him and plant my shoulder into Atlas's gut, tackling him into the statue. I feel the impact of our bodies crashing through the statue, instantly shattering the sculpture of the man responsible for ruining my life. The rocks pour down on top of us like light hail at the beginning of a storm.

I feel Atlas's teeth bite down on my neck. The breath catches in my windpipe as his fangs crush my trachea. I grab a chunk of Ventur's nearby body and thrash it into the wolf's temple to get him to let go. The open wound is nearly healed by the time I stand up.

A Blackblood is unfortunate enough to see two Lycans standing off and decides to land between us. This creature has picked a fight with the wrong wolves, and though Atlas and I are vehemently opposed to one another, we enjoy briefly teaming up to kill the demon that stands between us. Atlas grabs the beast's shoulders and I rip its head clean off, rearing the skull back to throw at Atlas. I launch the bloodied head at the red wolf and watch in dismay as he catches the lobbied head like a dog going after a tennis ball. His bloodied fangs snap shut on the Blackblood's cheeks and he shakes his dead prey like a wolf playing with its food. The Blackblood's body drops between us and Atlas spits the head onto the corpse.

I jump off the wall of a nearby building and launch myself into the air, fist cocked back and ready to rearrange Atlas's face. His silver eyes snicker as he uses my momentum against me and flips me midair to crash on my back. I dodge several blows as his fist punches the ground once, twice, three times where my head just was.

I bring my knees into my chest and plant my feet on his stomach, kicking off to send him flying off me and into the building behind him. His heavy body breaks through the mortar and disappears into the darkness of the home. I hear several humans scream at the sight of a Lycan lying in their living room uninvited. There are few things I can think would be more frightening as a mortal than a wolfman breaking into your house in the pitch black while everyone sleeps.

The screaming ceases as I hear several throats slit by claws. I can hear the victims' blood dripping to the floor from here. My ears twitch as each droplet hits the ground. Those people's deaths are on my hands. No matter, it just makes the list of guardian angels supporting me that much greater.

Atlas and I walk down the street exchanging blows like boxers. At this point we are just throwing any strike we can with as much force as we have left. We both pant uncontrollably, and though we have no sign of external injuries, we are both broken inside irreparably. The human body is not meant to push to the limits our Lycan beasts have, and the toll we each feel is tremendous. We each grab whatever props we can to try to catch one another by surprise. Atlas rips a door right off a hinge and flings it at me. I duck beneath it and scoop a fistful of dust and throw it in his eyes.

While he is blind I take full advantage of his defenselessness. My claws open his skin up from his shoulder down to his hip bone. I dig both hands in and separate the flesh from healing instantly, pulling it apart like magnetized curtains. I can see his ribcage and the muscle surrounding his inner bowels. I thrust my hand beneath his sternum in hopes of clasping my hand around his lungs or heart. Both of his hands wrap around my wrist to keep me from making any forward momentum. His flesh begins to heal while my fist is still in his chest cavity. I can feel the muscles tightening around my palm so tight that I can't pull it free.

Atlas uses this to his advantage and snaps my forearm in the same place the thyrops's dead body once did. A yelp escapes my wolfish snout. I pull the limp arm free and hold it close to my chest as I feel the bones reconnect and calcify. Atlas uses my moment of weakness against me. I feel his claws slash open my neck and blood rushes up my mouth and over my tongue like hot, red vomit. I suffocate on the blood momentarily. Atlas throws a devastating hook into my temple powerful enough to make me fall to one knee. My eyes go dark and my ears ring so loud that the sound of warfare around us fades completely.

Get up, bastard! The beast shouts at me. My body listens unwillingly as I stumble to my feet in time to avoid Atlas's kneecap flying for my skull. I spin on the ground and kick his single leg out from underneath him, toppling his body over to come crashing next to me. I mount him and rain down as many blows as my muscles will allow. My arms burn from the incessant action. I want nothing more than to lay on my back and rest while I stare at the stars. But Mordecai's training taught me long ago there is no rest for the wicked.

And I am the wickedest of them all.

My knuckles break as I pummel them into my opponent's face, rearranging the bones of his snout and skull. If I can't decapitate him, the next best option is to cave his cranium in on his brain to the point of no return. I feel his neck snap from my left jab. Wolves do not run. Blood flies from his mouth from my right jab. Wolves do not retreat. He yelps from my left hook. Wolves do not feel fear. The Lycan's left eyeball pops from its socket from my right hook. Wolves show no mercy.

I pull my left fist back to throw the finishing blow but am interrupted as an unforeseen force crashes into me. My body contorts as a dead Blackblood is sent on a collision course through the sky. It is like the gods saw that I was gaining the advantage in the battle and decided they could not allow me to be the victor. The heavy corpse rams into me and sends me flying. I roll several feet to the side and throw the dead body off me, looking into the sky to see the Undead responsible for the interruption in my attack. The amethyst eyes stare down at me with a smirk of superiority.

By the time I regain composure, Atlas is standing once again, one of his eyes missing from its socket, the muscle that held it connected to his head severed by the force of the blows. I look down and see the eyeball rolling on the ground from the collision. By the time it ceases all movement, its iris is pointed directly at me.

It no longer glows silver. It is just a regular eye. Devoid of emotion. I take a step forward, placing the ball of my foot atop the eyeball. I feel it squish and pop beneath me and twist it into the dust of the ground below.

Atlas watches me with amusement. He feels nothing toward the eye that's provided him vision his entire life.

There is a word for men like him in this world.

Lundis taught me about them.

Psychopaths, he said. Men who cannot feel traditional emotion. Men forced to put on a mask and fake their feelings to the outside world. And as I watch Atlas's snout flash a smile at the destruction of his eyeball, I know he is one of these rare men who feel no emotion. The sort of men who do what they do for no particular reason other than to make others experience the same emptiness in their hearts.

Atlas may not feel emotion, but he can still feel pain.

And that alone is good enough for me.

What are you standing here for? The beast shouts, *Attack him!*

I need to shift back into a human.

What do you mean?

I need you to trust me. I know how to beat him.

As do I! Cut the bastard's head from his neck!

I can't. He heals too fast and I can't get a killing blow lined up on him. He mirrors my fighting style too well.

You better know what you're doing.

If I don't, we're both dead, and you can tell me "I told you so" for an entire afterlife.

I shift back into a human and Atlas makes no move to attack me. It is common etiquette among Lycans to not use such a moment of vulnerability to blindside another. It would be like bringing a bow to a swordfight. Even men like Atlas respect such boundaries.

The second my bones are rearranged in the form of a human I plant my feet and leap into the air. I feel it distort around me and carry my body further. I don't look back to see if Atlas follows. I know he is committed to killing me. I can feel his presence like a force of physics.

But I need to continually distract him so he doesn't catch on to my plan. I ram into an Undead archer in midair and rip his bow and quiver out of his possession. Quickly, I notch an arrow and face downward. Sure enough, Atlas's human form flies after me into the night like a shooting star. Like his Lycan form, the man now misses a single eye, but I can see his remaining silver eye shining up at me as he pursues me.

I release an arrow in his direction and don't wait to see if it hits him. I have to keep moving. Though I have been a Lycan my entire life and had the advantage as one, I've only just learned to fly. The sky is Atlas's domain, and if I let him catch me before we've reached his final resting place, I'm dead.

The winds whip against my whiskerless face as I climb further into the atmosphere. Unlike the surface far below, it is freezing up here. The sweat along my skin turns to ice crystals. What little breath I can manage comes out as a cloud of ice.

All around us the Blackbloods and Undead press on in their meaningless war. Like the fire in Queensmyre, this is my doing, and there is no stopping it until it has run its course and turned to smoke and ashes.

"Get back here coward!" Atlas screams from a world away.

Wolves do not run, except when they have a plan. This fight cannot be won by brute strength. Our hour-long duel proved that. And unlike Sylvian and Dagon, I will not battle for multiple days for this to end in a stalemate. No, this fight will be won by whoever is cleverer. And though Atlas was raised by Bloodlust, I was raised by Lundis. We are both pupils of the same man, but now I will show why Lundis's wisdom is more powerful than Bloodlust's cruelty.

I look back and see Atlas has closed the gap between us by half the distance. I notch an arrow and let it fly, then throw the bow itself down at him to distract him further. He is like a dog. Keep its mind occupied in the moment and it won't even notice you're taking it to the vet until it has arrived.

I bump into Undead and Blackbloods alike, never keeping my flight path straight and narrow. Atlas is obviously faster and more agile in the sky than I am, so I must make my clumsiness his own problem. I use the nearby soldiers to kick off of and change my trajectory, never giving the slightest indication of where I am leading Atlas.

But like a wolf with his eyes on prey in the distance, he does not focus on the trap I am leading him to. Every Undead and Blackblood soldier Atlas passes is met with a swift end. As I turn around to see how close he is, I watch as he rips the wing clean off the back of a Blackblood, sending it plummeting toward the ground to be squashed like a bug.

As we enter the orbit of the atmosphere, everything strikes me as calmer up here. The curvature of the world below makes life on earth seem like nothing more than vanity. Fickle warriors fight fickle wars as if it matters which king is in control of it all. My body is covered with a thin sheet of ice that begins to make flight more difficult. I flip my body around and take off back toward the earth fast enough to feel the heat of friction burn my skin.

After several seconds of falling, I see the destination I set off for out of the corner of my eye. For this plan to work, I can't spare a moment of hesitation. I cannot misstep. I must be the master of my own fate.

The gods will not intervene in our battle out here. We are several miles outside of Sygon now. The war waging in the distance has no impact on us anymore. It is just me and Atlas and the iconic red lake known as Askamyre below us. If Atlas has caught on, his flight doesn't indicate it to me. He is soaring through the sky like a high velocity arrow. Nothing is going to stop him from catching me, and his superior experience in flight now shows as he catches up to me in a few measly seconds. Even if he catches me, I will not falter. I am ready to die to make sure this psychopath doesn't endanger this kingdom a minute more.

I slow my descent right above the center point of the lake, right where the depths will be deepest along the body of water. I hover above the water and turn to face Atlas. The crazed, demonic man dives at me like an eagle shot out of the sky. It is obvious from his momentum that Bloodlust did not teach him geography as Lundis did for me.

I take a moment to look him in his last remaining eye. For the briefest second, I almost feel bad for the man. I think back to the horrors I endured for the twenty-four moons I was a slave to Bloodlust. And here is this man that has been manipulated by the Blackblood leader for his entire life. I cannot imagine what such a life of darkness would look like, to watch your father be murdered by a demon while trying to protect your family, then for that demon to wear his skull as a reminder to you.

I can see emotion on Atlas's face. It is not written plainly for the unobservant eye to notice, but instead in the devilish details. The man's unrelentless pursuit to prove himself. His unwillingness to quit. The dance with death he walks on a daily basis. Deep down in the darkest pits of his heart, there is still that fearful little child too small to protect himself from the demons in life. And so to survive, he learned how to serve them.

Sylvian the First had two wives, and it is said my lineage can be traced back to Damon himself through his daughter. The legend goes Dagon's family died out throughout the years. As I look at Atlas's rage-filled silver eye, I know that to be a lie. Dagon's family has walked this earth all these eons that my family has ruled. What caused them to go into hiding may never be known. But it doesn't matter, because Dagon's bloodline dies with Atlas.

I can feel the wind blow past me as I dodge Atlas's advance at the last second, barely getting out of his way in time to avoid the impact of his body. The water below booms as Atlas makes contact faster than a falcon at the peak of its dive. A torrent of water shoots upward like a natural hot spring. I feel several droplets touch my skin and burn my flesh. The pain alone reminds me how doomed I felt when I fell into these waters myself.

If it hadn't been for Creon pulling me out, I would now be a lifeless gargoyle resting on the floor of Askamyre, never to be seen again by humanity.

But Atlas has no such friends present to save him, and so I watch as the surface of the red waters bubble as Atlas fights beneath their surface, slowly losing oxygen as his feet turn to anchors. Though I can't see him through the murky, bloodlike water, I can only imagine how he writhes in agony as the medusian bacteria enter his skull through his open eye socket, attacking the fleshy surface of his brain. I no longer feel the same envy toward him that I did in Yueltope.

Back then, I thought he was everything I wanted to be in life.

I convinced myself he is the hero of this story.

The only man fit for saving the world from Ventur and Bloodlust.

But he was just another villainous pawn this entire time.

And though I am certainly no hero, I am the lesser of two evils.

Though the gods will curse for what has happened, Atlas dies so I may live.

My silver eyes stare down at the waters as they settle. Barely any bubbles climb to the surface anymore. The water grows still with every waking moment. It is so motionless that an onlooker would never suspect a body would lurk within.

The world will forget about Atlas.

The histories won't even mention his name.

Fortune only favors winners in the game of life.

But it is his fault for challenging me.

The gods have never been kind enough to let me die. I am their personal entertainment. Their voodoo doll. A sinner they line up to cast stones at. They throw any and every torturous reaper in my path they can to watch me prevail miserably. Why would Atlas think they would be so kind as to let him bury me in the ground?

Vere mori skathen. The Sylvian creed. *We conquer our demons.*

Atlas is no Sylvian.

Though his eyes were silver, he never conquered his demons. Atlas's demons conquered him, and he will never see the light of day again because of it.

56

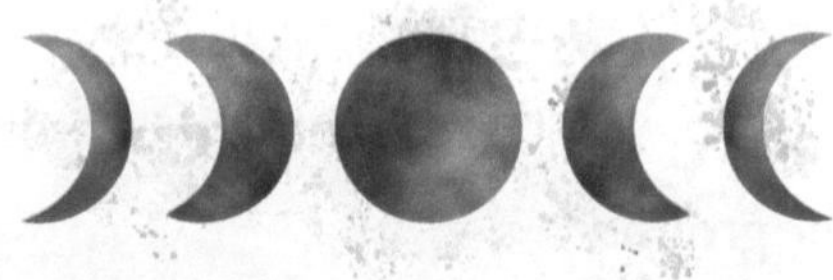

A Nightmare

The sun peaks on the horizon as I drop to the lake's sandy shore. My silver eyes disappear, but for once, I don't pass out from the exhaustion. It is a step in the right direction. My several day coma gave me the rest I needed to access my powers in full. I lay on my back and watch the sun rise in the distance. Luna's nearly full body sinks below the horizon. The stars have faded from the sky. All fighting in Sygon must take an intermission for the daylight.

And while the Undead are away, the Lycans will play. It is up to Urriah and his tribe to instill order in whatever humanity is left while the sun is up. I want nothing more than to pick myself up and fly back to my daughter's aid. But Sephora is in Crixus's care now, and I know she would die for my daughter.

For now, I enjoy the early morning warmth and bask in its glow. My body is so heavy that I feel as if it is me who is covered in stone.

"How can something so beautiful cause so much pain and suffering?" Crixus once asked as we laid awake staring at the moon. I could ask the same question about the sun. Though Luna is the bane of all Lycans' existence, the sun is our savior. And every savior must equally be a reaper. Though Solis causes the Undead a great deal of pain and suffering, it is the only force in this universe that gives Lycans the upper hand. And now, I will use Solis's daylight to my advantage.

"What do you plan on doing, after all of this is over?" Crixus once asked. I didn't have an answer for her when she asked it. But now?

I know now what I must do, though the thought of it is so daunting it makes me wish I was dead. Sygon was a set up all along. A mere plan for Bloodlust to effectuate his ascent to the Areopagus Throne. He never really cared about taking control of Sygon this entire time.

"I knew you could do it," Vesper says. I sit up and stare at the glimmering ghost of my wife. It feels like an eternity since I last saw her. I have never seen her image in the daylight before. Our entire life she was confined to the darkness of night. Now that she is dead and a figment of my imagination, she is free to walk the earth no matter the hour of day. She sparkles like translucent glass under the sunrise's potent light. Her pale face is as beautiful as the day I first met her. Her eyes are pale lilac.

If you truly love me, you'll keep fighting.

Her words are still written on my heart.

"Vesper..."

"Bloodlust is not the man you knew as a child," she continues, not entertaining the emotions that well deep inside me. "I told you before, Syrus. Bloodlust is planning on unleashing the Muzzled on them the next full moon. Tonight, he will unleash your fellow prisoners on Areopagus like I said. He will turn all of them from gladiator to soldier."

"Why didn't you warn me Sygon was a trap? If you knew this whole time this was his plan, why not tell me to head straight for Areopagus?"

"Because he had our daughter," Vesper replies sympathetically. "You needed to play his game in order to win her back, and to remember who you are, Syrus. You are ready now. He did not anticipate for you to survive Atlas's wrath. He thinks you are dead now, which gives you the upper hand in the battle to come."

"Battle to come? I can't make it to the Areopagus by tonight, Vesper. It is nearly a thousand miles away."

"You can fly now, Syrus. That only takes a few hours at altitude at best. You can be there by the time Solis crests in the sky at noon."

I am dumbfounded at my wife's persistence. My body can barely move after the fight against Atlas, and she would have me fly across the kingdoms to intercept Bloodlust and Ventur as they engage in the bloodiest war this earth has seen since the War of Flesh and Fangs. Yet the longer I sit here in silence, the more I realize there is no excuse available to me.

"Bloodlust said it himself. Sylvian the First turned Dagon's entire army of wolves against him. United all Lycans under his cause against their master. And now Bloodlust marches an entire army of Lycans to Ventur's gates for the night of the full moon. You can turn the tides of this war in your favor before it even begins, Syrus."

"But... I..." I breathe a sigh of exhaustion. Vesper is right. Bloodlust has planned this entire crusade on the contingency of my death in Sygon. I look down at my feet, then look back at her. My breath catches in my throat. It is no longer Vesper that stands before me, but instead the old hag I encountered in Queensmyre.

"You..." I stutter, "You aren't Vesper..."

"I never have been," she smiles excitedly. "I have always been what you needed me to be. In your darkest moments, every time you've forgotten who you are, I have been by your side."

"But Vesper..."

"Has never visited you as a ghost, Syrus. It has always been me. Even when you were in Bloodlust's custody, it was me."

"Who are you?"

"You wouldn't believe me if I told you." She grins. Her face is filled with wrinkles. She looks as innocent as a child.

"Try me," I reply.

"Some would call me a Fate. Some would call me a Muse. You may know me as the Summoner. I see the strings that attach themselves to living beings and move them forward through time like marionettes. And I have taken a special liking to you, Syrus Sylvian. I admire your unwillingness to die. No matter what the Creator has thrown in your path, you have refused to bow to the reaper. You've faced many dark hours in your life, and dark hours attract dark eyes."

Tucked behind the crone's sagging ear is a single flower—a Thanatos rose. I recognize it from the native regions of the Neverglades. Kateri used their petals to concoct powerful healing powders.

"It can't be..." I stutter. "It was just a play... Alabastur's story, all those years ago... The one about Enchantress... You can't be..."

"All stories are rooted in some truth, so here I am," she replies. "Alabastur may have written that play based on my life's story, but that doesn't mean I ever truly died."

"But you were never real... It was just fiction..."

"Reality is stranger than fiction, Syrus Sylvian. Surely you know that by now."

"Then the visions? What was the point of showing me my past?"

"To free you of the hold it had over you, as with Crixus. You both needed to know your predicament was not your fault. You needed to know you have someone watching over you, the same person that got you through those parts of your lives."

"And that person is you?"

"Who else?"

"And Creon's vision of the future? What was the point of that? Was that some attempt at scaring him into subordination?"

"No," she shakes her head, "That was the truth, Master Sylvian. Just as Ventur betrayed your father, so too shall your right-hand man betray you. The war you fight in the physical world is far more than flesh and blood. The Creator resents me and the death I carry with me. He has failed so many times in putting an end to me, so therefore he does his best to kill my best soldiers."

"Like my father?" I ask, realization setting in. I understand now why my father went to seek her counsel all those years ago.

"Now you are seeing the bigger picture, Syrus Sylvian. Hear my words, this war is much bigger than you and Bloodlust and the Areopagus Throne. This war goes back to my inception; back to Luna's affair with Cratos; back to the Equinox; back to the death of my husband Caspian. Solis could not put an end to me, so now the Creator sees me for the threat I am. I am the Summoner, and you are the one I've summoned to claim the throne. The Creator would sooner see Ventur or Bloodlust rule over the world he's created than concede to the soldier I've selected. I am forever the thorn in his side, the reaper that culls all life he creates, and I will not stop until I control all that he has created."

The woman vanishes like a mirage without time for me to question her any further. It is all like some bad joke. All of a sudden I'm forced to question my sanity once more, which I haven't done since the confined darkness of the mountainous prison. I almost wish I was going insane. At least then I would be free to run away from the burden the hag just placed on me. But deep down I know the truth. I am not going crazy.

There is much more going on behind the fabric of reality.

The Creator and his Devil are drafting teams to go to war, and the Devil has just selected me as her first pick. Now I understand why everything I've ever loved has died. It isn't me. It is my guardian angel. Like in the Alabastur play, everything she touches dies. She has been forming my life, tragedy by tragedy. Slowly making me dead inside to be her perfect soldier.

I now know what is at stake. The entire balance of the world's peace rests on my shoulders, and I've just learned I'm on the wrong side of the fight. I am putting all I love in this world in danger just by continuing to exist. But if I don't comply with the Summoner's demands, there is no telling what will happen to Sephora.

When you bring a child into this world, you make a vow to yourself to do whatever it takes to protect that baby.

If claiming the throne is the cost of protecting her, I don't care if it is the Devil herself that prompts me to do so. I will take back my kingdom if I have to make the moon bleed in the process.

The sound of wings flapping through the air breaks my trance of dread. I'm met by Wolfsram, who eagerly perches on my shoulder. The raven has followed me through the night in hopes of feeding on my most recent kill. Unfortunately for him, Atlas's body will never be seen again.

"Syrus!" he squawks eagerly.

I chuckle. I never would have thought I'd be so happy to see a bird again. After all these years, we are finally reunited. Best friends who've been separated against their will. I stroke the feathers along the back of his neck and he lifts his beak to the sky with joy.

"What now!" he asks.

"I need you to carry a message for me," I reply, still staring at the sunrise in the distance.

"Revenge!" he cries out, reading my mind.

"Precisely," I affirm. "Tonight, we will have our revenge."

About the Author

As a law school student by day and writer by night, Devin Thorpe spends a lot of time reading. He struggled making friends as a child, so he spent most of his free time creating epic plots for his action figures to enact. Now that he is an adult, he's put down the toys and picked up the pen in an effort to share these stories with the world. If even one person enjoys getting lost in the stories he tells, he will consider himself successful. With his Rottweiler, Atlas, his German Shepherd, Cato, and his girlfriend, Kristina by his side, he has all he could ever want in life.

www.ingramcontent.com/pod-product-compliance
Lightning Source LLC
Chambersburg PA
CBHW020452310726
48979CB00016B/2613/J

* 9 7 9 8 9 9 0 0 1 1 0 7 6 *